My Dear MISS DUPRÉ

AMERICAN ROYALTY
BOOK ONE

My Dear
MISS DUPRÉ

GRACE HITCHCOCK

BETHANYHOUSE
a division of Baker Publishing Group
Minneapolis, Minnesota

© 2021 by Grace Hitchcock

Published by Bethany House Publishers
11400 Hampshire Avenue South
Bloomington, Minnesota 55438
www.bethanyhouse.com

Bethany House Publishers is a division of
Baker Publishing Group, Grand Rapids, Michigan

Printed in the United States of America

Library of Congress Cataloging-in-Publication Data
Names: Hitchcock, Grace, author.
Title: My dear Miss Dupré / Grace Hitchcock.
Description: Minneapolis : Bethany House Publishers, a division of Baker
    Publishing Group, [2021] | Series: American royalty ; book 1
Identifiers: LCCN 2020042368 | ISBN 9780764237973 (trade paper) | ISBN
    9780764238086 (casebound) | ISBN 9781493430000 (ebook)
Subjects: LCSH: Romantic suspense fiction.
Classification: LCC PS3608.I834 M9 2021 | DDC 813/.6—dc23
LC record available at https://lccn.loc.gov/2020042368

Scripture quotations are from the King James Version of the Bible.

This is a work of fiction. Names, characters, incidents, and dialogues are products of the author's imagination and are not to be construed as real. Any resemblance to actual events or persons, living or dead, is entirely coincidental.

Cover design by Koechel Peterson & Associates, Inc., Minneapolis, Minnesota / Jon Godfredson
Cover photography by Ron Ravensborg

Author is represented by The Steve Laube Agency.

21 22 23 24 25 26 27   7 6 5 4 3 2 1

For Dakota,
My Heartbeat

And he hath put a new song in my mouth,
even praise unto our God: many shall see
it, and fear, and shall trust in the Lord.

Psalm 40:3

One

NEW YORK CITY
NEW YEAR'S EVE, 1882

Willow Dupré twirled on the ice, spreading her arms and guiding her body around the other skaters on the frozen lake of Central Park. The crisp morning air nipped at her cheeks and brought life to her limbs that ached from the long hours working behind her father's desk, which was something she was unused to doing. Since Father's illness, the ice was the one place she could truly release the pressures of assuming the throne of her family's sugar empire, for there was no risk of gliding by one of her paunchy board members. Willow arched her arms above her head despite the seams of her sleeves digging into her shoulders, keeping her hands in her fur muff, and spun, loving the whirl of her short, fur-trimmed crimson cape about her, not minding the hairpins pulling loose from her stern bun, releasing her chestnut locks to tumble to her slender waist while her winter cap miraculously stayed firmly in place.

"My dear Miss Dupré!"

She started, nearly losing her footing along with her thoughts. She flung out her arms to balance herself and turned to find a handsome gentleman she dimly recalled from a past season, stumbling across the frozen pond toward her in gleaming skates with leather straps over his boots that were far too loose to do much good. She allowed him to take her hand in his, scrambling to recall his name. *Kind eyes and impossibly deep voice.* "Mr. Friedrich Blythe." She dipped her head in the place of a curtsy. "I did not know you skated."

He chuckled and stroked the tip of his thick ginger mustache into a point and sent her a wink. "It's hard to believe, for as you can see, I'm such a natural on the ice. But I haven't skated since I was a boy. I heard that you enjoyed the sport, so I came in hope of seeing you."

"Oh?" She gave him a tentative smile, unsure as to why Mr. Blythe would seek her out when he had not done so in the year since they had met. A giggling pair of children wove around her and brushed passed Friedrich, the light touch sending his arms to flapping wildly as he attempted to regain his footing. Willow strode forward and seized his coat sleeve, steadying him lest he knock himself to the ground with his floundering. "Hold on, Mr. Blythe! You won't perish today."

Laughing, Mr. Blythe slowly released his hold on her arms, his cheeks reddening. "Thank you. Well, uh, as I was saying, you cannot imagine my pleasure when I received one of your coveted invitations last night."

Willow blinked, truly confused. Mother was hosting their annual New Year's Eve party tonight, but those invitations would have been issued two weeks ago. "Invitation?"

"Yes. I happen to have mine with me, if you would like to see it?" Mr. Blythe withdrew a golden scroll secured with a lush, burgundy satin ribbon from his greatcoat and handed it to her, bobbing from the motion.

She slid the ribbon off and unfurled the scroll to read the engraved summons,

To Mr. Friedrich Blythe, you have been selected to attend a

competition, along with twenty-nine gentlemen, beginning the thirty-first of December to win the hand of our daughter and heiress to our empire, Willow Dupré. Should you accept, you will court Miss Dupré alongside the other suitors in an attempt to win her heart and marry within six months.

What on earth? Willow crumpled the invitation in her fist without reading the rest and shoved it into her muff, shivering. "I apologize for the confusion. This has to be a jest. My parents would never think of something so outlandish, so—" *Degrading.*

He chuckled, removing his stiff hat and running his fingers through his thick locks before setting his hat firmly in place once more. "Come now, Miss Dupré. You do not have to be coy with me. The city is already humming with the news."

"But I am not playing the coquette, Mr. Blythe. I truly think there has been some sort of misunderstandi—"

He grasped her hand and lightly tugged, sending her skates into a gentle glide toward him. "Now, I know it is breaking the rules of the game to contact you before the ball tonight, so it is with the deepest remorse that I must bid you farewell, my lady, but not before I bestow upon you the first of many tokens of my affection." Mr. Blythe wobbled into a bow and kissed her gloved hand and straightened, giving her a smile filled with hope as he withdrew a nosegay of withering white flowers with tiny golden hearts. "From my mother's conservatory. My apologies for their state, which is due to my lack of foresight, but the sentiment of the white jasmine is what I hope to convey."

"Extreme amiability?" she interpreted, remembering its meaning from Mother's required hours of studying the secret language of flowers, including the ever-popular floral dictionaries. Sliding the small bouquet into her muff, she shook her head to wake herself from the haze of his charm. "So, this is not a hoax?"

Mr. Blythe's grin faltered. "You mean to tell me that you truly did not know of the invitation to court you?"

9

"Absolutely not. I knew, of course, about a party tonight, but do you think I would have allowed *these* invitations to have been sent if I had known? Please excuse me, as I need to sort through this mess." She dipped her head in a dismissive nod before gliding to the opposite side of the pond, weaving around the throngs of skaters going and coming from the three-storied skaters' tent with concessions in hand, her focus on her things atop the park bench at the edge of the landing. Lifting her plain navy skirt, she tromped through a snowdrift, not minding the snow seeping through her stockings at the tops of her boots, and perched on the freezing bench to unfasten the buckles of the leather straps securing her skates. She tugged her feet out of her skating boots and slipped on her walking shoes. Gripping the skate straps in one hand, she marched down the park's freshly shoveled path toward the Inventor's Gate, leading to her home on Fifth Avenue. She would get to the bottom of this nonsense at once.

"But, as it *is* true, you will not be stopping the competition, even if it is a bit untoward, will you, Miss Dupré?" Mr. Blythe called, disappointment edging his tone as he trotted up behind her, his skates nowhere in sight.

She took a second glance at him, surprise fluttering to life in her stomach. *He is genuinely excited about the invitation to court me.* Willow drew in a breath and gave the handsome fellow her prettiest smile, adding a modicum of kindness to her reply. "I am certain the annual New Year's Eve party will continue as planned and I will be happy to receive you. As for a competition, I can say with confidence that it will *not* occur. Now if you will excuse me, Mr. Blythe, I need to be on my way," she finished and darted off, disregarding etiquette for once. Her neck burned with the shame of the rumor as she skirted around couples, street vendors, and children with their nannies pushing prams at tremendous speeds, taking chase after them.

"Willow! Willow Dupré!"

She caught sight of her dearest friend waving frantically to her from down the avenue, and at the darkness in Flora's expression, Willow's heart plummeted. *Father.* She raced to Flora's side, hopping over and around patches of blackened ice. "Is something wrong?" Willow panted, pressing her gloved hand to her side where her corset pinched her, preventing her from taking a full breath.

"Yes! Why did you not tell me about this competition?" Flora crossed her arms, the golden curls framing her face atremble. "I had to find out from Marcy Mae Lovett, who knew all about it because her brother, Archibald, received his invitation last night, delivered by one of your own servants."

"Is that all?" She released a nervous laugh, which turned into a groan that even Flora had heard of the fraudulent invitation. Willow motioned for Flora to continue walking with her. "I only just found out myself and am about to put an end to this rumor."

Flora's expression clouded before her eyes widened and she dodged a flying snowball, sending the three mischiefs responsible a glare that could melt the snow, and brushed off her immaculate sapphire cloak. "End? B-but think of the men vying for your hand. I am fairly green from envy that my parents did not think of such a thing for me. And as for it being a rumor, haven't you noticed the murmurs about the city of those who have not been invited to your annual party?"

Willow slowed, the whispers of the past weeks of socialites not receiving invitations now making sense.

"Aren't you at all excited at the prospect of having your pick from society's elite gentlemen?"

Willow resumed her frantic pace. Her parents had some explaining to do. "I would have been when I was a debutante nearly six years ago, but I'm twenty-four now and having all those men seeking me out for marriage is *exactly* why I must put an end to it, and the means of said courtship is mortifying.

Now everyone will think I need my parents to make a favorable match when the fact is that I am simply too busy to take the time to find a husband worth the taking."

"After years of lessons at the university and working at your father's side for the past few years, you need to take time for yourself. How else are you going to find a husband?"

"I don't have time for a husband. This is the second Saturday I have had off from work since Father's heart attack this summer. Monday was the first time the doctors allowed Father to set foot in the Dupré Sucré office, and even then it was only for an hour or so. I have a family and a business to support and I do not have time for this sort of thing." She pulled the offending invitation from her muff and waved it in the air.

Flora snatched it away at once, clutching it to her chest. "Take care or you will lose it and have some *random* gentleman showing up at your ball." She stuffed it back into Willow's muff. "Take a breath and relax. The sugar refinery will be fine without you at the helm for the duration of this competition. Besides, your parents wouldn't have issued invitations for a courtship if Mr. Dupré wasn't recovering. It is time you cease thinking only about running the empire and turn your attention to having someone at your side *besides* your father," she replied as Willow climbed the steps to the Duprés' gray stone mansion at the corner of Sixty-Eighth, pausing to knock the snow from her boots against the doorframe. "It has been years since you have even looked at a man for anything other than a business deal, Willow. You have been labeled as New York's wealthiest spinster."

Willow gritted her teeth, suppressing her scathing riposte. "You know I prefer the term *bachelorette*."

"Bachelor girl sounds utterly nonsensical, even in French, and it will never become vogue to be an old maid. You are a *spinster*, dear, and I am but six months from being considered one myself," she added with a shudder. "Yet what am I to do now when all the good ones will be snatched up in your competition?"

Willow rolled her eyes. "Fine. This spinster needs to get to the bottom of this ridiculousness, so if you'll excuse me—"

"But I wanted to hear what your parents have to say," Flora protested, kicking a hardened lump of snow from the top step, sending it toppling down to the sidewalk.

"You and I both know I'll tell you all later," Willow reassured her friend before slipping inside. After handing her skates, hat, and wrap to the footman, she followed the echoes of voices.

Willow found her parents seated in the drawing room, heads bowed together and deep in thought, while her twin sisters half her age, Philomena and Sybil, kept their gazes fixed on the chessboard in front of them.

"Do you know anything about this?" Willow asked as she crossed the room and dropped the crumpled gilded invitation onto her mother's lap and planted her fists at her trim waist.

Father nodded to Mother. "You best tell her, Christine."

Setting aside the abused invitation, Mother rose, clasped her hands before her pristine blush skirt, and sent Willow an apologetic smile. "Let us speak privately in the adjoining room. I would rather the girls not hear our reasoning, William," she replied in a low voice, wrapping her arms around Father's waist, assisting him up from the settee and handing him his cane.

So, there is truth to the rumor. Willow groaned and followed them into her mother's private sitting room, waiting until Mother drew the French doors closed before asking, "Why would you do this to me? Do you know how humiliating it was to be told of this scheme by last season's most eligible bachelor, *Friedrich Blythe*? He has grown a rather large mustache since we met, so I almost didn't recall his name until it was too late. And what about our annual party? I have been reassuring our usual guests that their invitations must have gotten lost! And now I find out you have had an entirely different list in mind?"

"I do feel rather bad on that score. However, I sent round a note to our usual guests this morning, explaining things." Mother took her by the arm, shushing her with an admonishing tilt of her brow, silently reminding Willow to choose her next words carefully so as not to upset Father. "Have a seat, dear, and we will explain everything."

Willow rubbed her temples and stared at the fresco on the ceiling, attempting to gather her emotions. If she had not spent every waking moment buried in office ledgers, she might have noticed—she might have stopped this nonsense. "You both know I have no wish to marry at the moment, especially with having the company to run while you recover, Father. Why, then, do you two feel the need to marry me off in such a rush?"

Father rubbed his thumb over the intricate carved ivory head of his cane. "I know it seems sudden, but we received word from the doctors this past week and it was not what I had hoped to hear."

Any anger she harbored faded at the mention of her father's illness. Willow looked to the stooped man before her, amazed at how an illness could transform a person. Father seemed so much better than he had only last month, but of course he had seemed fine *before* the heart attack. *What aren't you telling me?* "You will recover, won't you?"

"The doctors say that I will recover, but not to the extent we had hoped. They have given me six months of working half days to retire or they fear I will suffer a second attack from the strain."

Mother pulled a handkerchief from her sleeve and balled it in her fist, blinking away her tears.

Willow sank down beside him on the mauve velvet, swallowing the lump in her throat. He would not wish to hear of her disappointment, her fear over his condition. He would only want for her to be level-headed. "Then I will take over, of course, but this does not explain the need for me to secure a husband by June."

"The shareholders do not approve of your taking over the business without me at your side to guide you, and with the doctors' new orders . . . I am afraid that I cannot be the partner with you as we had hoped for all these years." He stroked her cheek with the back of his hand as the fireplace crackled. "Which means, if the shareholders do not approve of your leadership, they may sell their portions to our biggest competitor, Wellington Sugar, who, as you well know, is always trying to lure them into selling him their shares in an attempt to gain a foothold in our family's legacy and eventually take control. So far I have managed to keep the shareholders through their sense of loyalty and promises of wealth, but if Wellington manages to secure those shares, along with that last bit from your rather unpredictable cousin . . ." He sighed. "We stand to lose a great deal, as Wellington will gain majority if your cousin Osborne sells."

Willow's lungs became heavy, her breath catching with the weight of the threat. She reached out for Father's hand, her first concern for his health and the second, closely after, of the sugar refinery her grandfather and father had spent their lives building. She thought of her little sisters and looked to her mother and father. She could not be the reason for the Dupré empire to fall. "I know I could do the job well. I have studied by your side for the past few years and taken classes at Cornell. I have journals upon journals of ideas on how to improve the company while bringing in even more profits. Surely the board will see—"

He lifted his hand, staying her argument. "You and I both know that you are as capable if not *more* than any gentleman. But businessmen wed all the time to secure their footing in the world. If you wish to be treated as a businessman, er, business*woman*, you must make certain sacrifices for the good

15

of the company. So, I must ask you, are you truly ready to wed someone in order to reign?"

Willow had longed to be treated as an equal since she was a young girl, and her father, forward-thinking as he was, had made certain to educate and train her to take over as he would have any son. And any son of his would have had to marry for the betterment of the business. She was no exception. "Yes," she answered.

Her mother nodded in approval and patted Willow's hand. "We knew you would be willing. However, we have always dreamed for you to have a union of love, like your father and I." She sent Father a look that made Willow shift in her seat. "Which is why we have devised a plan, that is admittedly rather outlandish, for you to find the love of your life while satisfying the board's demands," Mother added as the sounds of furniture being moved around down the hall reached them.

"The thirty gentlemen callers," Willow finished, a flicker of hope warming her. Surely one out of so many would be tolerable, maybe even attractive.

"Exactly. One of them will help you secure your future as queen of the sugar empire." Father rubbed his hands together, betraying his excitement. "Now, your mother and I have personally chosen the thirty potential suitors from the families of New York's elite Four Hundred set. You will have six months to select one of them to help you run the company, to be your king, your spokesperson if you will. You, of course, will retain control, but this will give the shareholders comfort at the thought of a man by your side, guiding you. Even though, in reality, he is merely your proxy and a male figurehead. And yet I am hopeful that the man you choose will be a partner to you in life *and* love."

A male figurehead? Her anger flared at the backwardness of the situation. *The board is acting as if I am not able to hold property. This isn't the 1840s.* "So, what do you suggest? I waltz into the ballroom tonight and select the best male like a prize bull?" She snorted.

Mother sent her a pointed look. "That is not ladylike."

Willow grunted, twisting her disheveled hair into a stern knot at the base of her neck and snatching one of Mother's crochet hooks from the sewing basket beside her chair and sticking it through the knot to keep it off her neck until she could have her maid see to it. "How else am I supposed to feel?"

"Chris." Father looked to Mother with a gentle smile, halting her correction, and turned to Willow. "No, Will. Not like a bull. During your six months, you will eliminate the men whom you discover a lack of connection with, until you have found the one you wish to marry, effectively ending the competition with a wedding."

"In six months?" Willow repeated, doubt, along with anger and hope, churning her stomach.

"Yes," they answered together, her mother's pursed lips and her father's white knuckles squeezing his cane further impressing upon her the seriousness of the situation.

"And if you need advice on whom to choose, we are always here to talk. Still, with matters of the heart, we understand that sometimes you need to speak to someone besides your parents, so we sent a note to Flora just before you arrived, asking if she would be available to offer you advice throughout the competition if you need it." Sensing her turmoil, Mother placed her hand on Willow's shoulder, offering her strength in that quiet way of hers. "Remember, in order for your father to rest his heart, you *need* to do this. Giving control over to your cousin is not an option . . . not after Osborne's past actions."

For Father. She could do it for him and his heart. She would earn the respect of the shareholders in time, but at this moment she did not have the luxury of time to garner the support needed to rule. A husband was her only choice. She straightened her shoulders. "Very well. Let the hunt for a king begin."

"Wonderful." Mother clapped her hands and rustled over to her desk, removing a thin portfolio and setting it into Willow's hands. "Now, I wasn't going to show you this, but since you are being so accommodating, it might help relax your nerves. These are the candidates in no particular order. If you wish, you can peruse their photographs, their names, and read over their short biographies before they arrive at eight." She continued to rattle off her expectations for the evening while Willow sat staring at the portfolio that held her future.

"You can do this, Will." Father patted her hand. "I hope you find one amongst the gentlemen who sparks your interest. Each one has been carefully vetted by your mother and I *and* our solicitor, so whomever you wish to wed is yours with our blessing. Granted, of course, the young man is willing." He chuckled.

With false bravado, Willow flipped open the portfolio to find a stack of papers with a small picture glued to each page. The first was a stocky, dark-haired gentleman with a jovial countenance. Above him read *Harold Harolds*. She bit back a laugh at the banal name combination and scanned the paragraph under his picture. She turned the page to the next gentleman and the next, curious to see whom she would find, but before she was even halfway through the stack, the grandfather clock rang five times, and at its ominous reminder, her mother sprang into action, frantically tucking the documents away and sending Willow upstairs to transform from a prim businesswoman to an American princess.

Two

I *wonder if my parents could have fashioned a more un-comfortable means of finding the love of my life.* Willow grunted and tugged on her cream gloves and twisted in the gilded looking glass, smoothing the satin front of the elegant powder-blue gown with small butterflies delicately perched in the cream tulle about her shoulders and at the bottom of her skirt where it melted into a ruffled lace hem. Atop her chestnut locks nestled a tasteful diamond coronet set in gold with a matching piece cascading down her neck and a delicate ring of diamonds encircling her wrist. She reached for her diamond chandelier earrings and tightened the screws, securing them so they would not fly off during dancing. No matter how nauseated she felt, at least she would sparkle in the candlelight and hopefully distract the guests from her pallid hue, which was exactly what her mother had intended.

As the minutes ticked past to the hour of her impending demise, Willow felt sick with what she must do to run the company she had dreamed of ruling alongside her father since girlhood. It was never meant to be this way. *Stop this,* she chided herself and mopped at her glistening forehead with a handkerchief. There was no sense in wallowing in self-pity. It was her responsibility to the family and the people she employed to do what was best for the company. *But what of love, Lord?* She prayed and fought back the emotion clouding her throat and set about controlling her thoughts and hopefully with them, her sentiments. She would not risk the livelihoods of so many for the sake of a fantasy.

She strode into the hall, where Father stood waiting, handsome as ever in his black evening coattails with its satin lapels and crisp white bow tie as he leaned on his cane. He slowly crossed the hall, his cane thudding on the thick burgundy carpet. "You are exquisite."

Willow dipped her head, her tears returning. He had never been so moved over a dress before. *But it is so much more than a dress. This is the beginning of his releasing my welfare into the care of another, of his retirement and of my ruling.* She straightened her shoulders and pecked him on the cheek in silent thanks.

"Shall we?" He offered her his left arm and rested so heavily on the cane in his other hand that she wondered how they would maneuver the stairs with every eye upon them.

Ignoring her misgivings, she placed her hand on his. She could do this. For the business. He guided her to the secondary staircase that led into the ballroom that Mother had built solely for the purpose of making grand entrances. Father paused at the corner of the long hall, the light from the ballroom splaying before them. One more step and all would see them.

"If you wouldn't mind, keep your hand steady on my arm, Will. I am afraid that if I don't take the stairs just so, we may tumble and ruin your mother's well-laid plans for your grand entrance."

She patted his arm. "Lean on me."

"I always do." He cleared his throat. "I am proud of you, Will."

At his words, she exhaled a ragged breath. *Cease being so*

emotional. You've made grand entrances countless times . . . the only difference is that your future husband is downstairs. She schooled her features and nodded to her father, and they continued around the corner. Then at the sight before her, she stumbled over the hem of her skirt. The massive twin crystal chandeliers sparkled overhead, bringing light to the horrifying fact that the only female in the gilded ballroom was her mother. Unlike their usual balls where Willow could hide in the crowd, thirty gentlemen with ten footmen serving hardly constituted a crowd, so there would be no hiding tonight. Willow moved back, fully intending on retreating, but it was too late. One of the men had spotted her, and word blazed through the suitors, all of them turning toward her. She plastered on a smile, hoping it disguised her rising terror. She could face a hostile boardroom, but thirty wealthy gentlemen dressed in their finest coattails intending to capture her in the net of matrimony? She would rather confront the boardroom.

A footman in scarlet livery at the bottom of the stairs sounded her arrival with a blast from a trumpet, sending her cheeks flaming once again. She squeezed Father's arm. "*Mother.*"

"Keep smiling and nodding," Father whispered between clenched teeth. "This is only the beginning. I should have warned you that your mother is leaning wholly into the American royalty theme. She could not be dissuaded."

As if she could hear him, Mother motioned them toward a trio of gilded thrones upon a mahogany platform set along the center of the main wall. Willow's knees weakened, dread seeping through her bones. Of course, her mother would do this to her—any excuse to showcase their fortune and send a message to society that they were the wealthiest family on Fifth Avenue.

Releasing her at the bottom step, Father lifted his hand. "Gentlemen, allow me to present the lady of the hour, the future queen of the Dupré Sucré empire, Miss Willow Dupré."

The men cheered, and Willow kept her head high as she strode down into the mass toward the thrones. The gentlemen murmured their greetings, smiling and bowing to her as Willow passed and inclined her head to each. Taking the two steps up to the platform, she followed the red carpet to stand before the men and gave herself a few seconds for the applause to dim. If word returned to the boardroom that she had vacillated . . . She gripped her satin fan and stood straight. She must appear strong, capable, despite her desire to bolt to the nearest door and make her escape. *Please, Lord, let my voice not waver. Let me not bring shame upon our legacy.*

"Gentlemen, I believe you were all as surprised as I when you received the invitation for this competition." She paused, their nervous laughter filling the gilded ballroom, and fastened her gaze on a redheaded fellow in the front. Friedrich Blythe grinned boldly at her, and she dipped her head to him in a silent greeting, causing the men around him to regard him warily. "I am honored you all have chosen to attend tonight, and I look forward to getting to know each and every one of you as my *potential* suitor."

Amid the cheers, Mother glided forward in her gold brocade and satin gown, lifting her egret feather fan with a twirl to garner the men's attention. "Throughout the evening, if my daughter chooses for you to stay, she will present to you a crown of laurels, which you may accept if you wish to continue on this journey with Miss Dupré." She gestured to a table to her left, draped in an imperial purple cloth bearing the crowns.

Crowns? If only the earth would open and swallow her. Nevertheless, Willow kept on, displaying nothing but complete trust and support for her mother as the men murmured, some elbowing each other and clapping hands on shoulders while others shifted about, determination lining their expressions.

"Should you accept, you will then be invited to reside in the guest rooms on the third floor for the duration of your time in the competition. Now, please form a line to Willow's right and introduce yourself to Miss Dupré and let us enjoy the evening before us." Mother turned, beckoning Willow forward once more, and she and Father assumed their seats behind her. Willow folded her hands around her fan and waited for the men to shuffle into a single file. The first gentleman strode forward and bowed to her, giving her a cheeky grin from beneath an unfortunate frizzled, thin brown mustache. "It's an honor to meet you, my dear. I am Lord Peregrine."

A lord? How did her parents manage to lure him to the party? Perhaps he was a titled gentleman with no funds to support his estates. She sank into a curtsy. "The honor is mine, Lord Peregrine. Do you reside in New York or are you only visiting?"

"Residing until the future is decided." His brows and mustache waggled up and down in unison. "Meaning until I find *Lady* Peregrine and then I can return to my estate in England, which is in need of a woman's touch. But given your business is here, perhaps an arrangement of sorts can be made."

Fortune hunter. Willow settled and spent the next few minutes listening to him regale facts of his social standing before tactfully excusing him and summoning the next gentleman, a Mr. Montgomery, who mumbled so low and quickly that Willow had a difficult time understanding anything but a smattering of words that she strung together for context. They conversed for only a few minutes before she met a dashing fellow, who introduced himself as Mr. Digory Pruett. Her head was already swimming with names and faces by the time she found herself laughing at charming Mr. Starling's parting jest and turned her focus to the man standing before her.

Taller than most, with broad shoulders and a fine jawline and high cheekbones that were accentuated by rather long, tousled dark hair that held an auburn tint, his bright emerald eyes pierced her own. His nose appeared to have been broken a time or two, but instead of diminishing his looks, it added to his aura of power. She certainly had not seen *him* in the portfolio. Her lips parted, yet her mouth had gone dry, trapping any greeting.

"It's a pleasure to finally meet you, Miss Dupré. I am Cullen Dempsey." He bowed before her extended hand, the deep timbre of his voice that held a hint of Irish brogue drawing her to him. "I must say this was an unexpected honor your parents paid me, and I hope to be worthy of their attention."

A smile caught at the corner of her lips. Handsome *and* polite. Maybe this process wouldn't be as painful as she thought. "The pleasure is all mine, sir." She curtsied as the music filled the air. She caught sight of his finger tapping against his pant leg, keeping perfect time with the dip of the violins. "Do you play music, Mr. Dempsey?"

He laughed and shook his head, shoving his hands into his pockets and rocking on his heels and back toward her. "Unfortunately, I do not, but I *do* enjoy dancing. My mother forced me into taking lessons as a young man to lend me a much-needed air of refinement, but little did she know how much I would come to adore them."

"Oh?" This was the first gentleman she had ever met to confess such a thing to her, but she supposed if one was so fortunate as to possess the physique of a Greek god, one could get away with owning a love for dance and live.

"But I shan't spill any more of my darkest secrets quite yet. If I may have the honor of the opening dance, I can perhaps tell you more?" He glanced over his shoulder to the remaining handful of gentlemen and added, "As soon as you greet the others, of course."

Her heart did a strange little flip. Why was she acting like a nervous debutante? In all her twenty-four years, she could not recall reacting so to a man. No, it was only the excitement of the evening . . . that or it was Cook's rich tray that Willow had consumed while she was dressing paying a call. "I look forward to it, Mr. Dempsey."

He took her hand and bowed but did not kiss her hand as the others had done, and she was shocked to discover her disappointment. Her gaze trailed Mr. Dempsey's retreating figure, admiring his confident gait as he joined the crowd of men about the buffet table, until Father cleared his throat and announced the next gentleman, a regal-looking fellow only an inch or two shorter than the Irish titan, Mr. Dempsey.

He bowed to her, the streaks of gray in his ebony hair catching her eye. "Miss Dupré, it is wonderful to see you again. I hope you remember me as well as I remember you."

His rich tone, sun-kissed skin, and sparkling brown eyes brought forth a rush of memories. "Mr. Quincy? Of course! How could I forget the young man who fished me out of the ornamental water in Central Park? Your gallant efforts to help a twelve-year-old girl have not been forgotten by me or my friends."

"I was wondering if you would recall." He chuckled, handsome as ever, revealing a dimple in each cheek that she well remembered. "I hope you do not mind a man nearing forty paying you call tonight."

She grasped his hand in hers. "Your kindness turned a potentially devastating moment of my girlhood into a romance of legends that all in my circle of friends spoke of long afterwards. And since you are here, am I to assume correctly that your marriage to Miss Lexington did not occur?"

"Shortly after our engagement, her parents announced that they were moving to India and she went with them." He gave a short laugh. "Tired with me and my dull inclinations, I believe was her explanation."

Her heart burned against the insult inflicted upon the kind Mr. Kit Quincy of her girlhood fancies. "Her fickle and foolhardy choice is my gain. I am delighted you have joined us tonight."

He bowed and kissed her hand. "It does my heart good to hear that my age is not a factor."

"Never. Rather, it is a draw to me." The moment the words left her lips, she realized how scandalously blunt she sounded. Feeling her cheeks heating already, she curtsied and motioned for him to pass. "Please enjoy some refreshments and find me later." She greeted the next gentleman and the next until, at last, she found herself face-to-face with a familiar gentleman. Willow gasped. "Teddy Day?" She held out both her hands to him. "What a marvelous surprise!"

"The one and the same, though I go by Theodore these days. It is wonderful to see you, Will!" He pressed a kiss atop her hand. "Imagine my surprise when I received your parents' summons."

Theodore, the once-scrawny blond boy she and Flora had played with during their summers in Newport, had transformed into a masterpiece worthy of the Metropolitan Museum. *Pity I did not run into you sooner and we could have avoided this entire nonsense.* But even as she thought it, her gaze flashed to Mr. Dempsey and Kit and back to Theodore. "A good surprise, I hope?"

"Lovely, like you."

She dipped her lashes at her childhood friend's compliment, but could not keep her smile from betraying her pleasure. "I should be quite vexed with you for flirting when I haven't seen you in nearly a decade," she teased, giving his arm a playful little shove like the old days, but found his arm to be solid and corded with muscle. *Oh my.* She cleared her throat and stepped back into the safe arms of propriety. "What has been keeping you from visiting, Mr. Day?"

He grinned even as his brows lifted at the use of his surname. "Mr. Day, is it? I see I have a lot of ground to recover. I haven't been by because my mother wanted to have me educated abroad in her country and I have only just returned from Paris to attend to my father's riverboat-building business in New Orleans these past six months. I had planned on leaving the business

26

in the care of my older brother, Carlisle, while I summered in Newport this coming year, and I would have come calling on you then. Mayhap if I had returned to New York sooner, I would have stood a chance of garnering your attention. Now, I'm certain I am too late to request the first dance, but . . . ?"

Cullen could not keep his attention from returning to Miss Dupré, who was laughing with Mr. Day. When his mentor had managed to covertly secure an invitation through the Duprés' solicitor, Cullen had agreed to the plan, secretly wondering what was the flaw that had kept the heiress from marrying all these years. He took in the graceful curve of her neck and the bloom in her complexion that did not at all resemble the old-maid image he had prepared himself to encounter. After seeing her on the staircase, he thought perhaps her personality had kept her from wedding, but meeting her and watching her interact with the others, he found her to be kind to each man who approached her, even the ones with less desirable traits, like the unfortunate mouth-breathing lord, and when she laughed, the petite beauty all but spellbound him. *Nothing. Nothing is wrong with her.*

Watching her evident interest in Theodore Day as she laughed again and took his arm to descend the platform, Cullen felt an undeniable twist in his gut. He set aside his plate, upset at the sliver of jealousy lodged within him. He had only just met the lady, and yet he could not shake the desire to be the one causing her to laugh. He tensed, waiting for Theodore to move along so that he could steal her away, but as the last fellow in line, Theodore was in no hurry to leave her. And judging from the looks of the other fellows, they were either too petrified to interrupt or too busy enjoying the fine food. *Time to cut in.*

Cullen finished off his pastry, rolled back his shoulders, and snatched a sugar cube from the buffet table. Keeping it in his fist, he approached her and dropped the sugar cube behind her at her hem. "Why? What is this?" he announced, drawing Miss Dupré's attention away from Theodore.

She turned, her brow lifted in a question.

He bent down and scooped it up, opening his hand to reveal the cube in his palm. "You dropped your calling card, Miss Dupré." Her lips parted, gaping at him. Did she find him foolish? Well, even if it was a silly jest, he was committed and so kept his expression somber.

Theodore rolled his eyes while Miss Dupré giggled into her fan and shook her head. "How utterly ridiculous, sir, but it is a good thing I dearly enjoy laughing and have little opportunity to do so at work."

Cullen grinned, tossing the cube up in the air and catching it before depositing it into his waistcoat pocket. "'Tis a pity when one smile from you lights up the very room."

Theodore moaned and moved closer to Miss Dupré as the stringed instruments began playing. "Did you find that line right under the sugar cube idea in a courtship book, Dempsey?"

Before Cullen could deny that claim, Mrs. Dupré tapped Willow's shoulder with her fan. "I do believe it is time for you to open the ball, my dear."

She nodded as her mother reclaimed her seat at the thrones and turned to Theodore. "Please excuse us, Mr. Day."

"Gladly, for that means the second dance awaits us that much sooner, my lady." Theodore bowed and bestowed a light kiss to her hand.

She curtsied to Theodore and rested her hand atop Cullen's, sending his pulse to pounding. He had not been expecting such charms from a lady well into her twenties who, by all counts, should have been married the moment she was of age, given her family alone.

As the violins began the Viennese waltz in perfect time, he chasséd side to side with her before drawing her into his arms, twirling them about the dance floor. "Tell me, Miss Dupré, how are you not already spoken for by at least a dozen suitors?"

She inclined her head to the men encircling the ballroom floor, who were staring at them. "As you can see, I have over two dozen suitors."

"True." Cullen spun her around, pulling her ever so slightly nearer.

"What about you, Mr. Dempsey? Why did you decide to join us tonight? I cannot fathom your having any lack of potential brides."

Direct. He liked that. "I have been too focused on building my business to attend society's call."

"Not even for a ball here or there to meet someone?"

He caught a glimpse of the gentlemen over her shoulder as they twirled past and couldn't help but grin at the scowls on Houlgrave's and Lord Peregrine's faces. Cullen leaned down and lowered his voice so that she alone would hear. "No one really knows this, but as we are courting, can I trust you?"

Miss Dupré nodded, her wide sapphire eyes serious. "Of course. I am not one to betray a confidence."

"My shipping business struggled for years following my father's untimely death, and after taking rather drastic measures, we are only now recovering. I have not been able to step away long enough to seek out a bride, but now that I am respected by men in our set, I feel as though I can offer a woman more than my charming personality and impeccable dancing skills." Cullen winked to soften his confession, as if the losses of his past had not nearly crippled him.

"I am so sorry to hear of your father's passing. I cannot imagine the pain of losing one's parent." The rims of her eyes reddened in sympathy as if she had experienced such fear before. He had heard of her father's illness but had not realized until now how close she was to her father . . . something he had not felt since he was a young lad.

29

"Thank you. Whenever I think of the fine childhood he gave me, the sting of his loss dulls to an ache." *Even though he destroyed the rest of my memories,* he silently finished. It had been nearly six years since his father's passing and yet it was still difficult for Cullen to recall the pleasant memories of his father. When Cullen had met some of his father's more nefarious connections, he was disgusted to discover that the foundation of the family's business had been built on the backs of their fellow Irishmen, whom Father had paid mere pennies. And he had obtained the money through gambling with dangerous men, who in turn incurred staggering debts—debts Father had paid with his life. "But enough about me. Tell me about yourself, Miss Dupré, and what it is like to be a woman in business."

Three

"Have you decided whom to crown?" Mother asked in the powder room, adjusting a gather at Willow's bustle.

"Isn't a coronation ceremony taking things too far?" Willow stepped back from the floor-length looking glass, grazing her diamond tiara with her fingertips and contemplating removing it then and there.

Mother swatted away her hand and lifted a single finger in warning to leave it be. "It is a *symbolic* coronation. Besides, one can never take a theme too far. You are an American princess, so be proud of it. Flaunt your position a little for once. You were not always this serious if you recall, but once you started those business classes with your father and then at the university, you changed into this somber creature."

"I'm not all that serious," Willow protested, returning her attention to the looking glass to avoid her mother's piercing stare. "I have been laughing throughout the evening, especially so with Teddy."

Mother moved around her, her hands fluttering over Willow's hair and correcting every strand out of place. "Because he reminded you of a time when you did not carry such responsibility.

You can be business-minded and be a *woman*. Allow yourself to enjoy flirting. Revel in the romance of it all."

"I do not possess the luxury of being the carefree girl I once was, not when the board is run by men who would use my femininity against me."

Mother paused in her administrations, drawing a steady breath. "Well, you best make this season the one exception so you do not sentence yourself to a life alongside someone you could not possibly love. You say it is humiliating to be given as a prize in a competition, but now that you have met the gentlemen, you must see how genuine they are and the honor they are paying you by being vulnerable in coming here tonight. The least you can do is show them the respect they deserve by *continuing* and being your truest self." She placed a hand on Willow's shoulder. "You do not take only after your father, you know. Being a bit carefree never hurt anyone."

Willow chewed the inside of her cheek. She had seen her friends marry one by one, some for love but most because it was expected. She had not taken much time to think of love, not since she was a young girl. But, in listening to Mother's arguments, Willow found herself agreeing that she could not afford to marry a man she did not respect or enjoy being around. *Maybe Mother's outlandish idea may not be all that silly. What better way is there to find a husband on such short notice?* "You may have a point."

"Of course I do. Now, I have thirty laurels for you to bestow at the end of the evening. The men know the significance, and I can guarantee you, each and every one of them desires a crown. Speaking of which, have you decided on any gentlemen you wish to keep or perhaps release?"

"Well, they are all so nice." Willow selected a fresh handkerchief and tucked it away in her bodice in case she began to sweat when the time to crown arrived.

"Nice? Be honest, dear. I will not judge you this once."

Willow laughed. "Very well. Clark Watson is friendly enough, but he is far too comfortable discussing my money."

Mother clicked her tongue and pinched Willow's cheeks to bring about the desired heightened color. "Bad form."

"Agreed." Willow pulled her face out of Mother's reach. "And Mr. Thomas Mosely is guarded and comes off rather cold, because he thinks everyone in attendance tonight, including myself, wants something from him."

Mother's mouth twisted to the side, betraying her disappointment. "Pity. He is quite handsome. Are you certain that is a good enough reason for dismissal?"

"I am afraid so. He is too guarded with me, and if I am to feel comfortable asking a gentleman to stay and court me, he must be more open and trusting."

"What about Sebastian Jones?"

Willow adjusted her elbow-length gloves. "He is a kind-hearted fellow, yet he was so nervous that he kept reverting the conversation back to cheese, a topic which I thought would be exhausted after a single sentence. Instead, he went on and on for the entirety of a waltz on the makings of a good strong cheese. In case you did not know, one of the oldest European cheeses known to man is gouda. And do you want to know why it is yellow?"

"Good heavens, I do not think I do." Mother sucked in a breath through her grimace. "I am guessing his breath matched his topic?"

Willow shuddered. "Yes."

"I cannot abide cheese, but perhaps we could make allowances for him, as this evening is quite odd?"

"I would not feel right dismissing him on so trivial a thing."

"And what about Mr. Kit Quincy?"

A dream. Willow paused, trying to think of an appropriate response to having her girlhood crush in attendance tonight. She bit her lip to keep her smile in check.

"A finalist at last!" Mother sang out and clapped her hands. "And what of Mr. Grubb?"

Willow sighed. "How terrible is it that I do not wish to be called Mrs. Grubb, no matter how wealthy the man?"

"I told your father that would be an issue. And unlike the cheese fellow, one cannot change his surname as easily as his breath, but there are still scads more men left for you to sift through." Mother pushed her toward the door. "Therefore, it is time you hand out the first laurel crown to the man you favor most, at the moment of course, to encourage the few shy ones in the group to come forward to get to know you, lest you do not bestow them a crown by the evening's end."

"Very well."

Mother patted her arm, her eyes sparking with mischief. "That's my girl. Pick a handsome one. I want cherubs for grand-children to parade in front of the society matrons."

Shaking her head, Willow went to do her mother's bidding, knowing it was easier not to protest. Besides, she had decided as to which one among the gentlemen she would give the first crown. She moved with purposeful strides to the imperially draped table bearing the crowns and snatched up a laurel crown before she could change her mind. The gentlemen parted before her, their focus on the leafy crown in her hand. Looking about the room, she craned her neck around a group of men and discovered that the French doors leading to the balcony were open. Greeting the men in passing, whose grins faded once they realized they were not her mark, she drew a deep breath and strode out into the frigid night.

His broad back was to her, with his eyes on the stars shining through the clouds, unaware that she was behind him. Willow paused mid-stride. What was she doing approaching a gentle-man with the intent of asking him to stay and court her? She regarded the crown in her hands, feeling more than impetu-ous. Who was she to invite men to pay her call? Only Queen

Victoria was allowed such liberties during her courtship, and despite everything her mother had told her, *Willow* was not a queen. She could retreat now and call this whole thing off and perhaps save whatever shred of pride she had left. Willow took a step back, but her heeled slipper caught on her hem, letting loose an extensive *rip* and sending her careening backward. She threw her arms back to catch herself, but as her fingertips brushed against the stones, his hand wrapped around her waist, pulling her up against his hard chest, the action dispelling the entirety of her breath. *Heavens. The man truly has been carved from marble.*

"Miss Dupré! Are you injured?" Mr. Dempsey's emerald eyes, which she could now see held flecks of amber, skimmed her for injuries.

"I am so sorry. I did not mean to disturb you," she whispered as she righted herself, her limbs weakening at the touch of him. *Compose yourself, Will.*

"Nonsense. Are you well?" he asked again, his wondrously solid arms still about her.

May they never depart. Her limbs and mind would never regain their strength at this rate. She pushed herself back from Mr. Dempsey and rested a hand on the balcony, the freezing rail waking her and reminding her why she was out of doors on New Year's Eve without a wrap in the first place. "Yes, I, uh, only wanted to ask . . ." Willow averted her attention from his bright eyes to the avenue below with its carriages passing to-and-fro and tugged off a leaf from the laurels she still grasped, rolling the leaf between her forefinger and thumb, the action staining the fingertips of her glove.

Cullen Dempsey's brows lifted at the object in her hand, understanding lighting his features at what it represented. "You wished to ask me something?"

"Don't be afraid to be a little carefree." Her mother's words echoed in her heart. She gave him a tentative smile, her shoulders

twitching from the chill. The sooner she got this mortifying business over, the sooner she could seek the warmth of the ballroom. "Mr. Dempsey, would you do me the honor of accepting the first crown of the evening?"

He bent and pressed a soft kiss atop her gloved fingers, the pressure of his lips stilling her tremors. "The honor is all mine, my dear Miss Dupré. I heartily accept."

She lifted the laurels and found that she had to rise onto the tips of her toes to reach his head, but at his crooked grin, she found herself wobbling again.

He caught her by the waist to steady her once more. "Allow me to help," he murmured and bent his head down far enough for her to crown him.

"There." She looked up to him, blushing furiously at the many pairs of eyes crowding in at the long windows for such an intimate moment, the men skewering Cullen with their gazes.

"Looks like the men shall all be aiming to take me out of the running now." Cullen laughed, sending her a wink.

"If the man I choose cannot withstand a little animosity, he will not survive in the sugar business," Willow teased, willing her cheeks to cool. "But in all seriousness, there are many who wish for my family's empire to fall into another's hands." *Wellington Sugar being the first and my cousin closely thereafter.*

"Any wrath incurred is worth it to know I have miraculously found favor in your eyes, Miss Dupré. And I thank you for the honor. Shall we dance to celebrate?"

But before she could answer, Cullen twirled her into the warmth and onto the dance floor, calling for a polka from the orchestra and spinning her thoughts into a jumbled mess from the first hop into the lively chasséing dance, his crown of laurels inexplicably staying in place as they whirled.

"May I cut in?" Archibald Lovett requested halfway through the dance, pulling her focus from Cullen to a man only an inch or so taller than herself.

Cullen bowed and, as he departed, whispered, "Thank you for the chance to get to know you. I do not take the honor lightly."

She curtsied to him, her chest heaving from the exertion of the dance, cheeks blazing yet. *I best keep my fan within reach when I am around Cullen Dempsey in the future.*

Archibald bowed to her, his dimples adding to his dandy appearance. "Miss Dupré, my sister has told me simply everything about you."

"Marcy Mae, yes?" She placed her hand in his as he counted the beat and off they twirled.

He gave a short, barking laugh. "That girl dearly loves to gossip and has the gift of gab, so she had no qualms in informing me all about your debut season, the beaus you could have had, and your unusual inclination toward winter games."

"Oh?" She giggled. It seemed that Marcy Mae was not the only loquacious member of his family. *Thank goodness, else I should pass out attempting to polka and carry on a conversation.*

"Yes, and I told her that it was quite a shame you and I have not met before, for I would have loved to toboggan-race with you as a child."

Archibald might be just the candidate to help me set aside my responsibilities for a day and enjoy life. She tilted her head and answered coyly, "Perhaps you still can."

"If I were invited to stay, it would make my life complete to race you down a hill in Central Park," Archibald replied, his voice bright with enthusiasm.

"Then I will have to arrange a toboggan race *if* you can stay," she whispered, spotting a dark-haired gentleman approaching Archibald from behind as the song came to a close.

"May I have this next dance?"

After Archibald left her to Mr. Noah Walden's care for a slow waltz, the men cut in one after the other until the clock chimed midnight, sounding in the new year. The men cheered around Willow and escorted her to the thrones, where Marvin, the mansion's youngest footman, held a silver tray to her bearing a glass of punch while four other footmen dispersed into the group of men with more drinks until all had a glass in hand.

With a smile over her shoulder to her parents, Willow lifted her glass to the gentlemen. "Happy New Year to all!"

The men returned her toast with thunderous shouts and applause. Teddy, who stood nearest to the platform, took her hand in his and lifted it to his lips. "To the happiest of new years for you, Miss Dupré."

Willow dipped her head in thanks. "And to you, good sir."

Mother pressed a kiss to Father's cheek and rose, quieting the room with a mere lift of her hand. "I loath to end the festivities, but it is time for Willow to bestow the remaining crowns. The chosen men will be able to continue their conversations with Miss Dupré tomorrow afternoon during your first group outing. Mr. Dempsey, since you have a crown, please stand behind Miss Dupré and wait for the others to join your rank. Let the ceremony begin."

"Hear, hear!" called Friedrich Blythe from the back of the group, clearly excited over his chances.

Setting aside her glass, Willow sent him a smile. While he had not grabbed her attention quite like Cullen, he was certainly one of the kindest gentlemen she had met in a while, and it would not do any harm to invite such a handsome fellow to stay until she was certain he was not the man for her. "Thank you all for attending tonight. I enjoyed each and every conversation. Unfortunately, I will not be distributing all thirty crowns tonight, as it would not be fair to continue on with some gentlemen who I am confident are not my future husband."

A murmur trickled through the men as if it were unfathomable that they could be passed over for another.

"But," Willow continued, "as this *is* a search for my husband,

I hope you can understand that I am only acting on my instinct. I do not wish to offend anyone." She lifted a crown, her gaze finding her dear friend. "Theodore Day."

"My queen." He trotted up the steps to join her on the platform and bowed to her. Willow placed the crown atop his blond curls, her fingers tingling as she inadvertently touched his temples. She clandestinely shook her hands loose as he assumed the place behind her on her left beside Cullen as directed by Mother.

Willow took up the third crown of the night. "Friedrich Blythe," she called, smiling at his reddened ears. She continued calling names, crowning the gentlemen one by one who had left a positive impression on her that she wished to explore. "Archibald Lovett . . . Harold Harolds . . . Clyde Billings . . . Sebastian Jones . . . Chandler Starling . . . Frank Keating . . . Kit Quincy . . . Ernest Lennox . . . Noah Walden . . . Oscar Seaborne . . . Digory Pruett . . . Alexander Houlgrave . . . and last but not least, Taylor Kemp." She paused after distributing the sixteenth crown and folded her hands, looking to the crowned men standing behind her as those remaining before her frowned. "Thank you for taking time out of your busy schedules to give me hope in finding a partner, but I will not be handing out any more laurels tonight."

Protests filled the room as the remaining gentlemen shifted uneasily. Like any business deal that did not go through, Willow needed to tread lightly and with respect. She looked to each man before her, praying they heard her next words. "Please do not feel slighted as I struggle along in this journey. I simply mean to—hopefully—find not only my partner in life but also in . . . in love. Please forgive me for any transgressions I unintentionally commit in the process."

The rejected suitors bowed one by one as they left her, politely extending her their best wishes. But judging from Lord Peregrine's twitching mustache over his pinched mouth, Willow knew he was gravely offended, and she braced herself for his indignation. Before he could unleash his vexation upon her, Father was at her side, ushering him out with the other thirteen men to the foyer, where Mother would be offering them each a small but costly gift of appreciation as they departed.

Once the doors closed with a resounding *boom*, Willow turned her attention to the sixteen gentlemen remaining, all looking statuesque in their Olympian crowns, and a rush of hope filled her at the thought that these men were *her* suitors. And one of them was her future husband.

Cullen tossed his crown atop one of the two carved walnut beds in the burgundy guest room. As so many other gentlemen were staying on and the second-floor guest rooms were not an option for propriety's sake, he had to share. The room was smaller than he had expected it to be, given the affluence of the family, but judging from the gold leaf painted liberally about the chamber's moldings, it held more wealth than the finest room in his home. As the Dempsey family had once possessed a vast fortune, they lived in one of the coveted addresses on Fifth Avenue, though not on the most desired mile, but due to his family's current lack of funds, it was falling into disrepair that no amount of cleaning could disguise.

His gaze fell on the fine Louis Vuitton flat-top trunks with *T. D.* on the crimson-striped cloth exteriors next to his worn steamer trunk with its curved top. While the cost of a new wardrobe was staggering, he had a façade to manage if he wanted to outpace the others. Yet judging by Theodore Day's trunks, the gentleman had never known hardship. And since Miss Dupré had a past with Theodore, Cullen realized he would have a rival in the fellow and could not afford to become friends with him. He needed this win, not only for his business but also to repay his mentor the fortune his family owed him.

"Ahh, so we are to be roommates," Theodore called from

the doorway, shedding his coat and neckcloth at once, studying their opulent chamber.

"Seems to be," Cullen replied, sitting on the edge of the bed nearest the fireplace, silently laying claim to it as he too removed his neckcloth.

Theodore kicked off his shoes and fell atop the opposite bed, sighing and crossing his arms behind his head. "What a surprise Will turned out to be."

"Will? Her father?" Cullen's brows furrowed, confused as to what the man could possibly mean.

Theodore yawned and adjusted his pillow, closing his eyes and clasping his hands over his chest. "No, Willow. Her father always called her Will, so I did too."

Will. Cullen frowned, not caring for such familiarity coming from Theodore's mouth. *Stop. If you start caring, you will risk everything.* He kept silent and began unpacking his trunk, waiting for Theodore's breathing to become even, signaling that he was asleep.

At the steady snore, Cullen took a seat at the walnut desk and, ignoring the twinge in his soul, pulled open the middle drawer, removed a single sheet of stationery, and penned a note.

> *H,*
> *Made it through first round. Plan is in motion.*
> *C.*

Four

Theodore held the lavender neckcloth up against his jacket. Frowning, he tossed it atop the bedcover in favor of the rich plum hue he recalled Willow had favored so long ago. Fitting it about his collar, he grinned at the thought of the fine lady she had become since he had last seen her. As a child, she had her pretty little nose buried in her newspapers, brewing new ideas for running the factory as she memorized stock numbers and business news to impress her father, always keeping her hair in a simple braid down her back while their mutual friend, Flora, wore hers in a waterfall of curls. As a lad, he had favored Flora's beauty, but over the summers spent in Newport, Willow's thirst for knowledge drew him to her, and Theodore had begun to see the lovely creature behind the economic books.

But when he had turned seventeen, his mother had decided it was time for him to study abroad, and he and Willow had been obliged to part ways. He had thought of her often over the years, until he had met Bernadette and began courting her. He sighed, shaking his head free of the memory of Bernadette's alluring, fanciful nature that he had come to realize was merely disguising her traits of an overgrown, petulant child. He only wished he had discovered her true heart before she had broken his by eloping with his old chum.

Now that he was free again, however, and permanently returned to the States, he was thankful that his path had once again intertwined with Willow Dupré, who had fully stepped into the role of a strong business-minded woman. And while he could see Mr. Dupré in her, her mother's gentler side was there in Willow's eyes, in her thoughtfulness that softened her direct nature. For it seemed that while Willow's serious side had quelled her humor in later years, he had caught glimpses of it last night when he had made her laugh . . . and when Cullen had danced with her so masterfully. It was the only time Theodore regretted not taking more dance lessons. Shrugging off the thought of Cullen, Theodore finished tying the knot and tugged on his coat, eager to finish his toilette so he could finally see her again and pick up where they had left off nearly a decade ago.

Cullen stepped through the shared bathroom in his robe, rubbing a thick ivory towel over his drenched hair, steam following him into the room. Theodore nodded to him and reached for his petroleum pomade and set about taming his wild curls, having given up attempting to make small conversation for the morning, as Cullen had answered only in single sentences, offering precious little in return. Theodore assumed Cullen's aloof attitude was either from a shy nature, which he doubted, judging by the man's confidence on the floor alone, or because of Cullen's recent climb to the top rungs of the social ladder. His mother had warned him of the parvenus who would be vying for Willow's hand and reassured him that while his opponents might have scads of money, it was *new* money and therefore far less desirable and valuable than old money with an old name to go along with it.

With his deep-rooted Knickerbocker heritage from his great-grandfather, and distant strands of French nobility from his mother's side, Theodore was sternly reminded by Mother that he could offer Willow something she desperately needed—an old name to back her business and bring credit to her as the new ruler. At the time, he had merely nodded respectfully while secretly dismissing such a snobbish view, but he was beginning to realize that it *did* indeed give him an edge over some of the men like Cullen, an edge Theodore found he desperately wanted now that Willow had returned to his life.

He ran a comb along the sides of his hair, wanting to look impeccable for his first meeting with Willow since the crowning. The moment he had seen her on the grand staircase, Theodore's boyhood infatuation and this strange sensation of hope had begun to swell within him. If Willow could come to think of him as a suitor, he did not particularly care if her affection began because of his old name so long as it ended with their finding a bit of happiness as a couple. He had seen firsthand the error of marrying for power or money and he would never sacrifice his chance for a happy marriage for the sake of shoring up his retirement or his legacy, which was why he had refused every young woman so far . . . until Bernadette and now Willow. While some of the other gentlemen spoke of feeling somewhat repulsed by her business nature, Theodore admired her drive and saw beyond that wall of hers into the heart of the girl he once knew, and he could not wait to get to know her once more. If love found them, he would gladly surrender his position in the family's riverboat-building business down South and claim his old New Yorker heritage to support Willow in building her empire.

At the snap of suspenders behind him, Theodore noticed Cullen was stretching around him to catch a glimpse of himself in the looking glass as he shrugged into his vest. Theodore gave his hair one more brush, tossed aside his comb and pomade atop the writing desk, and crossed the small chamber to look out to the avenue far below to find Willow returning to the house, seeming rather winded by the color in her cheeks and the hand pressed to her side.

"Eager to start the day?"

Theodore fairly jumped at Cullen's deep voice. "Uh, yes," he replied, shocked that the silent Irish giant had willingly spoken at last. "And yourself?"

"Quite."

Well, that's a start. "If you'll excuse me, I believe Miss Dupré has returned, and I want to catch her before the others have a chance."

Willow tromped up the steps, pausing to kick the snow from her boots against the doorframe, hand her wraps to the footman in the white marble foyer, and smooth her sapphire overskirt. It had taken an hour's walk in the park to set her temper to rights after reading the atrocious headline in this morning's papers. She shuddered as her eye caught another copy on the circular foyer table, the thick letters fairly shouting *American Heiress to Wed Victor of Competition*, followed by an outrageous article on how the mothers and daughters of New York would be up in arms at Willow's stealing the season's crop of the most eligible bachelors. She leaned over the foyer table, resting on her palms on the polished mahogany, and exhaled, attempting to gain back the peace from her walk. *Lord, what am I doing?* She didn't know how to flirt, much less court. Last night she had managed to make it through with few blunders and one slightly torn hem, all of which were plastered across page five of the papers.

"Good morning, Miss Dupré."

She glanced up at the familiar voice and could not help but smile at the perfection that was Teddy Day. "Mr. Day, good morning."

"May I escort you into breakfast? Your mother caught me

on the way down and asked me to take you in." He held his arm out to her.

Facing the men would be much easier with Theodore at her side. For even though she had agreed to this scheme, she still quaked at the thought of the outlandish goal of this season—although the scheme wasn't really much different from a debutante's first season, only far more structured. But, as it had been years since her first season, after last night's ball, she had retrieved an old favorite romance novel from her mother's bookcase that she hadn't read in years and took a few notes on the heroine's flirting that could prove useful if she were courageous enough to attempt flirting. She threaded her arm through his and tried batting her lashes, a favorite coquetry of the heroine. "I would like that very much."

"Do you have something in your eye?" He reached into his pocket and offered her his handkerchief.

She ceased batting and accepted the token, dabbing at her eyes to hide her mortification. "Much better. Shall we?"

The butler, Beckwith, opened the door to the dining room that was being used as the breakfast room—and all other meals now to accommodate the large party—bowing to them.

"Good morning, gentlemen," she called, keeping her voice cheery. The men, some seated, others clustered about the room and at the end of the line at the buffet table, turned their attention to her, plates already stacked with scones, pastries, meats, and all the delightful foods that breakfast could offer. She swept her gaze over the impressive group, enjoying seeing them in an informal setting after last night's ostentatiousness.

"I'll fetch us some coffees from Beckwith," Theodore whispered, and the moment he left her side, Chandler Starling closed the gap, his expression bright as he swallowed his mouthful.

The gangly fellow set aside his plate at a vacant place on the table and bowed to her. "Miss Dupré, wonderful to see you. What an adventure this has been already."

An adventure is one way to word it. She smiled at his enthusiasm. "I trust you are comfortable in your room?"

"Quite. Thought it was amusing, though, that I, being the youngest in this competition, should be paired with the oldest gentleman for a roommate. But I suppose that means he will not be waking *me* from coming in late after cards."

In the light of day, she could see that Mr. Starling was *far* younger than she had originally thought. She bit back asking exactly how old he was, knowing her parents had selected him for a reason and she had best find it out before insulting him by asking his age. *He might just have a youthful face.* "I am certain you will get along famously with Mr. Quincy. He is a man of great character."

"My ears are burning." Mr. Kit Quincy's voice brought her round.

"Mr. Quincy, you are looking as handsome as ever," she blurted, her eyes widening at the grin she remembered so well from her girlhood. Kit had been exceptionally handsome in his youth, and now, well, he had managed to become even more so. Starling gaped at her before letting loose a hoot.

"What is so amusing?" Teddy returned with coffees and handed one to her.

"Only that I should pack my bags and leave with Mr. Quincy in the house." Starling slapped his knee, shaking from suppressed laughter as if the very notion was absurd. "None of us stand a chance, as it seems Miss Dupré fancies him."

Thankful to have something to divert her attention, she encircled the cup with both hands, taking a long sip and looking everywhere but in Mr. Quincy's eyes, which brought the nearest gentleman, Mr. Pruett, to her side. The men continued to greet her throughout the morning, and she took note of their attire and any personal choices they had made to stand out, such as the blossom on the lapel of Friedrich Blythe's high-buttoned morning coat.

"A purple lilac, sir?" She finished her cup and handed it to the footman before tracing the bloom with her fingertip, recognizing its meaning for first emotions of love. "Isn't that a bold choice for the second day?"

"The flower never lies," Mr. Blythe quipped.

She laughed. "Wherever did you find it at this time of year? The flower shops are surely closed this early in the day."

Pulling it from his lapel, he lifted the flower to her. "I grew it in my personal hothouse and sent for it this morning. May I?" At her nod, he fixed it to her braided coiffure. "There. Now it is even lovelier."

Mr. Seaborne came alongside them, pulling her away into another conversation in which she nearly perished from the scent of stale coffee lingering on the gentleman's every breath. Even so, Willow nodded through the tête-à-têtes, keeping an eye out for Cullen's appearance. Her mind spun with how to respond to their stream of questions, so much so that she did not remember half of her conversations. Why hadn't she listened more closely to her mother's incessant tips on how to work a room? Mother, at one point in her own debut season, had six suitors. And while her mother's accounts over the years of her successful season and bits of advice seemed rather trivial at the time, Willow now wished she had listened more attentively. But then she never would have thought she would have six suitors at a time, much less sixteen!

"Looks like you could use a cup of strong coffee," came a deep voice at her elbow, the hint of brogue sending chills up her spine.

She turned to find Cullen holding out a steaming cup toward her. "I will never turn down a cup of coffee." She took a sip and fought a gag, her cheeks bulging to keep from swallowing. She quickly turned her back to him and dribbled the coffee back into the cup. "*Unless* it does not have a single cube of sugar in it." She coughed and smacked against the bitter taste and reached for a fresh cup from the butler and for the sugar pot, then dropped four lumps of sugar into the cup. While she was at it, she added a generous amount of cream until it was the perfect hue.

"So, the sugar queen has a sweet tooth. Why am I not surprised?" Cullen chuckled.

She smirked and took a long draft. "Much better." She sighed in satisfaction. "You may mock me, sir, but it is an occupational hazard. A queen cannot rule a sugar kingdom without believing in her product. And I am a firm believer in *Dupré* sugar."

A footman appeared at her elbow and presented a note to her on a silver tray. Nodding her thanks, she opened it to find Mother's scrawling penmanship, detailing the first outing she had planned per Willow's suggestion last night, along with the list of men who would be in attendance. She excused herself from Cullen and moved to stand at the head of the table, setting her cup down long enough to fold her hands around the card in front of her skirt to keep herself from fidgeting.

"Gentlemen? May I have a moment?" Willow waited for the room to quiet and all to turn to her while the staff quietly rustled about the room, removing used dishes and refilling cups. "Before I issue an invitation to join me for the first outing, I need to address today's headline in *The World*. I'd like to remind you all of the contracts you signed before you entered the ballroom not to disclose any of the details of the competition until *after* I have selected a husband." She lifted her hand to stay the gentlemen's replies. "And please, do not think I am accusing you, for it could have been anyone, even our trusted staff, but perhaps see this as a *friendly* reminder that this is not a game to me. Like you, I have taken time away from my business to be here today. Let us respect one another and not treat this like a holiday."

"Hear, hear!" Teddy called, lifting his cup to her. "And I would like to add that it is our duty as gentlemen to inform the lady if we hear of anyone who has anything but the purest of intentions." His gaze pierced her own. "She is too dear to trifle with."

Willow's cheeks tinted at his magnanimous words. He had always been kind, but after working with hardened men every day, Willow could see that his kindness held a strength and his striking eyes possessed a gentleness that drew her. "Thank you, Teddy," she replied, forgetting herself and using his childhood sobriquet and at once regretting it as the men beside him elbowed him, others snorting and murmuring their disapproval. "My apologies. I always think of you as Teddy and I am afraid it tumbled out. I will try my best to adjust to saying Theodore— I mean, *Mr. Day.*" She turned her chin to her shoulder at her stumbling.

"I don't mind," he said with a grin. "In fact, I quite like the sound of it when it comes from you."

"Miss Dupré." Mr. Blythe approached her, taking her elbow. "May I steal you away for a moment to the conservatory where it is more private?"

"Oh." Willow looked down at the card in her hand and back to Mr. Blythe. "Well, I was going to take some of you on an outing today, but of course you may speak with me. You are my beau, after all." She gave a nervous giggle and rested her hand on Mr. Blythe's arm, allowing him to lead her out into the hall, away from the others.

"Why didn't I think of that?" Teddy muttered under his breath as they passed, causing her to swallow her happiness at the realization of how much he was already invested in her.

"I hope you didn't mind my interruption, but I did not see how else I could speak with you alone."

"I am so glad you did. The conservatory is one of my favorite places to find a bit of peace during the long winter, and I think you will find it most interesting." Willow motioned him down the hall, through the parlor and out the rear door into the humid warmth of the conservatory, which had another door leading out to a small courtyard that she frequently used when there wasn't so much snow.

The pair walked in silence amongst the buds and full blooms while he scanned the room as if searching for something hidden. "Aha! Here it is. I hoped your mother would have it, as it is a hardy plant that likes cooler weather but usually dies with the first frost. You must have an exceptional gardener to cultivate such blooms off-season." Mr. Blythe plucked a bloom before tapping his chin and selecting a second and a third flower. He showed her to the bench and took the seat beside her, offering her a blue flower. "Allow me to translate for you. This is a forget-me-not, and as you can guess—"

"It means to remember the giver." Willow finished, tucking it into her hair beside the lilac. "How could one ever forget Friedrich Blythe?"

"Fritz, if you will, and it is easier than you might think." He lifted the second flower to her, a small blossom with an orange throat.

Easy to forget? Was there a reason that the most eligible bachelor remained single for another season? "Fritz. It suits you. And you must call me Willow, but please, only in private. My mother would not approve of such informality and so soon."

"Willow." He drew out her name in a whisper, twirling the flower by its tiny stem. "This is an orange blossom and it holds a dear message. Your pure heart is only matched by your beauty." Before she could respond, the third blossom with a vibrant lavender hue was placed in her hand, his fingertips brushing her palm.

"Thank you, Fritz."

He beamed at the sound of his name from her lips and closed his hand over hers, encasing the delicate blossom with their hands. "And at last, the orchid, which represents royalty. And to me, Miss Dupré, you are everything a queen should be. Kind, lovely, and full of grace."

She pressed the back of her hand to her cheeks and neck, overwhelmed by his fervor. Was this how all his previous ladies felt? His presentation *was* rather flawless, but looking into his ardent gaze, she could read nothing but genuineness. "And you know this from having spent one evening with me?"

"Your character is in your very name, which means *graceful*, or at least it is one of the many interpretations."

"How do you know so much about flowers and their meanings?"

"I have been fascinated with blossoms since boyhood, and my dictionary of the language of flowers is quite frayed." He chuckled, shaking his head. "Which may seem ridiculous to most, but I am clandestinely working on a dictionary of my own with a dash more information I have gathered over the years, as well as experimenting with the forced blossoming of flowers year-round, which is why I am so impressed that your gardener has mastered the technique, and I must speak with him to compare our methods. Forcing blooms is all about the soil and temperature and of course how you have the bulb potted."

Willow's lips parted in surprise at his passion lying beneath the flowers. "Not at all ridiculous. How marvelous to have a botanist calling upon me."

He shrugged dismissively. "No, not quite a botanist. I study whenever I get a moment, but Mother stoutly refuses to allow me to study formally since she considers that a trade, and I, being a Blythe, descended from English lords, should never have a trade."

"How heartbreaking." She could not fathom what it would be like to have her passion for running the business denied to her by her own mother.

He chuckled and ran his fingers through his brilliant ginger locks. "Not as heartbreaking as losing one's inheritance a year from coming into it, so I study in secret, and if she ever looked in the cabinet of my study, she would find row upon row of botany literature hidden inside." He chuckled. "My flowers are actually located next door where my mother will never find them. My neighbor readily agreed to allow me the use of her conservatory, as I always give her the blooms."

"Then we must make certain your mother does not discover your secrets until *after* you can claim your inheritance." She fitted the final blossom in her coiffure. "But I must admit, Mr. Blythe—"

"Fritz, please," he corrected, his fingers steadying the flowers in her hair and tucking them more securely in place.

She froze at the intimate gesture. When they had been in the dining room, they were so closely watched that she had not thought of it . . . but his touching her hair while alone with her was quite another matter. She leaned back from him and rose. "Fritz, I must admit that your sudden interest in me after meeting me years ago has left me wondering—"

"Of my intentions? You are right to ask. While you *did* catch my eye last season—" he coughed, rising—"time got away from me."

"Along with numerous courtships?" She gave him a wink, continuing their procession amongst the flowers. "I believe I have heard of at least one maiden last year who was certain you would propose."

"Ah, yes, that would have been Miss Hughina." He clasped his hands behind his back. "I will not defend myself. Instead, I must reply with a question. How are we to know who is the right one if we do not sift through the ones who are not? How are we to know what we desire in a partner until we see what we do not want in the actions of others?"

She well remembered her own parade of suitors in the years past. Who was she to judge him? *After all, I am in the most outlandish competition man has ever known . . . well, unless one considers that Esther was once in such a competition to become queen of Persia.* "That's fair. Well, besides courting a few of the ladies in New York and studying botany in secret—"

"Pardon me, Mr. Blythe," a nasally voice interrupted, "but might I have a word with Miss Dupré?" Mr. Harolds appeared from behind a potted palm, his eyes impossibly magnified behind his round wire spectacles that he had not donned for his photograph or for the ball, which explained why he had tripped so much during their waltz the previous night.

She rested a hand on Fritz's sleeve. "Forgive me for cutting short our conversation, but I would love to continue it soon. Perhaps you could join me along with a few others for tobogganing this evening?"

"I would enjoy that very much. Until then, my dear Miss Dupré." He bowed and grasped her hand in his, slowly lifting it to his lips. At Mr. Harolds *harrumph* of disapproval, Fritz whispered, "Willow."

Mr. Harolds grasped her by the elbow and steered her to the bench beside the fountain with cherubs flying just above the bowls of the second and third tiers. "I must say that you have quite the impressive head, Miss Dupré."

Seeing his earnestness, she squelched her ungenerous laughter, biting her lip at the absurd observation. "Thank you. But, uh, do you mind my inquiring as to *why* you were thinking such a thing?"

He blinked rapidly behind his bifocals, which she was beginning to recognize as his nervous trait. "I am a phrenologist. I study the shape of one's skull to determine the patient's humor. I have been studying the men, and I find that Mr. Dempsey and Mr. Blythe possess exceptionally good skulls, revealing their honest natures. I have not had much of a chance to ascertain the humors of the rest of the men, but I am certain, given time, I will be able to help you weed out the bad eggs from your overflowing basket of suitors, if you will."

She scrunched her brows together, not entirely certain how to reply. She had heard of the fad of seeing such doctors from some of the ladies in her charity group but had dismissed it as ludicrous and focused on the task at hand. "How thoughtful."

"You seem confused. Allow me to demonstrate what I mean." Mr. Harolds eagerly forced her to take a seat on the marble bench athwart from the fountain.

"No, I wasn't confused. I, uh . . ." But his fingers were already weaving their way through her locks and began pressing into her skull, the man muttering away to himself. "Sir, please, you shouldn't bother yourself." She leaned to the side, and he merely sidestepped with her movement, feeling away. "Mr. Harolds."

"Oh no. This will not do at all." His brows lowered as he pressed his fingers methodically over her skull in the same place he had already prodded.

"*What* won't do?" she inquired, unable to keep her voice from rising. While she certainly did not fully believe in the science behind the shape of one's skull revealing the mystery of personal traits, it did not bode well for a phrenologist doctor to exclaim over the ridges of her skull. "I know I have a bump at the back of my skull, but it is not cause for alarm . . . is it?"

"Well, while the dips and slopes of your skull suggest a benevolent nature, I find a shocking lack of—" He sucked in his breath as if his findings were too scandalous to reveal.

"Shocking lack of what, sir?" She attempted to pull her head away from the man, but his bony little fingers were surprisingly strong and were now at her temples, and there was no hope for escape now.

"If you must know, *philoprogenitiveness*."

She blinked. "I beg your pardon?"

"Philoprogenitiveness is a love of children or offspring." He halfheartedly continued prodding her head. "After this discovery, I will have to take some time to evaluate the possibility of a future with a woman who apparently would not make a very good mother."

Willow gasped at the man's audacity and attempted to extricate her hair from his fingers. "*Excuse me?*"

"Pardon me, Miss Dupré, are you in need of assistance?" Cullen's deep voice filled the conservatory.

"Mr. Dempsey!" She moved to stand, but Mr. Harolds, lost in his own world, kept her effectively pinned to the bench as if she were a butterfly he was adding to his morbid collection.

Cullen crossed the paving stones to her side and snatched back Mr. Harolds's arm with ease, taking a few strands of her dark hair with it. "Excuse me, sir. I believe you have forgotten that Miss Dupré is not your patient."

Willow sent the horrid man a scowl, her fingers rubbing at the sore spot on her scalp where Mr. Harolds had inadvertently pulled her hair. *While you are considering, consider that perhaps I do not wish for a charlatan for a husband.* "Thank goodness you saved me," she whispered to Cullen, taking his arm and resisting the urge to run from the room.

"Well, I think we both know who will be dismissed come next crowning ceremony," Cullen mumbled through the side of his mouth, guiding her into the parlor.

She snorted and paused by the looking glass above the fireplace, pulling the pins from her hair and removing the now-crumpled flowers. Her braid tumbled to her waist, and she began raking loose the braid with her fingertips.

"Miss Dupré, whatever are you about?" Cullen whipped his back to her, crimson staining the back of his neck that was barely visible under his dark hair.

"Pardon me for my state of undress, but I have to put my hair to rights lest the man informing the papers suggest lurid behavior." She twisted her locks into a loose bun and reapplied the pins. She would have to summon her maid to repair it once she was finished issuing her invitations for this evening. "There."

She laid a hand on his shoulder. "It's safe now. I am prim-and-proper Miss Dupré once again and no one will be the wiser."

He sent her a crooked grin. "Oh no? How can you be certain that I am not the rat? Tomorrow's papers could tell all."

She threaded her hand through his arm, pulling him along through the parlor, the platinum-leaf walls shining in the light splaying through the windows. "Why, because our resident phrenologist said you had the construction of an honest skull and therefore an honest face. And as you know, he is a professional, so it *must* be true."

He threw his head back and laughed. "An honest face? That's a first. When most people see my nose—"

"They think you are a hooligan?" she finished for him, daring to risk teasing him, even though she had no idea how he had obtained such an injury.

"Indeed, for no businessman would sport a broken nose if he were a *true* gentleman."

Willow paused outside the dining room door, echoes of the men's banter floating out to them. "Well, I tend to be a fair judge of character, and until I find out otherwise, which I hope never happens—" she gave him a pointed look, imitating her mother—"I will be happy to have you around." She sighed. "We best return or they may send out a search party."

"But I *am* the search party and I only just found you," he whispered, his hand wrapping around her wrist. "And I have had a burning question to ask you."

Her heart hammered in her chest at the intensity in his brilliant eyes, the raw power in his arms that she could sense in the gentle tugging of his hand. She could easily forget herself in those eyes and arms. He could ask her anything and she would be forced to tell him by the spell he cast. She longed to spend more time with him and find out his story and exactly how and why his nose had been broken, but she had a schedule to keep. "Yes?"

He leaned so close, his breath heated her ear. "What is your favorite color?"

She blinked, the spell vanishing. "Oh, um, green, I suppose?" She inwardly cringed at her declaration. Until she had met Cullen, she had always preferred powder blue, but one look in those eyes and no other color could compare.

He laughed. "Don't you know?"

"I wasn't prepared for a quiz today, sir." She winked, striding toward the door before pausing to look over her shoulder at him. "It is definitely green." Willow sauntered into the fray, the gentlemen at once surrounding her, and she spent the next half hour speaking with each of her beaus.

Glancing at the clock over the massive, carved fireplace mantel, Willow knew she had to close the morning visit if she was ever going to finish her paper work in time for an evening of tobogganing. She looked about for a way to see the whole group, but being rather on the petite side, she needed a platform. She pulled out a chair from the table and, gathering her skirts to maintain modesty, stood upon it, clapping her hands to garner their attention, though her being on the chair seemed to do the trick at once.

"It has been a delight visiting with you all this morning. Now, in order to move things forward, I'd like to invite a small group for an outing this evening, so please listen for your name. If I do not call your name, that means there will be another outing planned, so please do not think I have forgotten you." She turned her attention to her friend. "Theodore Day."

Teddy hooted and shot over to her side and took her hand, bumping her chair and startling her into seizing his shoulder for support. "That's my girl. You hold on to me and I'll take care of you," he teased, sending a flame up her neck.

Will I never cease blushing around these gentlemen? "Fritz Blythe."

Fritz grinned and joined Willow on her other side, sending her a curious look.

The flowers. She inwardly groaned, hoping Fritz did not feel slighted or realize that her hair was arranged differently. "Archibald Lovett."

Archibald bowed to the group. "Sorry, gents. I will be certain to take care of our sweetheart this evening."

She looked to the phrenologist and suppressed a sigh. She had already decided before coming in this morning that she was going to invite him, but after his debacle in the conservatory, she was fairly certain he would not make it to the next ceremony. Still, remembering what her mother had told her before this all began, she summoned a bit of kindness. *"Everyone deserves a second chance to make a better first impression."*

"Mr. Harolds."

The phrenologist tucked his hands behind his back as he joined them, blinking away behind his glasses. "All right then. All right then," he murmured over and over excitedly.

"And last but not least, Cullen Dempsey." She smiled at the fifth gentleman. "Would you all do me the honor of accompanying me on a tobogganing adventure in Central Park?"

Five

Those left behind grumbled, but Cullen paid them no mind and followed Willow's swishing skirts out the front door into the soft snowfall, not knowing what to expect when one was courting a woman with fifteen other beaus. Having come to know Fritz some throughout the day over billiards and cards, he was almost relieved to have a comrade on the outing to alleviate the awkwardness of so many gentlemen courting the same woman. *Comrade?* No. He gave up comrades when his father died. He had business associates who thought they were friends. He shook that thought from his head. Even though Cullen was fairly certain that the gentleman had little chance with Willow, he had to focus on the prize, who was now heading toward the carriage. With five gentlemen and one lady on a lover's outing, there would be precious little time with Willow unless he was smart.

And getting her to talk about the factory during that short amount of time would be next to impossible. He rubbed the back of his neck. Wellington was not a patient man, but even he surely did not expect Willow to hand over the keys to her kingdom so swiftly. He shoved his hands into his pockets and rubbed the lone coin inside his left pocket between his thumb and forefinger, a sore reminder of his family's fiscal state. He needed this victory. For Mother and Eva Marie. If only he could reverse time and sell Father's shipping business to cover the debts, surely it would have been better than this ever-present force driving him into the ground. *But if I don't find anything to send Wellington by the end of the week . . . he may make good on his vow to destroy my father's legacy, sullied as it is, and Eva Marie's future along with it.*

Cullen kicked at a lump of snow on the bottom step. No matter the cost, Eva Marie must be protected. It wasn't her fault that in his grief he had ignored God and trusted the wrong man, had put himself *and* his family at the mercy of a Machiavellian tycoon.

Theodore trotted up behind Miss Dupré and adjusted her fur cap to a jaunty angle and offered her his arm, making Cullen kick himself for wasting time wallowing in thought. Frowning, he yanked on his gloves and followed Theodore and Miss Dupré like a puppy, with Archibald, Harold, and Fritz yapping at their heels. Willow laughed at something Theodore had whispered in her ear and surreptitiously glanced over her shoulder, meeting his gaze before she stepped into the carriage.

He lengthened his stride and closed the gap, but to no avail as the others had already scrambled into the best positions at either side of her and across, leaving him to squeeze beside Archibald and the miserably cold window.

Fritz waggled his brows at Willow from his position beside her. "May I ask what the prize is should one of us win the race?"

"A private dinner with me." Willow settled her skirts. "Though sledding was my idea, the dinner was my mother's. She is the one who will be planning all our future outings, as I have, to put it in Mother's loving way, 'not a creative bone in my body.'"

"A worthy prize indeed," Cullen replied over the men's laughter, enjoying seeing her lashes dip at his words.

Archibald, seated directly across from her, rested his elbows on his knees in a boyish manner that irked Cullen. "Shall we be sharing the toboggans, Miss Dupré?"

"No. Nice try, however. I am quite proficient, and this will be a fair race down the hill, even though it is a rather small hill."

"I wouldn't think you would have time for such frivolity." Theodore winked to soften his words while Cullen leaned forward to catch her response.

"I don't usually." Willow flipped her hands out, shrugging. "But winter has always been my favorite season, and as I am on a forced hiatus from going into the office until I find a husband to help me run the company, Mother wishes for us to have a bit of fun."

Forced hiatus. So, she wasn't happy with finding a gentleman in such a fashion. He had suspected as much, for despite her smiles and support of her parents during the ball, she was holding back something. And that something was probably what would interest Wellington and keep him off his back for another week.

"Sometimes we must force ourselves to take a moment from our frenetic lives lest we miss the beauty surrounding us." Theodore propped his face in his hands. "And in your case, *I* am that beauty," he added, making her laugh.

It seemed this fellow was always bringing a smile to her, despite her reputation of having a rather serious nature. Yet was it truly her nature or merely the attitude she was forced into assuming as a woman in the workplace? He would have to endeavor more to discover who Willow Dupré really was beneath the surface. The carriage wheels crunched to a halt on the fresh snowfall, and without waiting for the driver, Cullen shot out the door and almost slipped on a slick patch, then caught himself against the carriage before anyone could notice and lifted his hand to assist her down. Thanking him, she fitted her small hand into his, sending a jolt through his arm. He did not release her but instead led her up the hill to where he spotted a row of sleds awaiting them with one of the Duprés' footmen standing beside the sleds. They followed the recently shoveled path that the staff must have dug for the occasion but was even now filling up with the slow, steady snowfall. "I have a confession, my lady."

"Another confession?" She withdrew her hand and tucked it inside her fur muff. "Are you an expert in winter games as well as a dance instructor? When you told me you adored dancing, I had no idea you were so proficient."

"I am pleased that you found my dancing matched my enthusiasm for it. Actually, I . . . uh, have never had the opportunity to sled."

She tilted her head. "Surely you jest. I would have thought that you, being the largest of the bunch, could have done this blindfolded and seated backwards. Did you grow up elsewhere?"

He grinned. She *had* noticed his form. "I grew up in New York City, but my father did not believe that playing was an important aspect of boyhood, so I am afraid I never had the chance to learn."

"Then you must allow me the honor of teaching you." Taking his arm, she tugged him over to the longest toboggan, which could have easily fit three or four children. "I'll steer for the inaugural race down the hill, and you should be able to take it from there."

Cullen rubbed his gloved hand over the back of his neck. "Isn't that somewhat improper?"

"We are sledding, you are my beau, and we are supervised by all at the park, including a footman in my father's house. What is improper about it?" She settled herself onto the emerald sled, taking up the golden ropes at the front. "Push us toward the edge of the hill and hop on."

Seeing the jealous light in the other men's scowls, Cullen moved quickly, leaping onto the back of the toboggan, and with Willow squealing in front of him, Cullen held on to her petite waist as she expertly steered the toboggan to the bottom of the hill. A snowball smacked his neck, the cold sliding down his collar to his spine. He hooted and released her waist to wipe it off and half fell from the toboggan.

"Don't let go!" Willow shrieked and grabbed at his hand, wrapping it about her.

Cullen braced against the hail of snowballs being thrown at his back from the men when Willow turned to say something and was struck by a snowball in the jaw, sending them toppling over. "Willow!" Cullen kept his grip about her waist, taking the brunt of the fall and keeping her cradled against his chest. They sank into the snow, Willow rubbing at her jaw where an angry red splotch marred her pale skin. "Miss Dupré? Are you badly injured?"

She giggled, despite her watering eyes. "Not as bad as the fellow who threw it will be."

Theodore's toboggan slid toward them, and he leapt off. "I am so sorry, Will! I was aiming for—"

"You?" And with a battle cry, she raced after him, leaving Cullen colder than ever, seeing the comradery between the pair as Willow dropped a handful of snow down the man's collar. Scores even, Theodore pulled his sled behind him, already heading back up the hill with Willow on his arm.

Cullen seized his sled's rope and trotted up beside Willow. "Hold up. I think I might need one more lesson. One that preferably does not end with us falling off."

Her eyes sparkled at him. "If you need a second lesson, perhaps Mr. Day can be persuaded to teach you." She motioned to Fritz, who was waving to her from the hilltop. "I'm afraid I am already spoken for this next round. Mr. Blythe wishes to sled beside me."

Theodore snorted. "That will be a firm *no*, Miss Dupré. We both know that Dempsey did not need a lesson in the first place. You sit on a board and hold on to the rope attached and do not let go. How hard could it be to steer oneself?"

"Fairly difficult." Cullen grinned at Willow.

Theodore lined up his sled with the others at the top of the hill. "Nice effort, Dempsey, but enough practice. I say let's race. I want my private dinner with Miss Dupré."

Harold bobbed his head in agreement, rubbing his spectacles with his plaid scarf to remove the fog created from his heavy breathing into his equally heavy scarf. "Quite right you are, old boy. And there is no time like the present to begin our first race of the evening."

Cullen suppressed his riposte because he feared any response would come off as desperate and insecure, both of which he was shocked to find he actually felt. So, instead of giving in to those disconcerting feelings, Cullen aligned his sled with the others.

"On three," Willow called, positioning herself on her sled and taking up the ropes. "One. Two. *Three!*" The footman shoved off her sled and sent her careening down the fresh powder.

Cullen pushed off with the other men but fell behind at once. He glanced over his shoulder and noticed Harold had waited to take off, his focus on Cullen. *Strange fellow.* Cullen attempted to direct his infernally slow sled toward the middle where the group had packed down the snow when a streak blazing down the hill caught his eye. He glanced back in time to see Harold barreling toward him, a maniacal grin peeking over his scarf.

Willow made it to the bottom first. Laughing more than she had in a long while, she hopped off and turned to gloat when she spied Cullen's sled speeding toward a tree trunk. "Cullen!" She screamed a warning, but before his name left her lips, his sled cracked into the base of the tree and he was thrown, his body falling lifeless in the snow. *Lord, no!* She seized her skirts and ran, her boots sinking with every pace up the snowbank. "Cullen!" she cried again, falling to her knees beside him. She groaned as she turned him over, her heart sinking at the sight of a gash at his hairline, blood streaking down to his jaw. *Lord, please let him be well.*

"Did you see what happened?" Fritz dropped down beside her, pulling off his gloves and feeling for Cullen's pulse.

"It was Harold. I saw him deliberately cut in front of Dempsey." Teddy shook his head over Cullen, glaring at Harold. "It is a *friendly* competition, not a gladiator match, Mr. Harolds."

"I didn't mean for him to run into a *tree*, Theodore," Harold snapped. "I only meant to beat him out."

"His pulse is strong." At Willow's questioning look, Fritz added, "Mother tends to give in to a fit of vapors at the first sign of my occasional rebellion. The doctor showed me how to feel for her pulse before summoning him."

"I should think his pulse would be strong. He seems like a solid enough fellow. One could hazard to guess that the tree would yield before his skull." Harold snorted.

Though Willow had never wished to strike a man more, she suppressed the urge to do so. It wouldn't do Cullen any good. She studied the rise and fall of his chest, calming her racing pulse with the steady rhythm. Harold was at least correct on one account. Cullen was stronger than any man she had ever met. "I'll deal with *you* later, Mr. Harolds, but we need to get him to a doctor. Teddy, will you help me carry him?"

"Of course." Teddy moved to pick up Cullen when he moaned and brushed away Teddy's hand.

"If you think I'm going to allow you to carry me . . ." Cullen mumbled, holding his head. "I am perfectly capable."

Willow threw her arms around Cullen's neck before jerking back, remembering herself and the gentlemen watching her. "You had us all so worried."

"Which makes my accident almost worth it to see you fawn over me," he said with a smile, which then melted into a scowl as he again lifted a hand to his head. "I didn't think the next man to knock me out would be you, Harolds."

If this giant of a man was in pain, Willow knew it had to be agonizing. She shook her head, dismissing his comment. "That's your injury talking. Please allow Mr. Day to assist you into a hired carriage." She lifted her hand, staying his protest. "While you are residing under my family's roof, you *will* see the doctor, Mr. Dempsey. Any argument you make will be grounds for dismissal." But with one look at his smirk, Willow knew he saw through her falsehood.

Heaving a long-suffering sigh, he pulled himself to a seated position and allowed Teddy to drape his arm over the man's shoulder and hobbled down the hill to hail a carriage.

Willow turned to the remaining men. "The rest of you, please return to the house. Our time is over."

"A bump on the head hardly constitutes canceling our evening." Harold huffed, adjusting his scarf to cover his mouth again. "You don't need a physician to tell you that when you have a head doctor with you. Give the man some headache powder and put him to bed. He will be fine come morning."

Head doctor? She gritted her teeth against the man's arrogance and drew a deep breath. "Mr. Day, I'll be right behind you," she called after them, still stunned at the turn of events. She had wanted this evening to be carefree. Instead, she had found out the true character of Mr. Harolds and found him wanting . . . even more than he had been in the conservatory, which she could have dismissed as nervousness until his blatant cheating. *No wonder the man is single.*

Willow crossed her arms over her chest, wishing she had her muff that she must have dropped in the commotion. "Gentlemen, I requested Mother to create today's outing as a test. First, being out of doors to perform a child's game was meant to test your willingness to adapt and please me. Second, the race was meant to show if there were any dishonorable ones among you. While this may seem like a puerile activity to you, I do not want a cheater to run the empire at my side." She looked pointedly at Harold.

"You are going to cut me because I took a simple liberty in a child's game?" Harold clenched his gloved hands.

"A cheater with a bad temper in a child's game does not belong in my office. If one cheats in something small, the temptation to cheat when it comes to millions is too great. Thank you for your time, but I think you should leave us, Mr. Harolds."

"Pardon me, Miss Dupré, but you might wish to reconsider your rash decision given my family's place in the Four Hundred. I'm not like most of your suitors, who are merely the grandsons of the members of high society. The Harolds family are *all* members of the Four Hundred, and if you slight me, imagine the repercussions to your business."

Archibald took a step forward, rolling his shoulders back. "You forget yourself. I am in the elite set as well as Fritz here, old boy."

"I do not believe I said elite." He gave a chortle. "I meant that the Harolds family are part of the *elect* of Mrs. Vanderbilt." He turned again to Willow. "No. I shall wait at the mansion until we can speak in private and you do not allow your feminine emotions to rule."

Willow tilted her chin. "Even if you are in the Vanderbilts' elected inner circle, I do not appreciate your insinuation, nor your tone. Again, I thank you for your attentions, but do not bother waiting for me at the mansion. I want you out by the time we return."

His eyes set to blinking wildly behind his spectacles. "Willow, aren't you being a little hasty? Anyone could tell that injuring Mr. Dempsey was not my intention."

"I would listen to the lady. You have had your say. It is time to leave before more damage is done." Fritz closed the gap between himself and Willow, offering her his strength. For a flower-loving fellow, his form did not reflect it.

Courage bolstered, she straightened her shoulders, the last shred of compassion vanishing with his insistence. "It's *Miss Dupré*. I'll say this once more so you do not misinterpret my meaning. I do not desire a cheater for a suitor, so if you would be so kind as to pack your trunks, I would be most grateful." She marched down the hill and noticed a man in a greatcoat with his cap pulled low next to a tree, scribbling away with a pencil, his body inclined toward her. *Reporter.* She sucked in a breath. Feeling the fool for her public humiliation of Mr. Harolds, she pretended not to see the man and hurried to the hired carriage, where Teddy was depositing Cullen, a crowd already gathering about them. When they spied her and the three gentlemen following down the hill, the gossip flamed to life.

"Why, it's Willow Dupré. You were right," a gentleman whispered to the woman on his arm.

"So it *is* true," an elderly lady commented to the girl at her side, loud enough for Willow's ears to start to burn.

"Of course it is true," said the young woman. "She has more than a dozen men vying for her hand."

"In my day, we had, at the most, three suitors at a time, but we *never* went out together like a . . . well, it's outlandish, that's what it is."

"Outlandish? I wish my parents would have done this for me," the young woman sighed.

"Miss Dupré! I believe my invitation was lost in the mail," called a gentleman from the back of the group, waving his stiff hat in the air and distracting her from the elderly woman's revulsion.

Approaching the carriage, Willow lifted her hands, attempting to keep the crowd from pressing forward. "Please, move back and give us a moment of privacy. Can't you see Cullen's hurt?"

"*Cullen*, is it? She is already calling them by their Christian names? Scandalous." The elderly lady huffed, and even the girl seemed taken aback by such a liberty.

Willow pressed a hand to her waist at her gaffe. The onslaught was growing out of control. Her chest constricted at the group crowding ever nearer when Teddy grasped her wrist, pushed her into the carriage, and deposited her onto the seat next to Cullen.

He leaned halfway into the two-seater closed carriage, his russet eyes finding hers, calming her. "Go with Dempsey and see that you keep him awake. I'll deal with the reporters."

"Thank you, Teddy." She captured his hand, not caring about the onlookers at this point. It was too late for propriety today when all her blunders would be published in the morning's post, which would no doubt result in half a dozen more morning lessons from her mother on the art of courtship.

"Anytime, my lady." He secured the door and called up to the coachman, "You know where to go."

The carriage rocked to life, pushing her back into Cullen's shoulder, who moaned from under the coach's plaid that looked like it had seen far too many passengers in between washings.

"I did not think getting alone time with you on a group outing would require running my sled into a tree. But hopefully that warrants my winning the unaccompanied dinner with you by default."

"I am so sorry about all this, Cullen. I never thought that one of them could be so vicious."

"We should have read Harold's skull." He sighed, shaking his head. "It would have saved us both so much trouble."

She held her hand over her mouth to suppress her laughter. "You jest, but Mr. Harolds firmly believes in the shape of—" The carriage hit a rut, sending Cullen to wincing and her mirth into concern. "Does your head throb terribly? Oh, I pray that you are not concussed. We should be arriving in a few minutes."

He dropped his hand from his head and reached out for hers.

She slowly lowered the tips of her gloved fingers to graze along his callused palms and he grasped them. "Please do not worry yourself. It's not as if I haven't suffered worse blows, *mo chara*."

"What do you mean?" Her breath caught at the insinuation.

"Sorry, it means *my friend*."

She smiled at the term, warmth spreading from her heart through to her numbed limbs. "That's not what I was referring to, sir."

He shifted and looked out the window before meeting her gaze. "In the ring."

Her jaw dropped, all falling into place . . . his massive build, his confidence, lightness of foot, broken nose, rough hands. "You are a *boxer*."

"*Was*. When things weren't as stable for Dempsey Shipping, I, uh, took hold of the one boyhood pastime I was allowed and turned it into gain," he admitted slowly as if it pained him to do so.

"Often?"

He sighed and pushed up the hair over his ears, showing rather battered ears that were shriveled in some places and enlarged in others. "Often enough to acquire boxer's ear. Though it is not as bad as most, it is enough to send my mother into a fit for having done this to myself."

Her eyes widened before she could catch herself. *So that's why he wears his hair longer than is in fashion, but not long enough for a decent queue, which would reveal his ears.* "I see. Were you any good?"

He grinned, lifting his chin. "Do you remember reading anything about a fighter dubbed *Wild Man*?"

She gasped, remembering the countless articles the men in her office had devoured on the boxing champion. "Who hasn't heard of him? You cannot be serious."

He spread his arms wide, swaying with the turn of the wheels. "Well, you are looking at him. And because I have had

71

so many knocks in my time in the ring, I know the signs of a concussion, which proves my devotion to allow you to take me to a doctor even though I know what he is going to say and how to treat it."

She openly stared at him. How could she have *not* recognized him until now? She herself had been caught up in the mania of his career, but she supposed that one would look quite different clean-shaven and wearing a well-tailored suit. And thinking of his suit, she now knew for certain of his muscular chest. "My father will never believe it that the Irish Wild Man is courting his daughter."

"You may, of course, tell your parents and sisters, but, uh, I would prefer to keep my alternate identity from the others. I am attempting to leave that life behind me . . . after the last fight. I would hate for the papers to find me. They only know me as the Irish Wild Man and that I answer to Cullen, but it is a common enough name in New York to provide anonymity."

She nodded, recalling the stories covering the tragedy of his final fight only six months ago. "Never fear. I will tell my family and naught anyone else. Your secret is safe with me, Wild Man."

The carriage halted, and Willow hopped out and lifted her arms to him.

"I can manage without your assistance." He gave her a half grin that told her he thought her sweet but woefully unable to help him.

"Yes, you can manage, but I would feel much more comfortable with my arms around you."

His brows lifted, his mirth spreading to his eyes. "Such an indecent proposal, my lady."

"Oh, hush. You *know* what I meant." Unwilling to allow her embarrassment to overwhelm her, Willow grasped his forearms and helped him down, ushering him up the brownstone's steps. She dropped the knocker against the mahogany door.

Cullen swayed, and she gripped her arms around his waist,

holding him upright with all her strength. "Mr. Dempsey!" As his weight sagged against her, she sank to her knees. Then the door opened, and the butler's jaw dropped at the sight of Cullen's unconscious form atop her.

"Miss!" He moved to hoist Cullen up, and Willow managed to scoot out from under him. Cullen's substantial muscles and height made the elderly man groan with the effort, so Willow at once ducked under Cullen's arm and helped to shoulder him inside.

"If we can take him straight into the doctor's office, I'll fetch Dr. Philpott from dinner. He is only two doors down, visiting the Pruett family. What name shall I give him, and what is wrong with your gentleman?"

"Willow Dupré and Mr. Cullen Dempsey," she grunted, the butler's brows rising at the name. She shuffled forward and glanced at Cullen's lolling head, his thick neck bending backward at an angle that made her uneasy. "I don't know what happened. We were talking one second and then he collapsed the next."

"It happens more often than you would think at our front door. So much so, one would think the doctor would have hired a younger footman by now to help me in these times of crisis. How did Mr. Dempsey come to sustain injuries?" he asked as they staggered down the hallway.

Willow explained in a rush, and the butler nudged open the study door with his boot. The pair of them lowered Cullen to the settee, his legs dangling off the short piece of furniture whose dark-green velvet matched the walls of the small room.

The butler eyed her. "I am hesitant to leave you alone with him, miss, but someone has to fetch the doctor."

"Sir, I assure you, my reputation is safe enough with a cook in the house."

"Very good, miss. I shall return in a quarter of an hour." He hurried out the door.

Willow knelt beside Cullen and stroked his hair from his forehead to find that the gash had finally ceased its flow, leaving a streak of crimson from his crown to his neck. "Cullen? Can you hear me?" She bit her lip. She had read about some patients waking, or ending a fit of hysteria, when receiving a kiss. She rubbed her head. *Or am I remembering a fairy tale instead?* She looked to his full lips. *It couldn't hurt to try, could it? For medical purposes . . .* She leaned toward him, pausing a breath away, second-guessing herself. His lashes fluttered and he caught her about to *kiss* him. Her cheeks flooded with warmth. She jerked back. "Thank goodness," she whispered. "You had me worried. I did not hear your breathing."

"Is that the excuse you are going with?" The corners of his mouth turned upward, and his hand found hers. "I'm sorry for falling on top of you."

She waved her hand dismissively, as if this were a normal occurrence and not one that had shaken her to her core.

"I suppose I should thank you for not listening to me. I am not a fan of doctors, so I am apt to neglect myself if it means saving myself from being poked and prodded by a physician."

"Speaking of whom, I should check the window and see if I can spot him."

He held fast to her hand. "Stay."

"What can I do?" She glanced over at the basin atop a desk. "I could wash your wound?"

"Nay, lass. But you could check to see if I am breathing again." His half smile and hand drew her closer.

Her gaze locked upon his lips. "I was only checking for your good, sir."

The front door slammed, and Willow scrambled to standing, folding her hands before her skirts as the doctor strode into the room and reached for his black bag on the desk.

"I hear you had yourself quite the spill. Tobogganing seems a rather juvenile way for a gentleman to be spending his time."

Doctor Philpott retrieved a stethoscope from his bag, his disapproval coating his tone.

Cullen chortled. "A man will do all manner of ridiculous things if it means he can please his lady."

"So it seems." The doctor frowned, unamused, before turning an eye to Willow and pointing her to the door.

Six

Willow stifled a yawn and rested her head against the cool glass of the carriage window, watching as it wheeled her onto the Brooklyn Bridge. The rushing waters below churned her stomach. She pressed a hand to her corset, thankful she would never have to take the dangerous ferry to and from the island again. She had heard of the tragedies of ferries sinking in the past and would never forget the cramped trips returning home in the evening with the odor of perspiring workers filling the stale air. She returned her notice to the center of the bridge where the masses of pedestrians were ambling across.

She pressed her handkerchief to her forehead, aching from the early morning after last night's debacle, waking not only to find the post's latest scathing headline but also a stack of papers the courier had delivered to her father at dawn, which he promptly delegated to her. For this one meeting, her father had lifted her office-visits hiatus because he wasn't feeling his best. The confession, she knew, cost him greatly and she did not take it lightly. If Father wasn't feeling his best, a doctor would no doubt be visiting the house in her absence.

She rubbed her fingers along her hairline, hoping to alleviate the pressure before she stepped into the hostile boardroom.

Judging from the courier's pile of papers now organized neatly in the portfolio beside her, today's meeting would discuss the new year's business plan. Unlike years past, last year had not been quite as lucrative as projected, no doubt due to Wellington undercutting their prices again and again. Unlike Wellington Sugar, however, Dupré Sucré was renowned for its quality, which in turn made them the sugar of choice for teahouses and hotels across the nation. And she needed to recover those national orders if she was ever going to bring the sugar to international use, although such a change would have to wait until she found the best possible property in France—and until her new crown was accepted by her fellow board members.

Sighing, she picked up the paper again. While her parents were pleased with the press surrounding the competition, Willow did not enjoy the negative light cast upon her. She studied the article, hoping that if she memorized the style and tone of the anonymous author, she could perhaps catch the one responsible for leaking the story to the press, for she could no longer explain away the shocking amount of detail. It had to be one of her suitors. She needed to ask Flora's opinion. She would know what to do. She was always reading those mystery dime novels.

Her head pounded, and she closed her eyes as her façade threatened to crumble. In front of her parents and all, she was supportive, but in the few moments she had alone since this whole thing started, she did not feel like the confident woman she had portrayed and she felt exhausted. *Lord, how am I supposed to do this? I know precious little of courting and even less of love.* She bit her lip against her welling tears. *And if I am honest with myself, I am terrified of choosing the wrong man, Lord . . . and of them only wanting me because of my wealth. Is it so wrong to wish for love as well as a partnership?* She drew in a steadying breath. *I cannot do this alone.*

At the carriage's slowing, she swiped at her nose and eyes

and rolled back her shoulders. *First things first.* Sighing, Willow tossed the paper aside, grabbed her portfolio, and climbed the stone stairs into the factory's offices. She nodded to people in passing, only pausing for pleasantries with those who asked about her father, while others brushed by, too busy to take notice of her. She opened the heavy, carved mahogany door to her shared office with her father and inhaled the scents of leather and sugar, blinking in surprise to see her father's assistant, Maurice, rising from her father's desk, scattering a few papers to the floor in his haste.

"Willow? You're here!"

She arched her brow at his familiarity and merely stared at him, allowing her disapproving silence to do the speaking. While Maurice was only five years her senior, he was not allowed to call her by her first name without her permission, which she had never given.

"My apologies, Miss Dupré. I was only arranging things for your father's return today. I wasn't expecting you since, well, the competition and all."

She pulled off her gloves a finger at a time to give herself a moment to reply as she sank into her father's wing-back leather chair, sending Maurice scurrying over to the hearth, where he nervously took up the poker and worked at the logs in the already-crackling fireplace. "My father was not feeling up to making the trip in the cold, so he sent me in his stead for the board meeting." At the low rumble of voices on the other side of the French doors that separated the office from the boardroom, she added, "It sounds as though most have arrived, yes?"

"Not just arrived, miss." Maurice glanced at the papers on the floor. "The meeting began fifteen minutes ago, and I was sent here to your office to search for a document and—"

"What?" *They began a half hour early?* She surged across the room, flinging open the pair of doors.

The talking came to an abrupt halt as Mr. Crain, one of the

more vocal members, glanced over his shoulder at her, his fist propped against his back as he leaned over a stack of papers on the table. His barely concealed sneer appeared at once, and the men halfheartedly rose at her arrival, muttering their greetings.

"So glad you could finally honor us with your presence, Miss Dupré." Mr. Crain lifted the folded newspaper in front of him and let it drop to the table. "Judging from this morning's articles on your many upcoming outings with your beaus and then your heartless dismissal of Mr. Harolds, we had thought it would have been too distressing for your father, much less yourself, to make an appearance, so we began. For a woman who has fifteen men to contend with at home, surely you have enough on your hands without adding the six here in the boardroom." He chuckled at his own jest, the members joining him, whispers of her being a love-sick schoolgirl filling the room. The only one who remained silent was Mr. Lowe.

She pursed her lips, her heel tapping on the hardwood as she stood behind her father's chair at the head of the table, resting her hands atop the width of it and waiting for their laughter to wane. "You and I know full well the reason why I am going through with this competition." She stared at each member of the board. "To satiate *your* request that I rule with a husband at my side, even though I am more than capable of taking over the company upon my father's impending retirement. However, I respect your opinions and am doing my best to see to your demands." *But that respect is clearly something we do not have in common.*

"And we appreciate your taking our suggestion seriously, Miss Dupré." Mr. Lowe dipped his head to her, which she returned.

At least one of the members respected her. The tension in her shoulders lessened a fraction.

"Well, you can hardly hold it against us for not waiting for a Dupré to be present when your father is ill and you were not certain to appear, given your current situation." Mr. Crain assumed his seat without waiting for her to sit first, a slight she did her best to ignore as the rest of the men followed suit save Mr. Lowe.

She assumed the head seat, opening her portfolio. "Well, I am here now. Where shall we begin?"

"Allow me to catch you up to speed, Miss Dupré." Mr. Doyle leaned back in his chair and drummed his fingers against one another. "Before you arrived, we were discussing how it's a shame my son was not extended an invitation, given our connection. Did you intend to slight me?"

"How could I when neither you nor your son is a part of the Four Hundred set?" Willow quipped, lifting her chin, but as her words settled over the room, Willow knew she had made a grave mistake. She had torn the veil of civility that had barely covered the group. Horrified, she lifted her hand at the murmurs filling the room. "Pardon me, sir. That did not come across as intended."

"Oh, I think it did, Miss Dupré, and you should take care not to insult those of us who are considered *new money*, for you should remember that you too are a parvenu like the rest of us, and just because you have enough wealth as a means to cross the threshold into that oh-so-sacred club, you are not our superior by birth."

Willow bristled. While she had not intended to cause such a reaction, to apologize to a man like Doyle drew upon every ounce of decorum that her mother had painstakingly instilled in her over years and years of lectures. She folded her hands and looked directly at him. "Mr. Doyle, I misspoke and I extend my most sincere apology. I replied in haste and do not wish to cause offense."

"As women are prone to do, they give in to their emotions and expect us to dismiss their moments of weakness." He narrowed his gaze as if waiting for her to blame her femininity. "A boardroom is no place for such weakness—a fact which your cousin Osborne readily reminds us. Tell me, Miss Dupré, how does it feel to have even your own blood out for your dismissal?"

She stared at him for a second, then two, before she flipped through her portfolio. "Now, gentlemen, shall we take a look—"

Mr. Doyle rose and leaned over the table, his knuckles whitening under his weight. "If it were not for your father, I would be selling my shares to Wellington without a moment's hesitation due to your puerile actions this day. Business is a man's game. Wellington knows how to run a company."

She straightened her shoulders at the insinuation. No, not insinuation, blatant insult against her femininity. "As do I. And as you very well know, we have been established a great deal longer than Wellington. Vendors respect us for our name *and* our quality."

"A name that you continually pollute with your parade of suitors," Crain tossed his hands in the air, the men nodding in agreement. "The papers have made you a laughingstock. It is only a matter of time before you drag the company into fiscal ruin with your outlandish behavior."

Willow repressed her scathing retort. "I assure you, any marriage will only strengthen my ability in running the compan—"

Crain held up his hand, mirth lining his features. "Running? Did you say *running*? No, no. Now that we are being *honest*, allow me to stop you there. Once you have a husband, this pretense of running the company, as you say, this childish play will vanish the instant you become a wife. The place where you should be is in the home, and then we can all stop gratifying you like you are one of us."

Willow tore her gaze from Crain and looked to each in attendance, silently begging them to argue on her behalf. But as the seconds ticked past and no one rose to her defense, she stood, folded her hands behind her, and walked to the floor-length window that overlooked the heart of the factory. She observed the workers below, operating at a steady pace. "Whose name is on the building, Mr. Crain?" She heard a throat clear behind her and the scrape of chair legs against the wood floor, but she kept her attention on the factory floor, where a young man was lifting a heavy burlap sack marked with the crimson insignia of *Dupré Sucré*. "Mr. Crain?"

"Dupré," he spat out at last.

She turned on her heel, studying the boardroom floor now as she paced the room. "And did you attend the university for business classes? Did you study at my father's side for the past four years? Did you spend the past two decades listening to how sugar is refined? How it is grown, imported, and exported?"

He harrumphed.

She skewered him with her gaze. "Because *I* have. I challenge anyone here to say he has a more rounded education on the refining of sugar than I. If any one of you can best me, then I see no reason why I should dedicate my life to overseeing this factory." She held her head high, knowing that her worth was not in this man's opinion of her, nor any man's on earth. She turned to Mr. Doyle, his face as red as his cravat. "But if you want to sell your shares, I would be happy to pay you double for them."

Mr. Doyle snorted, resuming his seat. "Even at double, it would not be worth it to sell."

"Then I suggest you show me a modicum of respect, for it is *my* name and not yours that sells sugar. Now, gentlemen, shall we continue? I was reading an article about the British Royal Navy and I had an idea on how to streamline the production with the use of an updated conveyor belt."

Theodore took a seat on one of the benches facing the pond in Central Park. He watched a lone skater on the ice with her back to him. When she had sufficient speed, she tucked her arms over her chest and simultaneously crossed her ankle atop her skating leg and spun, sending her navy skirts whirling and blurring her face, until at last she slowed enough to glide onward and he recognized her. *Willow*. He started to rise to call out to her, then spotted her brushing at her cheeks with the back of her hand. He hesitated, trying to decide if he should speak, but she kept gliding with her head down, unaware of his presence. He sank down again and continued watching her in fascination until her right blade struck something and sent her slamming onto the ice.

"Will!" Theodore shot from his seat and scrambled toward her, his shoes slipping on the ice with every step and making little progress. Dropping to his knees, he crawled until he managed to make his way over to her side as she was pulling herself up to her elbows, moaning and holding her side where she had landed. He helped her to sit and gently turned her face to examine her cut chin. "It's a gusher."

"It looks worse than it really is, I am sure." She pulled her chin out of his hand and gave him a shaky smile. "Well, this is mortifying."

"Why? It's just me." He sat back on his heels and held out his hand to her.

"Because I do not normally fall and can evade most lumps in the ice like this, but I wasn't in my right frame of mind." Taking his hand at last, she pushed herself to standing with the other and swayed, pressing her wrist to her temple.

"You *are* hurt, Will." Theodore rose unsteadily and tightened his grip on her for fear she would fall a second time.

"Only my pride." She grimaced but still held on to his arms, tottering.

"Your pride along with your head, apparently." He scooped her into his arms and proceeded to carry her off the ice, his feet sliding every which way.

"Teddy! What are you doing? Put me down. You're going to get us both killed with your attempt to play the knight."

He took one slippery footstep after the other. "If I fall, I'll see to it that you land atop me."

Her arms wove about his neck, sending his pulse to racing. His left leg shot out, and she tightened her grip at once, pulling her face to his, their lips a hairsbreadth apart. "But people will see."

He turned to reply when his lips inadvertently brushed against hers, stealing his words. All that was left was the thought of what it would be like to lean in and fully kiss her. What it would be like to have such a clever, lovely woman to call his bride . . . He looked away. Being this close to her was stirring something inside him that he had thought long departed. After all, hadn't he used his one chance to fall in love with Bernadette? He cleared his throat along with his thoughts. "Why should that matter?"

"My reputation for one. And secondly, I cannot afford to be seen as weak or in need of anyone's help, especially not after my meeting this morning," Willow added, oblivious to his thoughts of kissing.

Ahh, the meeting. And judging by her damp lashes, it clearly had not gone well. At her struggle once more to be set down, he tightened his grip on her. "Everyone needs help sometime, Will. And sometimes admitting that need shows more character than being strong, stubborn, and alone."

"I am not being stubborn." She lifted her chin, which did little to prove her point as blood was dribbling down to her cream jabot.

Laughing at her outrageous claim, he ignored her protests until they were off the ice. He gingerly set her down on the bench, his heart pounding as he gently took her ankle in his hand.

She gasped, moving her ankle from his touch. "Teddy, I can manage."

"And have you keel over and be left to answer to your mother by myself? No, thank you. See, that is a perfect example of admitting that I need your help without injuring my pride. Sit tight and stop being so bossy." He pulled the leather straps and unfastened the silver buckles, tugging off her skate boot before reaching for her other foot. At her sharp inhale, he paused with her stockinged calf in hand. "Will?"

"I am well." She glanced behind her. "Please make haste or I will not be sorry for bossing you about. I think there is a reporter nearby."

"Relax. It could be anyone." Even so, he made quick work of the last strap and fitted her walking shoes before withdrawing his handkerchief from his pocket and holding it to her chin, dabbing with the greatest care. "I hope I am not hurting you."

Her hands twisted in her lap. "It's only a mild injury, but I'll keep close to the settee for the rest of the day if it would put you at ease."

"It would." He moved to take her in his arms again but paused at her lifted hand.

"Thank you, but I can make it home without the scandal of you carrying me." She commandeered the handkerchief, holding it to her chin.

"That's a relief to be sure." He sent her a wink and rose, at once aware of the snow that now dampened his clothing. It would be a glacial few blocks.

"What were you doing way out here anyway? Why aren't you enjoying the warmth of indoors over a cup of chocolate?"

He gripped the straps of her skates and helped her to stand, watching her for any signs of discomfort. "Not to complain, but living with so many gentlemen, I need to get away every now and again from the swirling manly anger, and what better way is there to refresh one's mind than with a walk amongst nature?"

Willow threaded her arm through his and leaned against him as they walked, keeping the cotton handkerchief pressed to her chin. "I agree, which is why I come here far too often. Although I do ache for the summer months spent in Newport when I can be away from the city."

"Really? What about your business? Won't you need to be near the factory, being the new leader?"

"I do when it is necessary, but Father always claimed that it was important for him to take time with his family, and that is why he hired a good foreman and has a handful of assistants he can trust to carry on without him and to summon him when needed. In such cases, he would take the ferry back a few times each month for any important meetings that needed a guiding hand."

Theodore pulled her closer, feeling a shiver run through her. "Well, while we wait for the warmth of summer, would you like to share a pot of chocolate to warm up your bones?"

She sighed. "Are you a phrenologist, too? Because you utterly read what was inside my head."

Theodore shook his head, laughing. "That was appalling, Will." He tugged her arm and guided her onto Park Avenue toward a nearby teahouse.

"But you are always making me laugh, and I was looking for the first opportunity to return the favor. It is the best I could come up with, as humor is not my forte." She paused on the sidewalk, lowering the handkerchief. "Are you certain I do not look like I just came from a brawl?"

He took her face in his hands and adjusted her fur stole over her collar to hide her stained lace jabot and pocketed the bloodied cotton. "There. With your stole tugged up, it helps to hide it."

She lifted her brows. "I do, then?"

He shrugged. "Yes, you look like you came from a brawl, but I am certain people will think that the other brawler looks far worse than yourself."

"How comforting." She smirked. "You are incorrigible."

"I'm only teasing. It bled a lot at first, yet it seems to have clotted now and shouldn't show unless you sit up straight. So, be certain to hunch your shoulders as much as possible."

She laughed, revealing the infinitesimal dimples at each corner of her bottom lip. "Good, because bloodied or not, hot chocolate must be had."

He tucked a curl behind her ear and stepped off the curb to cross the street. He couldn't allow himself to fall again, not after Bernadette. After declaring his love, his Parisian sweetheart had chosen another and, in the process, broken his heart, making this competition that much harder because he truly liked Willow . . . more than he should at this point. He was not in love yet, of course, but he could see their relationship heading in that direction and it petrified him.

She looked sideways at him, and he knew he had to break the silence, but all topics besides her disastrous business meeting fled and it would not do to remind her. What were those topics Mother had told him to raise? *The weather.* He looked to the darkening skies. *Nothing to discuss there that wouldn't obviously be contrived conversation. Health.* He glanced to her chin. From past experience, he knew he should not press her too much on an injury. *Family!*

"How are the twins?" he asked. "I haven't had the pleasure of visiting with them yet."

"Philomena and Sybil are faring well, though Mother and Father have insisted that they do not interact with any of the suitors until we have narrowed it down at the second laurel ceremony. Which is wise, for I do not want them to become too attached to someone who will not be around for long."

Theodore sucked in a breath through his teeth and held the door to the teahouse for her. "Well, that does not bode well for me. The last I saw of the twins, they were still in the nursery. I would love to see them again. Unless you are planning on getting rid of me?"

She bumped into his shoulder in the marble foyer of the teahouse. "Not unless you are the undercover reporter who has been blabbing to everyone that I tend to bite my poor nails to death whenever I get lost in thought, but even then, I think I could find it in my heart to forgive you for the sake of our past."

Warmth swelled Theodore's chest. *She at least remembers our time as fondly as I.* He tucked her a little closer to him under the guise of keeping her from being jostled by a passerby and followed the waiter to a table in the corner near one of the front windows before ordering them each a cup of chocolate, one with a lump of sugar and ample cream.

"How did you know that was how I liked my hot chocolate?" She unbuttoned her cloak to reveal a well-tailored albeit stern navy suit beneath, but kept the fur stole in place, raising her brows in question, silently asking him if her cut was visible.

He mimed for her to hunch her shoulders more until the cut was hidden. "Perfect. As for the immoral amount of sugar in your beverages, your name stands for sugar across the nation. So, understandably, you have a sweet tooth."

She smirked, mirroring his expression. "But what if I did not?"

"I know you better than you think." Theodore held his response until the waiter finished setting their full china cups in front of them, placed the chocolate pot in the center of the small table beside a crystal vase with a single rose, and departed. "Now, returning to the subject of the competition, I need to know . . . do I have a chance?"

Willow set down her hot chocolate and slowly slid her hand across the table, her fingertips brushing the top of his knuckles. He allowed himself to hold her hand, then released it at once, knowing what such a display could cost her should anyone recognize them.

"Yes, Teddy. You have a *great* chance. And I promise that I will not string you along if my heart tells me otherwise."

He lifted the crimson rose from the vase and held it out to her. "Then that's all I can hope for . . . at least for now, my dear Miss Dupré."

Seven

"What do you mean, Day happened upon you?" Oscar Seaborne crossed his arms over his broad chest, his agitation slipping through his smile as he towered over Willow from her place upon the stool, plucking the strings of her harp in the middle of a rather difficult sonata. "I thought this was supposed to be a fair competition." He gave a short laugh and turned the page of the sheet music on the stand for her, his shadow blocking the next note in the flickering candlelight that her mother had insisted was more romantic than using the gaslights.

She guessed at the notes, the immediate discord making her flinch as she hurried on to the next note to disguise her blunder.

"If I had known that I could have 'happened upon you,' I would have sought you out, as well. This is the second time in two days this has occurred. And I am certain, being a business-woman, that you know there are ten of us who have not yet even been out with you." He sent her a wink to soften his words.

She paused, the unfinished melody irking her fingers, yet Mr. Seaborne had a point. She leaned forward, using her shoulder to set down her gilded harp before straightening the sheet music, gathering her patience. She folded her hands atop her golden

skirts in an attempt to remain sympathetic, but it was growing difficult, as her chin was throbbing and her dull headache
had now reached her temples. She shifted uneasily and caught
Teddy edging toward her despite that their being together any
more today would further disquiet the men. "Mr. Seaborne,
you are absolutely right. I apologize for the breach in etiquette
to you and to the others."

He coughed, reddening a bit. "Thank you for recognizing
that . . . this hasn't been the easiest competition. I never thought
I would be in a situation where the woman I am courting is also
balancing fourteen other relationships."

She smiled, dropping her gaze to her hands. "Me neither,
and I know I am doing a poor job of it."

"I am not usually a jealous sort of fellow." He ran his hands
through his wavy brown hair. "But, with this competition, I
find that every little moment is heightened and could have a
thousand other implications for my future. Frankly, it is all
rather exhausting."

Willow jerked her head up to look at him. Mortified. Here
she was thinking only of herself and *her* future. She had never
thought it could possibly be as hard for the men as it was for
her to picture a future. And if they happened to be able to build
an idea of a life with her, and she hadn't even glanced their
way in a day . . . she shook her head, knowing how she would
feel if the situation were reversed. "I hadn't thought of that."

He shrugged. "You have had enough to worry about."

"Well, that is no excuse, but I do have a little surprise in
store that may help alleviate your frustrations about not having any time today." She rose from the stool and faced the rest
of the men in the music room and gave a brilliant smile. "I
will be joining you for a special dinner that my mother has so
graciously arranged for us." At the mutterings about the room,
she pictured it from their perspective. What could possibly be
special about a dinner? It is not as if they hadn't already had

several dinners with her. Willow looked to Mr. Lennox, who was whispering to Mr. Pruett. "Mr. Lennox, do you have a comment that you would like to add?"

He shuffled, uncomfortable that Willow had heard him, his left eye twitching behind his monocle. "I was simply thinking that the only ones at a dinner table who can visit with you are the ones in your immediate circle. The rest of us look like fools staring and wondering what jest was made to cause you to laugh."

"This dinner is special, as we shall be having an indoor picnic dinner." She beamed at their cheers, relieved to have done *something* right today, and crossed the room to pull the bell cord to signal the staff, lingering for a second with her hand against the wall for support when Cullen joined her, his hand at her elbow.

"Theodore informed me of your spill. You should take care not to overdo it."

"You are one to speak. What are you doing out of bed?" Despite her scolding, Willow's heart leapt at being near him again after their almost-kiss at the doctor's, and without thinking of what she was doing, she relinquished her hold on the wall and eased her weight onto Cullen's hand, allowing his strength to support her. "I should have taken Mr. Day's advice and kept off my feet, for I fear I am making a mild headache much worse due to my innate desire to please everyone."

"Is that an invitation to carry you to the nearest settee?" he teased, but she caught an unmistakable gleam of desire to carry through with his scandalous proposal.

"And risk the jealousy of the gentlemen? I fear some of their tempers are worse than Mr. Doyle's on my board."

"I am not certain who Mr. Doyle is, but I assure you, it is well worth it to me to risk any jealous revenge if it means I can hold you in my arms between the space of here and the settee. I can manage the men, though something tells me you can more than hold your own against an irate, irrational suitor."

His faith in her warmed her. Most times she acted more self-assured than she felt, hoping that one day she would eventually possess her father's confidence in the workplace. "How is your head?"

"I have had a nasty headache since the accident and kept to the conservatory for a moment of quiet, but this afternoon, your sister Philomena found me and was quite helpful in offering me a homeopathic remedy to help aid the headache powder into functioning more efficiently. And Sybil worked to raise my chances in the competition by divulging all sorts of diverting stories about you over chess." He grinned. "I told them they weren't allowed to visit with any of us suitors yet, but they said they had permission from your mother, given my circumstances."

Touched by her sisters' thoughtfulness, she pressed a hand over her heart. "Oh, Phil. I wouldn't be surprised if she attempted to open an apothecary one day. And dear Bil better not have told you anything terrible about me."

He waggled his brows at her last question and merely shrugged. "Perhaps. As for the apothecary business, I would not doubt Phil's ability to do so. After all, with her sister pioneering the business world, it would not be that outlandish for her to wish to become an apothecary." He rubbed the back of his neck. "The peppermint concoction she gave me has me feeling much better already."

"Oh. That's why you do not smell like yourself." She froze as the words left her mouth, realizing just how reprehensible they sounded. "If you'll excuse me, I best check on the others." She dropped her hold on him and was crossing the room to speak with Fritz when she caught Mr. Seaborne's conversation in passing.

"Of course, she doesn't exclude Theodore, nor the other three from the previous outing," Oscar complained under his breath to Digory Pruett. "How are we supposed to have any time with her when competing against everyone at once?"

She winced. Again, she had not thought of that. Willow could just imagine the headlines tomorrow, declaring her ineptness. Skirting away from Mr. Seaborne, she joined Fritz and engaged him in small talk until the doors opened and the servants entered behind Father on his cane and Mother, who directed where the plaids were to be spread over the Persian rug and pillows were to be strewn about, wicker baskets bulging with goods atop each blanket to enhance the picnic aesthetic Mother sought.

Mother excused her from Fritz and pulled Willow away to speak privately. "There is nothing quite so relaxing as a picnic, is there, dear?"

"And being relaxed is exactly what I need at the moment with fifteen men's gazes on me. Thank you." Mother was truly surprising Willow with her unique ideas to drive her together with her beaus. In the past, she had dismissed her mother's suggestions, yet now Willow was beginning to see her in a new light. Even though Willow took after her father, there was a reason why Mother and Father complemented each other.

Mother winked at her. "That's why I thought of this. Many years ago, my mother did the same for me and my beaus to create an enchanting atmosphere while eliciting jealousy to bring about a swifter proposal from my favored suitor."

"And did it work?"

"Your father proposed within two weeks of courtship, so I'd say so." She sighed, smiling and nodding over the room, pleased with her work. "It looks magical. I wish your sisters could join you, but I think we should attempt to keep them apart from your beaus a little while longer. At least until you have narrowed them down." She nodded toward Cullen, who was helping a footman spread a blanket. "But I'm afraid they rather like him already."

Willow lowered her voice. "They have no worries on that score. I agree, however, that they shouldn't mingle yet, though

I will miss their feisty additions to the conversation. Please tell them that I will stop by their room tonight to catch them up on all the details."

Mother nodded toward Digory Pruett and whispered, "Now, how about you ask Mr. Pruett to be your partner for dinner?"

Willow bit her lip. "I was hoping to speak more with Mr. Quincy."

"Very well, but do try to visit with Mr. Pruett at some point this evening." Her lips pursed at a footman's arrangement of a blanket over a Louis XIV chair. "A picnic is supposed to aid in a feeling of comradery, and a chair does not accomplish that." She clicked her tongue and swept off to see that the blankets were arranged to her exact specifications as Father sank into his oversized wing-back chair beside the fire, propping his feet up on a stool while conversing with Mr. Starling and Mr. Jones.

Willow scanned the room and found Mr. Quincy speaking with Cullen in the corner, both their forms inclined in her direction as if covertly keeping an eye on her movements about the room. Such a strange business to be courting so many at once, but a little bit of awkwardness could not be helped. She approached them, smiling at Mr. Digory Pruett and Noah Walden and Archie Lovett in passing. "Mr. Quincy? Would you mind joining me?"

An undeniable excitement sparked in his blue eyes. "My dear Miss Dupré, I thought you would never ask."

Cullen shifted, obviously perturbed. "You still owe me that private dinner, Miss Dupré."

"Soon," she promised as she took Kit's arm, then walked toward the room's arched alcove and semicircle of floor-length glass doors where a blanket was spread, providing them with a modicum of privacy. Sinking onto the plaid, her skirts billowed about her in a golden cloud while thoughts of her girlhood infatuation came flooding back.

"It feels like a fortnight since our waltz. I half thought that you had forgotten me." He flipped open the basket and peered inside.

"You know, you don't need to wait to speak with me whenever I come to the library to visit. You can come to me." She leaned forward and whispered, "And I give you permission to seek me out, but do not tell the others, else I will never get anything finished."

"It shall be our secret." He lifted out two crystal glasses from the basket and handed one to her before retrieving a corked, frosted bottle of what appeared to be lemonade, sending her mouth to watering.

"Ah, looks like there is enough room for three." Fritz plopped down on his side without invitation, bracing himself up on his elbow, his hand holding his head in such a boyish, carefree manner that she did not have the heart to scold him for his indecorum, though she did not wish to share her time with Kit Quincy.

Kit's jaw tightened and he openly glared at Fritz in a rare show of annoyance. "Hardly."

Fritz sat up at that, the jovial light in his countenance fading. "Sorry, Kit. I won't stay then, but I do have something for you, Willow." He reached into his coat and retrieved an envelope and handed it to her.

She turned it over, finding it blank. "What is this in regard to?"

He sighed theatrically. "Do you know nothing of romance, my lady? I shan't spoil the mystery. Open it later." He winked at her before hoisting himself to his feet and leaving her with Kit.

"Do you enjoy picnics, sir?" Willow insouciantly slipped the envelope into her hidden pocket that she required her seamstress to include in all her dresses, including her evening wear, and took a sip of the cool, tart lemonade.

Kit removed a delightful meat pie for two from the wicker basket. "Quite. And what a novel idea to have one indoors."

"Thank you, although it is not of my design. I was recently accused of not having enough excitement in my life, which is why my mother is planning all sorts of strange activities for us to do. She says it will help me bond with my future husband and bring me in touch with my younger self."

Using a silver pie knife, he scooped a generous portion of meat pie onto a plate for her and handed it over with a fork before fixing his own plate. "Now that I think of it, it is rather brilliant to create opportunities for adventure, amusement, and of course romance, to aid in speeding up the process that typically can take a few seasons to fully blossom." He lifted a steaming forkful of pie and popped it into his mouth. "If I recall correctly, you always had a knack for adventure that landed you into trouble. And the last we spoke, you also mentioned harboring an affection for me after my rescuing you."

"Mr. Quincy! Such a thing to bring up over dinner." She could not halt the blush from burning her cheeks. She set aside her fork for the cool glass again. "I told you that in a moment of nostalgia and I regret it sorely now."

"Come now. There is no harm after all these years to admit to such a thing." He raised his glass to her. "I brought it up to thank you. For it gives me courage to dare to hope."

She took in the masterpiece before her with his broad shoulders, dark complexion, with streaks of gray appearing at his temples. "As long as we are being candid . . ." She kept her voice low despite the steady hum of conversations about them. "What is the draw for you to be here? You are wealthy and . . ." *Dashing and impossibly kind.*

"And?" He raised his brows, waiting.

"And, well, good-looking and sweet, if you must make me spell it out." She laughed, taking a tiny bite of pie. "What can I possibly offer you that would tempt you to endure such a competition? You could have anyone you like. You *should* have anyone."

He set aside his fork, propped up one knee, and rested his arm on it. "I know why you are hurrying into a marriage, Willow. As you are aware, my cousin is on the board, Mr. Lowe, and he mentioned to me the ultimatum."

She swallowed hard. She had feared word would get out. "So, you know that they do not respect me . . . that they find me wanting as a leader." The shame nearly overwhelmed her. It was one thing to receive such news from her parents and endure the board's judgment behind closed doors, yet it was quite another to discuss it with a man she so admired.

"I think you may need to reexamine yourself, Miss Dupré. While there is a gap in our ages, yes, and I have lived a bit more of life than you have, I have kept an eye on you for years."

"Years?" She ran her finger along the rim of her glass, her heart hammering.

"A platonic interest, of course, for I was engaged for part of the time. But during that period, I found you to be kind and brilliant and devout. You are more than your business, your family, and wealth." He took her hand in his. "You have an inheritance that is incorruptible, which will never fade away."

Willow dropped her gaze to her plate at the reference to the book of First Peter, her breath catching, touched. Never had a man spoken to her thus. *More than my wealth? More than my name?* Unbidden tears filled her eyes, but to disguise that fact, she reached for the basket on the pretense of looking for dessert. They finished the rest of their meal over talk of Kit's pursuits and were just beginning on his aspirations when Cullen approached her with a bow.

"Miss Dupré and Mr. Quincy, I apologize for interrupting, but I noticed you had finished your dessert and I was wondering if I may take a turn with you, Miss Dupré?"

"Of course." She placed a hand on Kit's sleeve. "Thank you for the lovely conversation and encouragement. I look forward to finishing our discussion at a future time."

"My pleasure. I meant every word." He rose with her and bowed.

"Right this way, my lady." Cullen escorted her to the adjoining room, where a silver pot and two cups awaited on a side table before a fire, along with a sweet nosegay in a crystal glass of water.

"How lovely." She clasped her hands to her chest. "Did you do this?"

"I think it was the Fae." He winked at her and continued to hold her hand as she sat on the tête-à-tête love seat with its backrests that curved in the shape of an S, which allowed them to visit face-to-face while still maintaining propriety. Though her mother had acquired the piece of furniture when Willow came of age, she had not made much use of it as yet, much to her mother's dismay.

He reached for the pot. "Allow me." He poured her a cup of chocolate and handed it to her, their fingertips meeting for half a second. "I wanted to apologize for ruining your outing and then collapsing upon you at the doctor's front door." He ran his hands through his hair, revealing a battered ear. He settled onto the love seat, teacup in hand.

"It wasn't you who ruined the outing. It was Mr. Harolds. And besides, it is not every day that the damsel gets to rescue the hero in distress." She sent him a brazen wink and sipped from her teacup.

Cullen laughed softly. "No one would ever accuse you of being a damsel, Miss Dupré."

"I do wish you would call me Willow in private. It seems rather silly to be so formal after our adventure last night."

"Then you must call me Cullen."

She blew on the hot beverage. "I do believe I have already taken that liberty a time or two."

"You never needed my permission. I like the sound of my name on your lips." He reached for the nosegay and extended it to her. "Flowers for the lady?"

99

Willow's fingers had just encircled the stems when a glass shattered behind her, sending them both to their feet and her chocolate to splashing on her hem.

"You *cad*!" Mr. Seaborne bellowed from the doorway, his white collar stark against his crimson neck.

Willow's jaw dropped. *Whatever is he upset about now?* "Mr. Seaborne. You forget yourself."

Cullen tilted his head, his brows lowering to a point as he set aside his cup and reached for Willow's. "And why am I a cad?"

Mr. Seaborne gestured to where they sat, the vein in his head becoming more prevalent. "You robbed me of my special moment with Miss Dupré."

Willow's stomach dropped, the lingering taste of chocolate turning bitter. *The Fae? Oh, Cullen.* "Oscar, *you* planned this?" She lifted the nosegay and gestured to the set behind her.

"Of course I did. I gathered those blooms myself and had the servants prepare the rest."

Cullen groaned. "My apologies, chap. I did not know."

His nostrils flared. "How could you *not* know that it wasn't meant for your use? Who do you think would have set up such an interlude?"

Willow was unwilling to allow his jealous wrath to fall solely on Cullen's shoulders, broad as they were. "I am so sorry, Mr. Seaborne. I should have realized—"

He lifted his splayed fingers. "You were not to know, miss. But, Dempsey, you have no such excuse. I *just* told you that I had something special planned."

Cullen rubbed his forehead, muttering, "That's what I get for being distracted. I had asked the staff to set up something special for us too, so I assumed—"

"Assumed?" He gave a short, bitter laugh. "I waited all day for this moment with Miss Dupré, and you took it from me by your arrogant postulations."

Oscar's voice brought Teddy into the room. "What is going

on? Seaborne? Are you still on about this being a fair competition? I hardly think that a few extra hours with Miss Dupré while at the *doctor's* office warrants such a pernicious outburst."

Oscar clenched his fists. "Shut up. This is not about you."

Teddy's expression took on a dangerous light that she had seen in him only once when they were children, and someone had taken to bullying her. "Be a man, Seaborne. You want to woo Miss Dupré? Then *woo* her and cease this simpering."

Oscar snorted. "Says the man who *also* broke the rules and went to the teahouse with her this very afternoon."

"How on earth would you know about the teahouse? Have you been following us?" Willow's voice rose.

"That is neither here nor there." Oscar waved her off.

Is Oscar the reporter? She clenched her jaw, forcing herself to keep silent on that score. It would not do to accuse a suitor unless she had proof.

"Dempsey, you are a cheat," Oscar continued. "Give me the satisfaction of a fight that you so adamantly denied me earlier . . . unless you wish to add cowardice to your growing list of inadequacies?"

Her eyes met Cullen's in a silent question.

Cullen crossed his arms and leaned against the carved marble mantel. "I think not."

"You would deny me a second time?" His chest heaved.

"You best consider yourself fortunate and walk away, sir," Willow warned, stepping toward Oscar, reaching for his arm to guide him away. "It is best not to act in the heat of jealousy."

"Are you suggesting that his form is superior to mine?" Oscar's voice lowered, his hurt evident. "This isn't about jealousy anymore. My honor is being called into question."

She dropped her hand. She was bungling the situation again. She rubbed her forehead and turned to Cullen. "What's this about a fight?"

101

"Apparently, Seaborne found a grievance with me in that I had extra time with you as well and did not immediately inform the entire group of what occurred on our outing." He looked pointedly at Oscar and moved to Willow's side. "I had thought that a *head* injury was an indication that I had been whisked away to a doctor and not a romantic tryst."

Her cheeks warmed again at the thought of her indiscretion with Cullen. She was the one who had leaned. She was the one who had lost her head. But Cullen, ever the gentleman, had not spoken of her brazen mistake. Even if Cullen was the man she would marry, she needed to keep her kisses until she was nearer the end of the competition for fear she would regret giving one to someone she would eventually dismiss. Yet she was lying to herself if she hadn't thought of that moment with remorse, that she had not felt the pressure of his lips on hers.

"I am afraid that our Seaborne is rather thick and should see a head doctor of his own, as I keep telling him that *nothing* untoward happened," Cullen added.

He lunged for Cullen, who easily dodged his blow. Teddy was not so lucky, for Oscar's wayward blow sent him reeling backward over the love seat, narrowly missing the stone hearth.

"Oscar!" Willow gasped as the irate suitor charged for Teddy. Cullen leapt in front of her, shielding her from Oscar as Archie appeared and pulled her out of the way. "Stop this at once!" she yelled over the chaos.

Ignoring her shouts, Oscar jabbed over and over at Cullen, continually missing his target. And when Teddy stirred, rising to his feet, Oscar made a move toward him. Willow watched as Cullen's powerful body slid into position. He planted his feet and landed a blow to Oscar's jaw, sending the man reeling backward, slumping onto the love seat, unconscious.

"Are you hurt, Miss Dupré?" Cullen's stormy eyes found hers, and he took her hand in his, his thumb rubbing the back of her hand.

She nodded slowly, breathless at his transformation from gentleman to fighter and back to gentleman. She had never been permitted to watch an actual boxing match, but she felt this was likely what it felt like. Thrillingly alive.

"Good." He straightened his jacket, his glare flashing to Oscar.

"For a man who no longer wishes to fight, you certainly put an end to that quickly," she whispered, unable to keep the admiration from her voice.

"I wouldn't fight for just anyone."

"How kind. I didn't know you held such affection for me." Teddy draped his arm across Cullen's shoulders. "I assure you that after today, the feeling is mutual. I'd fight for you any day."

Cullen shrugged him off. "You know I was speaking of our sweetheart, Day. Don't think this means—"

"I'll consider you a friend for life, no matter the outcome. Meaning that when I wed Miss Dupré, 'tis no matter, for I shall still consider you a friend," Teddy replied, tucking Willow's hand into his arm in a possessive manner.

But she slipped from his side and let her fingertips brush against Cullen's for a moment. "Thank you for stopping him before it got too out of hand." She turned to Oscar and knelt beside him, patting his hand in hopes of reviving him. How could she not have recognized his jealous tendencies sooner? She supposed she saw his hubris as a show, perhaps because she never really thought of herself as one to capture suitors' attentions. Rather, her fortune did the speaking for her. She shook her head. Because she had once again underestimated the men, she had let things get out of her control.

Oscar blinked, the rage gone from his eyes, chagrin now in its place. "Miss Dupré. I didn't mean to react that way. It's just I had been looking forward to that moment with you all day and then to see him?" He ran a hand over his face and rose, extending his hand to her, which she ignored. "I went mad with jealousy. Please believe me, I'm not usually like—"

"Mr. Seaborne, I am appalled by your behavior. You are to leave at once. Your trunks will follow as soon as the servant finishes collecting your things." Mother stood in the doorway, bringing all to attention at once, the others in the music room craning to look past her and see what was going on in the adjoining room. "Outbursts will not be tolerated."

"Mrs. Dupré . . ." Oscar coughed, adjusting his collar. "It's not—"

"You should have considered the consequences before such a display of wanting character." Mother called over her shoulder, "Beckwith, will you please escort Mr. Seaborne out of the mansion?"

"Miss Dupré?" He turned pleading eyes to her. "You know I didn't mean to let it get so out of hand."

Willow bit her lip. As much as he held her in affection and she understood his disappointment of his ruined plan, she could not marry someone with such a jealous side when she worked with men all day every day. "I'm sorry and I thank you for your time."

He hung his head for a moment, exhaling before straightening. "Best of luck to you then, Miss Dupré." He kissed her hand and followed the butler out, causing the men to stir, watching with open jaws and elbowing one another as Oscar made his disgraceful exit into the hall, where the butler escorted him to the door.

Mother motioned Willow to her side. "Willow, your father and I have decided that having the men under such circumstances in New York is not creating a natural environment and is instead promoting hostility. So, to preserve the integrity of the process, we have decided to move you and your *eight* suitors to Aisling Manor in Newport."

Willow gasped. *So many?* "Eight? But there are fourteen now with Mr. Seaborne gone and—"

Mother lifted her hand. "Your father and I have our reasons. I have sent for Flora to help you make your decision." She turned to the men. "As you may have guessed, gentlemen, tonight Willow will perform the second crowning ceremony. We have only so many guest rooms on the third floor of our Newport residence, and we fear the close quarters are negatively impacting your ability to be amiable with one another, which has prompted this rather drastic cut." She turned on her heeled slipper. "I suggest that if you have not had time with my daughter, you had best create time between now and the ceremony. You have one hour."

Eight

After Mother closed the French doors of the music room behind her, Willow turned to the group of men before her, knowing the first two she would cut . . . and despising the fact that she had to send away four others. *But who?* Her gaze rested on the few men she had spoken to only briefly: Sebastian Jones, Clyde Billings, and Frank Keating. How was she supposed to know if she had a connection with them if she had not spent much time with them? But seeing Fritz's grin from across the room, her gut twisted. In their time together, she had thoroughly enjoyed their conversations. Still, she hadn't felt any spark, and if she had not felt it yet, she doubted she would by June. And as much as it pained her, she could not hold him for friendship, especially when she didn't even know where he stood. "Fritz? Can you join me, please?"

He bobbed his head, his wild mop of red curls bouncing as he waded through the group to her. "I was hoping we could speak," he whispered and followed her into the conservatory, his hand on her elbow gently guiding her to a bench. "There was something I was meaning to tell you in that letter, but now, since it looks like you will not have a chance to read it before the ceremony, I will have to tell you in person."

"I see." She ran her hand over the silk ruching at her waist. How did one go about telling a friend that she might not be able to become attracted to him, especially when one was last season's most sought-after bachelor in the city? "I wish I could have read it too, but, uh, we need to talk."

His smile faltered. "Oh, dear. I am afraid I know that tone. So, your bringing me aside is not for a pleasant talk."

She rested a hand on his shoulder. "I am afraid not."

He inclined his head away from her, brushing his fist over his eyes. "I wish you could have sent me home that first night rather than allow me to hope."

Her heart dipped at his reaction. "Fritz, how could I have sent you away when I was still uncertain? I did not wish to dismiss you if there was the possibility of making a favorable match. I'm very fond of you and I wish I could ask you to stay. Yet you are so exceptionally kind that I cannot in good conscience keep you when   "

"When you've found me wanting?" A hint of a smile appeared at the corner of his thin lips. "And my being uncommonly kind is supposed to make me feel better somehow?"

"It's not that." This was not at all going like she had envisioned. She had not thought he would be so hurt, especially since they had only had a few conversations together. "If we simply had more time . . ."

"Which you can give me if you are willing."

She turned her chin to her shoulder, blinking. She had not expected to feel such a tear in her heart in dismissing him. *Am I making a mistake?* She sniffed back her tears. "Oh, Fritz, I'm sorry."

"Don't say that. While you may not feel something now, who is to say that I won't grow on you in the future weeks? You know me better than those other blokes." He tugged her hand as if he could draw out her answer in doing so. "It's enough for me to stay hearing your confession to liking me. Still, you need to know where *I* stand before you make a rash decision that will later haunt me."

"Haunt you? But we hardly know each other," she whispered.

"That is where you are wrong. If I cannot persuade you, open the letter."

She withdrew the envelope and broke the seal, a pressed red, double pink flower fluttering onto her lap, her breath catching at the meaning. *Ardent love?* She ran her fingers over the dried flower, her heart performing a strange staccato.

"Yes, I love you. I love you more than I ever thought possible, and that is the only reason I feel no shame in asking you for more time at your side. I can prove that we are a good match, if you will only give me the time to show you."

"You *love* me?" She immediately thought of all the little moments Fritz had taken during the group outing and throughout the week to seek her out, his bright countenance, his thoughtfulness with each flower he had presented to her. And with the flower in hand, proclaiming his heart, she felt an awakening inside her, a longing to be cherished by more than just her family. She swallowed the lump in her throat. She had always been content with her sweet corner of the world, but now? She looked up at Fritz. Willow did not know if he was the one, but if she had such a reaction to his declaration, what else might lie between them, given time?

"Do you not believe in love at first, or in my case, second sight? Because I do love you." He lifted her hand to his lips and kissed it. "Most ardently . . . Willow."

Against all reason, Fritz was in love with her, and she could not dismiss his declaration. She expelled her breath and smiled at him. "I cannot return your affections yet, sir, but maybe, someday, I can."

His eyes widened. "Truly?"

She dropped her gaze. "I did not realize where you stood

before, and if you truly love me, maybe you are right. Maybe there is something that I missed which only time will reveal."

Fritz jumped to his feet, pulling her up with him. "Thank you. You won't regret this." He bowed over her hands before kissing them and releasing her. "Thank you."

Willow dipped her head at his enthusiasm, smoothing out her skirts, still a touch flustered. She accepted his arm, certain her cheeks were blazing, and returned to the room full of her remaining suitors, her gaze flowing through the men. *Now, who shall not receive laurels in his stead?*

Archibald Lovett approached her and handed her a glass of punch, which she downed in one unseemly gulp that had her cheeks bulging and Teddy shaking his head, grinning.

Archie chuckled as she set aside her cup on a passing footman's tray. "Your meeting with Fritz was that bad?" Without waiting for her reply, he added, "May I steal you away?"

"Certainly." She threaded her arm through his and ventured out into the hallway so as not to be too far from the library but far enough to give them a semblance of privacy.

He turned to her, their faces at the same level. "Marcy Mae told me that if I did not make it until at least the next cut, I would be a disgrace. I beg of you, allow me one more chance to win your heart and avoid bringing dishonor to my family."

She laughed. "Never fear, Archie. While we have not spent a lot of time together, the time we have spent has been lovely, and I do not intend on sending home a fellow who has the uncanny ability to make me laugh when I should not."

He exhaled heavily, theatrically wiping his brow. "Thank goodness. Marcy Mae had threatened all sorts of things if I failed to continue. First, I was going to lose my collection of neckcloths to the fire," he said, counting off the list on his fingers. "Closely followed by my shoes taking a swim in the pond in Central Park, a fact she was so adamant about that I did not have the heart to tell her the East River would have been a better choice due to the pond being iced over."

She squeezed his hand. "Then I am doubly thankful that we get along so well to spare your wardrobe a fate worse than death." Bidding Archie farewell, Willow drew a steadying breath, hoping that a few moments alone would help clear her mind.

"Oh, good. I was worried I would have to search the length of the house before I found you," Flora called from the foyer, her wraps still on and the footman taking chase after her to acquire them.

"Thank heaven you came, Flora!"

"Of course! When your mother sent a carriage for me and her note about the crowning ceremony and the remaining suitors you had to sort through, I knew it was more important than my staying with the family to entertain Lord Peregrine. It is one of the advantages of having four sisters. I can escape and no one notices." She surrendered her wraps to reveal a rose satin dinner gown and pulled Willow up the grand staircase, making her way at a clipped pace to Willow's chambers. "Now, we do not have much time, so tell me everything about your beaus."

Willow laughed softly, following her inside. "Well, let's at least wait until I close the door, lest my sisters overhear and inform the suitors."

Flora paced before the fire, rubbing her hands up and down her bare arms. "Teddy, of course, is still in the running?"

"Of course. I'd even dare to say he is one of my favorites."

Flora paused, dropping her hands. "But not *the* favorite? Who else do you like?" A slow smile lit her features. "Is the elusive Miss Dupré losing her heart so soon?"

Willow sank atop the tufted footstool before the fire. "Mr. Dempsey has surprised me."

Flora continued her pacing. "Mr. *Cullen* Dempsey, correct? I feel like I have heard of him before." She shrugged dismissively. "Although that would not be unlikely given our circles. Now, there is no need to discuss your keeping the charming Mr. Kit Quincy, so I'll continue on with my list. Any thoughts on Mr. Pruett?"

Willow nodded, thankful to be shifting Flora's focus away from Mr. Dempsey. It was all so new, she wasn't quite ready to begin discussing him, even with her dearest friend. "Mr. Pruett is a bit of an enigma at this point, but Mother and Father like him, so I am leaning toward keeping him if he will have me."

She arched a single brow. "Oh, he will have you. His family is elated that he has even been extended an invitation. I know so because Mr. and Mrs. Pruett dined with us two nights ago. What about Mr. Walden?"

"Noah Walden is as handsome as a gentleman should be and as wealthy as they come. Though I have only spent a dinner at his side, I want to know him more."

"Good enough for me." Flora continued her march to the window and back to the fireplace. "And Mr. Houlgrave? He seems nice."

Willow twisted her lips to the side. "Yes, but he's quite uninformed about the sugar-refinery business."

"And that's a problem?" Flora stopped short, her hand pressing to her chest. "Because I must remind you that *I* am ill-informed as well and you still love me."

Willow laughed, stretching her hands to the flames. "It is when one is a major sugar importer."

Flora grimaced. "That's unfortunate. Any feelings for Taylor Kemp? He is quite a boaster if I recall, and I was surprised that you kept him past the first night. Just a number I thought if ever there was one."

"Flora!" Willow gasped, dropping her hands to her lap.

"Well, it is true. Do you want me to be honest or do you want me to cushion my words?" She crossed her arms and pursed her lips.

Willow waved her on and kicked off her slippers, stretching her stockinged toes. "Fine. Be honest. But do try to be kinder."

"Fine," Flora returned. "Clyde Billings?"

"Nice but dull, I'm afraid."

"Now who is being unkind?" Flora giggled. "And Sebastian Jones?"

Willow gritted her teeth into a smile. "Would I sound impossibly cruel if I admitted the same is true for him? Nice, but again, dull."

Flora shrugged. "It makes my job easier. And the last one I wanted to ask you about was that dear boy, Mr. Starling."

"I think you just outed the reason why I first thought he must go. However, as the son of a newspaper tycoon, he has proven himself to be quite the candidate. He has brilliant business instincts." The china clock above the mantel began to chime and with a sigh, Willow stood, shaking out her skirts and slipping on her shoes, thankful for the moment of respite. "Thank you for coming, Flora, but unfortunately, I'm afraid I don't have time to discuss Mr. Keating, Mr. Lovett and Mr. Blythe. Though, I am fairly certain in my decision on whom to keep now thanks to you."

"Wait, isn't there one more?"

Willow brought a hand to her mouth. Once again she had forgotten poor Mr. Lennox. "Ernest!"

"Yes, the eye-twitcher." Flora nodded. "Well, judging by the fact that you forgot him, I'd say that one is an easy choice." At the rapid knock on the door, Flora clapped. "My work here is done. Go! Off with you. Remember the good I did tonight and do not forget to send a handsome rich fellow my way when you give him the boot, but do make certain he is interesting."

Cullen discreetly swiped at his temple, hopefully removing any signs of stress. He shifted from foot to foot as he stood at the base of the platform, staring up at Willow and the six men behind her. Theodore Day, Fritz Blythe, Kit Quincy, Archie Lovett, Chandler Starling, and Digory Pruett. Had he done enough to earn another crown from Willow? At the beginning of the ceremony, he was confident that she would award him with laurels, but she continued to call the gentlemen, including that adolescent Chandler, over him, until there remained only two crowns. He glanced sideways, eyeing the remaining men—Clyde Billings, Frank Keating, Ernest Lennox, Noah Walden, Alexander Houlgrave, Sebastian Jones, and Taylor Kemp.

Cullen shifted from foot to foot at the waning slots. Surely the confusion over the pot of chocolate would not be his undoing. He could not lose his family's legacy over a stinking pot of chocolate. He pulled at his neckcloth that had become unexplainably tight, but if he was honest with himself, Cullen truly would be sorry if Willow dismissed him. He thought of how tenderly she had cared for him at the doctor's home and of their little tête-à-têtes that were the brightest moments of his day. He studied her in her comely gown of gold with its yards of delicate tulle and rosettes cascading across her shoulders and down to her slim waist. He did not want to go without hearing her sweet voice call his name. *Stop. Do not let your heart become even more invested in this girl.* For like Wellington always said, *"To love is to be weak."*

Mr. Noah Walden stepped forward, his focus on the crown in Willow's grip. "Before we continue, may I have a word with you, Miss Dupré?"

She faltered with the crown in hand. "Certainly. Shall we adjourn to the parlor?"

As they left, the men shifted. "What's he doing stealing her away? The time for chatting has ended," Mr. Jones grumbled beside him, shoving his hands into his pockets.

Cullen slipped away from the group and stood just outside

the door to the parlor and held his breath, catching bits of conversation.

"The thing is, Miss Dupré, and I mean no offense, but I respect you too much to continue on when I do not think I could marry a woman I am not attracted to—"

Cullen winced at the man's blunt tone. How could anyone look at her pretty turned-up nose, bright eyes, and sweet smile and not be drawn to her? Cullen strode back to his post, ecstatic that one less man stood between him and Willow. But, watching Willow leave the parlor looking flustered, his elatedness ceased at the thought that Mr. Walden's words had bothered her.

Willow returned to her place before the thrones. "Mr. Walden has decided to leave, and with him, he takes away a crown." She picked up one of the laurels and handed it to the footman, who was standing at attention beside the table, leaving a single crown. "I cannot offer a crown to a man I had already dismissed in my mind. Forgive me." She lifted the final crown and sent the group an apologetic glance before announcing, "Mr. Dempsey, will you accept the final crown?"

He released his pent-up breath at her words, his pulse slowing as he climbed the steps to her and knelt. "The honor would be mine, my dear Miss Dupré."

Setting the crown atop his head, Willow clasped his hands in her own and gently tugged him to standing.

He leaned to her and whispered in her ear, "You had me worried."

"I can't have you becoming too confident in my feelings, sir, for where would the fun be in that?" She motioned for him to stand with the others behind her and folded her hands in front of her skirts and faced the rejected suitors. "My apologies, sirs, but if you were not crowned, it is the end of our time together. I give you my heartfelt thanks for taking the time to court me, and it is my prayer that you all find the bride of your dreams."

The men murmured their disappointment, the crowned fellows looking as relieved as Cullen felt, though he was surprised to see Clyde in the rejected suitors. He was a nice fellow, and he had thought that Willow would at least give him more time, and yet Cullen appreciated her ability to decide with confidence. Besides, every suitor rejected was another obstacle removed to his receiving the ultimate final crown. He straightened his shoulders at the thought. At the first ceremony, he had been intrigued with her, but now, having spent time with her and her sweet family, his motives had somehow begun to shift. He *wanted* to be the last groom standing, not only because of her wealth but also because of the way she treated him, as if he were special to her. *Him . . . special.*

He swallowed, feeling a pressing on his soul. He bent his head from side to side, cracking his neck and attempting to ignore that still, small voice. But wasn't his ignoring the Lord's correction the reason why he was in this mess in the first place? And seeing the pure light of Miss Dupré's nature in her acceptance of him and his boxing secret, he could not use her for his own gain. And if he was to have any chance at redemption and continuing forward, Wellington had to release him from his promise.

"I was honestly worried for you, Cullen."

Cullen started. "What?"

Theodore handed him a cup of coffee as Willow escorted the rejected group from the house. "Thought for a moment that she might cut you."

Cullen gulped the coffee in a single draft, despite the scalding temperature, hoping it would help his courage return. "Sure you were. You know that Willow and I share a strong connection."

Theodore squared his shoulders, his jaw tightening and the jovial light vanishing from his expression. "Be that as it may, I have a connection with her from years past, and I hope you remember that when it is I standing by her side at the end."

Cullen shuffled the cup from hand to hand, having the feeling that neither of them cared for the other's admission. "I need a second cup," he mumbled, crossing over to the footman with the silver pot and motioning for him to fill it up with a nod of thanks. He would pay for drinking so much later.

Willow returned, smiling brightly at the culled group. "Gentlemen, I will retire early tonight, as you all should, for we will be leaving on the train for Newport in the morning. Thank you to each and every one of you for choosing to stay for me. Your kindness . . ." Willow paused, laid a hand over her heart, and cleared her throat. "Your kindness gives me hope."

She was moving to depart when Cullen darted forward and caught her wrist in the hallway, thankful for the single flickering gaslight sconce that offered precious little light. "Willow," he whispered. "Thank you for keeping me."

She gave him a soft smile. "I know it was a little wicked of me to keep you for last, but I thought, out of all the men, you would know that I, uh . . ." She dropped her gaze. "That I wish to spend more time with you."

She cares for me? Even in the darkness, he could see how much that confession had cost her. She was in all sincerity, and he was a cad for the way he was using her. He swallowed back his pain. *Pain?* Perhaps he truly was falling for her. He dropped her wrist. He couldn't do this. Not with Wellington breathing down his neck. His feelings were growing at an alarming rate and it would not do to linger. He would speak to Wellington tonight. "And I you," he admitted.

"I'm guessing you made me wait for your answer as a means of revenge?" She laughed, misinterpreting his silence as agreement and not for what it was—guilt. "Good night, Mr. Dempsey. I look forward to our time tomorrow." She slipped away to the stairs.

Instead of joining the other men in the library for celebratory drinks, Cullen snatched his greatcoat from the hall tree

116

and marched out into the snow, determined to speak with Wellington. He hunched his shoulders against the sharp wind and kept one foot in front of the other until he was standing before Wellington's parlor fire.

"This had better be good." Wellington slammed the door behind him. "Miss Davenport has proven most eager for my attention and I intend to ask for her hand, and more importantly, her massive dowry."

"Felicitations, sir," Cullen said, stretching his numb fingers toward the fire. In his haste he had forgotten his gloves.

"Get on with it, boy, or I fear the lady's kisses will cool, along with her eagerness to prove herself to me." He shoved his hands into his pockets. "And I do intend on letting her prove her devotion to me *before* I get down on one knee."

Cullen barely disguised his disgust in time. "I will keep it brief, sir. I have come to tell you that the Duprés are moving the competition to Newport, and I in good conscience cannot allow this arrangement to go on any further. I will, of course, continue to fight for her hand, but only because I wish to and not because you are forcing my hand as a means to repay my debts. If we wed, I will pay you back *with* interest, but that is all. I cannot betray her confidence in me anymore out of a sense of loyalty to you. If I win her hand, it must be done honorably."

Wellington smirked as he trilled his fingers against one another, moving to his desk where he stopped and shifted his paperweights here and there before speaking. "So, when did you fall in love with our sugar queen, Miss Dupré?"

Cullen's throat caught. "I never said—"

"You did not have to. Your betrayal of my confidence is enough to shout it from the rooftops. How could you so quickly forget that it was *I* who created you? You were *nothing* before I helped you, and you will be nothing again if you dare to defy me." He tossed a paperweight up into the air and caught it, turning it over in the firelight, the crystal's reflection catching along the ceiling's dark mahogany coffers.

Perhaps he had once again underestimated the man. "Sir, I meant no offense."

"But you have given it and it has been taken." Wellington flung the paperweight into the fire, shattering it against the stones. "Listen, Dempsey," he began, his tone deadly, "you will either give up this fool notion of being an honest man and fulfill your promise to me, or I will make good on my threat and I will have your business. *And* I vow to destroy any chance of your sister making a decent match."

At the mention of Eva Marie, Cullen took a single menacing step forward, his fists balling. "I think you have forgotten who you are dealing with. You had best watch your words."

"As should you, or perhaps I will persuade your sister to allow me to take her hand in marriage."

Cullen snorted and paced to the wing-back chair, sinking down in a feign of confidence, realizing too late that it was a tactic Wellington himself had taught him. "Do you take me and my family for fools? My mother would never consent to it, and besides, what of Miss Davenport?"

Wellington batted the air as if she were a fly. "She will serve her purpose, but she is nothing compared to your sister, who bears a remarkable resemblance to the woman I courted years ago. Your mother is a well-preserved woman, but I think it would make my success complete to, at last, have her daughter by my side." He laughed, shaking his head. "I do not know why I haven't considered it sooner. I was your mother's second choice, after all. Why shouldn't her daughter be mine?"

Blood rushed to Cullen's head as he fought the urge to strike the man. He knew the scores of women Wellington entertained and conquered. No amount of wealth would save his sister from certain heartbreak should the two wed. Cullen could warn her, but he knew the moment Eva Marie sensed any threat against

118

her brother, she would not think twice of sacrificing herself to this wolf. Cullen squelched the impulse to fight, knowing that any blows here would reverberate to his family. He slowly rose and bowed. "Consider my request withdrawn. It will never happen again, sir."

Wellington withdrew a cigar from his coat pocket and set to lighting it by candle flame, taking a long draft, keeping Cullen on the line as always. "Good, now tell me what you have garnered from living in the household thus far."

"Nothing that you don't already know." Cullen turned on his heel, leaving the man to his sordid evening. He paused at the bottom step and drew a deep breath. *Lord, I know I haven't sought you in a while, but would you show me the way out of this pit I have thrown myself and my family into?* He lifted his face to the dark sky above, the snowflakes drifting down upon his cheeks. Silence.

With a grunt, he trekked through the snow, unable to return to the mansion yet, with Wellington's latest threat weighing on him, when he passed a policeman and then a second. He looked up to find a precinct on the corner, his insides twisting. What if the way of escaping Wellington was to betray his confidence to the law? Cullen had spent years at Wellington's side, and during that time he had witnessed hundreds of illicit dealings. He had prayed and this could be God's answer, but that peace of old was not as strong as before . . . but he could sense it nonetheless. He glanced over his shoulder and crossed the street, stepping inside the brick building.

A stout man behind a large desk looked up at him from his thick ledger. Without setting aside his pen, he lifted a single brow. "How can I help you, sir?"

Cullen cleared his throat and bent his head to the side, cracking his neck as he did every time before entering the ring. Peace rested in his soul at last. *Lord, lead me to someone trustworthy.* "I would like to speak with a detective."

Nine

Theodore kept his back to the wind and followed Archie Lovett up onto the Wickford Station platform to find Willow standing under the roofline of the platform, her arms crossed against the damp chill. The fellows were diligently attempting to impress Mr. and Mrs. Dupré, so he edged away from the group when he saw a girl on the cusp of womanhood approaching Willow from behind and brushing her fingertips on Willow's crimson sleeve. He paused mid-stride, listening.

"Miss Dupré? I had to tell you thank you for keeping my favorite with this last cut. How drastic it must have seemed to you for your mother to ask you to cut the group down so quickly and without warning."

Willow's focus flicked to the newspaper clutched in the girl's arms with what Theodore could guess boasted the latest headline regarding the competition. She smiled at the girl, bending down to speak with her. "And which is your favorite, miss?"

"Teddy, of course!" she giggled, her golden curls bobbing

with her excitement. "I fairly melted when I saw that was your sweet name for him. I have always adored *Little Women* and thought that Jo should have married Laurie, who everyone knows she fondly called—"

"Teddy," Theodore interjected, wrapping his hand around Willow's waist, surprising her with the action but sending the girl practically into a faint. "It is a pleasure to meet you, Miss . . . ?"

"Daisy," she replied, breathless, Willow seeming to be all but forgotten at his appearance. "My friends will never believe me when I tell them I met you."

The train whistle blew its warning, steam shooting out from behind the wheels onto the platform and enveloping them as the conductor appeared at the back of one of the cars, checking his watch. "Miss Daisy, it is truly an honor. But, if you'll excuse us, Miss Dupré needs to board and take her seat. And I'll be certain to do my best to win her heart and hand for you and your friends." With that, he tipped his hat and scooped Willow into his arms, which sent Daisy into a fit of giggles, and charged up the steps into the vacant drawing-room car the Duprés had secured.

"Teddy! Put me down." She pulled her right hand from her fur muff and clutched the brim of her chapeau. "You can't keep sweeping me off my feet just because you feel like it." Willow pressed her hands against his chest as he entered the opulent car with its luxurious polished wood, high ceiling with a small chandelier in the middle, and nontraditional seating arrangement with chairs positioned about the car in a cozy fashion to encourage tête-à-têtes.

"You know my little doting supporter outside is loving this, and besides, I had to give her something delicious to impart to her friends." He proceeded to carry her to the tufted bench seat at the back of the car, thankful for the heavy emerald velvet curtains at the windows that would give them a few moments of privacy from the platform and suitors' passing gazes, when she scrambled out of his arms, righting her crimson traveling jacket and glancing through the glass and out onto the platform. But instead of sending him daggers, she shook her head for laughing.

"I did not know you were such a politician in your ability to win over the hearts of America, but I think you have given your supporter quite enough fodder for one day."

Theodore tossed his hat atop the emerald tufted seat and crossed his arms. "I won't deny it because it may help sway your decision to know that people listen to me. It may prove valuable for you to choose me to help you rule with my ability to gain the businessmen's attention."

Willow dipped her head, her mirth vanishing, and he was at once reminded why she must be having this competition in the first place. "Will," he said, his concerned tone bringing her attention up from studying the carpeted floor, "I did not mean to insinuate that you could not do this on your own. I only meant that I could be of help to you if you chose me."

She sank onto the seat. "But you see, it's true. That is the reason you are all here. The board thinks of me as a girl playing at business and that I need a husband to rule the company. Hence the sudden parade of suitors."

Theodore joined her and wrapped her gloved hand in his, wishing he could pull off the kid glove and kiss her hand. "I had guessed as much, and you resent this fact?"

She shrugged. "Before New Year's Eve, I was not in a place where I wanted or needed to choose a husband . . . and I must admit, I found the whole idea humiliating." She swallowed and whispered, "And absolutely terrifying. I have no idea what I am doing, Teddy."

He leaned so close, he bumped into her chapeau, sending the giant curved egret feather dancing across her cheek. "And do you still feel that way?" he whispered as the sounds of many entering the car reached them. But he kept his focus on her, unwilling to look up and see anyone but her.

She brushed off flecks of dust from the lapel of his coat. "Now I have hope that perhaps I could find happiness if I had the courage."

"Courage? It's falling in love, Will."

"To fall in love is to lose control of one's heart." She looked up at him. "I wish I could be honest with you, because people are so often dishonest with me, yet I'm afraid that if I say what I am thinking, I will come to regret it."

"Say it."

She closed her eyes and murmured so that only he could hear as the men gathered in the center of the car, muttering as if they did not wish to take their seats until she stood to better their chances of sitting with her. "I need to choose a husband in time for a June wedding."

"Yes, we know." He chuckled to dislodge the lump of disappointment within his throat.

"With that stated up front, I am *beginning* to feel things for a few of you . . . you in particular. Even so, it is not love I feel for any of you."

"Not the best phrasing, but your message is all I desire." He took her hand in his. "Look, Will, if you do not find a husband by June and do not feel love for anyone in particular, just a general fondness . . . perhaps you could consider a pact with your friend of old." Fritz paused and looked like he was about to join them on the bench, but Theodore scowled and waved him onward.

"A pact?" she whispered and shifted in her seat so that her back was to the window, where a gaggle of girls had appeared, pointing and squealing.

"That if you do not find love, we will marry and hope a love will grow in time. I will save you from the board, and you will save me from a broken heart, because these last few days with you have reminded me of my boyhood yearnings for the pretty girl on Bellevue Avenue, and of that wretched first summer I was forced to spend away from you because Father did not want to leave the business in New Orleans and then again, when Mother decided it was time for me to study abroad. Those summers away from you. . ." He shook his head, unable to put into words the pain of those first unexpected partings. "Just promise me you will think on my offer?" *Because I am falling irrevocably in love with you and cannot stop it.*

"Thank you. I am honored to have your affection. I will seriously consider your offer before I decide my future."

The twins tapped on the glass outside the car with their parasols, their lips pursed and their brows raised in such an exact imitation of Mrs. Dupré that Teddy and Willow both laughed, breaking the tension. They rose, Teddy's hand lingering around hers, yet Kit Quincy was there at once.

"May I join you, Willow? I wanted to ensure I requested a seat beside you for our train luncheon, if that is agreeable?"

Willow slid her arm through his and allowed him to guide her away from Teddy. "A perfect arrangement, sir."

Kit assisted her to one of a pair of chairs that were inclined toward each other. "Pardon my abrupt change in topic, but, uh, I know you are looking for honesty in your gentlemen."

She stiffened, fearing his next words. *Please do not excuse yourself from the competition like Mr. Walden did.* The thought jolted her that she would be so shaken by his departure. The competition, against all odds, was working. "Of course. What is amiss?"

He removed his greatcoat and reached for her crimson jacket as the warmth of the car grew with the closing of the doors behind the twins. "I do not like to come bearing tales, but I feel I must inquire and be done with it. I have been asking the fellows this morning if they knew anything about Cullen Dempsey's history, and most said that they had not seen him prior to this competition."

"He has only recently joined society," Willow returned, her chest tightening. Why was he asking about Cullen? Kit did not strike her as the invidious sort to stir animosity toward anyone.

"Yes, but . . ." He leaned toward her, his elbows on his thighs. "Forgive me for pressing, but did he confide in you regarding his past?"

She expelled a breath. "Of course." She glanced at the opposite end of the car, where Cullen sat between the twins, drawing away on one of their sketchbooks they had brought along to pass the time. "Mr. Dempsey was quite forthcoming but requested that I refrain from spreading the word among the gentlemen."

"Thank goodness." He chuckled and leaned back in his chair. "And now that I have done my duty in informing you of a possible danger to your heart, I shall set it aside. Let us talk about having an outing all our own in Newport. As you know, I have a mansion there as well as a yacht. Perhaps you would like to see my home or take a picnic lunch aboard my yacht?"

"I would love to." Her heart eased after his tumultuous question, even as her gaze rested on Cullen with the twins, who were giggling over his attempts to draw, which must have been poor indeed to elicit a laugh from Mother over the tableau while her father disappeared behind his copy of *The World*.

"Then I will speak with your mother and arrange a day." He leaned back as Fritz joined them, pulling over a chair to sit directly across from Willow.

Fritz, in his usual fashion, made himself at home. "So, the luncheon? Am I too late to ask to sit with you?"

"I had thought the furniture was bolted down." That annoyed look appeared on Kit's face again.

Fritz grinned. "Not this one."

Kit lifted a brow. "I highly doubt that."

"Well, it was the loosest, and I managed to yank it free, which only slightly tore the carpet. So then, can I join you two?"

Willow shook her head, suppressing her laugh behind her hand, lest her mother notice Fritz's destroying of private property. "Anyone that determined to dine with me shall."

The carriage rolled down Bellevue Avenue under the graceful boughs of barren trees lining the avenue as they passed mansion after mansion. The carriage turned left down a cobblestone drive before turning once more and passing through massive, elaborately designed black cast-iron gates that were held open on either side by footmen in crimson liveries. The gravel crunched beneath the wheels as the gray stone mansion came into view, and Cullen couldn't help but gape at the size of the summer "cottage" by the sea that Willow had fondly told him about. This was far larger than her New York residence, and judging from the magnificent exterior alone, it was a palace fit for a queen.

"I was relieved that you told Miss Dupré of your past." Kit broke the silence from his seat across from Cullen, snapping his book shut and bumping into the trunk beside him in the packed carriage, filled to the brim with the others' belongings.

Cullen sat upright. "What did you say?"

"I asked Miss Dupré if she knew of your past, and when she confirmed it, I happily let it lie."

And for the first time, Cullen realized from where he had recognized Kit Quincy—the gentlemen's social club that Wellington frequented. He had only gone there a handful of times to relay messages to his mentor, but Cullen distinctly remembered seeing Kit in a corner of the room, watching him greet Wellington. But Cullen kept himself from stiffening lest he appear guilty. "Why would you feel the need to bring my name up during your limited time with her?"

"I did not feel comfortable staying silent after I knew the identity of your mentor. When I saw you that first night, I wondered how on earth you were approved as a suitor, but I held my peace until this last cut."

Cullen swallowed back the bile in his throat. Of course, he did not say that Willow did not know the entirety of the truth yet. If Kit had approached him before he had spoken to the detective, who had in turn connected him with a Pinkerton agent, Cullen did not know what he would have done. But if the truth got out now and ruined his chances of freeing himself from Wellington and honorably securing Willow's hand . . . But Kit was an honorable man, and if he said he would not press the issue, he would not. "Thank you for telling me."

"I was only looking out to save her from potential heartache, but as she knows and you are still here, she must hold you in great affection to let your past—or your undesirable connections—*not* sway her." The carriage halted, and without another word, Kit opened the door and left him.

Cullen hopped down from the carriage and glanced ahead to the second carriage, where Willow had decided to sit with Archie, Theodore, Chandler, Digory, and Fritz. He had meant to spend time with Willow, but when he overheard Theodore's and her whispered conversation, his heart sank, and along with it his jovial spirit of getting out of the city and away from Wellington and his fleet of spies. He was allowed enough space then to compile the condemning information he had collected on Wellington over the years into a journal, including names, dates, and illicit activities, all to be delivered to the agent. However, Cullen knew Wellington was a master at covering his tracks and planting the blame elsewhere. The journal was merely the first piece toward securing his freedom from the tyrant and redeeming his name with Willow when the time came to tell her the truth.

His gaze flicked to Kit joining the others. Cullen hung back and observed the fellows in their comradery, angry at the possibility of her wedding another. While Willow confessed that she was having feelings for some of the men, she did not say whom . . . even though he was fairly certain she meant Day, since she hadn't refused his half-baked proposal. *But surely a marriage of convenience is not all Willow wishes for in a partner?*

At the thought of marriage, the prospect of his sister wedding Wellington, should Cullen fail and the man carry through on his myriad of threats, made Cullen's stomach revolt. While Cullen's initial agreement to the competition was for a debt owed, Heathcliff Wellington's latest threat was enough to drive him to such desperate lengths as to continue to lie to the woman he was falling for more and more with each passing day for the sake of catching Wellington in his own web. But, since Cullen was truly beginning to feel more than affection for Willow, was he really lying that much, especially since he was now trying to take down her company's greatest threat instead of helping Wellington steal her throne? He clenched his fists and kicked at the drive, sending a spray of pebbles into the air. He loathed this sense of helplessness, something he was not used to feeling. After years of settling matters with his fists, anything else felt like a sign of weakness.

"Cullen!"

He turned at the sweet voice, a smile involuntarily springing to life at the sight of Willow strolling out of the ring of gentlemen and tucking her hands into her fur muff.

"While it was kind of you to visit with my sisters, why didn't you seek me out on the ride over?" She fell into step beside him, tilting her head to indicate where they should walk. "Is something amiss?"

He shrugged, his hands finding their way into his pockets as they followed the path that led around to the left of the house, where a massive weeping willow stood, its stripped branches swaying in the breeze flowing from the cliffs and ocean beyond. "You seemed pretty preoccupied with Day's proposal and then, with the throng of admirers surrounding you for the entirety of the train ride to Newport, I never had a turn."

She sucked in her cheeks and grunted. "I see. You heard what Teddy said?"

Cullen inwardly cringed at the sobriquet, raking his hand through his hair and clenching his jaw so that he didn't say something stupid. *This was supposed to be a simple task. Win her hand and her heart, not be broken in the process.* Such hubris. He shouldn't be feeling such things for her, not this soon in the game, and yet here he was, lost in her eyes. "Yes."

She measured his response and continued their walk toward the tree. "And does it bother you?"

He cleared his throat. "That you have feelings for others here? I am a man. Of course it does." He looked over his shoulder at the others, who had begun to follow them. *Never a moment of privacy.* Straightening his shoulders, Cullen decided he did not care if he made a fool of himself in public. He took her hand in his, rubbing his thumb over the back of her hand. "And do you want to know why? Because what can I offer you compared to Day? A debt-ridden business? A failure of a businessman as your partner?" *Having a connection with Wellington built over years of mentorship?*

She followed his line of sight to the men quickly approaching. She pulled him around the back side of the tree, the large trunk hiding them from view. "That does not sound like the confident man I know. Who put such doubts in your head? If my mother and father approved of you, why shouldn't I?"

How could she tell that Wellington had put those doubts in his mind? He gestured to the manor by the sea, letting his silence speak for him.

She pressed her hand to his cheek and turned him away from the house and back to her. "Cullen. I do not care about your money. What I care about is this." She rested her hand over his heart. "The only gold I care about is in here."

He dropped his gaze. His character was even more wanting than his bank account. "Then I shall endeavor to be worthy of your trust." *Lord, I don't know if I will ever be worthy of Willow, but help me not fail her.*

Her brilliant smile erased her frown in an instant. "Good. Now, how would you like to go for a stroll about town with me this week? I can send round a note when I am ready?"

"I'm already counting down the minutes until I receive your summons, my dear Miss Dupré."

Ten

A message for you, sir," a young footman announced. He held a silver tray out to Cullen, bearing an envelope with *Cullen Dempsey* written across in a pretty scrolling hand.

Cullen fairly dropped his cards in his haste to snatch it up, ignoring the three gentlemen at the card table protesting his halting the game. But after a week of waiting and seeing Willow at mealtimes and for fleeting, stolen moments before she turned away and asked the other gentlemen for outings before him, and Kit Quincy twice, Cullen did not care. He broke the seal and read the long-awaited summons from Willow, thankful he had worn his favorite morning suit of gray. Tucking the letter into his pocket, he adjusted his dark moss-green neckcloth and called out to Fritz in the adjoining library, "Blythe, take my place, will you?" And at a clipped pace over the marble floors, Cullen crossed into the great hall and to the stairs and the open-air sitting room on the second floor, where Willow stood beneath the middle arch with her back to him, her attention focused on the expansive grounds below and the breaking waves beyond.

"I have been anticipating our rendezvous all week, hoping and praying that you had not forgotten me." He lifted his brows at the small feast on the table and then to the two painting stations that faced each other.

Willow dipped into a curtsy. "Never. I am sorry I kept you waiting, but I have been having difficulty juggling everything, and Mother insisted that I pay some of the others a call first lest I offend them." She gestured to the stands. "I thought we would enjoy painting over an early luncheon." She rubbed her hands up and down her sapphire satin brocade sleeves, drawing her embroidered cream shawl tight against herself, the gold tassels swaying in the breeze. "I thought the weather was mild enough for a partially outdoor activity, so the twins suggested painting and arranged everything. The servants brought wood for the fireplace but seem to have forgotten to arrange and light it." She pointed at the two tin pails beside the stone fireplace.

"Then allow me." Cullen crossed the room and found the matchbox atop the carved marble mantel inside an ornate stone box. Squatting down, he arranged the wood, stuffing bits of paper here and there before striking a match and lighting the papers, coaxing the fire into a blaze with the poker.

"Only one match needed?" Willow's skirts billowed about her as she sank down beside him, watching him work. "It appears as though you have done this before."

He shifted in his crouch to study her, wondering how much to disclose. He didn't need to ask if she had ever lit a fire to know her answer. "Many times."

She looked at him expectantly. "But don't you live on Fifth Avenue?"

He gave her a lopsided grin. "And have you never wondered why we haven't visited before? My house is the one in disrepair at the far end, on the not-so-desired part of the avenue, nowhere near the park." At her lips parting, he knew she was picturing his derelict home. He gave a little laugh and poked at the fire. "For as long as I can remember, my family kept only the bare minimum of servants at our home—employing a cook, a maid, and a butler—so there were never enough shoulders to bear the load. After my father's death, I took it upon myself to light the fires in the house until we could afford to hire someone to light them for us. Yet when I discovered my action disheartened my mother to see how far we had fallen, I decided to find another way of staunching the bleeding that was our finances." He leaned back on his heels, watching her as she lifted her palms to the warmth of the fire.

"Boxing," she said, rubbing her hands together. "And was it lucrative?"

"Enough to give my mother and sister a few new dresses for the season. Enough to patch the roof, hire a second maid, and keep our cook and butler." He shrugged. "It wasn't a lot, but it was enough to fool my mother into thinking the business was picking back up . . . until I received my first broken nose. Whenever I had black eyes, I explained them away as a brawl that had gotten out of hand at a public house, or I stayed at the office until they faded. But the second broken nose . . ." Cullen grinned at the memory of his mother's wrath when she discovered his double life. "After that, I entered only those matches with the highest stakes."

Understanding flickered in her eyes. "Which gave you notoriety after you almost beat the new heavyweight champion."

He nearly dropped the poker. "You've read about *my* fight with John L. Sullivan last year?"

She hugged herself against the lingering chill. "I am not only interested in business matters, you know."

Not only was she intelligent and beautiful, but of all things she had followed his career. The ember in his heart blazed. He removed his morning jacket and spread it over her shoulders, his hands lingering around her arms for only a moment.

She laughed. "You are speechless!"

"Only because most consider boxing a barbaric sport and,

excuse me for saying, especially so for the ladies." He rested his hand over his heart. "I am honored."

Willow extended her hand to him and gestured for them to stand. "My interest in the sport began as a by-product of my working with men. At first I did not wish to be ill-informed, and then it turned into a passion. But, unfortunately, I have never attended a match as per my father's orders for he agreed with society. Boxing matches and proper ladies do not mix, not even for the purpose of furthering business relations."

He assisted Willow to her feet. "And how is it going balancing the business from afar?"

"I don't know how Father does it some days, but I know expertise will come with experience and time." She set aside his coat, tied a pinafore over her dress, and reached for a paintbrush, motioning for him to take up one, as well.

"Please tell me we are not painting landscapes." Cullen grunted as he moved behind his own station and reached for the smock, pulling it on over his clothes that he could not afford to ruin with a stray drop of paint.

"I thought it would be a good exercise to paint each other."

"While I do not deny my gifts of dancing and boxing, I am sorely lacking in creative talent, especially painting."

She giggled, nonplussed. "That's what the twins implied, which will make this a much more diverting experience, especially given our time limit and that I too lack the gift of art."

Picking up a brush, he dipped it into the paint of the ready-made color palette, using the time to gather his courage to ask another question in the most nonchalant way. If he was going to maintain his façade of assisting Wellington, Cullen needed to find something that would keep Wellington pleased while setting numerous traps to catch him. For despite Wellington's list of crimes, Cullen knew from his time learning from his mentor that no roads would lead back to Wellington . . . but, as the agent said, Wellington trusted him. Cullen was the agency's best shot of taking down the crime lord. "If you need assistance, maybe I can help? I am not just a pretty face like Theodore, you know. My failures have proven quite useful as a lesson on how *not* to run a business."

This brought a smile to her lips, summoning those delightful dimples at the corners of her bottom lip. "Well, we have conquered America's sugar industry, but with my officially taking over the business in June, I am attempting to expand to a factory in Paris and then in time distribute Dupré Sucré to all of Europe."

He shifted, leaving a smear on his painting. He blended it into the oval that was to be Willow's face. Wellington would devour this information. Perhaps it was enough to keep him satisfied for the remainder of the competition and let him court Willow without the subterfuge . . . well, without the subterfuge regarding Willow. Perhaps he could even tell her about his taking Wellington down so that her business would be safe, along with his family. And for the first time, to his shame, he thought of others who would be free from his mentor's iron fist should he succeed, the merchants Wellington had blackmailed, the politicians he had in his net, along with the hundreds of Irish families in Wellington's disgusting housing who were at the mercy of the landlord who employed them, paying them pennies and continually raising their rent . . . like his father had been planning to do before he was murdered.

He cleared his throat against the memory. "And do you have a lead, or do you need help securing one?"

She blended colors on her palette. "I have been searching for the perfect factory for about a year now. And for my plan to work, I need to find a factory already built and available, all at a fantastic price."

"Quite the undertaking. Have you had any luck?"

She withdrew a telegram from her pocket, her happiness lighting her face and her paintbrush dangerously close to dripping on her hem. "I received a reply today, in fact. I can hardly believe that this dream I have had since I started training is finally coming to fruition."

Please don't let me read it, he silently begged, and kept painting. If he read it, he feared it was something he would be forced to put into motion that he could never reverse. And even if he *was* working with the Pinkertons, wouldn't destroying a dream of hers be unforgivable? "How fortunate."

"Isn't it?" She fairly squealed and flapped the telegram victoriously above her head, accidentally spattering her paint onto her pinafore, her girlish action betraying the depth of her attachment to the property. "I cannot wait to talk to the board about the potential acquisition. This is exactly what I need to make my mark on the business, to prove I am more than just a figurehead." She set aside her brush and went to the buffet table and lifted a journal Cullen hadn't noticed before. "I have all sorts of ideas in here on how to improve the business and the workload." She trilled her fingers on the binding. "If only I could get the board's support, I know I could make them a fortune. Once it passes, I would love to get your opinion on how to best ship the product."

"I would be honored to take a look. I would also advise you to act quickly and send your acceptance." *Before the agent encourages me to send a telegram to Wellington, telling him of your plans.* Wellington would not need to search long before finding the property.

"I wish I had the freedom to act without consulting the board, but alas, that is not how my father does business, so it will have to wait a few weeks until the next meeting. Still, I will bring my completed proposal, along with my father, to ensure the best possible reception."

A few weeks. By then it will be too late. Cullen swallowed hard, his mouth gone dry. *Lord, let me not be the reason for the death of her dream.*

The gong of the hall clock sounded, signaling the end of her time with Cullen. He sighed, recognizing it as well, and tugged on his morning jacket. Willow popped a strawberry into her mouth and put the finishing touches on her painting, albeit unwilling to cease her excuse for studying the model before her. In the course of their conversations and her showing Cullen her business journal, she was finding that his soul matched his outward appearance. He was more encouraging of her work than any man, besides her father, had ever been. His love for his family was evident, and his small confessions that she knew pained him made her feel closer to him than to most of the others. Like his broken features, she could tell there was a hurt lying within him concerning his father and his past business dealings. And she hoped, given time, he would come to trust her enough to completely confide in her. "I wish we could linger, but I am supposed to take tea in town." She removed her apron and draped it over the wooden stool beside her station. "I quite enjoyed our morning of painting, which you will now reveal to me."

He leapt in front of his picture, at once dispelling any seriousness between them. "Oh no. You will dismiss me on the spot. You do not want to see this."

"Oh, but I do." She gently pushed him aside, then gasped at the painting that looked as if it had been completed with a blindfold in place. Laughter burst from her as she struggled for breath.

"Come now. Your painting can't be much better," he said, leaning around her to look at her canvas, and joined her merriment over the appalling painting. "Shall I throw them over the balcony and aim for the fountain below?"

"Absolutely not. You might hurt Mr. and Mrs. Swan who are

currently swimming in it." She stayed his hand. "I will treasure your painting of me forever." She looked to the barely touched feast behind them. "It is a shame to waste such preparations. Let's bring some food to the library for the others."

She moved to pick up a tray when Cullen bumped into her back, sending her forward, grabbing wildly at the table. But instead of finding the hardwood top, her fingers caught on a silver tray, sending whatever it bore up into the air as Cullen grabbed for her waist. He pulled her up against himself, even as he lost his own footing, and together they tumbled to the floor, the silver tray landing with a resounding crash. Willow gasped as bits of gravy dribbled down her face and into her mouth. She raked her fingers over her eyes and nose, flicking the cream away, and found Cullen's hair had taken the worst of it, along with his suit jacket. "Oh, Cullen, your suit. It's ruined."

"I have another. Yet there is not another Willow Dupré. You could have broken something on these stones."

While he tried to disguise his dismay with a jaunty grin, she could tell the loss bothered him. His suit bore no signs of wear, and after their conversation, she knew it had cost him dearly to outfit himself for her competition, and here she had gone and ruined one because she could not keep her footing while around him. *And speaking of footing* . . . She reluctantly released her hold about his neck, sat up, and brushed back a gravy-spattered lock of hair from his forehead.

"Miss Willow!"

She grimaced and glanced over her shoulder to see the butler standing behind them, slack-jawed.

"I never in all my days . . ." Beckwith sputtered, rushing to help her, but Cullen waved him off.

"No sense in sacrificing your suit as well, Mr. Beckwith. I'll attend her." Cullen's hands wrapped about her waist and lifted her to her feet, the perilously slick gravy-covered stones throwing her against his chest once more.

Nicolette, her lady's maid, appeared behind the butler, a stack of linens in hand. "Oh, dear! Let's get you changed, miss, before your mother finds you in such a compromising state."

Anyone else wish to witness my disastrous first call with Cullen?

"Willow Dupré!" Her mother's gasp sent Willow scrambling away from Cullen's gravy-soaked shirt that was far too revealing to endure for long. "What on earth are you doing?"

"Having a bit of breakfast," Willow replied evenly, folding her hands in front of her skirts when Flora appeared from behind Mother, looking all too happy to see Willow in such a predicament with Cullen.

"Flora!" She moved to embrace her, but Flora sidestepped her.

"Oh no, you don't. You keep those hands to yourself, missy. I don't want to ruin my new frock."

"How long will you be here? And what brought you here?"

"I'll be in town for only a week because I have to return to New York for a ball at the Astors', and then I am here for as long as you need me. And when I say *here*, I mean I will be staying at my aunt's house, as yours is full."

"You two can continue this later. If word of this gets leaked to the papers, we will be ruined," Mother whispered. "Take the back way up to your room, Mr. Dempsey. Nicolette, see to Miss Dupré. She has a tea to get to in an hour with Mr. Starling."

"Nicolette is not a miracle worker, Mrs. Dupré," Flora mumbled out of the corner of her mouth, earning a scowl from Mother.

"Until we meet again, Miss Dupré." Cullen bowed to her, keeping a straight face despite the gravy.

Flora's grin spread as she giggled and seized Willow by the arm, propelling her toward Willow's bedroom. "So, tell me, is this some new sort of beauty treatment? If so, can I borrow one of your gentlemen and try it for myself?"

Eleven

Theodore leaned against the library's windowsill, watching the snowflakes drift down from the gray sky and melt within seconds upon landing on the patchy grass below, when he noticed Cullen exiting the mansion from a side door, hurrying down the drive with long, purposeful strides. *Where is he off to now? And why isn't he taking the carriage?* He straightened, cracking his knuckles. This was the third time Cullen had clandestinely disappeared since his brunch with Willow nearly a week ago. At dinner last night, Willow had again asked everyone to be vigilant in finding the informer for the papers, and knowing Cullen's propensity for writing letters in the night when he thought all were sleeping, Theodore turned away from the window, having the excuse he needed to follow Cullen.

"I have a mind for a walk. See you in a bit, gents," he called to Fritz, Chandler, Archie, Kit, and Digory, all murmuring in return, having their heads buried behind their cards. Donning his greatcoat, hat, gloves, and scarf, Theodore braced himself against the damp cold and struck out into the blustery day, determined to find out whom Cullen was writing to and why. He knew Cullen was a businessman, and yet he wrote with the dedication of a lover. *And if he is playing with Willow's heart . . .*

Theodore shoved his fists into his pockets and hunched against the buffeting wind, following Cullen down the street until he turned right onto Bellevue Avenue. Theodore adjusted his scarf to cover his mouth. If Cullen was headed to town, it would be a good twenty minutes of miserable hiking before they arrived.

While he knew Willow admired Cullen, he did not know how she could feel so attached to a man she had just met. And who was to say that, because Cullen had managed to secure an invitation, he was worthy of her hand? His anger kept him warm through the cold until, as he suspected, Cullen headed straight into the post office. Theodore leaned against the corner of the building, watching the window of the shop as Cullen handed the man a sealed letter.

"Teddy?" Willow exclaimed behind him.

He started and turned away from his view of the window lest Cullen spot him. She was a vision, draped in a crimson cape with an ebony fur-trimmed hood and matching muff. "Willow? I didn't know you were coming to town with Flora." He nodded at the taller woman standing beside Willow, her blond curls framing her pointed face, her powder-blue coat contrasting with Willow's. "Pardon me. I meant to say Miss Wingfield. Old habits are hard to break."

"We are old friends." Flora gave him a brilliant smile and dipped into a curtsy. "My first name is more than proper, Teddy. Since it is my last day here for a while, Willow has finally given in to my demands to shop."

"A trial if there ever was one." He winked at Willow.

Willow looked down the avenue behind him. "No carriage? You didn't *walk* here, did you?"

He nodded, unwilling to give up his true reason yet. "But now that I've discovered you two, I may not need to take the walk back?"

Willow placed her arm through his without waiting for an invitation, bringing warmth to his chilled body that she would feel so at ease with him. "Of course. I know shopping isn't the most exciting outing for you, but I desperately need some time out of the house, and Flora mentioned that with Valentine's Day approaching, I had best get shopping in case I have to place something on order. Can you survive a little shopping?"

"While I wouldn't call shopping for seven suitors a small task, you could say I was trained for lengthy shopping trips from a young age. My mother went to Paris only every few years to be fitted for her Worth wardrobe instead of every season, so as a boy I would spend most of our time abroad sitting in some designer's shop, waiting for Mère to finish up, which she *never* did in a timely manner."

"I think I would have melted from boredom," Willow commented as they passed a milliner's shop, its vibrant collection of chapeaus in the display window bringing Flora to a halt.

She pointed to a hideous crimson glacé straw hat with an upturned brim on one side, complete with multiple matching feathers and a tiny stuffed parrot. "It is so horrid that I think I must have it," Flora said.

Willow tugged her friend away. "Not while I'm here to stop you."

Flora clicked her tongue, moving along. "Listen to you. How could one be bored shopping in Paris?"

"It happens more often than one might think," Teddy said with a shrug.

Willow grinned. "And I can only shop if a great many interludes for tea and pastries along the way are promised up front. If not, I perish from fatigue."

"I often did nearly die, but my mother always said she was training me up for my future wife." He glanced down at Willow, loving the color creeping into her cheeks just as he knew it would.

Flora paused at a storefront display of a mercantile, pressing her gloved fingertips to the glass. "I love the look of this one. I think I can see a bolt of fabric that would be perfect for sewing the first of those little doll dresses I was telling you about for my cousin's baby."

"But she is still months away from having the baby."

"Cornelia will be having a girl. There is no doubt in my mind, so I better start sewing now to have the present ready in time," Flora said and reached for the door.

Theodore held the door for the ladies and took up a position a few yards back beside a display of books, assuming he would be doing a lot of watching, and was surprised when he found Willow at his side, holding up a gold neckcloth to his jaw.

"Just as I suspected. It suits your eyes to perfection."

Theodore shifted closer to her. "Is that so, my lady? Are you going to purchase it for my Valentine's Day gift?"

"I may if you should last so long," she returned, her eyes sparkling. "Although Mother would say that a neckcloth is too intimate a gift."

"Not for a future fiancé. And speaking of which, are you still considering my offer? Or do I need to provide some persuasion?" His hand cupped her cheek, her full lips calling him. He just might kiss her in this store, as the snow seemed to have kept other shoppers at home, for the three of them were the only ones inside besides the clerk.

"Teddy," she whispered, turning her head to look behind them.

"No one is near," he returned, closing the gap between them. He leaned down and swept her into a kiss that he had dreamed of for years. Her lips melded into his as she swayed into him. He drew in a breath of her scent of strawberries and vanilla, and even though he was loath to release her, he gently, reluctantly pulled back, finding her sapphire eyes bright with a light he had never seen in them before. "Willow, I want you to know that—"

At the deep throat-clearing behind him, he looked over his shoulder and saw Cullen with his arms crossed, his brows narrowed into a fierce glare, and Flora standing behind him with a bolt of cloth draped over her arm, pale and stricken. Theodore returned his attention to Willow, whose skin appeared to be on fire. "Willow, I—"

Without a word, she slipped away, grabbing Flora by the wrist and practically dragging her out the door, leaving the bolt of fabric in a heap on the floor, the tie forgotten on Theodore's shoulder.

Cullen surged forward, dropping his arms, his fists curling inward, stopping an inch from Theodore's face. "How *dare* you take such liberties with Miss Dupré. Have you no respect for the lady? For her good name?"

Theodore swallowed back his rising guilt for the indiscretion, yet he did not wish away their sweet kiss. Rather, he felt cheated that such a tender moment had been shared with *Cullen* of all people. "I resent your claim that I have no respect for her. It is because of that respect I wished to share such a moment with her." He straightened his collar. "And if you had not noticed, *Will* seemed to enjoy it as much as I."

Cullen's jaw clenched, his fists twitching. "We will see about that," he grunted, then charged outside to join the women, no doubt.

At the store manager's glare, Theodore scooped up the goods and purchased the bolt for Flora and the tie for himself, a memento of their first kiss. Waiting for the clerk to wrap the goods, Theodore scowled as the sting of Cullen's words lingered. *Who is he to judge?* The secret trip to the post office still piqued him, but if Willow had truly enjoyed their moment, he did not have to worry for long. He would win. He knew it. If only he could get Willow to see that he was more than a friend . . . more than just an emergency plan. He could be her everything.

Willow had never been so mortified in all her life. To have her first kiss ever turn into the most public kiss of all time was simply more than a woman should have to bear. Her fingers flitted to her lips. It had been surprising. One could even say *lovely*.

"Willow, if you want people to respect you as a businesswoman, you cannot go around town kissing your beaus for all the world to see," Flora hissed, her cheeks blazing as she pulled Willow toward the carriage. "You have *six* other suitors. Are you going to sample their lips before deciding?"

"Flora!" Willow gasped, tugging her arm away from Flora's iron grip.

"Well, how do you think it will make your suitors feel after you smooch one of them and send said kisser home? And how will your future husband feel when he discovers you have been going around kissing your sweethearts in such a devil-may-care manner?"

Willow stopped short, hurt that her friend would say such things to her . . . and it stung because if she allowed herself to stop and think about her actions, she knew Flora was right. Even so, Willow was too embarrassed at the moment to own up to her own folly. "But you know I did not kiss just any one of my beaus. I kissed *Teddy*."

"I *know*." Flora's voice dropped into a growl, her complaints coming so fast and mumbled that Willow couldn't understand her.

She grabbed Flora's arm, staying her. "Why do you care so much?"

Flora crossed her arms. "How could you ask me that? I came all the way to Newport, taking time away from the season in New York City, to help you. I am missing not one, not two, but three balls in coming here this week. I am only saying that you should keep your lips to yourself."

"If you are going to be in such a foul temper, maybe you should ride on ahead while I speak with Cullen and *walk* home." She braced herself against the wind sweeping down the main street. Anything would be preferable to suffering through Flora's righteous anger.

"Fine." She whirled, flouncing to their carriage waiting at the corner.

Willow at once regretted her words, but at the angry swish of Flora's skirts, she knew that distance was what Flora needed, more than a halfhearted apology. Willow would have to make it up to her tonight before Flora's departure in the morning.

At the sound of boots approaching, Willow drew a deep breath and turned to face Cullen. At the sight of his stormy expression, her heart hammered, knees weakened, and she never felt so confused in all her life. "I am sorry you witnessed that, uh, moment. I am certain it was as awkward for you as it was mortifying for me to be caught in such a tableau." She averted her gaze from him. *As sweet as it was.*

Cullen lifted a hand, stopping her, then ran his hand through his hair and secured his hat. "It is part of the competition. I realize that, but yes, it was not easy to witness." He cleared his throat, a hint of a smile appearing. "But if I had known that you were giving away kisses, I would have gotten in line."

Willow drew in a sharp breath and opened her mouth to give him a piece of her mind when his wicked grin lit his features, his shoulders shaking in suppressed mirth. "You, sir, are a cad." She swatted at him with her muff, laughing as he easily dodged her, breaking the tension between them.

"And yet you keep me here because you like me." He grasped her hand and folded it over the crook of his arm.

She warmed, remembering her first kiss had almost been with him. *But he was unconscious, so it doesn't count.* "Yes, I do."

"Then I will endeavor to put aside your other relationships from my mind and focus not on the terrible parts of this situation but rather the wonderful part of being with you." Cullen pulled her closer as they walked back toward the mansion.

"And I shall as well. When I am with you, I am with you," she said, passing the nearly vacant Newport casino, the sound of a lone tennis ball being hit to-and-fro catching her ear. "I didn't know they played in the winter season. This place is full during the summer months."

Cullen stuffed his hand into his pocket, rocking back on his heels and forward. "I've never seen a real tennis court. Can we watch for a moment? Are we allowed inside?"

"Of course. During the summer months, my family attends a myriad of social events, including lectures and dances in the theater in the back." Willow tugged him through the arched corridor and down the mosaic-tiled hall. They strode through the open double doors to see the lawn tennis court in the center of the grounds, where two gentlemen were volleying despite the cold, though the club's two wings encircling the lawn aided in blocking the wind.

"Do you recognize the players?"

His gaze rested on her and she thought of what it would be like to spend a lifetime of melting into the arms of such a manly sort of gentleman. He wasn't like the others with their refined mannerisms and soft hands. She had noticed during their time together that his hands were callused and showed signs of a hard life that she could only imagine. She did imagine, however, that with those scars came a strength of character that she wished to have in a partner. And knowing the way he took charge of securing creature comforts for his mother and sister, she admired him all the more for his sacrifices. She shifted away from him and rested her hand on the rail that kept the spectators from encroaching upon the court, focusing on the two players beginning their set. "No, I do not believe I do."

What is wrong with me? Kissing one man one minute and thinking of a life with another the next? She was not that sort of woman, and yet here she was, opening her heart to Cullen Dempsey. Conversation was never awkward between them, and any silence that enveloped them felt comforting instead of strained like it did with the others. Still, Teddy was the obvious choice, the safe choice, no matter how swoon-worthy her fans thought him, or she herself thought him only ten minutes ago. There was a sort of magnetism between her and Cullen, though he had never acted inappropriately with her, never *truly* requesting a kiss but only teasing.

"Willow?" Cullen waved his hand before her face. "Did you go somewhere?"

She ducked her head. "My apologies. Sometimes I get lost in thought. Did you ask me something?"

He shook his head and laughed. "My sister says I often drift, as well. I asked if you enjoy tennis?"

"Tennis?" She blinked as the sun peeked through the clouds, splaying a halo over her suitor's head . . . as if she needed any more reasons to become distracted. "Every summer. This place only opened a few years ago, though." She pushed away from the rail. "We had better head back."

He cast one last look to the players and then followed her.

To get away from her thoughts that threatened to distract her to no end, she asked him the first thing she could think of, keeping her hands firmly in her muff so as not to take his arm again. "So, your sister, is she married?"

"No. Eva Marie is just sixteen and thankfully is not yet out in society." Cullen seemed to have sensed her unwillingness to take his arm and shoved his hands into his coat pockets. "I shudder to think of suitors paying call to her in two years' time."

"Ahh, to be sixteen again." She lifted her eyes to the clouds, reminiscing when the twins were little, keeping her mother busy. Her father had been strong then, and she was beginning to take her first classes at the university. The wind blew her sideways into Cullen, but she quickly looked away from his intense gaze to Chateau-sur-Mer, the gray stone mansion of Father's political friend, Mr. Wetmore.

"Oh? What were you doing when you were sixteen?"

"Attending Cornell."

"Cornell? At such a young age?" His jaw dropped and he halted.

Willow had hidden that fact for so long that the telling of it made her admit, "I could have gone a year earlier, but Mother wished me to have another year of girlhood before I studied to take over the business. At the time, it was difficult to hear because I was so hungry for any morsel of knowledge. But I thank her for her intervention. Sixteen was young enough, and now I cannot imagine how I would have handled classes a year sooner than that." She pulled him along, unwilling to be spotted outside a family friend's mansion and have the matter brought to the attention to anyone still in the parlors of Newport. "I have the rest of my life to work and to learn, but that last year was well spent with the twins."

He whistled through his teeth. "I knew you were smart, Willow, but I had no idea I was in the company of a genius."

"Far from it. I merely had a lot to prove, especially once I saw that Father was never going to have a male heir. It was up to me to carry on the family business. And so I became my father's apprentice." She bit her lip, realizing she had asked about his sister and here she was rambling about herself. "Forgive me for the digression."

"On the contrary, I found it fascinating." He pulled his hat down to keep it from blowing away in the wind and turned down the lane that led to the mansion.

"What does your sister enjoy?"

"She is a little butterfly and would flit about town if she were able, spending all her pin money in one outing and have to come begging for more."

"And does she get it?" she asked before remembering that *of course* he did not have the extra funds to spend.

"I wish I could, for I know young girls can be cruel when one in their circle is not vogue. Unfortunately, there is only so much I can do to shield her from the burden brought on by our father's death." He paused. "I suppose I shouldn't say his death was a burden, but it is the honest truth. I wasn't ready to assume the family business. My father had ill-prepared me for it. I was at Columbia during his passing and had to leave before I completed my degree. Not to make excuses for my business decisions, but that is partially why the shipping business was recently in such a dire position."

She could not imagine having to take over the business after her father's death, much less when he had not prepared her for the role. "How did you pull out of the depression?"

Cullen shrugged. "It was not easy. One of my father's old friends approached me with an offer to mentor me and give me a loan, which is being paid off to this date due to the high interest rate. But at least the business is thriving once more, and my workers no longer fear for their positions."

She nodded. "Thank goodness for friends in this cutthroat world. I wish my father had a few of those friends working in the sugar-refinement industry. Of course, as you know, the only other big sugar company is owned by Heathcliff Wellington."

He coughed, studying the skyline before them. "So I have heard."

Willow laughed, shaking her head. "I'm sorry. I tend to get carried away whenever business is brought up, which is why Flora is my only remaining friend. The others, over time, fell to the wayside with their marriages and babies and total lack of interest when it comes to matters of sugar."

Cullen paused outside the stone wall that surrounded her family's estate. "The ivory tower, though beautiful, can be a lonely place."

"But effective when attempting to get business completed in a timely fashion," she quipped, and rubbed her hand up and down her arm. "Come now, let's send for a pot of chocolate to enjoy in the library with the others."

"Already done!" Fritz called out, trotting up to them through the main gate. "When Flora and Teddy returned without you, I sent for hot chocolate and thought I'd come out to meet you both. And once you warm up, it's time for the games to begin."

"Games?" Willow allowed Fritz to take her arm.

"Archie, Kit, Digory, Chandler, and myself have set up the badminton net in the library, so I hope you are ready for a long afternoon that will end in certain defeat."

Twelve

Mother stormed into Willow's bedroom and tossed the morning's paper onto her lap. "First, you leave Teddy behind in town, and now to find out that you kissed him in *public*? You might as well have announced your engagement! Is this your way of ending the competition? Because it is unwarranted to have it announced so vulgarly in the post." Mother clenched her hands at her sides. "Your father and I have given you room to court and *this* is how you are going to respond? Like a naïve schoolgirl? Kissing one man and walking home with another?" She lifted her focus to the cherub-and-floral mural on the ceiling and exhaled. "Please tell me this is a grievous falsehood."

Willow bit her lip, glancing at the headline: *Sugar Queen Bestows Kiss upon Devotee Favorite*. Willow inwardly cringed, knowing Mother was right. She raised her lashes to the looking glass of her vanity to see Nicolette putting the finishing touches on her hair for yachting with Kit Quincy. *She won't breathe a word of this downstairs*. She called forth her courage and twisted in her seat, grabbing the back of the chair and admitting slowly, "It was only *one* kiss."

Mother expelled her breath and sank onto the settee, reaching for Willow's tea service. "That should have been saved for a private moment, or at least for your *fiancé*." Mother clicked her tongue. "Truly, Willow. Have I taught you nothing?"

Willow ran her finger along the rim of the cup atop her vanity, keeping her focus on the painted gold, knowing Mother was glaring at her in the looking glass's reflection. "Pardon me for saying so, but what did you expect would happen when you and Father wish for me to court so many men at once? And as for word getting out about the kiss, I have warned the men again and again not to breathe a word of this competition to the press, and yet you and Father seemed more than happy about all the publicity that this has brought about for the sake of our standing in society and in turn our business."

Mother pinched the bridge of her nose. "Yes, of course we were happy, but, Willow, did you really have to kiss a beau in town?"

"Perhaps you are correct. Even so, if I do not allow a kiss to happen between myself and someone I am seriously considering when the moment is right, how am I supposed to know if there is a spark?"

Mother laughed sharply. "I never thought I would say this to you of all my daughters, but you have read too many of my romance novels." She set her cup in her saucer, her scowl replaced with a soft smile.

Willow joined her mother at this, the newspaper in one hand, her teacup in the other. "Well, you did give the novels to me."

Mother poured her a second cup, watching the steam curl upward before she spoke. "My dear girl, if the right beau so much as kisses your hand, there won't be any spark. There will be a current pulsating from your hand directly to your heart. So, you do not need to go about kissing fellows left and right to find out. Consider the heartbreak you are giving to these gentlemen by your actions."

"Flora told me the same." Willow twisted her hands, regretting that she had waited until midnight to seek her friend out and apologize. She would have to make it up to Flora upon her return to Newport.

"Wise girl." Mother lifted the paper from Willow's grasp. "In any event, I think it might be time we find the informant. This article is too detailed for it to simply have been wired to New York. This was written here and sent by courier."

"Whoever it was has made this process far more difficult than needed, but we do not control where the men go when they are not on an outing with me. Teddy was in town yesterday, along with Cullen, and I have complete confidence in them."

Mother turned to the maid, who was tidying up now. "Nicolette? Have we hired anyone new? Someone who would not have a sense of loyalty to the family yet?"

Nicolette paused in gathering Willow's nightclothes. "We have hired a new scullery maid, but she is the daughter of the cook and looks up to the family as if you all were royals."

"Well, that's a relief." Willow met Mother's gaze. It would have been particularly hard if one of their own had turned on them. "We'll have to go down and meet her after dinner."

Nicolette grinned. "She would faint for sure." Her smile faded. "But, now that you have brought up the subject of a possible informant, I feel compelled to tell you that the maids have been speaking about the contents of Mr. Digory Pruett's chamber."

Mother snapped to attention. "What have they found?"

Nicolette twisted her hands beneath the pile of fine clothes.

Willow rose, resting a hand on Mother's shoulder. "They will not be punished for gossiping. Please, tell us. I need to know. This is my future and my family's livelihood."

"The maids found a journal, piles of telegrams, and . . ." Nicolette paused as if unwilling to continue.

"And what?" Mother leaned forward.

"They didn't mean to snoop." The maid dipped her head. "They were making the bed when one of them found a portfolio hidden underneath, and, uh, they dropped it and scattered dozens of clipped articles, all about Miss Willow and the competition."

"I see." Mother pursed her lips. "That does seem rather incriminating, for who else but the author would wish to keep them?"

"Well, until we know more, I do not think we should go charging at Mr. Pruett, demanding answers. For if it is not the case . . ." Willow paused as an equally horrible thought occurred to her. What if it *wasn't* him and there was another in their midst who had ill will toward her? *And what if I am already falling in love with him?* She straightened her shoulders and gave her maid a reassuring pat on the arm. "Thank you, Nicolette. You have potentially saved me from heartbreak and future scandal. Please inform the other maids that while I do not generally condone snooping, in this instance I am relieved they did so even if it was by accident. They have no need to fear any repercussions. I am grateful for their loyalty to me and my family. Will you please have one of them fetch the papers for me after they clean Mr. Pruett's chamber? I will think of how to handle it upon my return with Mr. Quincy."

"Certainly, miss." Nicolette curtsied and hurried out to do her bidding.

"Such a breach in etiquette to take from a guest's room, but I fear it cannot be helped." Mother rubbed her forehead. "If only your father were here to handle this."

"He's gone?"

"Yes. He received a telegram from your cousin last night and left early this morning on the first train out with Flora. Your father is calling an emergency meeting with the board to discuss the company's future."

"Without me?" Willow's voice rose. "I should pack. This business with Mr. Pruett will keep until I return. Father's health is too delicate—"

"While I agree with you, your father insisted on going alone and that you stay and focus on your men."

"What has happened?" She gripped Mother's arm and sank down beside her, bracing herself for the worst.

"Osborne has returned to New York. He hasn't been back since . . ." Mother's gaze flicked to the door left ajar.

"Since he turned the board against me after Father's heart attack and nearly convinced all to sell their shares to Wellington," Willow finished quietly. "Nothing good ever comes from Osborne Dupré becoming suddenly interested in the business."

"Which is why your father left, even though you are courting seven gentlemen, to deal with your ungrateful parasite of a cousin." Mother picked at her nail bed as she always did when she was nervous. "After what Osborne did, I am surprised that he is daring to show his face around your father, but I suppose your little exploit in the shop gave him the courage he needed to try to take action once more with the board."

Willow buried her face in her hands and groaned at her stupidity. How could she have given in to such a moment of weakness? The board already hated her because she was a woman, and this—this could seal her fate. "And if the board agrees with him . . ."

Mother rose and began pacing the room. "They won't, not while your father has breath in his lungs. Perhaps he can finally convince them to sell to him and be done with this whole wretched threat of Wellington's."

"It will take more than an offer from Father. They know how much we want those shares and how much Wellington will pay for them. I doubt we could sell enough assets within the week to cover the amount he would offer. Until this next sugar run, the majority of our fortune is tied up in stocks, the factory, the next shipments, and our residences." Willow fidgeted with the lace at her cuff. "I kept enough aside to purchase the new factory in Paris and I would surrender the money in a heartbeat rather than relinquish those shares to Wellington. But, the question remains, is it enough?"

"Osborne's arrival could not be timed more poorly for us. We are always at our weakest in this season, especially after our inexplicably slow year." Mother shook her head, groaning. "I told your father not to invest so heavily and to keep cash on hand. But no. He says it takes money and risk to make money."

"Which is why Osborne is moving in now. He must have heard about Father's latest investment." Willow twisted her hands in her lap. "I can sell my jewels. We could even sell this place if Father is willing, although we would be hard put to sell it at a fair price given the timeline."

"Sell *Aisling Manor*?" Mother's voice cracked. "Never. Your father and I built this place when you were a child. I would rather sell our home in New York before I part with this." Mother rubbed her temples. "We have simply stretched ourselves too thin for a buyout at the moment."

"Which I will do as soon as we rebuild our equity. No matter the cost."

Digory sank into the wing-back chair across from Cullen's place beside the library's fireplace and sighed. Cullen glanced up from his newspaper, giving it a little snap and returning his focus to an article on Wellington, hoping Digory would take the hint and try not to satiate his ever-present need to talk.

"I wish you could have seen how much I outshined poor Kit yesterday over our billiards competition with Willow, and without even trying." He gave a sharp bark of a laugh. "Willow put on an impressive show, though, and I must admit it made me like her even more."

Cullen shifted in his chair and snapped the paper again, then reached for his cup of coffee on the side table.

"So, I might steal a kiss on our next outing. But I'll have

to wait until she gets back from her day of yachting, which I suppose is one of the many downsides of competing against so many for her attention."

At this, Cullen folded his paper and rose, abandoning all hope of reading his paper in peace. "I would prefer you would refrain from such things as *stealing*, Mr. Pruett." He glared at him and joined Fritz, Archie, and Theodore at the card table, when the sounds of giggling turned his attention to the door, where Philomena and Sybil stood, hands to their mouths, focused on Digory.

"Steal a kiss? You think Will likes you?" Sybil bounded to Digory's side of the couch.

His shifted away from her paint-stained fingers, offering them a smile that betrayed his annoyance. "Shouldn't you two be in the nursery?"

"Of course not. We are twelve." Philomena rolled her eyes. "We were passing and heard your ridiculous claim, and because we are nice, we have decided to warn you. Do *not* try kissing our sister. Mother just told her that she shouldn't do that with anyone but her fiancé."

"And we *know* you are not he," interjected Sybil, not in an unkind manner but as if it were only a matter of fact.

Cullen counted out the cards, swallowing back his amusement.

"Don't you have someone else you could bother?" Pruett snapped, getting to his feet and brushing off his sleeve where Sybil had brushed against him, the hurt in her face plain.

"Don't be rude, Pruett. You best remember that you are staying in *their* home." Cullen threw down his cards, the men rising, protesting with him. Cullen strode over to the girls and bowed, extending an arm to each. "Excuse his manners, my ladies. I, for one, am honored you decided to join us. I was hoping for a bit of diversion. Would you like to take me for a drive in your pony cart to town? I need to visit the sweet shop, and I would love your help in selecting the best sweets for my sweetheart and her sisters."

At their eager nodding, he threaded their hands through his arms. "Let's go ask your mother first and then we shall be off."

Permission secured and pony cart summoned, the three headed out the front door. But when Cullen lifted Phil into the cart, he found a scowl in place. "I am sorry Mr. Pruett was so uncouth. Do you want me to punch him for you?" he asked in a playful manner, though secretly he wished to throttle the man for being so cruel to the kindhearted twins.

"Thank you, Mr. Dempsey, but Sybil and I can take it from here." She leaned over to her twin and began whispering away, and Cullen did not envy whatever they had in store for Pruett.

Cullen snapped the reins, enjoying the novelty of riding in a pony cart with the twins. The two reminded him so much of Willow, he felt as if he were receiving a glance into her childhood. They did not even have a chance to become cold before they arrived at the sweet shop. As Cullen tethered the horses, he noticed Agent Flannery leaning against the doorframe of the post office across the street twenty paces away.

"You ladies go inside. I'll be right behind you. Please be certain to find something that Willow will enjoy." The girls scurried inside before the instructions had left Cullen's mouth, and he turned to face Flannery strolling toward him.

"Wellington is getting anxious." Agent Flannery rubbed the pony's nose as if he were having a casual conversation with Cullen. "Do you have anything that might keep him content instead of cutting you and your future loose?"

Cullen shoved his hands into his pockets and cleared his throat. "As a matter of fact, I do, but it might be too precious to share."

The agent scowled, pausing in his patting the horse. "What is it?"

The words stuck in his throat. He could trust Flannery,

couldn't he? "Information on Dupré Sucré's next big move—a factory in Paris."

Flannery's brows rose, and he gave Cullen the first signs of a smile that he had ever witnessed from the agent. "That's good. And you don't want to give this up because . . . ?"

"Because it is Miss Dupré's dream." Cullen glanced over his shoulder toward the shop's window, seeing the twins pointing to candies on the shelves behind the proprietor. "If only I could warn her, tell her what I am about—"

Flannery's scowl returned from beneath his bowler hat. "You cannot risk her dismissing you."

Cullen shrugged. "I don't think she would if I tell her everything."

"And risk everything? Look, it's not just your family and your business on the line. Wellington has hurt thousands and deserves to spend the rest of his days behind bars for his crimes." Flannery crossed his arms. "My sister married one of his factory workers, and within a year of living in Wellington's overpriced slums, she was dead. His tenancies are deathtraps for anyone with weak lungs. Only the hardiest survive past fifty."

Cullen bit the inside of his mouth and nodded. Of course, Flannery had skin in the game. He knew firsthand the manipulation of Wellington. At first, he made you feel understood and valued, and then, once you were indebted to him, his talons would sink deep and never release their hold until you had given him everything he wanted from you in the first place. *What does Wellington have over his factory workers to keep them there?* "My sincerest condolences for your loss and I understand, truly I do. But, if I wait too much longer to tell her, there could be no recovery."

"I don't want your condolences. Write Wellington, keep quiet, and save our people from this madman."

Cullen bowed his head. "Very well." But as he spoke the words, he felt the pull between himself and Willow fray. *Lord, help her forgive me for this. And please, let there be a way I can tell her everything . . . before it is too late.*

Kit guided the yacht to her family's dock with remarkable ease. Judging from his expertise, he probably did not even need the two crewmen to work the lines and sails. She gripped the straw brim of her boating hat to keep it in place in the wind, studying him. Kit had shed his coat and rolled up his sleeves after an hour of working. She admired his tanned, corded arms. If the other men had witnessed Kit's sailing today, she was certain they would no longer tease him for his age. "How old are you, Kit?" she called to where he stood behind the polished wheel.

He threw back his head and laughed. "Am I showing my age?"

"Not at all." She bit her lip for her blunder. "I was merely thinking that the others would be jealous of your skill."

"I was twenty-five the first time we met."

That day was etched in her girlhood heart for all eternity. "Thirty-seven is hardly old, sir."

"For a young lady, yes, it is. Especially when a young lady has half a dozen suitors to choose from to marry." He motioned for a crewman to take over at the helm. Wiping his brow with the back of his forearm, he took a seat on the plaid beside Willow and reached for a bottle of water and uncorked it, pouring a full glass and downing it before continuing. "I know our age difference does not appear to be much now, but if you think ahead, you will realize that one day, you will be married to a man in his seventies and you will be in your fifties. Do you really want to be a nursemaid to your husband when you should be running your business, hosting parties, and chasing grandchildren?"

She took a sip of her own water at the mention of children

"I doubt that would happen." She gestured to him. "You are in better shape than most young men."

He shrugged. "It could happen, though, if I fell ill. And what of having a husband who will in all likelihood perish before you, leaving you a widow for a decade, perhaps longer?"

She grasped his hand to cease his flow of reasons why they should part. She was not ready to release him, not while the memories of young Willow's love still lingered in her heart. "Those things do not matter to me."

He stroked back a stray lock of her hair that had escaped her braided coiffure. "Do not be blinded by my show of strength today. Perhaps it was unfair to demonstrate my skills in sailing in hopes of winning your admiration. No, my dear, you must consider carefully and decide which future you wish to live. A long, happy marriage with, let's say, a childhood best friend? Or a shorter yet still marvelously happy life with an older man?"

As the crewmen dropped anchor, Kit hitched himself up and helped her to standing, then saw her safely out of the yacht before taking her up the cliff walk to her home in silence.

"Thank you for the lovely day, Kit." Willow turned to face him on the rear stone steps of the mansion. "I will carefully consider your words, but you should know that any woman would be honored to be your bride."

He caressed her cheek. "Thank you, Will—"

A bloodcurdling scream wrenched them apart.

"What on earth?" Panicked, she gathered her skirts and bolted inside, following the screaming up the stairs until she reached the third level to find the men gathered in a mass at the door of one of the guest rooms. "Let me pass!" she cried, pushing her way through the group, having no idea what she would find. And there in the middle of the room, in his untucked dress shirt and evening trousers with his suspenders halfway on, stood Digory, his hair a vivid pea green.

"Who did this to me? Who is responsible for this?" he shouted to the onlookers, his face a crimson color. "Who?"

Willow pressed a hand to her mouth, her fear giving way to hysteria, her shoulders shaking from suppressed laughter as the men surrounding her bent over double with their laughing.

"What is going on?" Mother cried, her ivory skirts trailing behind her as the men parted before her. The corner of her lips twitched at the sight. "Well, Mr. Pruett, you had best dress, for there is nothing that can be done about your hair at the moment, and there is no sense in missing a good meal. You have half an hour." Mother clapped her hands to the group and sent them all scurrying back to their rooms, whispering to Willow, "You must tell me everything tonight, but first you need to change."

Dressing quickly in an emerald evening gown with a cream lace trim, Willow cringed at what she had to do. After such a lovely day with Kit, spending half the time thinking there was a traitor in her midst, she had made up her mind. Striding down the hall and taking the main stairs, she flung open the double doors to the parlor, where her suitors stood waiting with the family for dinner. She focused on Digory, whose green hair seemed even more vivid properly combed into a pompadour. The men murmured as she crossed the room, her heeled slippers clicking on the polished marble. "Digory, might I have a word?"

He grinned, bounding to her side with a bow. "You may have a hundred words if it pleases you. Ah, I see you have decided to wear my colors tonight." He gestured to her green gown, earning more laughter from the men.

Usually his jests were just the thing to bring a smile to her face, but this rather nasty business of his secret stash of papers was plaguing her.

He interlocked his fingers and cracked his knuckles. "I have not found the culprit responsible for turning my hair green, but when I do . . . boy, do I have a surprise in store for him."

Silently, she led him to the conservatory. Unlike Digory's hair, *this* greenery helped to clear her mind. She ran her finger over the length of a potted palm leaf, absentmindedly tearing off the tip. "I do not know how to begin, so I simply must push through because this will be rather awkward for the both of us."

Digory's jovial smile faded into a serious line, his eyes brimming with concern as he gripped her hand in his. "You can tell me anything. I can see you have doubts. Give me a chance to help alleviate your fears concerning our relationship."

She freed herself from his hand and his smooth words. "Forgive me for what I am about to ask, but the maids found a stack of papers under your mattress and brought the matter to me. I am quite concerned that I have found the reporter in you." She met his gaze, searching for a flicker of guilt.

He released a short, shaky laugh. "How does one keep his secret yearnings a secret with all the onlookers about the place, my lady? The writings are simply a reminder of my time here and a token that I might share with our children one day as proof of our fairy tale."

I wish I could believe you. "Then may I ask with whom have you been corresponding? The maids said they have seen many a letter posted from your hand and found the stack of letters in your room." Digory reached out to her to brush back a lock of her hair, but she moved out of his reach. "Mr. Pruett, please take this seriously. It may seem like a game to you, but I need to know if your intentions are pure."

Digory's hand stilled. "Don't you believe me when I say they are mere tokens of my affection?"

Affection? Does he truly care for me? We have only had two outings together since arriving in Newport, and one was with Kit in the room! She had only kept him because her parents seemed to like him. And while she had hardly expected anything but interest from the men, now *two* had declared their hearts, laying them at her feet and now Digory was confessing having feelings for her, too? She was not the sort of woman to take a declaration lightly, and this whole competition was turning her stomach with hope, excitement, dread, and above all, fear. Fear that she would hurt someone. Fear that she would hurt herself if someone did not return her interest. Fear that there was a traitor in her midst, waiting until the end to break her heart.

"What do you want from me, Miss Dupré?"

She paused in her pacing when the maid appeared in the doorway, holding a tray with a stack of papers. "Please forgive me, but I sent for the papers to set to rest this allegation. For the last shred of privacy in this horrid affair, I have not looked at the documents. Can you show me? Perhaps I am being overly cautious, but it would put my heart at ease. I cannot continue on with you if I do not trust you." She waved the maid forward and removed the top letter from the pile and handed it to him. "Would you mind reading this to me? Or at least in part?"

He sighed and broke the seal. "I meant to send this out with the morning's post." He cleared his throat and looked into her eyes for a long moment before lowering the page enough for her to read along with him. "'Dearest Mother, these past weeks with Willow have been the happiest I have ever known. And while we haven't spent much time together, I can see qualities in her that I wish for my children. Children, Mother. Can you believe that I am even thinking of having children when I have thought naught of my future before? But that is what comes from knowing Willow. She is kind, beautiful, and smart. I suppose that falling in love with someone would take more time under normal circumstances, but she has been so trusting and vulnerable with us, it is impossible not to follow suit.'"

She pressed her hand to her mouth, lifting a horrified gaze to this man who had poured his heart onto the page.

"Shall I continue?"

"Digory, forgive me," she whispered, tears threatening to close her throat.

He sighed. "Of course, but you must realize this will be difficult for me to forget. I was falling in love with you, Willow, and I fear this may slow the process for me."

"I understand. Thank you. Now, if you'll excuse me, I need to take a moment to gather my thoughts on what to say to the group to explain my appalling behavior." She drew herself up and passed him, slipping through the vacant library. Willow continued walking across the great hall until she ducked into the alcove under the stairs, taking refuge on a chair in front of the small marble wall fountain. *Am I so wretchedly incompetent, Lord, that I would accuse a man who loves me of being false?* She wrapped her arms around her waist, rocking back and forth, realizing that if Digory was not the reporter, then the likelihood of someone else in her following being a traitor was that much greater. *Lord, I cannot take much more of this. I don't know what I am about and feel at a loss in handling the hearts of these good gentlemen. I never wanted to—*

"Miss Dupré?" the butler called, keeping a respectful distance from her, his eyes averted as she swiped at her cheeks with the back of her hand. "Your family and suitors are waiting for you to go through to the dining room."

"Thank you, Beckwith. I'll join them in a moment." Drawing a steadying breath, she gathered herself. She still needed a king. And now she had only seven remaining suitors . . . and one of them was out to break her heart.

Thirteen

Cullen nocked an arrow to the bowstring and aimed at the target on the back lawn of Aisling Manor, facing the cliffs with the waves breaking in the distance. Holding the bow so that the arrow's fletching brushed against his cheek, he drew in a breath and, taking in adjustments for the wind and hoping his shot was true, released the arrow. It hit the target's outer circle, bringing laughter from the remaining suitors of the house. Cullen shrugged it off, laughing with the others. He was just happy to be out of the mansion and enjoying the warmth that had banished all traces of snow. "At least Miss Dupré did not witness it."

"Where is she anyway?" Fritz asked, looking behind them to the mansion. "She was supposed to meet us ten minutes ago."

"Can you believe that Pruett dismissed himself from the competition?" Theodore commented as Fritz took his position as next in line.

Cullen stiffened, thinking of Willow's contrite speech at dinner nearly a week ago that had resulted in Digory brooding about the mansion for the following days until this morning when they had discovered his room empty save a note addressed to Willow.

"I am not surprised, not after what Willow accused him of doing." Fritz adjusted his stance and took aim, sending the arrow dead center. "Of course, had I known who he was writing to, I would have spoken up at once and saved Willow the pain of humiliation."

"I wouldn't be too hard on yourself. Cullen is always scribbling away too, but you *know* he is writing to his mother, as he would never out Willow to the papers." Theodore snorted.

"And how do you know that?" Cullen lifted a single brow. "Willow wishes for us to be vigilant in finding the leak, and if you think me incapable of writing to the papers, isn't that being rather lax?"

"No sense in pretending, chap. We have been in this competition for not even a month and you are already acting like she is the light of your life." Archie clapped him on the shoulder. "I mean, it's one thing for Teddy to act so because he has known her for years, not weeks."

And what if she is the light of my life? Cullen ignored Archie's teasing and focused on Kit's shot, his chest heavy with the news that was certainly the reason behind Willow's delay in joining them. He had seen the telegram arrive before they moved outside for their archery contest, and if it was not from her father, as he suspected it wasn't, he had the sinking feeling it was in regard to the Parisian factory. "If you are so certain that she is not the love of your life, you should withdraw, Archibald."

"I did not say that. I only said that it is far too soon to have you all acting like love-sick puppies," Archie responded, taking his shot and smiling with the result, which was only slightly off the second ring. "Chandler, Kit, and I are the only sensible ones among you, it seems."

Sensible or senseless? Cullen adjusted the leather bracer on his forearm.

"Speak for yourself," Kit chuckled, releasing his arrow. "I

hold Miss Dupré in the highest regard. She is kind, beautiful, and clever, and I would be honored to call her my wife."

"If she would only give me more time, I know I could woo her away from you ancient chaps," Chandler grumbled.

Still scowling from Kit's declaration, Cullen turned his back to the group and faced the house with its open-air sitting room on the second floor, where Mrs. Dupré and her twin daughters sat watching them from beneath the arches, when out of the back door came Willow, her canary skirts billowing behind her in the breeze as she descended the stone steps, her shoulders looking tense even from this distance. He set his bow on the table the servants had set up for their use, and with his hands in his pockets he left his jacket behind, crossing the lawn to meet her halfway. "Willow?"

She looked up at him, her eyes red. "I lost the Paris factory."

He reached out and took her hand in his own. "I am so sorry."

"And the worst part is that I lost it to *Wellington*." She spat out his name. "I do not know how he even thought of the building, unless Father mentioned it to the board and Mr. Crain told Wellington to spite me. It really is the only way he could have found out, because I know you wouldn't tell anyone." Her bottom lip trembled as a tear escaped.

He pulled out a handkerchief from his vest pocket and handed it to her, hating himself for causing her such distress. How could he ever recover if she found out? He shouldn't be here. He had done what Flannery had asked . . . and Wellington. He had found a way to hurt the Dupré empire in return for his freedom and his family's future. Perhaps Wellington would be satisfied at last. Perhaps he *could* stay and be with Willow without Wellington's further demands driving them apart. Did it really matter that Wellington had procured Cullen an invitation through a debt owed by the Duprés' solicitor? Would that offence truly be enough to keep him from her side in the end once he had taken down Wellington?

He felt his heart seize at the sight of her tears. His lies had wrapped themselves over and around his soul, and they were slowly exorcizing the life from his veins. *Lord, please, get me out of this pit.* "What can I do?"

She blew her nose into the handkerchief and balled it in her fist. "Short of finding me another factory? Help me take my mind off work and do not tell the others about the factory. I would rather they not know of my failed business venture just yet if I can help it."

He pulled her closer and wrapped his arm about her waist, walking with her to the table. "Fellows, our dear Miss Dupré is in need of some cheering up, so what say you?"

The men cheered, clamoring about her and performing such ridiculous antics to draw a smile from her that Willow could not help but have her spirits lifted by their efforts. At Cullen's fourth shot in a row that sailed to the left of the target, Willow joined the men in their playful jeering.

"Allow me to show you how it is done." She strapped on a bracer over her sleeve, taking the bow and positioning her body. She drew the bowstring along with her breath and released them simultaneously. And her arrow buried itself in the ground to the left of Cullen's, the men all shouting their comforts, blaming it on the wind, the sun, anything other than her skill, while Cullen kept silent, grinning.

"Well, I know now who not to ask to have my back when in a medieval battle," Cullen laughed. "Do you have any other talents you would like to boast of, Willow?"

Willow grabbed for a second arrow, pointing it at the sky. "Fritz and Chandler are right. There was a wind. And you all were distracting me."

"Miss Dupré?" A maid called from the steps as she hastened down to the lawn and toward them. "Miss Dupré," she panted, pressing a hand to her plump waistline. "I have come to fetch you. Your father is home."

Willow fumbled with her bow. "Is he unwell?"

The maid shook her head. "He is as well as can be expected, but he seems quite out of sorts. He wishes to see you right away."

The men shifted, their concerned gazes burning into her. "I'll be in at once." She turned to the men, but they waved her on. "Thank you." She dropped the bow and arrow into Cullen's arms, gathered her skirts, and ran to the house, praying that Father was well and wondering if he knew about Paris already. She almost hoped he did know. She had been disappointed enough in herself without having to admit her failure to her father, the one man who trusted her opinion as much as any man's. She did not slow until she spied the twins scurrying out of the parlor, pouts in place.

"I don't see why we can't talk with him, too." Sybil crossed her arms, frowning at Willow.

"Father sent you both away?" Willow panted, smoothing down her hair.

"He sent us to change for dinner." Philomena gave her twin a pointed look. "And you know better than to complain when he has been so ill and just returned from traveling. He is never in his best mood then." She shook her head. "I would not wish to be in your shoes, Will."

Willow bit her lip. "It's as bad as all that?"

"Worse," they replied in unison, taking the stairs.

Willow let herself into the parlor and closed the door, turning to find Father sinking into his armchair beside the fireplace and kicking off his shoes. Lifting his stockinged feet to the fire, he closed his eyes, enjoying the warmth as Mother moved to stand behind him, rubbing his shoulders and bringing a soft smile to his lined face, before he sat up and drew Mother around the chair to face him.

"Father? You wanted to see me?"

He waved her forward, his weary spirit evident in the dark circles under his eyes. "Yes. I will not beat around the bush, my darlings. The news I have is not good."

Mother knelt before him, concern etched into her expression. "Your health?"

"It held, thank the Lord. The trip home was harder than expected, but I am speaking of the meetings I have had." He looked to Willow. "The board says that waiting until June to choose your groom will not suffice, because with a recent surge in orders, that will be a pivotal month this year for our business. If we do not wish for Osborne to take over the company, you need to marry by April first, which will give the new ruler time to adjust before the major shipments go out."

Willow's jaw dropped, her news about the Parisian factory fading into the horror of the board's latest demand. "B-but that means I only have three months until I am *married*?"

Mother moaned, placing her head in her hand as she rested back on her heels. "And only three months for me to plan a wedding without even knowing the personal tastes of the groom."

Father nodded, his mouth in a grim line. "With that in mind, I think Willow's crowning ceremony should happen on, not after, Valentine's Day. Until then, meet with the gentlemen you are uncertain about and make up your mind, and plan to keep only three."

"Three?" She sank down on the rug beside her mother, breathless. "Will the board never be satisfied? I wish to heaven Grandfather had never sold those shares."

"As do I, but this is what we have to deal with, and no amount of wishing can change it." He leaned forward, elbows propped on his thighs. "Will, if you desire to rule, you need to take this request seriously. Are you still willing to continue?"

Could she endure *another* abrupt change in her life? "They are being unreasonable."

He pushed himself to standing, the ladies rising with him, and Mother handed him the cane. "I know. Take some time thinking on it tonight. If you decide by morning to continue, I no longer want you to spend half your time locked in your room, sending missives to the company and answering work letters."

"But your health," Willow protested.

He held up a hand. "It's only until April. You have a partner to find, and your mother has a wedding to plan. Now go find a young man you are uncertain about and take him for a hike on the cliff walk."

"Even though it is warm out, the winds down there will be positively frigid." Willow crossed her arms, still in shock over the news.

"Then the unpleasantness will bring out both your true natures all the more quickly for the other to discover."

Willow paused, knowing it was dangerous pressing her father when he was weary from travel. "There is one more thing . . . the matter of the reporter." Willow filled him in on her findings and of her accusation of Digory.

"Such an invasion of privacy cannot occur again. I will not have you or the staff searching the men's things." He scowled, picking up the poker and stoking the fire. "And why the sudden need to find the reporter? He has been writing about you for weeks, and you know your mother's and my stance on the issue. It is not necessary to distract yourself with this trivial matter. We have dealt with reporters for decades and will continue to do so."

"Because I lost the Paris property. I have no other choice but to invade their privacy to cease this attack on our business." *And my love life.*

He slowly set aside the iron and leaned against the mantel, his shoulders hunching at this bit of news. "For that I am sorry. But if you cannot trust them, how can you expect to marry one of them? Ignore the papers and focus on what is important." With that, he sent her on her way.

Instead of seeking out a gentleman, she fled to her room, desperate to be alone with her thoughts. She fought the urge to slam the door, knowing if she did, it would bring unwanted attention, and right now she needed to pray. She twisted her hands and paced the length of her room, wrestling with her future and raging against the board's contemptible demands and quaking at the thought of what could happen if she chose the wrong man.

"It's too much, Lord. I can't." At last, she sank to her knees beside her bed, tears streaming. "I have tried to adapt, to honor my father and surrender my idea of the perfect future, but I don't know my next step and I'm terrified, Lord. What if this new future for me is not as good as the one I have planned for, hoped for since girlhood? Is this it? Am I to be stuck in this mire of pleasing people for the rest of my life, even if it means giving up my own dreams? What if I say I'll continue and—?"

Footsteps sounded overhead from one of the guest rooms, breaking her prayer. She pulled herself onto her comforter and crossed her legs, reaching for her Bible atop the nightstand, seeking the comfort of the psalm she had glanced over the night before, half asleep for her nightly reading. Now she returned to the fortieth psalm and read it again, pausing at the third verse.

"'And he hath put a new song in my mouth, even praise unto our God: many shall see it, and fear, and shall trust in the LORD.'" She lifted her gaze heavenward and breathed, "A new song." That is what she desired. Her old dreams would never come to pass . . . but perhaps God had something better in store, something that would turn her sorrow into praise. She removed a card from her desk and copied down the third verse, holding it to her heart. "Lord, my dreams have been dashed, and with them my carefully laid-out plans for my future. I beg you to give me a new song, a new dream for my heart to hold on to, a promise of a better future. If this competition is more than about finding a partner, show me what I should do, Lord. Show me whom to choose."

Fourteen

Theodore crumpled the morning's post and tossed it into the dining room's fireplace, watching the headline *Sugar Queen Misses the Mark* curl in on itself, followed by the scathing exposé on Willow's ineptitude with a bow *and* with securing a Parisian factory, along with some letters printed from the public regarding whom Willow should choose. Alone, he stoked the fire, stabbing it until the paper disintegrated into ash. It was time to end this invasion of Willow's goodwill and privacy. Fritz was too besotted to do anything so vile, so Cullen's clandestine trips to the post were the obvious place to start. He could not discount Archie and Chandler, even though he had never seen the fellows act as anything other than the ideal gentlemen while at the mansion. And then there was Kit, but the action seemed out of character for the man, and besides, what need did he have of the extra income from the articles? And since Cullen was the poorest of the lot, Theodore's investigation would start with him.

At the sound of the men coming down the stairs for breakfast, Theodore set aside the poker, rose, and edged around them, giving each a nod in greeting, and retreated into the great hall where he heard the gentle strains of a harp. He smiled to himself. He had not heard her play Chopin since their summers in Newport when she had been forced to study an instrument as part of her training as an heiress. Slipping inside the music room, he found Willow in a simple gown the color of a robin's egg, the morning light upon her hair, her fingers dancing across the strings. As if sensing him, she opened her eyes to find him at the door.

"Teddy." Willow's smile did not reach her eyes as she set down her harp.

"That was lovely. You didn't need to stop," Theodore admonished, folding his hands behind his back. "Is something amiss?"

She shrugged. "Only that I have just finished reading a most horrifying article. Did you see it?"

He sucked in a breath through his teeth. "I'm afraid everyone will have by noon. We need to stop this reporter. He is going to destroy your chances of the board taking you seriously."

"He already has." Willow rose, tugging her waistband straight. "And besides that, I want to know if this mystery author was the informer behind Wellington finding out about Paris. I spoke with Father and he did not disclose the deal with the board after all. The only way Wellington could have found out is if someone here went through my things and discovered the telegram and my plans."

"You were pretty animated the day you received that telegram, if I recall correctly. Though you did not show me, did you share it with anyone?"

She bit her lip and looked away. "The only suitor I told was Cullen."

He snorted. "And you did not immediately suspect him? That's rather uncharacteristically naïve of you, Will."

"I didn't actually show him the telegram or share the address—only the general idea." She scowled, crossing her arms. "Be that as it may, I cannot think Cullen would betray my confidence, not after all he has divulged to me and all that we have shared together."

Shared together? What, like a trip to the doctor's office? Painting? He swallowed back his retort and pulled at his neckcloth that seemed to have tightened. "If you say so, but let's not speak of your time with Dempsey, shall we?"

She folded her hands in front of her skirt. "I'm sorry. It is growing more and more difficult not to speak of you to one another. It feels as though I am doing something erroneous by courting one while the other is professing love."

Theodore halted at the thought that she might have a deeper connection with someone else, but remembering their kiss, it was hard to imagine. "Professing *love*? Who has told you that he loves you?"

Willow rested a hand on his arm. "As you said, it is best that we do not discuss the others now that the group has narrowed so much."

He fought the urge to shake her off and demand to know who else had fallen in love with her. He cleared his throat. "Fine, but we need to find the culprit, who very well might be one of the gentlemen. Shall we take a note from the maids' book and search the rooms together?"

"I'm afraid that will not be possible." Willow rubbed her forehead. "Father was very clear that I cannot have the maids search through the gentlemen's rooms."

"But you can allow them to take advantage of your generosity and destroy your livelihood?"

"It could just as well be someone from the outside who is the informant," she snapped.

He lifted his hands in surrender. "I'm on your side, remember? I *know* you really don't believe that it's someone on the outside like your parents keep reassuring you."

Willow grunted. "I just thought your attack on Mr. Dempsey was rather pointed."

"I am only looking out for your best interests." He held out his elbow to her, intending on taking a turn outside the grounds before breakfast. "I want to help you."

"If we do this, we cannot tell anyone else," she whispered as he held open the side glass door and they slipped out onto the terrace. "Mother and Father do not want me to catch the reporter."

He jerked his head back. "That is nonsensical. How could they possibly still want him around? Even after all that he has done, destroying your reputation with the board?"

Willow pursed her lips. "They say it is improving our business to have so much news, and with an impending wedding, the public will forget all the scandal printed before and love me and my new ruler forever, giving me the most support an heiress has ever received and making me one of the most powerful magnates in New York City, which will then force the board members to treat me with respect."

Theodore chewed the inside of his mouth, nodding. "That is actually a brilliant outlook. Regardless, I'm here for you, and if you want this lack of privacy to end, it will end."

"I do."

"Very well. Shall *I* search the rooms for clues while the men are at breakfast, as you are forbidden to do so?"

"I think after Digory's secret stash of love letters was discovered, the culprit will have hidden any evidence far better than a half hour's search will unveil." She wrapped her hands about his arm and pulled him down the steps into the gardens. "I have a better idea, and *you* are just the one who can help me."

Willow shifted from foot to foot outside the front door, waiting for the post to arrive as she had done every day for the past two weeks after she had entrusted false secret stories with each of her suitors, waiting for one of them to appear in the papers.

She loosened her grip on her silk shawl, as the morning was proving to be the warmest since their arrival. She stared at the watercolor sky and watched the clouds part and dawn peek above the barren trees, a sea gull screeching in the distance. Part of her longed to read the headline of the morning paper and discover the traitor behind the false news and have done with it, while another part ached at the thought of finding one of her suitors in a lie. At the sight of a rider coming up the drive, Willow rolled from her heels to her toes and back, huffing at the overwhelming anxiety building in her chest that was slowly tightening and climbing up to her throat.

The rider no longer gaped at the sight of her outside. Instead, he reached for his cap and lifted it to her in greeting. "Good morning, Miss Dupré."

She nodded, her attention on his satchel as he retrieved the post and handed it to her before turning and urging his mount into a trot. Her fingers trembled, and she dropped the mail in her haste to open the paper and read the headline. "Well, that takes care of that." She finally had her man. Willow folded the paper and ducked back inside, pulling off her wraps before heading to the library.

The scullery maid started from her place before the fire and moved to rise, but Willow motioned for her to stay, smiling her thanks as she tossed her things atop one of the couches and sank into an oversized chair for her entertaining read that would divulge all sorts of delightfully fabricated tidbits, including a false business plan that would hopefully send Wellington down a rabbit trail. But the article did not humor her in the least, and she found herself watching the maid, kneeling on a sheet before the fireplace and brushing the soot into her pan before dumping the contents into a tin pail.

Willow ran her hand over her face, the truth stinging. How could she not have known it was Archie before? The articles had been heavily focused on the others, yet whenever he was mentioned, it was quite favorable . . . well, besides one article where he must have attempted to throw her off the trail by disparaging himself for his dandy habits. *Clever fellow*. But she couldn't keep her happiness at bay, for she was so relieved that it was not Cullen or sweet Fritz who had betrayed her. Though she had never really suspected Kit, she was relieved all the same to be certain she knew the culprit's identity. He had most likely hoped she had blamed the only person openly connected with the papers, but Chandler Starling was a man of honor . . . unlike Archie. Now she could use *him* to reclaim her foothold by continuing to feed him false stories that Wellington would no doubt read and attempt to use for his own gain. The thought bolstered her, despite the horrid feeling of being found a fool, especially as she thought of her parting with dear Digory Pruett, whose only fault had been that he loved her—well, the idea of her. And if she did not think of her cringeworthy accusations toward him, it was comforting to at last be in control again.

The maid rose with a pail in each hand, one filled with soot, the other bearing remnants of the wood she had used to build the now-crackling fire. She curtsied to Willow before disappearing to tend another fire, while the men's voices echoed in the hall, announcing their arrival for breakfast. She rubbed a hand over her face before giving her cheeks a little slap to awaken her senses. *Let the acting commence.* She tossed the paper into the fire and set the few letters addressed to her father on the silver mail tray on the foyer table and hurried to the dining room, where the men had already formed a line, piling food on their plates from the buffet table, but Archie was not among them.

Kit turned with a full plate, and his genuine smile warmed her heart. "Willow! What a pleasure to have you join us for our breakfast. No tray for you with the twins this morning?"

Willow lifted her hands. "As you know, my duties have been placed on hiatus until the competition is over, so Mother thought it best that I join you all every morning from now on." *Given I have two less months to choose a husband.*

"Huzzah!" Fritz bowed to her and presented her with a lovely rosebud.

"Enchantment," Willow interpreted, smiling up at him. "How did you know I'd be—?"

"The scullery maid told me you were joining us. The staff are all aware that I must select a flower from my dried collection or your mother's conservatory before seeing you each day, so they informed me of your possibly joining us. Most thoughtful of them."

"Indeed." She affixed the bud to the buttonhole at her throat. At least she knew for certain where Fritz stood, and it brought her comfort.

Cullen cleared his throat from behind them, holding two cups of steaming coffee. "Pardon me, Fritz, but you seem to always forget that there are others here wishing to greet their lady."

Willow's heart fluttered in that strange way it was in the habit of doing now whenever Cullen was in the room.

Fritz bowed to her. "I shall leave your side only long enough to stuff my face with the delightful fare the kitchen has prepared before returning to your side, my lady. So you best make haste, Cullen, with what you want to say before I return to claim her."

"Cup of coffee for you, Willow?" He offered her one of the cups. "I've added the necessary cream and sugar to make it palatable for you."

She laughed, accepting it with a nod. His emerald eyes never left hers as he lifted her free hand to his mouth, the pressure of his full lips sending tremors through her. Then she remembered her mother's words. Yet with so little time remaining in the competition, she needed to be certain before bestowing her affections on anyone. This was not one of her secret romance novels where a couple could be together in the end just because of a feeling, or the fact that the hero was swoon worthy. She needed a partner in life. Beauty could fade, but a heart truly devoted to the Lord would not. *God, give me discernment.*

At the sight of Teddy, Chandler, and Archie in the doorway, Willow froze. She studied Archie's confident posture. When there had been so many others, he had blended in quite well, but now his disguise was crumbling, despite his show of lightheartedness. She lifted her coffee cup and flicked her finger against the china in rapid succession, turning the men's attention to herself. "As this has been such an unseasonably warm few days, who wishes to go on a trip to Bailey's Beach with me today?"

Fifteen

Cullen gripped the sides of his bench seat in the cozy cab as it jostled and pulled onto Bailey's Beach, the men hooting and hollering their excitement over an outing to the seaside on the warmest day since their arrival. In the back of the cab sat the men's valets, with Willow's maid in the corner of the wagon clutching the handle of Willow's carpetbag, which most certainly contained her bathing costume should she desire to wade into the water or sunbathe. Cullen, having no valet, carried his own satchel, which held a bathing suit he had never worn before, having no opportunity to slip away for a week by the sea due to the demands of his usual day-to-day life.

The open carriage rolled to a stop in front of a line of small wooden cabanas, where everyone piled out, Willow laughing at one of Chandler's jokes again. He peered down the beach and found only a few other residents here and there on the shore, along with a handful of bathing machines at the ready should any of the more modest bathers wish to use them to access the water. The beach curved into a jetty of boulders on either side, forming a barrier to block much of the wind, which Cullen guessed aided in the exclusivity of the beach, the proprietor keeping away anyone who did not pay for membership or own one of the cabanas. While it was not exactly a very pretty beach with its brown water, foul-smelling seaweed dotting the sand, and shards of broken seashells underfoot, he was secretly thrilled at the novelty of spending the day at the beach with Willow . . . even if he did have to share her with four others.

Willow clutched her straw hat with its navy band that matched her navy-and-ecru-striped gown. "Gentlemen," she called, "please use the blue cabana. I will be using the red."

His brows rose at the extravagance of one family having two cabanas at the far end of the beach, but he supposed nothing should surprise him in a land where cottages were the size of small palaces.

As if she sensed his thoughts, Willow added, "In a family of mostly girls, my father had the second built after he had to wait on four women to dress, along with any feminine guests, before he went for his morning swim."

Willow disappeared inside the red cabana, followed by her maid who carried the massive bag. Seeing as he had no valet, Cullen motioned the other men to the front of the queue, thinking they would dress in half the time. He was about to ask Kit about the sailing outing when he caught sight of a man standing atop an outcropping of rocks, staring directly at him before he tipped his bowler hat and revealed a balding spot.

Recognizing the man, Cullen's heart thudded in his chest. *Wellington's lackey.* "Excuse me, Kit. I believe I see a reporter watching us that I need to dissuade from staying."

"Really? Well, I won't hold your place in line." Kit winked and waved him on, then struck up a conversation with Fritz and Chandler while they waited for Theodore to finish up inside.

Cullen strolled down the beach toward Terrance, the sand finding its way into the sides of his shoes as he climbed up the rocks. He looked over his shoulder and found that Fritz had already entered the cabana, while Teddy and Archie were shouting, running for the water in their striped, cotton suits with their high necklines, shirtsleeves, and knee-length pants. Even at a distance, he could clearly hear their shouts as the frigid water first touched them, yet they were too absorbed in the fun of the day to notice his absence. The man extended his hand to Cullen. Cullen kept his hands in his pockets, refusing to shake the minion's hand. "What do you want, Terrance?"

"Wellington hasn't heard from you in a while. He wants to know what is keeping you so busy?" He grinned, revealing yellowed teeth, the third tooth on the right missing, a new development since the last time Cullen had seen him. "But I can see now for myself that it's the pretty young lady. Think I might stick around to see how comely them ankles are in her bathing slippers."

"What did you say?" Cullen's fists curled as he took a step toward the man, moving to close the gap.

The man lifted his hands and hopped off the rock onto the other, grassy side, completely keeping them from view of the bathers. "Look, I don't want no trouble. I only came to warn you. While he liked that whole Paris tip, he wants more. Send Wellington something by the end of the week or he's going to be forced into taking action."

"Like what?"

The man dug into his pocket and withdrew a note. "Or he will be sending this to the papers."

Cullen unfolded the note, his stomach leaping to his throat. *If this gets out, it will ruin all the work Agent Flannery and I have done and my betraying Willow's dream will be for naught.* He crumpled the paper and shoved it into his pants pocket. "Tell him to back off. I will have something for him soon." Without another word, he clambered over the rocks and jogged back to the cabana to change.

Archie shouted to him from the water, waving his arm over his head and trotting out with the aid of a wave, spitting away the seawater dotting his lips. "Who was that?"

Cullen stiffened before catching himself and rolling back his shoulders. "Reporter. Ran him off."

"Really? I did not recognize him." Archie ran his hands over his hair, wringing out the water and sending it trickling down his neck, his arms turning to gooseflesh in the cool breeze.

Cullen angled his head. "Why would you?"

He shrugged. "I have spotted many over the time we have spent with Miss Dupré. Thanks for watching out for her."

"If we don't, who will? I'll be out in a minute," Cullen said, gesturing toward the cabana.

Archie nodded, then charged back into the water, ramming Chandler in the back and crashing down with him, both yelling as they hit the water.

"I cannot wait to try on my new suit!" Willow clapped her hands. "Mother thought that yellow, though unusual for a bathing costume, quite complements my coloring."

Her maid grimaced. "About that . . ."

"What? Did something happen to it?"

Nicolette slowly set the bag atop the wooden table in the cabana that served as the Dupré women's changing area, which included a small water closet. "Your father didn't want me to say anything until we were in the cabana."

Willow's heart dropped. She waved her hand over her chemise, the stale air of the cabana strangling her along with this horrifying turn of events. "What did he do to my suit?"

"It is fine." She lifted her hand to stay Willow's rising voice. "But, when he heard about the outing, he wanted to see what you would be wearing."

Willow buried her face in her hands, the memory of her thirteenth birthday beach-day disaster flooding her thoughts. *No. Please not again.* "Please tell me he didn't tamper with it. It is a perfectly acceptable knee-length overskirt."

The maid lifted out the bathing costume, not the darling form-fitting gown of canary yellow with its sweet white trim and graceful flounce at the knee and the matching bloomers, but instead unfurled a shapeless black suit with no braiding in sight, its mutton sleeves falling limp in Nicolette's grip.

Willow gasped. "*No.* Where on earth did he dig up this monstrosity?"

Nicolette gritted her teeth. "He had me search your great-aunt Muriel's trunks in the attic." She spread the suit on the table, the waistline so vast it would swallow Willow whole.

Father expects me to wear this in front of a potential husband? "No. No." She crossed her arms and turned her back on the offending wool suit and faced her maid. "Please tell me you brought along the pretty yellow one *Mother* chose for me?"

"Your father insisted that since he could not be present for such an intimate setting as a beach day, that the yellow was too bold a choice for an unmarried, unaccompanied female."

"But you are here supervising."

"I am only doing as I was told, miss."

Groaning, Willow peeled off her silk stockings and stepped into the suit, squelching her protests. The hem reached to her shins, and as there was no waistline to speak of, she pulled the sash from her gown and wrapped it about her waist, cinching it. Nicolette then helped her into the matching black stockings and fastened her bloomers before she set about securing Willow's pretty yellow beach slippers that her father had not been able to confiscate, lacing them up to Willow's knees.

Willow turned in the narrow looking glass affixed to the water closet door. "Well, with the slippers and sash, I think I might look decent after all."

Nicolette cringed. "There is one more item your father *insisted* upon you wearing."

"Oh no." Her heart nearly stopped as she remembered Auntie Muriel's full ensemble.

"Oh yes." Nicolette reached into the satchel and retrieved a giant matching woolen mobcap and handed it to Willow. "Apparently, he would not listen to reason, not even from your mother."

Grimacing against the criminal piece, she shuddered as she stuffed her hair inside it. "I look hideous."

"I would not go quite that far, miss."

"That is a comfort." She snorted and reached for her beach cape, pausing when she did not see it among her things. "You did manage to talk him into my wearing my own cape, right?"

Nicolette withdrew the yellow cape with a flourish and secured it over Willow's shoulders. "If the sun is not too bad, perhaps you can get away with wearing it all day and hiding a suit that should be burned."

Willow gripped the cape front closed, mortified at the thought of Cullen seeing her in her great-auntie Muriel's suit. *Just make it through the day at the beach without showing your bathing costume. Easy.* For as much as she hated the ensemble, she would not ruin such a splendid day for the men. She strode out of the cabana and blinked in the sun, holding her cape tight as the wind whipped over the sand.

"There you are," Cullen called from his seat on the men's cabana steps. He took a look at her mobcap and grinned. "Afraid of the sun burning our hair, our we?"

"Trust me, my cap is only the tip of the monstrosity beneath this cape."

"Well, you cannot wear a cape in the water. You *are* going to join the others swimming, aren't you? Because I can tell you right now, no one will want to swim without you."

And there goes my plan to sit on the sand all day. "Do you think I would ruin everyone's fun over my vanity?" She answered with all the false bravado she could muster and gestured for him to follow her, heading to the farthest corner of the beach, where she pulled the ribbon securing her cloak and let it drop in his hands. He gave a low whistle, and she whipped around. "Mr. Dempsey!"

But as he was shaking with laughter, she adjusted the skirt over her bloomers and ran for the water, thinking it was the only way to hide the costume from the others. Lifting her arms above her head, she dove into the frigid water, giving a squeal of vivacity, lifting her head above the water's surface to find Cullen stroking clumsily toward her, his powerful arms accentuated by his now-wet suit. Her cap, soaked through, pulled her neck back from the weight, so she jerked it off and let it slip beneath the murky waters where it belonged. The others, having spotted them, struck out in their direction, shouting their greetings.

The group was enjoying the day, swimming and sunbathing, when the wagonette from the mansion arrived bearing picnic baskets. Teddy, Cullen, Chandler, Fritz, and Kit, hungry as they were, trotted out to meet the wagonette and carry the supplies to the beach, cutting the waiting time down before they could eat Cook's delightful creations. Lying back on her elbow atop the plaid, Willow shielded her eyes and looked to where Archie was climbing the rocks. She studied the waters and guessed they were nearing about half tide. She watched Archie as he moved farther down the rocks, his focus fixed on their bridge-like formation. "Archie!" she called. "Not too far. It is half tide."

He lifted his hand to his ear and shrugged as if he could not hear her. Willow could see the swelling of the ocean as he neared a narrow outcrop of rock, but as he had never been to Bailey's Beach before, he wasn't aware of the danger. "Archie, that's spouting rock! Take care." Yet he still did not hear her. She sprang to her feet and started toward him, watching as the water moved and swelled, growing ever nearer to the rocks. "Archie!" To her horror, he stepped atop the bridge of rock, balancing on one foot as if he were on a high wire. "Archie?"

She broke into a run, scrambling over the rocks and leaping to a dry patch at a pace she had not tried since girlhood, slipping on a slick spot. She sucked in her breath at the rock slicing her hand, but she did not stop. If he stood there when the spout of water exploded . . . "Archie!" she screamed as the water swelled again. She snagged his arm and jerked him back off the ledge, and he fell on top of her, knocking the breath from her lungs.

"What on earth did you do that for, Willow?"

But as she shifted beneath him, the water shot through the bridge, spouting fifty feet of raw power into the air, sliding them across the rocks before the water crashed back down, filling her lungs with seawater.

Archie gasped and dragged her from the spout for fear that it would explode again. Willow rolled onto her side and retched the contents of her breakfast on the rock.

"You saved my life," Archie panted, helping her to a sitting position. "Why didn't you just shout?"

Willow's hand throbbed to life now. She cradled the injured hand and suppressed a groan. "I tried, but you didn't hear me."

"And you hurt yourself to get to me," he added, his voice exuding misery.

And for the first time since she had discovered his clandestine mission, Willow sensed true remorse in his features. "Of course. I couldn't stand by and watch you get hurt when I could save you."

"Of course, she says." He stroked a wet strand of hair from her cheek. "Miss Dupré, you are not at all what I expected." He swallowed. "I—"

"Willow?" Fritz called from behind them, with Teddy, Cullen, Kit, and Chandler close behind him. "We saw you toss your accounts. What happened?"

She pressed her hem to her cut to staunch the flow of blood.

"Of course, that is all that the men see. Me throwing up my breakfast for the gulls."

"Then I shall become your troubadour, singing of your bravery, and soon no one will remember the part of your throwing up." She laughed as Archie helped her to her feet. "Let's get that hand taken care of and see you home, little lady."

Sixteen

Willow tucked Kit's heart-shaped valentine into the corner of her vanity's looking glass with the other five notes, smiling at the arch of hearts and sweet sentiments as Nicolette fitted Willow's delicate gold tiara encrusted with rubies into her elaborate coiffure. Tonight would be her last crowning ceremony before choosing a husband. And tonight she would turn Archie from her house. Even though he had been exceptionally kind to her since the rescue, and his articles reflected his change of heart while still betraying every bit of confidence she gave him, she knew that he would still turn on her if it meant getting ahead in his career.

"You look like a princess, miss." Nicolette held out the hand mirror to Willow.

She studied the coiffure. "Only because of your uncanny ability to take someone plain and make them appear special." She rose and moved to the floor-length looking glass, examining the crimson creation from Worth that she had been keen to wear since its arrival. She adjusted the folds in her bustle here and there, for once in the competition feeling almost completely happy.

After discovering Archie was the reporter, the last few weeks were blissfully sequestered for Willow as she spent her days courting her gentlemen and feeding Archie stories that had already

193

caused Wellington to make a few poor investments and increased the Dupré holdings, which she prayed in turn would result in the board's approval of her at last. The time away from the business had given her the peace she needed to focus on her future and what she would like to see in a spouse. With that thought, however, she knew her final decision was only six weeks away. How was she going to say good-bye to all but one gentleman come April? She thought of Kit's ever-present smile and willingness to please her, Fritz's sweet offering of flowers that he presented daily to her, of Teddy's kind heart, and of Cullen's smoldering gaze, along with the quiet moments of confidence they shared each day.

Mother burst into the room, shattering her thoughts. "Your maid forgot to take this." She lifted a diamond necklace that would drape her neck in a graceful waterfall of strands.

"Your wedding necklace?" she gasped as Mother fastened it about her neck, the splendor fairly blinding her. "It's a simple party."

"A party is never simple for you." Mother smoothed the diamonds. "I want the families—I mean, gentlemen—to remember everything that marriage to you means. This will serve that purpose."

She wished for the men to forget her status. The weeks spent in the competition had removed the carefully constructed layers over her heart until at last she discovered an old dream of her girlhood, for a man to love her for *her* and not for her wealth. Despite her feelings, she loved the way she appeared in the diamonds. Strong. They were her armor. Willow turned and embraced her mother. "Thank you. I shall take special care of them. I know how much this means to you."

Mother put her at arm's length, her tone overflowing with anticipation. "Let's go down now and narrow your gentlemen to the final *three*."

Willow nodded, even as her insides twisted over the third slot to bestow. She had hoped by now that the answer would have been clear, less painful. "I am anxious to find out what this evening has in store for us. All the men have been so secretive that I can hardly guess what is occurring. Nicolette did not even allow me to open my curtains today for fear I would catch a glimpse of the surprises being delivered to the house. If it had not been for Philomena and Sybil keeping me company today, since I'm not allowed to work, I would have gone mad with trying to work it out."

"Just know that what we have planned will help you with your choice tonight."

Mother slipped her arm around Willow, and they strode out, crossed toward the stairs, passing the balcony overlooking the great hall. Willow gasped at the sight. Thousands of scarlet roses filled the hall. The chandelier was decorated with garlands of the red blossoms, as was the mantel. The two tables at the far wall opposite the staircase were covered in gold silk, scattered with red rose petals, and decorated with matching paper cupids and hearts. Voices, both male and female, drifted up to her, yet she couldn't see anyone from her vantage point.

"Miss Dupré, may I have the honor of escorting you?" She turned to find Cullen dressed in coattails, his black silk lapels stark against his crisp white shirt and bow tie, his hair combed into a perfect pompadour in the front while still covering his ears at the sides. He bowed to her, his grin broadening, catching her admiring him.

"Ah, I see you won the draw. Fortunate fellow, Mr. Dempsey." Mother patted his arm. "Please excuse me while I see to our guests. Take care of my girl and come down at the signal."

"Guests?" Willow queried, but Mother had already disappeared. She turned to Cullen. "Can you tell me now what to expect? And what signal?"

He leaned one fist on his hip, the other resting on the marble column behind Willow's head, encasing her. "I cannot say. It will ruin the surprise."

She pulled her gaze from his and leaned over the marble balcony, taking it all in. "Everything is so lovely. Wherever did you find so many blooms on the island? Surely the little shop in town could not have supplied it all?"

"Who else?" He shrugged. "Fritz worked his magic and contacted all the florists he could find that carried the treasured roses and had them shipped. He wanted nothing but the best."

She turned around, finding that he was leaning closer, and nearly brushed her lips to his. "How thoughtful of him," she whispered, her lashes fluttering up to meet his Irish eyes.

He grinned and grasped her hand, twirling her under his arm and out into the middle of the carpeted hall but did not release her hand. "No more peeping before it is time! But let's hope you still think the party lovely after you see who is in attendance for a *Valentine's* party. I tried to tell your mother, but she was insistent."

"Oh dear. If you were disturbed enough to protest Mother's guest list for tonight, it must be rather terrible."

He sucked in sharply through his teeth. "Yes. And rather awkward if you ask me."

She tugged on his hand. "Cullen. You have to tell me who is in attendance now."

He stepped into her grasp, lowering his mouth to her ear. "Is that a command?"

"Yes." She crossed her arms and attempted to mirror Mother's look that was reserved for the sternest of commands.

"I'm afraid I may have to be locked in the dungeon for denying your command then. I am sworn to secrecy by the queen mother herself."

"You are incorrigible." She twirled away from him and back to the balcony, straining to catch a glimpse of the attendants.

"I've been wanting to tell you something, especially with the next crowning ceremony tonight." Cullen captured her hand once more, turning her to face him. "These weeks with you have been the happiest I have ever known." He swallowed. "I never thought it could be possible to feel such things after a short amount of time, but this is not a normal courtship. Being here with you and your family, it has brought something to life in me."

Trumpets sounded, wrenching them from the moment, but she placed a hand on his arm, unwilling to let the moment pass. "What have I brought to life, Cullen?"

"That, I will have to leave for another time. We best not keep your mother, or the surprise, waiting."

Knowing she would corner him at some point tonight, she took his arm and lifted her skirts in her free hand, then descended the grand staircase into the great hall, her breath catching at the sight of her suitors all standing in groups with those she assumed to be their families. She tightened her grip on Cullen's arm. *I am going to meet their families? All at once?* While she knew some of them from her years spent in society, she was *not* ready to converse with the families of her potential husbands, particularly not when she was sending away half tonight. "Are your mother and sister in attendance?"

He leaned to her ear. "They are standing beside the fireplace on the far wall, conversing with the twins, which is where we'll be pausing first since I won the draw for escorting you."

Willow kept her bright smile, nodding in passing to Archie's five brothers, Kit's two sisters and brother-in-law, a woman she assumed was Fritz's mother, Chandler's newspaper tycoon giant of a father and equally impressive brother, and Teddy's parents and his stoic brother, Carlisle, feeling more than uncomfortable that she could not stop to greet all. Yet Cullen's even strides did not pause until they had reached a regal woman whose beauty had not left her and a young lady beside her with pretty features, though she held no resemblance to her brother.

"Mrs. Dempsey and Miss Eva Marie Dempsey." Willow dipped into a curtsy, mirroring their own. "I'm honored you have joined us tonight."

"I would not miss meeting the first woman my son has written home about." Mrs. Dempsey returned her curtsy, and Willow could at once see Cullen in her eyes. "Has my son been treating you well?"

"Like a queen," she replied, looking up at Cullen, happy to find him more relaxed than he had seemed in weeks.

"Well, he'd better because I told him that you are American royalty and could end our standing in an instant." Eva Marie giggled into her painted silk fan, even as her mother flinched at the faux pas.

Then, as Mrs. Dempsey laughed away the discomfiture and began to chide her daughter, Mother clapped her hands.

"It appears everyone has *finally* arrived," Mother announced from her place on the second step of the grand staircase. "Each of Willow's suitors has come up with an amusement for us tonight. First, I shall introduce Mr. Blythe's selection. Tonight we will be picking hearts that have been cut in half, all in unique designs." She gestured to the box on her right. "This box is for the ladies in attendance to choose from to determine their partner, and the box on my left is for the gentlemen. The ladies and gentlemen will have to mingle and try to fit their heart to another's to discover who their partner will be for the rest of the evening. And who knows"—she raised her eyebrows to Willow—"maybe your partner will turn out to be your one true love. Line up, please. Willow and suitors, you all are first, of course." She held up a glass bowl to Willow, shaking the six halves inside. "Willow's suitors shall choose from their own bowl and then attempt to fit it to Willow's. Only one heart will match, which means the five remaining halves of the gentlemen's hearts in Willow's bowl will be added to the ladies' box, and at that point the rest of you may select your heart."

Knowing her mother would appreciate it, Willow lifted her hand above her head and reached dramatically into the bowl, and with the tips of her fingers she raised her half of a heart for all to see as the guests crowded round the boxes, eager to learn who would be Willow's partner for the evening.

"And this is why I never liked Valentine's Day parties, for they are far too risky," Cullen whispered to her while Teddy selected his paper heart.

"I know, but you have to admit, it's rather diverting and suspenseful." Willow giggled and fitted her heart to Teddy's, but the teethlike angles did not fit.

Chandler stepped up, his grin in place and heart held out to Willow's. "It would be nice to win something while under your roof, especially with my father and brother looking on."

Willow gave him a reassuring smile and lifted her heart to his, the mismatch evident. "I'm sorry, Chandler, but find me for the first dance?"

This seemed to raise his spirits considerably as he left her with a kiss to her hand, and then Cullen selected his heart and at once turned to Willow and tried to match it. They sighed.

"Well, we could only hope, but it looks like I will only be seeing you during the two second waltzes this evening," Cullen mumbled. "If I had wanted to spend the evening with another girl, I would have escorted her. But I didn't. I won the draw fair and square and escorted you."

Willow blushed with pleasure. "Never fear. We'll spend time together again later."

With an eager smile, Fritz held out his heart to her.

She moved forward and it matched perfectly. "It appears we are to enjoy the festivities together this evening."

"That's not fair. He must have rigged it somehow," Kit protested, though she caught his teasing tone. "I vote that we try again."

"Not so fast. I won fair and square." Fritz hooted, grasping her hand and threading it through his arm. "Cupid has favored us at last, Miss Dupré."

Mother stirred the remaining hearts in Willow's bowl into

the ladies' box and waved everyone forward to join in the fun when Willow spotted her friend.

"Flora? You returned to Newport just for my party?" Willow pulled her into an embrace, relieved that she would have someone impartial to speak to about the men.

"I told you I would return. After all, your Valentine's party is *the* talk of the city. Everyone was seething with jealousy that I was invited when it was supposed to be family members of the suitors only."

"You are one of my sisters. Everyone knows that. Now go choose your heart and we shall have loads to catch up on tonight. Will you stay with me tonight?"

"Of course." Flora nodded to Fritz and selected a heart, twirling around, flitting from man to man as she tried to find her heart's match while Willow's suitors hemmed her in, keeping Fritz from stealing her away.

At last, Flora stopped in front of Teddy and fitted her heart to his. She gave a gasp of pleasure and slipped her arm possessively through his arm. "Well then, I suppose that you belong to me for the evening."

"I suppose I do." Teddy grinned.

Willow sent Flora a wink. "Just see to it that you return him to me at the end of the ball."

Flora waved her off and pulled Teddy away, saying, "Now, what are your plans to support a wife? Spiritually, emotionally, and of course fiscally."

The twins approached Cullen, holding up a single half of a paper heart. "Mama said we could share *one* gentleman, and you are one of the last gentlemen left without a partner."

He grinned and fitted his heart to theirs. They squealed and tugged him away, demanding that he fetch them punch and plates of dessert posthaste.

"Alone at last." Fritz turned to her, sliding his hand into his inside breast pocket. "I wanted to give you something."

"Friedrich, you have yet to introduce me to your lady friend," called a nasally voice behind them.

He closed his eyes and exhaled with a groan. "So close." He turned with Willow to face a short, stout lady bedecked in a severe black silk gown trimmed in yards of delicate black lace with a matching onyx necklace. "Miss Dupré, I'd like you to meet my mother, Mrs. Blythe."

She nodded approvingly over Willow's gown, smiling. "So, you are the one who has my Friedrich making plans of a future?"

Willow curtsied to Mrs. Blythe. "It is difficult to plan in such an environment as this, but your son's daily thoughtfulness is the highlight of my day."

"Thoughtfulness?" She gave a disbelieving laugh. "Goodness me. Whatever has he been doing to set himself apart? He is never so thoughtful to me."

She bit the inside of her mouth, knowing that she could not tell of the daily blossoms with hidden messages in their petals.

"Speaking of thoughtfulness," Fritz interjected, saving her from replying. He reached into his jacket and retrieved not a blossom but a small package . . . small enough to contain a ring.

His mother began to fan herself wildly, sending her manufactured gray curls dancing about. "Oh, my boy, my precious boy."

Willow glanced at those around them, who were no doubt watching, but opened it anyway. Nestled in velvet, she found a delicate gold token in the shape of a rose with an engraved script. *A love token?* She had only ever read about them and seen the few love tokens Mother kept in her keepsake box, but never had Willow received one for her very own before. She lifted the script to the light and read aloud, "'If I had a flower for every time I thought of you . . . I could walk through my garden forever.'" She lifted the token to her heart, warmed at his words. "Fritz, that is such a beautiful sentiment."

"I wish I could take credit for Lord Alfred Tennyson's brilliance, but alas, I can only uphold the sentiment."

"More flowers." Mrs. Blythe heaved a sigh. "A fault I'm certain you are eager to mend, Miss Dupré." She rolled her shoulders back, her scowl rippling down her features.

Willow traced the gold rose with her fingertips. "On the contrary, his kind heart is something I need more of in my life." She slipped the token into her pocket and kissed him on the cheek, earning a smile from Fritz and a gasp from his mother.

"Will we never have more than a moment of this famed sugar queen's time?" Mrs. Dempsey flicked her egret feather fan back and forth, accepting the glass of punch from Cullen. He had just returned from setting up the twins in the corner, who were happily munching away on a pile of sweets. "She hardly spoke with us before she was called away. If Miss Dupré thinks she has a chance with you, she had best make a more favorable impression on me."

"Of course you will have more time. You wouldn't have come all this way if you were not going to visit with Miss Dupré and her family." Cullen arched his neck in hopes of catching Willow's attention from Chandler's family, but if tonight was like any of the other parties, he would be hard-pressed to receive more than a moment or two with the woman of the hour . . . but he would not be sharing that with his mother.

"One would hope." Mother lifted her chin and appeared to be observing the gold leaf coating every molding and the four crystal chandeliers adorning each corner of the center fresco. "Their cottage by the sea and this competition are as outlandish as the papers said. To have this many beaus and their families under the same roof is not natural." She fluffed Eva Marie's pink silk sleeves, and Cullen tried not to think how much his mother's and sister's new ensembles were costing them.

He waved over Marvin with his tray of punch, taking a fresh glass for himself. "Be that as it may, I am grateful to be here."

"You are a catch, Cullen. We may not have as much as the Dupré family, but you have a lot to offer her in yourself. What recommends Miss Dupré besides her wealth?" She took a long sip. "She is not that handsome."

Cullen stiffened. If only Mother knew of his past . . . maybe she would not be so quick to judge Willow.

"I disagree. She is as lovely as you described in your letters, Cullen." Eva Marie grasped his arm. "And even if Mother cannot understand the draw, I can see why she has so many suitors seeking her hand."

"Don't be naïve, Eva Marie. It is her wealth. Even if her looks *did* reflect her spinsterhood, the men would still flock to her side due to her millions. Good thing her little sisters still have years before they make their debut, or Miss Dupré's fortune would mean little against two fresh faces with fortunes tied to them, as well."

Cullen scowled, downing his glass of punch. "I know not what you are on about. Miss Dupré is by far the loveliest young lady I have ever met. Unconventional, yes, but if you could know her the way I do and see how kind she is to her staff, loving to her family, and devoted to her family's legacy, you would begin to understand why the six of us gentlemen wish to win her heart and hand." He clenched his jaw, taken aback by his own confession.

Eva Marie giggled into her silk fan. "I do believe our Cullen is smitten, Mother."

At this, Mother's stern expression smoothed. "Cullen, have you declared yourself to her?"

"Not in so many words, yet she knows of my regard for her." He shifted in his form-fitting jacket.

Mother gestured to Kit and Fritz on either side of Willow, leading her away from the great hall toward the parlor. "Regard? No, you must dismiss any doubts she has if you are to capture her attention from her other suitors, all of whom have much larger fortunes tied to their names than we do."

Cullen cleared his throat, perturbed that his mother and sister had found him out so easily, when the twins bounded up to his side. *Thank goodness.* "Come to ask for more treats from your escort?"

Philomena grabbed his hand, tugging it. "We want you to play blind man's bluff with us in the parlor. It's about to begin."

He grimaced. Why Theodore had thought it would be appropriate to play such a childish game was beyond him, but as all the suitors had to come up with one game each, he supposed Theodore gave Mrs. Dupré the first game that came to mind. The last time Cullen had played it was two decades ago at some laddie's birthday party. "If you'll excuse me, Mother, I must go. Eva Marie, be sure to take a heart from the box, or I fear there will be someone's relative roaming about without a partner."

With those words, the twins each grabbed one of his arms and pulled him into the parlor, where Willow stood in the center of the room, fitting a cloth over Theodore's eyes. Tightening the blindfold, she turned him thrice and released him, squealing as she darted from his grasp and ducked around a settee while Flora, Fritz, and some of the other guests flew about the room, evading being caught in Theodore's flailing hands.

Seeing Willow step behind the thick velvet curtain, Cullen joined her. "Can I hide with you?"

She lifted a finger to her lips, pressing her back against the window to give him more room.

Theodore sang out, "Blind man's—"

Willow peeked around their curtain, answering in unison with the rest of the room, "Bluff!"

Cullen watched as Theodore whipped about, disoriented from the answers coming in every direction. He seemed to have heard her melodic voice in the group, for he took a few paces nearer.

"We better move. He is getting too close," she whispered.

"We are safe yet." Cullen snatched her wrist in his, wishing they could continue hiding from the world. He pulled her closer, his secret burning within him. He had written Flannery three times since the beach trip, practically begging for permission to tell Willow, but each time he had been met with staunch resistance. Flannery said it would be soon, but with the competition ending in six weeks, time was pressing on his lungs. And during Willow's and his daily strolls and conversations on the cliff walk, he had to keep himself from confessing all more than once.

Theodore's grasp batted the curtain over Willow's head as a giggle sounded across the room. Cullen enveloped her in his arms and held his breath as Theodore moved away to capture the giggler.

Willow looked up at him, drawing his attention to her full lips. In all their moments alone, he had kept himself from kissing her. He respected her too much to kiss her with such a secret between them, but with their breath mingling behind the curtain, it acted as a charm, pulling him to her. He slid his hand from her shoulders to the base of her neck, allowing his fingers to weave through her hair. Then he lowered his lips, pausing a breath away. Her chin tilted up, and the curtain tore open, Theodore's hand landing on Willow's shoulder, feeling the elaborate sleeve with its rosettes.

"I've got you, Will."

Waking from his stupor, Cullen jerked away from her just as Theodore tore off his blindfold, his grin encompassing his face as he tugged her to stand in the middle of the room. "Now, it is time for you to pay the forfeit of my choosing in front of all."

The forfeit. Cullen's insides twisted knowing at once what Theodore would request. *No wonder Theodore chose this game*. He did not want to witness a second kiss between them. The first still plagued his nightmares. "Come now, Day, this is a child's game. No sense in following the rules further. Miss Dupré, would you care for some refreshments?"

Theodore shot him a glare. "No one likes a spoilsport, Dempsey."

Flora grasped Theodore's elbow, gently pulling him away from Cullen. "I believe the music is starting. Perhaps we should have a glass of punch before dancing?"

"Not until I collect my forfeit, provided of course that the lady's willing to grant me a kiss." Theodore sent Willow a wink.

With a laugh, she rose on her tiptoes and pressed a kiss to his cheek. "There." She turned and motioned over Chandler. "Now, Chandler, let us begin the dancing before the next game."

Cullen stepped forward. "Actually, my contribution for the night is teaching everyone variations from popular dances." He extended his elbow to her. "Which means the first dance, if my lady accepts, belongs to me."

Seventeen

Willow returned to the dessert table between sets and inspected the miniature heart-shaped cakes, cookies, and pastries, at last selecting a tiny frosted cookie and popping it into her mouth.

"Did you try this cake over here?" Teddy appeared at her elbow, scooping up a delicate, heart-shaped confection with a soft cloud of pink whipped icing.

Willow pointed to her full mouth and held her hand up to cover her lips, mortified at being caught in such a state, and accepted the sweet from him, even though she could almost hear her mother saying that eating so much in front of a suitor was uncouth. "Thank you," she said as soon as she was able and was about to take a small, and much more ladylike, bite, when Flora bumped into her elbow, mushing the icing across Willow's nose and mouth. "Flora!" she gasped.

Teddy chortled and pulled out his handkerchief, offering it to her. "You may need this. I cannot say for certain, but I think you might have missed your mouth by a tad."

Willow snatched the handkerchief and swiped it over her nose and chin before her mother could see.

"Oh dear. It is still all over your face." Flora clicked her tongue. "You might need a looking glass before the icing dye sets into your skin. But, as you blush so much, I don't think anyone will take that much notice even if it does set into your skin."

Willow sent Flora an exasperated look and curtsied to her beau as if nothing were out of place. "Please excuse me, Teddy, while I retire to the powder room to freshen up."

"I'll be right here, guarding the pastry table from Fritz," Teddy replied, discreetly stuffing another cookie into his mouth.

"Glad to see that you could spare a moment for Teddy away from Fritz and Cullen," Flora quipped, following Willow into the powder room.

Willow threw the spoiled handkerchief onto the vanity, reached for a porcelain pitcher, and splashed water into the basin. She dabbed a hand towel into the water and wiped at her cheeks, sighing with relief as the pink icing had left no trace on her skin. "Why on earth did you smash icing up my nose?"

"How else was I going to get you alone with all these men buzzing around you? And don't say that I didn't try before resorting to such measures, but what did you expect me to do when I came all this way to *help* you." Flora placed her hands on her hourglass waist. "Do you wish for my advice or not? Because, believe me, it would have been far easier to stay at home than to watch you with—" She shook her head. "It doesn't matter."

Willow paused in her ablutions. She had thought they would catch up tonight, but that would have been too late with the crowning ceremony at the end of the festivities. *Little wonder Flora is peeved.* "You are absolutely right. Forgive me?"

Flora nodded. "I wanted to let you know that Teddy is serious about you. He is . . ." She drew in a breath and looked pointedly at Willow. "He is *in love* with you."

Willow lowered the towel and turned to Flora, mouth slack. *In love? Teddy is in love with me?* While he had claimed to hold her in high regard, it was quite another matter entirely to confess such a claim to Flora. "He told you those very words?"

"Do you think he would have kissed you in town for all the world to see if he wasn't in love with you?" She appropriated the stained towel from Willow and tossed it into the bin under the vanity. "Your mother invited me here to help you discern who is worthy. Well, they all seem pretty worthy to me, and now that I know that our dear Teddy is in love with you, I need to take a stand."

"What kind of stand?"

Flora winced as if her words were physically paining her. "I caught a glimpse of Cullen holding you behind that curtain during the game."

"Nothing happened."

"I have a difficult time believing you didn't *want* Cullen to kiss you. You can't have all of them, Willow. You must either cease this kissing nonsense until you have made up your mind or cut Teddy loose."

Willow blinked, unsure of how to respond. "You think I am being cruel?"

Flora bit the inside of her lip and gave a single nod before reaching out and squeezing Willow's hand. "Not that you are *intending* to be cruel. I'm only telling you this because I do not wish to see you, or your reputation, hurt. You may have yourself fooled into believing that Teddy has only been caught up in the romance of the competition for your heart, but I know how much he thinks of you and that you've spent practically every afternoon at his side. It would be hard for any man you kiss not to think he has the greatest chance of winning your heart. Still, after those almost-kisses with Cullen you keep having . . . I'm not so certain. Almost kissing someone multiple times is more telling than kissing someone only once."

Willow did not like the direction this was taking. She turned to the looking glass and smoothed her hair, attempting to keep her temper at bay and *listen* to her friend's advice. "I try to give everyone equal attention. You will understand how hard it is to keep everyone content when the beaus come calling at your door."

Flora snorted. "Me get courted by multiple men at once? Did you know that when you narrowed your suitors to six gentlemen, my mother told me that I finally had the chance to snag the second-best gentleman in New York due to my association with you? She told me that since you have been given wit as well as scads of money, the men will flock after you first. I, however, only have my Knickerbocker pedigree and a modest inheritance upon marriage to recommend me."

Willow gasped. "What a horrid thing for Mrs. Wingfield to tell you. That simply is not true."

"With five daughters, Father didn't allot for more than a few million to go around. I am a poor American princess compared to you. At least until my father passes and we receive the rest of our inheritance . . . a truly dreadful thought. But we both know money is what lures gentlemen in our set into marriage more often than not."

"Nonsense. You are a beautiful, *intelligent* young woman with so much more than money to offer."

Flora gestured to the looking glass. "I am not naïve, Will. I know that you are the wealthier one in this relationship at this point in our lives, so after Mother's initial shock at your competition, she was actually excited to have your money married off and out of my way."

"You don't believe that, do you? What happened to your dreams of marriage to your own Prince Charming?"

"Don't we all lose some of the childhood magic of imagination?" She shrugged. "When society discovered Father's clause on our receiving our full inheritance until well after marriage, they stopped calling. Certainly, I may still dream of a knight in shining armor coming to sweep me up onto his mighty steed, but those were fairy tales. This is real life. There are no knights left after you have made your selection, for they shall all be captured by husband-hunting heiresses before they even look at me."

Willow was surprised to see such sadness in Flora's naturally bright countenance. But before she could respond, Flora shook her head and laughed.

"How did we get onto the topic of my wanting a love life? Tonight is about my dearest friend and finding you the perfect match. All I'm saying is to tread carefully for fear of crushing Teddy's heart underfoot. I couldn't bear it if he were hurt. Now, enough with this serious conversation. I have done my duty as your best friend. So, what are your thoughts on the others?"

Willow reached into her pocket and displayed the love token. "I thought I was ready with my choice *before* I met the families, but now . . . they are all so wonderful, I may have to reconsider my choices over the final slot." *At least Archie is out.* No matter how kind he had been in person and in his articles since the rescue, she knew the truth and would not forget it.

"Well, I've said what I needed to say about Teddy, but if you need help deciding, I'm here."

"Thank you, but I think this is one choice I must make on my own." Willow gestured to the door. "We best rejoin the others."

At the first strike of the grandfather clock at midnight, Mr. Dupré stood at the second step of the grand staircase, clinking his fingernail to his glass, calling all to attention a second time before he silenced the hall. "Gentlemen, if you will, please join Miss Dupré in the music room for the ceremony. As for the families, I want to thank you for coming out tonight. Your support will be remembered." He lifted his glass. "To Willow Dupré and her future husband."

The crowd echoed his toast, and Willow thanked the families she passed on her way to the music room, where a short column with three laurels atop stood before the Brazilian rosewood piano, the moonlight streaming in from the alcove's glass doors beyond. On either side of the piano stood a candelabra, the flames flickering in the silent room where a refreshment table had been set along the back wall, most likely for after the ceremony.

Drawing a deep breath, Willow took her place before the men, holding the first crown in her gloved hands, looking out at the gentlemen whom she had come to admire. Most of them had become her friends and, unlike the other ceremonies, she felt a tug of regret for having to send someone she had come to care for home.

"I know it may seem ridiculous to be so formal at this stage in our relationship," she began, "but as with every serious occasion, it must not be taken lightly. Tonight I will offer three crowns, and if you feel you cannot propose by the end of March, I will understand if you must refuse me tonight." She lifted the crown in her hands. "I know what accepting a crown means, and I pray that each one of you realizes how special you are to me." She paused at the emotion welling in her chest, surprised by the tears pricking at her lashes. *Why am I crying?* She lifted her fingers to her lips, attempting to gather herself. "Pardon me."

The men shifted uneasily before her. She cleared her throat and, with a smile, lifted the first crown. "Teddy."

A grin lit his face as he crossed the room in two strides and knelt before her.

"Will you accept this crown and all that it symbolizes?"

"Forever."

Her heart fluttered at his declaration as she set the laurels upon his head and motioned for him to stand behind her on her right. She drew a steadying breath and picked up the second crown when Kit took a pace forward.

"Willow? May I have a word in private?"

She blinked, uncertain as to what he was about. The last time a suitor stepped forward during the ceremony, he had left her. Her pulse pounded. She could tell his request took the group aback, and worry flickered across Cullen's features, but she nodded. "Of course. Gentlemen, please take your refreshments while I am away."

Kit gently grasped her elbow and led her through the glass doors of the alcove and out into the moonlit garden with torches at each bend in the gravel path, lighting the way along the evergreens and flowers. "Willow, I wanted to speak with you away from the others. Your speech touched me, and I feel I must confess something."

She looked at the crown still in her hands, her heart dipping. "You do not wish to accept a crown from me, do you?"

"It's not that I do not wish to marry you . . ." He took her hands in his, the torchlight revealing the pain lining his every feature. "I know a union between us would be beneficial to both of our futures, but—"

"But you want more," Willow finished.

"Yes." His brow creased. "I want my wife to be in love with *me* and only me." He stroked her cheek with the back of his hand. "I have come to think of you as a dear friend, yet I'm afraid I have hidden from you that I am rather a romantic and want more from marriage than a good business deal. And I respect myself and you too much to continue on in this way. If you loved me in the way I desire, things would be different. But I don't think you do."

She kneaded the heel of her palm over her heart, finding it was growing harder and harder to breathe. *Lord, why does this hurt so much?* She had been prepared to release Fritz tonight because she believed that Kit loved her, but now to discover that he did not . . . She sank onto the cast-iron bench beneath the garden arch with its dormant vines. "When did you come to this realization?"

"When Theodore tried to kiss you as your forfeit tonight.

Cullen, Fritz, and even Chandler were all in a rage, while I . . ." He ran his fingers through his dark locks, flicking his hand to the side. "I felt nothing but amusement. I figured I should at least be able to summon a bit of jealousy when it comes to another man kissing my potential bride."

"I agree." She wiped at her eyes with the back of her hand, sniffing.

Kit knelt beside her and rested his hand on hers. "I never meant to hurt you in guarding my heart. Still, I think it will be better for you and me to part now before it grows even harder to say good-bye." He swallowed, his voice gruff. "No matter how painful it is now, I know it will be worse if we delay."

She dipped her head, desperate to gather herself. "Thank you for being honest with me, Kit. I wish you nothing but the greatest of love in your future. And if you ever have need of anything in your lifetime, you always have a friend in me."

He squeezed her hand. "You are a queen of a woman, Willow."

"Kind until the very end." She smiled up at him. "Any parting words of wisdom?"

He helped her to standing. "Yes. But know that I am only saying this for no other reason but for your happiness."

"Tell me."

He met her gaze without hesitation. "I do not trust Cullen. I do not know him in the way that you do, but I have had dealings with him many years ago, and if he is anything like his father, even in the smallest of ways, he is not to be trusted."

She stiffened, absorbing this next blow. "Thank you."

He pulled her into his arms and rested his chin atop her hair. "Best of luck and brightest of futures to you, my dear Miss Dupré."

With a parting smile, she returned to the music room without him and prayed that no one else was hiding secrets from her. She looked at the remaining five and, at Archie's beaming face, decided her course of action. "As you can see, Kit has left the group, which leaves two crowns. But before I can continue, I am loath to inform you of a traitor among us."

The sugar cookie turned to chalk in Cullen's mouth, and he squelched the urge to cough aloud, his shoulders hunching and his neck tightening from the effort.

"You okay there?" Theodore clapped him on the back several times.

Cullen threw back his coffee. "Thanks. Food went down wrong."

"You'll want to hear this," Theodore murmured out of the side of his mouth.

Cullen set aside his plate and cup and joined the others in front of the column once more and focused on Willow, praying and hoping against all hope that she did not mean him. Her focus went from man to man, finally landing on him. His insides twisted. *God, let me have the chance to explain.*

She turned her gaze to the left of him and rested her eyes on Archie. "Archibald Lovett. You have exactly one minute to explain yourself before I throw you out on your ear."

Cullen's breath left him, even as his fists curled inward and he turned with the others toward Archie.

Archie gave a nervous laugh. "I-I don't know what you mean."

She pulled a newspaper from behind a cushion and slapped it against his chest. "I *trusted* you. My family trusted you. We allowed you into our home *and* our hearts."

His confident expression transformed into one of horror and then into a smirk as he snatched the paper from her hand, tucking it into his pocket. "Well, at least you showed your true colors in choosing to attempt to humiliate me in front of all instead of dismissing me in private. I liked you, Will, but now you've awakened me from the spell you cast since you saved me on Bailey's Beach, and I can cease this bowing and scraping to please you and get back to Dorothea."

Dorothea? Cullen's insides churned. Surely Willow had not mistaken a suitor's actions a *second* time.

"You aren't the reporter? You are courting someone else?"

"If you can have a half-dozen men at your beck and call, why can't I have one lady on the side? The odds did not dictate that I would win anyway." He shrugged and unfolded the paper, flipping to the most recent article on Willow. "Besides, it's time I claim the credit for my brilliant writing of the first weeks and get back to printing the truth about you instead of this love-tempered drivel."

She pinched the bridge of her nose as if trying to keep her anger at bay. "Why did you stay so long when you have what you needed and had your Miss Dorothea waiting?"

He smirked again. "Because my uncle Crain is on the board and wanted me to try to win in order to give him more sway in the business by, at the least, becoming your friend and confidant. As for myself, I wished for the fame for both my career and love life. Before your parents invited me here, I was merely one of Dorothea's callers, but you have made me desirable. Ever since joining this little competition, her mother has been most apologetic about her behavior toward me in the past, for if I am good enough for the sugar queen, I am certainly a favorable match for her daughter."

Willow rubbed her forehead between two fingers. "And if you had kept your cover and I had chosen you? What then?"

At the question, the men shifted. Cullen cracked his thumb, ready to beat the cad.

Archie shrugged as he pulled a peppermint from his pocket and popped it into his mouth. "If I did win, I'd have your wealth, and we both know that money covers a multitude of imperfections." He allowed his gaze to travel down her, his cheek bulging from the sweet. "Like the fact that you are nothing compared to Dorothea's beauty. Your wealth gilds you. Without it, you are a spinster wallflower."

Willow jerked back as if he had slapped her and Cullen started for him, but Willow lifted her hand, staying him.

"You do not have to be so cruel, sir."

Archie snorted and sauntered to the door leading to the hallway.

"Such words can only come from the heart, and that poor girl should be warned of your true nature," she called after him.

He clenched his fists at his sides, turning on his heel to glare at her. "You may think you are so high-and-mighty now, but your reign will never come to pass. My uncle will be moving for Osborne to take over, as well he should. The business world is no place for a woman." At her gasp, he added, "Do not take it upon yourself to act like the jilted maiden. You only kept me around because you found me charming and then I'm sure to feed me stories that showed you in a more favorable light, now that I think of it. And unless these fellows were as dull as tombs, charming does not win the race. Your heart was never in danger with me."

"How dare you?" Her voice trembled in such a way that made Cullen ache to wrap an arm about her, but he had the feeling to do so would make her even more irate. As much as he disliked it, he stayed planted in place and watched Willow fight for herself.

"How dare I? Willow, if I were truly interested in you, do you realize how cruel it is to keep me simply because I amuse you? Are you really that spoiled?"

She drew herself up. "I may be wealthy, but I am *not* spoiled. If I were, do you think I would stand to put myself through such a competition as this?"

"I can see your next headline now." He lifted his hand and arched the air. "*Sugar Queen in Competition Against Her Will.*" He sent her a wink. "Thanks for that parting gift, my queen."

Cullen couldn't keep himself back any longer. He seized Archie by the collar. "If you would allow me, Miss Dupré, I will see this fellow out the door before he has any more fodder for his outhouse articles."

"Thank you, Mr. Dempsey." The corners of her lips twitched into a shadow of a smile. "Good-bye, Mr. Lovett. I hope you are happy with the enemy you have made here today."

"*Enemies*," Theodore corrected as he, Chandler, and Fritz joined Cullen.

At these words, Archie's confident façade flickered, and Cullen could see the fleck of fear appearing in his eyes. Cullen grinned. How could Archie not realize that by printing all those stories, he was making powerful enemies of the new generation of New York society?

"It was all in the name of business, gents." Archie gave a shaky laugh. "You don't have to *all* play the devoted suitor because she can only wed one of you."

Theodore seized Archie's other arm, propelling him out along with Cullen. Theodore's voice lowered into a growl. "You should have thought of the consequences before you decided to play the spy."

Archie's protests surely reached the servants' quarters on the fourth floor, but Cullen could not think of anything other than the fact that he had so narrowly escaped being found out. Kit had left. He had no reason to keep silent and yet he must have, or else Cullen would have been joining Archie. He would write to Flannery again. There had to be a way or at least a timeline the agent had in mind of when Cullen could confess all to Willow.

The men slapped one another on the shoulders after depositing Archie outside in the cold and made their way back to the music room, standing in front of Willow with Theodore behind her.

Willow turned to them, puffy-eyed, but gave them a warm

smile each. "Thank you for your service, sirs." She lifted a crown in each hand. "And if you, Fritz, and you, Cullen, would be so kind as to accept a crown, I would like to invite you both to stay and continue to court me."

Cullen grinned and did not hesitate to kneel before her, but before he could express his heart, Fritz hooted and ran to her, lifting her in the air and twirling her around as Theodore applauded and cheered.

Setting her down, Fritz withdrew his pocketbook and opened it to lay a dried blue flower in her palm. "Blue violet, a vow of my promise of faithfulness."

"Thank you, Fritz and Cullen." She rested the delicate flower atop the column and crowned them both. She looked up at Chandler, sadness etched in her dark eyes. "Can I walk you outside?"

At his nod, she slipped her hand around his arm and rested her head on his shoulder as they departed.

The door creaked open almost at once, and Mr. Dupré thumped into the room on his cane. "Gentlemen. This has been a wonderful time of rest for my family and for you gentlemen to get to know her without the rigors of the city, but this life by the sea is not Willow's every day. To see if you are ready to take on life with Willow, you need to experience firsthand what it will be like to be wed to a businesswoman. And so this party concludes our time in Newport. Tomorrow we will adjourn to the city where you will study the business at Willow's side and, by doing so, help repair some of the damage that Archibald Lovett's articles have inflicted on my family. Gentlemen, please bid your family members farewell and retire to your rooms and ready yourselves for the trip to New York."

Eighteen

Willow braced herself as the wheels clattered onto the Brooklyn Bridge so as not to knock into Cullen with her father directly across from them. After a week of packing, traveling, and settling back into their New York residence, and a week of sifting through the piles of paper work delivered for her father, Willow was eager to return to the office and feel the pulse of the factory once more. It had been too long.

She glanced sideways at Cullen. Though she was initially opposed to having a suitor with her on the first day back at work, it did make sense to see how each gentleman behaved under the pressures of her day-to-day life. And with her father present, she knew Cullen's presence would not be a subject for teasing among the staff . . . well, not at least when *she* could hear them. "Thank you for coming with us to the office, Father. I need your support after all that has happened."

"With your cousin in town, it would be foolish of me not to attend the arrival of the new shipment, even if my presence does complicate our original plan of seeing if the pair of you

220

were compatible work partners." He sighed. "I'm afraid that Archie's articles, which your mother and I ignored in the hopes of your gaining fame and veneration, have taken such a turn that they have given the board and your cousin far too much fodder in the dispute of your right to run the company. We must do some damage control with the staff and workers." He turned to Cullen. "Mr. Dempsey, I would like you to take careful notes on how we do things at the factory. If you see any room for improvement, we are ready to listen. Because that's what makes a great company—the best company—not fearing suggestions and change."

Cullen lifted the notebook Willow had supplied him with this morning. "Quite agree, sir. Thank you for allowing me the honor."

Father waved him off. "It's more than an honor. I'm testing all the suitors later to see who remembers the most and who has the best suggestions for improvements. Never forget, Mr. Dempsey, that this is not an ordinary courtship. This is a competition, and the stakes are everything to me and mine."

"Yes, sir." His throat bobbed as he swallowed.

The carriage rolled to a halt at the company's wharf, and Cullen hopped out, holding the door for Willow's father and herself. Willow stepped out of the carriage to where the latest ship was docked and surveyed the workers moving up and down the plank, unloading sacks of raw sugar fresh from the Caribbean islands. They tossed the sacks into the arms of their fellow workers, who carried them to a giant cylinder storage house, handing the sacks off to a different group of burly men, who cut open each sack with a bowie knife and dumped the contents into crates. The crates were then loaded onto a conveyor belt and sent up to the top of a massive bin, where two other men poured the raw sugar inside until it was ready to be processed.

"I haven't seen a conveyor belt run on a steam engine before." Cullen stood at her elbow, writing furiously in his notebook.

Willow crossed her arms, engrossed with the machinery. "I was reading an article about an experiment that used such an engine. This is the first I've seen the new equipment in action."

"Fascinating."

"Glad you think so, as well." Willow studied the men, watching which ones performed quickly, as well as those who seemed exhausted, wishing she could find a way to further streamline the process for the men. Her gaze landed on a giant of a man, coated in sweat, hefting a sack onto his shoulder and dumping it into the bin. He used only one arm, as the other was in a sling. She nudged Father and pointed as the foreman caught sight of them. "Shouldn't that man be resting?"

Before Father could reply, the foreman reached them, tipping his hat. "Mr. and Miss Dupré and sir. It's an honor. I was sorry to hear of your health not improving as much as expected, Mr. Dupré. We all were." He averted his gaze, pretending not to notice the cane.

"Thank you, Jarvis. It's been far too long since I have been at the dock for a shipment." Father clapped the man's hand in a firm handshake. "And Miss Dupré wishes for her suitor, Mr. Dempsey, to see how things are coming along."

The man nodded respectfully to Willow. "Miss, I appreciate you comin' to check on the men, and you too, Mr. Dempsey."

"How is everyone? Have there been any accidents that have yet to be reported?" She gestured to the man in the sling, who was already lifting a second sack onto his shoulder in an impressive show of strength. "I do not remember hearing of an accident."

Jarvis pressed his lips into a thin line beneath his bushy mustache, looped his thumbs on his vest, and nodded. "In the rush with the season, and then overseeing the installation of that new conveyor belt, I haven't had much chance to write up any of them reports you've been requesting, miss, but do know that I fully intended to and I understand their importance."

She pursed her lips and nodded. Jarvis had been promising her those reports since Thanksgiving, so clearly he did *not* understand their importance. "Do you know that injured fellow's name? And why is he still working when he's clearly inhibited?"

"That's McClain." Jarvis scowled and clasped his hands behind his back. "I promise you, miss, he's carrying his weight. I would've dismissed him otherwise, except he's got eight little ones at home."

"Oh. I wasn't thinking of dismissing him, Jarvis, only about giving him leave. But with eight little ones at home . . . how is that possible?"

"I suppose he loves his wife." The man suppressed his laugh when he caught sight of her father's glare. "Beg your pardon, miss. Truth is, a man must do what he must to provide for his family, good times or bad."

Cullen nodded, keeping silent, though Willow knew he understood more than her other suitors about such motivation.

"So long as he's carrying his weight, we have no qualms." Father took her arm, tipping his hat to Jarvis. "Excuse us, we have a long day ahead at the office."

"Of course, sir. Have a good day." He tipped his hat to them and returned to his men.

"Aren't you going to give McClain time off with perhaps half pay?" Willow whispered, falling into step beside her father as usual. She had missed this time with him.

"One issue at a time. If we give McClain paid time off, the board is not going to be happy. And when the other workers catch wind of it, there will be a demand for back pay, and we cannot handle any more battles—not with your cousin threatening us at every turn. Come now, we need to visit the refinery. Mind your hem. You know how your mother detests it when you get it sticky." He leaned heavily on the stair rail and cane.

While Willow wished she could take his arm, she knew Father would not like appearing weak. Cullen moved to her side

223

at the wooden stairs, but she did not take his elbow. He seemed to sense her unwillingness to fall into their customary nearness, and she appreciated his allowing a respectful distance while walking at her side, giving her plenty of room as the warehouse door rolled open.

Willow was greeted with a blast of heat and strode along the walls to keep out of the way of the workers as they set about their various stages of removing the impurities from the sugar. At the top level of the warehouse, a massive kettle with boiling water popped and sizzled nearby, warning Willow to stay clear. She quickly made her way down the steps to the next level, where workers removed the sugar crystals left behind after the boiling process and placed the crystals into a cylinder bin that rotated at such speed as to separate the sugar into granules. As the workers moved swiftly about the station, she met their curious stares with a nod, hoping to set at ease the few employees with panic in their eyes, who then averted their attention to the task at hand.

"You don't come down here often, do you?" Cullen asked, his voice raised above the din of the machines as he followed Father's weaving path among the workers.

"Only a few times a year for random quality checks, or in this case to see how the equipment is handling under the pressure of so many orders."

The final station, at dock level, was Willow's favorite. She paused to watch the workers at the sugar table, setting about packaging the beautiful white mounds of sugar, readying it for market. As always, she paused and watched for the efficiency of the girls working the station and selected a package from the swiftest girl and the slowest, noting the quality of wrapping and weight. *Identical.* Satisfied, she set them in the loading crate, nodding to the young women.

"Where are the sugar cubes made?" Cullen's voice was moderate now, the ground level not nearly as deafening as the top stations.

"Different section of the factory." Willow pointed to a separate station, where more rows of girls were packaging the cubes.

Father gestured for them to move along to the ground floor exit. Soon Willow slipped outside with them, breathing deeply of the fresh air as they walked around the building to the office's main entrance.

"It's an incredible process." Cullen's eyes shone, his color heightened. She could tell that this trip had stirred something in him.

"Do you think you could find a passion for sugar making?" Willow wrapped her hand around his arm, pulling him to a halt.

"Absolutely."

"Even in our absence, our quality is king." Father grinned, stuffing his hand into his coat and thumping his cane, but his enthusiasm turned into a coughing fit.

Willow patted him on the back and took in Father's reddening face. She lowered her voice. "I'm afraid that there were too many steps. Why don't you take a moment to catch your breath? Perhaps you can take tea and rest on the couch in your office while Cullen and I go over the paper work with Jarvis."

"I cannot rest on my first day back. We need to find a way to increase productivity. The storage bin is too full of raw sugar, and there are many outstanding orders. I do not know how the production has dwindled given the pace of our workers and new system, but if we do not correct this, we stand to lose a great deal." He pinched the bridge of his nose, a sure sign that a headache was already bothering him.

"What would Mother want you to do?"

Father smirked, shaking his head. "We both know what she would say, Will."

"I'm your partner, and as partners we must lean on each other during hard times." She threaded her hand through his arm. "Go take some tea in the office while Cullen and I sort this out with the foreman. Trust me?"

He sighed. "Always."

Cullen admired her confident gait as she strode among rough men whom he would never allow his sister near and caught the attention of the foreman. Cullen tugged his coat into place again, gliding his hand into his pocket to ensure that Wellington's latest missive was still secure. Willow had happened upon him when he was reading it, and he had not yet had the chance to get rid of the message like he did with all the others, which he'd tossed into the fire.

Unlike the other messages, however, Wellington was no longer being subtle, the contentment with the Parisian acquisition having worn away. Wellington demanded more or else he would follow through and Cullen's lies would be exposed—along with his cover. If Flannery did not have enough to arrest Wellington in a few weeks, Cullen doubted Flannery ever would, and with that loss, Cullen would surely lose Willow once she found out that he had deceived her on this matter since day one. If he was able to give Wellington something irresistible, maybe the man would become lax in his vigilance to remain out of the picture. Yet even as the thought crossed his mind, Cullen knew it was farfetched. Wellington would never fall into such an obvious trap, not even one set by someone he trusted.

The foreman unlocked the door to his office, waving her inside, his face a wreath of concern. They moved into a small shack-like room with a Franklin stove in the center, a desk with two wood chairs on either side that faced a lone grimy window, and a poorly made-up bunk in the corner where a line of empty, expensive whiskey bottles rested beneath. Cullen narrowed his eyes at their labels . . . a favorite of Wellington. *How could a foreman with a modest salary afford such costly liquor?*

"Miss Dupré, there is no need for you to waste your time comin' to me. I can bring the ledgers up to you and your father in the main office. No sense you being chilled when I haven't added to the fire since this morning."

"I have the day slotted for work, sir, and it makes no difference if I do that work down here or up in the factory office. Not to worry, Jarvis, for I won't be staying for long."

"I have to see to the men." Jarvis fumbled with his ring of keys, clanking them together in a telling fashion. They were not welcome to stay, but Willow, ever stalwart, simply stared back at him in the room she surely owned. "I'm certain your father would not be pleased with me leaving you alone—"

"I'll be fine here with Mr. Dempsey to keep me company, and my father is aware of where we are, so there is no need to fret about your position being in jeopardy." She waved him along, then unfastened her cloak and draped it over the back of the wooden chair, stretching her neck from side to side before reaching for the thick ledgers atop the man's desk.

Cullen's heart thudded at the sight of her face lighting up with a smile when her gaze met his. He loathed himself for betraying her, but it was the only way to save his sister from a wolf who would ruin her and his mother and business with scandal and bankruptcy, not to mention the Irish workers ensnared in Wellington's net. Too much was riding on his ability to take down Wellington—too much for his heart to take the lead and potentially destroy it all.

"Could you assist me? It will go twice as fast if we work together." She walked around the desk, her hip bumping into a ledger and knocking it from the shambolic surface.

Cullen snatched up the ledger before it hit the floor and set it beside the other two. "I'm happy to be of service. I'm guessing we are looking for a cause of the deficit despite the increase in orders?"

Willow trilled her fingers atop the ledgers. "Correct. There is no reason why productivity is down when, judging from the workers' speed, the sugar orders should have no problem being completed, and we have no end of supplies being delivered."

Cullen nodded and removed a few mugs from the desk and set them by a half-filled bucket that appeared to be what Jarvis used for shaving, what with the flecks of cream and hair floating in the water. He shoved aside some old newspapers to make room for them before he dragged the second chair to sit directly across from her. Once more, his eyes darted to the empty whiskey bottles. This had Wellington written all over it. He knew Wellington's numbers were continually growing, sometimes without reason. *Has he stooped so low as to turn some of the workers against the Dupré family?*

It was the easy answer and the most likely, yet how could Cullen alert Willow to the fact that Wellington might have hired a saboteur without putting the case in danger? "Well, let me see if I can spot any discrepancies." He gave a short laugh as he flipped open the first book. "I must confess, however, I'm probably not as good as Day is with the books, judging from my past business failures."

Willow laid a hand on his shoulder. "I've full confidence in you. It has been years since your business *almost* failed, *and* you have been mentored since then."

Mentored by Wellington. If she only knew the truth, she would treat him like the pariah he was. He studied her, enjoying seeing this side of her as she tossed aside her plain navy hat and pored over the ledgers with a practiced eye.

After an hour of diligent searching, Willow leaned back and sighed. "I fear I see no reason for the numbers to be so down." She ran her fingers through her hair, ruffling her locks.

He pushed himself up and checked the coffeepot he had put on the stove. The handle singed his forefinger. Quelling a choice expletive, Cullen stuck his finger in his mouth and grabbed the two least questionable mugs available. He poured them each a cup and slid one to her, along with a grimy bowl of sugar, giving her an apologetic shrug at the lack of cream. She murmured her thanks, returning to her ledger.

Cullen drew a steadying sip. "Have you considered that Wellington may have hired someone on the inside of the factory? Someone to dispose of the final product or mayhap steal it and relabel it?"

Willow's gaze flashed up to him, her mouth agape. "Would he be so bold? That would explain a lot, especially why the numbers are not adding up after they reach production. While most of the workers are loyal to the company, there could be a few who may be dissatisfied with the change in leadership. But how would I go about exposing the one who is stealing the products from us?"

Cullen ran his hand over his jaw. If he could ask the Pinkerton Agency to investigate this on the grounds of Wellington's possible involvement, perhaps he could help Willow take down Wellington. "How do you feel about getting your hands dirty?"

Willow sat up straight. "I would never resort to any violence unless it was in defense of my being, or of course my family."

"I meant more along the lines of our going undercover and working alongside the factory workers to hear what we can for a day, possibly two if we uncover naught."

Her lips curved upward. "I like it."

"It will be long hours of hard labor. Are you certain you can handle it?"

"I may seem like a kid-gloved businesswoman, but I assure you, sir, I'm quite strong."

"Will your parents be fine with your stepping away from the competition for so long . . . and without a chaperone?"

"They will if they think I'm on an outing with you. And if

working girls do not need a chaperone while courting, I believe I will be more than safe with a former boxer nearby to protect me if needed." She extended her hand to him. "Will you join me in weeding out the traitor?"

"Nothing would give me greater satisfaction."

Nineteen

Doesn't Willow realize how humiliating it is to be paraded about on a public outing with a second suitor at this stage in the game? Theodore leaned against a red maple in Central Park and gripped his croquet mallet, his knuckles turning white as he observed Willow lining up her next shot. Fritz stood behind her, offering her completely unnecessary aid in how she should position her body and how he would angle the wooden ball so as to send it through the most hoops. Theodore grunted as he tore his gaze from them, lifted his face to the budding red clusters above him, and exhaled.

He *would* say something to keep the man from touching Willow's waist again, save for the onlookers surrounding their little playing field, who barely gave the trio enough room to play, much less converse in private. And no matter how much he scowled at the observers, they would not take the intimation and move along. At the fluttering lace handkerchiefs and tittering women waving to him and casting him what he guessed were their most alluring gazes, Theodore supposed that they would not easily relinquish the chance of finding out who was in the lead for Willow's heart . . . and heaven help the poor sap who placed second with all these women ready to pounce on him.

At Fritz touching her arm a second time, Theodore shoved off the rough bark with a grumble, took his aim, and whacked the ball directly into Fritz's and sent it rolling down the hill and as far out of bounds as he could have hoped. Fritz threw him a look before trotting down the hill for his turn, leaving Theodore alone at last with Willow . . . as alone as they could be with all of Central Park observing them, judging him.

"What's wrong?" Willow whispered as she adjusted her straw hat to shield her face from the sun, her attention focused on Fritz below trying to hit his ball out of the weeds surrounding the pond it had nearly rolled into. "You have been out of sorts all afternoon."

Theodore thought about swallowing back his true feelings, just as he had for the past few months. But if he and Willow were to wed, he knew he had to be honest with her, no matter how painful it was to admit his growing agitation with her. He ran his fingers through his hair, sending the ladies around them to moaning behind painted fans, whispering away. Exasperated, he gently took Willow's elbow and turned her to the trunk of the maple to keep the onlookers from trying to make out what he was saying. "You really wish to know?"

"Of course. If something is amiss between us, I want to know about it so that I might attempt to make amends."

Very well. He rested his hand above her head against the bark, leaning in as if they were sharing a sweet moment instead of the lover's quarrel brewing inside him. "Will, it's been a week since you first brought Cullen to the sugar factory, and since then you've brought him a second time, and Fritz too, which I understood, *at first*. But every single day since, I have found myself at home, *waiting* for my invitation to join you. How do you think this makes me feel when you are gone and I am left twiddling my thumbs, especially when I know we returned to New York to help you run the factory to see if we were a good match in business as well as in life?"

"Oh." Her lashes swept her cheeks, but he ignored her rising color and pressed on to the heart of the matter.

"And then when you finally do lift your nose from your ledgers to look at me, you ask me on an outing *with another suitor* and on display for all of New York to witness my mortification at seeing you with another man when you *know* how I feel." He lowered his brows to a point but did not take his gaze from her. This was too important. "We need privacy, Will. I cannot speak freely to you when I know another suitor is near."

She rested both hands atop her mallet handle, at last looking up at him. "You are absolutely right. I've been so caught up with trying to discover the discrepancies in the ledgers that I hurt you in the process." She rested her hand on his arm. "It was thoughtless and, I see now, hurtful. Please forgive me?"

But before he could reply, Fritz came trotting up again behind Willow, sweeping her into a waltz. Theodore kicked at Willow's wooden ball, mumbling, "As I said, no privacy." He glared at Fritz's back as they waltzed among the hoops.

"Miss Dupré!" a reporter called from the crowd. "Give us something to write about. Kiss him! Kiss him!"

Her cheeks reddened, though she gave no other indication that she had heard him. But Fritz must have, as he started to lean down to her, lips pursed. If Fritz wanted to play this way, Theodore would no longer hold back. Casting aside his mallet, he cracked his knuckles and strode toward the whirling couple as the crowd shouted for a kiss worthy of the newspapers.

Cullen stepped inside the dim Irish public house, scanning the room for Flannery, eager to share what he had observed while working as a factory laborer during the past week for Dupré Sucré. Cullen believed he had narrowed down the location of the theft to the loading docks. It seemed that at all points in the workplace, the amount of sugar remained the same, even when it was packaged. So the theft must have occurred *after* being packaged, which would mean the Duprés had lost significantly more money than if somebody was stealing the raw sugar directly from the cylinders, or even the crystallized sugar, but instead waiting for the entire process to be completed before stealing the products, which would most likely occur when the wagons left for their various deliveries. It would be easy enough if the driver was in on the theft . . . easier still if the foreman, or someone with access to the ledgers, was on Wellington's payroll. With this news in hand, he sank down on a chair across from Flannery and, in the hum of the pub, presented his findings.

For the first time since their meeting, Flannery's eyes were bright, his smile wide. "If this is indeed true," he said while tapping his notebook of Cullen's accounts, "all we need to do is find *where* the warehouse is that's storing the stolen goods, which should be easy enough now that you have narrowed down the point of exit. Then we need to discover how Wellington is getting paid for the product. If the money trail leads to one of Wellington's bank accounts"—he leaned back in his chair, grinning—"then we've got him."

Cullen nodded and ran his hands down his slack jaw. After all this time collecting documents, writing down what he had witnessed with Wellington's dealings, and presenting all he'd learned to the Pinkerton Agency, the answer was far simpler than he could have imagined. Despite all of Wellington's efforts in covering his tracks and using others as pawns, Wellington's weakness for collecting wealth, and therefore status, would betray him in the end.

"Do you know when the products are shipped out next?"

"In two days," Cullen replied.

"Then I suggest you involve Miss Dupré for the sugar caper."

Cullen's heart started hammering. "You mean I can tell her

everything now that I have helped you?" *Now that I can taste my freedom?*

Flannery paused as the barkeep brought him a steaming shepherd's pie and a tankard before continuing. "I think now would be a good time to have the lady assist you, as it would be a smoother way for you to tell her what is going on . . . after." He looked at Cullen pointedly. "Meaning *after* I find the money trail leading back to Wellington. Then, and only then, can you confess all to her. Since she was on the discovery portion of this sordid affair with you, perhaps she will forgive you for lying to her in the first place and accept Wellington's arrest as your redemption."

Cullen did not like the manipulation, but seeing as he had no other hope of winning Willow's hand, he nodded. *Lord, let this all work out. Because if it doesn't . . . I don't even want to think of a life without Willow Dupré.*

"Now, go find her. And make sure you aren't spotted leaving here." Flannery shoveled the layered mashed potatoes, peas, and beef onto his spoon, dropping his gaze to his paper.

Without another word, Cullen slipped from the table and headed toward Central Park where he knew Willow was on an outing. Cullen of the prior year would have disliked being alone with his thoughts, but now he had a sense of peace that God was using him. *Lord, thank you for this new purpose in my life. Please protect Willow from my past folly and let me be the man she believes me to be.*

The sounds of shouting broke his prayer, and the shouter sounded familiar. *Willow?* He broke into a run down the path, rounding Croton's Reservoir where he found Theodore and Fritz in an all-out brawl, and Willow keeping the reporters at bay with a croquet mallet.

"Miss Dupré! Over here, Paxton West with *The World*. Have you always been this inept with your courtships?"

"Miss Dupré! Will the winner of this fight win your heart?

235

My paper is doing a poll," another reporter called, waving his pencil in the air.

"I told you to go away and leave us in peace!" Willow's voice cracked as she raised the mallet higher. "And *you* started this brawl in the first place. Stop spurring Mr. Day and Mr. Blythe on!"

Cullen trotted up beside her, sliding into position between them. "I would listen to the lady."

The reporter blinked. "I recognize you."

Willow's wide eyes met Cullen's before she whirled to the reporter. "Of course. He is *my* suitor."

The reporter narrowed his gaze and then shrugged. "I have enough for tomorrow's story. Thank you for the fantastic headline this will bring, Miss Dupré."

The mallet swung, but Cullen seized it in time. "Let him have his five minutes of fame." Cullen rushed to the brawling suitors and grabbed the shoulder of each, attempting to pull them apart, but Fritz's wayward blow caught him on the mouth and he tasted blood. He spat onto the grass. "Stop this *at once*. You are shaming Miss Dupré."

Willow threw herself between Fritz and Theodore, arms spread wide between them, her glare dangerous. "The next one to land a blow will have my *mother* to answer to."

Theodore wiped at his mouth with his sleeve, rolling his shoulders back. "And the next time, Fritz, you even think about *stealing* a kiss for no other reason than to show off for a bunch of jackal reporters, I'll break your jaw."

Willow's eyes widened at Theodore's rare show of possessiveness, but Cullen's fists curled inward in agreement. If he had been on the outing instead, Fritz would be on his way to the hospital.

For his answer, Fritz retrieved his hat and shoved his hands into his pockets, making his way down the dirt path, while Theodore had the gall to scowl at Willow before doing the same, the reporters and crowd dispersing.

"Thank you for your assistance, Mr. Dempsey," she whispered. "If you hadn't stopped me—"

"That young reporter would have had the column of a lifetime." Cullen sent her a wink and tucked her hand around his arm, pulling her away. "Would you mind if I joined you three?"

She laughed, gesturing to the broken hoops and mallet. "I think our outing is over."

He turned her to face him before he glanced back to ensure that he would not be overheard. "Then I shall ask you now. Is your Friday free?"

Her brows lifted. "It could be."

"Then have your maid find you a gown that is worthy of a factory girl. We are going undercover, because I think I have found out how your company is losing money."

Twenty

Willow paid close attention to the head girl's instructions on how to package sugar, even though she felt like she knew the process so well that she could do it with her eyes closed. She stifled a yawn from the early hour and tugged at the thin, plain gown she had her maid purchase for her and returned her focus to the speaker, who was now giving Willow such a glare that it made her straighten at once.

"At Dupré Sucré, we expect perfection. A package any less will have to be ripped open and started over, which is a waste in packaging *and* time, and that will not be tolerated." She pointed to a long table in the back row of stations. "You're to work beside Marta. If you've any questions, ask her. You've got today to prove yourself before your position is given to the next girl in line. Remember, there are always ten others behind you willing to take less for more work."

Willow nodded and stepped up beside Marta, watching her fingers fly, folding the paper this way and that before measuring the sugar for the package, tamping it and adding a fraction more, then weighing and finishing off the bag. "Amazing," she whispered.

"Not once you get the feel of it," Marta replied, but Willow could tell she was pleased. "What do I call you?"

Knowing it would be foolish to use even her sobriquet, Willow reached for a bag and answered, "Christine. It was my mother's name."

The girl reached for a third bag and snorted. "Well, Christine, you best get a move on or the door will be smacking you in that bustle of yours before you even know you are fired."

Bustle? Nicolette had warned her against it for her working-girl ensemble, yet Willow decided to wear her smallest for the occasion, because going without it felt almost indecent. She fumbled the folding of the wax paper, though she had seen the women perform the task countless times. Still, no matter how many times Willow attempted to get those perfectly folded edges, nothing seemed to work. After about twenty minutes of reworking the same package, Marta took pity on her and showed her how to do it.

For the next eight hours, Willow toiled until her fingers stung from the rough paper edges, her only break being a fifteen-minute lunch, which she used to mingle with the other women to discover any bits of gossip that could prove useful. Cullen had told her of his theories but had asked her to try to rule out any wrongdoing at the packaging station, as he had not been able to look into it. She kept alert while at her station, looking to spot any sign of a saboteur, and as each hour passed, she was certain a thief was the only way that the business was suffering. These girls had the fear of dismissal hovering over them. They would not fall below the expected number in production. As the hour neared for her ten-hour shift to end, Willow's fingers ached to slow from Marta's frantic pace, but she didn't want to lose her position and have her work be for naught. She had decided she would need to come back a second day to find out more when the warehouse door slid open. Glancing sideways, she saw a man enter whom she had not seen around before.

He wheeled away one of the carts filled with product ready for market that would then be loaded into a wagon for local distribution.

"Who is that man?" she whispered to Marta.

Marta jerked her head up and at once returned her focus to the bag at hand. "He's bringing the sugar to the vendors."

"Yes, but what's his name?" Had she been so busy with the men that she had lost her pulse on the company? It was the Dupré policy to review the foreman's notes on new employees at the beginning of every month, and she had attempted to take it a step further by meeting everyone in her employ . . . but perhaps she was being paranoid. Yet she had not found any signs of foul play during her day with the women, although she supposed she would have to come back a second day if she were to make certain all was aboveboard at the packaging stations.

"How should I know? There are so many workers here with constantly rotating shifts, it's impossible to keep them all straight when one should be keeping her head down and *keep working*, which you need to do or we'll both get our pay slashed for gabbing."

A second man came for the other cart, and a third, and then came Cullen, dressed as the rest of the men in brown trousers held up with worn leather suspenders. His plain cotton sleeves were rolled up to his elbows, revealing his tan, corded forearms. He cut an impressive figure. His gaze flicked to Willow, silently asking if she was well.

She gave a discreet nod and waited for him to exit. "I need to use the necessary," she whispered to Marta.

"You should wait. We are almost done."

"I cannot." Willow shifted from foot to foot to emphasize her need.

Marta began to package at an even faster rate, a feat Willow didn't think possible. "Be quick. I'll tell the head girl when she asks, but I'll not be dismissed on account of you slowing our station."

Willow slipped out of the warehouse and watched the men load the carts onto emerald painted wagons, clearly marked with *Dupré Sucré* on the side in gold lettering. Cart after cart rolled out to fill up the wagons. When the last three carts arrived, Cullen moved to finish loading his, but Jarvis waved him away, not recognizing Cullen as her suitor in his workman's attire and grimy face.

"Special order. Leave them. Take your wagon to this address." Jarvis shoved a paper into Cullen's chest. "Do *not* be late."

Willow had triple-checked the orders in her ledger. There was *no* special order that she knew of. *Cullen is right. This must be where the thefts are occurring.* Sliding behind a row of rain barrels at the side of the building, she kept her eyes on the trio of carts. She settled to the ground, folding her legs underneath her, thanks to the simple style of skirt the factory girls sported, her bustle collapsing nicely beneath her weight. While she might be risking her position, it would be worth it if she actually saw the men stealing.

As the sun began to set and the heat of her body cooled, she longed for more than her dark green wool shawl for warmth, but she had waited too long to give up now, though her back and hands ached as if she had spent the afternoon rowing.

"Will?" Cullen's deep voice cut through the darkness. "Will? Are you still here?"

She dared to rise up on her knees and stiffly peek over the barrel. "Here," she whispered, waving him over. He darted behind the barrels, and she tugged him down to a seated position. "Quick. I hope we didn't alert the man picking those carts up." Her voice quaked from the cold, her shoulders twitching.

"You're freezing. Where's your cloak?" He shrugged out of his thick coat and wrapped her in it, the masculine scent of sandalwood melting her at once.

"Working girls don't wear cloaks," she returned, still shivering despite the warmth of his coat.

"Come here." He pulled her into his massive arms, tucking her head to his chest. To her surprise, she let him. "I'll keep a lookout."

It had been so long since she had been able to, wanted to, accept help from someone else. After her father's illness, she had no one to share her burden. But then Cullen had showed up with his grand ideas of helping her to save her business—Cullen, who always seemed to arrive at just the right moment.

"You should've signaled to me. I've been frantic searching for you."

She looked over her shoulder at him. "You were worried about me?"

"Certainly. Your parents would've had me thrown in jail for losing you."

Though he was jesting, the nearness of him was enough to make the world fade away. She studied his jaw, reached up and brushed the sharp outline with her fingertips, drawing his head down to meet her gaze, his dark hair falling down into his eyes. What had she done? She jerked her hand away and shifted to move, but his arms tightened about her.

"It is impossible not to love you," he whispered.

"Are you trying *not* to love me, sir?"

"And failing miserably."

Her heart thudded. *Say it, Cullen. Say that you love me and end this competition.* She ran her finger over the stubble beneath his sideburns.

His eyes flickered with a heat that Willow felt reflected in her own heart. "But I shouldn't. There are things in my past . . . and present that would make it too difficult for us to be together."

She turned in his arms to face him. "My father's solicitor has looked into each of my suitors. Father wouldn't present me with someone he thought would not be right for me."

He bent his lips to her, his warm breath bringing a longing to be nearer still to him. "Your kisses are not meant to be taken."

"For you, I shall gladly give one." She held herself perfectly still, willing him to kiss her at last.

He hesitated, then slowly slid his hand at the base of her neck and drew her to him, lowering his lips to hers. Willow's arms wrapped around his neck, pulling herself closer, wishing he would keep kissing her and that she could go on kissing him forever.

The squeak of a cart being moved shattered their moment as they both became aware of their arms tangled in the other's. Willow adjusted herself to watch the last cart being wheeled down the dock. Cullen took her hand and silently tugged her to her feet to follow the man to the end of the dock to where he loaded it onto an unmarked wagon, along with five other carts full of product.

"Looks like we'll have to trot to keep up. You ready for a run, Miss Dupré?"

But before she could reply, the wagon was on the move.

The wagon finally stopped in front of a warehouse Cullen had thought he would never have to see again. Memories of his father flooded his being as Cullen stood before the building he had allowed to fall into complete disrepair since that wretched day. Willow's heavy breathing wrenched him back into the present, and he turned to find her bent over double, her hand pinching her side. He closed the gap between them. "Are you unwell?"

She waved him off, gasping for air and motioning to the warehouse. "Shall we?"

Cullen's mind raced, attempting to find a reason why he could not go inside . . . but any lie he told now would be uncovered when Willow would surely follow through with an official investigation. "Now that we have discovered the warehouse, isn't it enough? Don't we need to return home? It's now eight of the clock and I am certain your mother—"

"I told her we were having our outing and I may have hinted that we were taking dinner at Flora's, so she will not expect us home until ten." She drew in a ragged breath and straightened, tossing Cullen his coat. "Aren't you dying to go inside and find out who owns this place? We ran all that way."

Cullen felt a stab of guilt and knew if he stopped to pray about what to do, he would know the answer, and he did not wish to lose her. Even so, he couldn't lie his way out of this. *Lord, please help me through.* He forced himself to lift his gaze to the derelict building, images flashing before his eyes. He shook his head free of them. "I cannot."

"What? Why on earth not?"

"Because I know the owner." He watched her small fists clench at her sides, and if he wasn't so full of regret for his rueful beginnings, he would have thought it endearing.

"Is it Wellington?"

"No." He turned to face her. "It's me."

She tilted her chin, confusion clouding her expression as she looked from him to the building and back to him. "You? But it looks like it hasn't seen use in ages."

He slowly nodded. "I abandoned it after I found my father here. There is an office connected to the back of the warehouse where he would conduct his business." *And entertain his mistresses and gambling partners.*

Willow pressed a hand to her chest, her eyes wide in the moonlight. "When you say *found* . . ."

Cullen ran his fingers through his hair. "I mean slumped over at his desk. The doctors say it was an attack of the heart."

Tears brimming, she reached for his hand. "You never told me it was that . . ."

"I didn't wish to alarm you, not with your father's present

condition. And besides, I do not entirely believe it was an attack. There were too many extenuating circumstances for it to be that simple." He thought of the piles of scraps of paper scribbled in drunken, hasty notes of debts owed, no doubt issued in the heat of gambling.

"I am so sorry, Cullen. I had no idea." Her eyes darted back to the warehouse. "I will not press you to go inside."

"But that does not give us much light on the matter at hand. Why would someone be using *my* warehouse?"

At the sound of the door being scraped open once more, Cullen pulled her into the shadows of an alley and watched as the wagon rolled out and a man in a greatcoat threaded the warehouse door handle with a long chain that showed signs of rust and fastened a padlock through the links.

Willow kept still against him until the wagon rolled away into the night. Cullen lifted a finger to his lips and slipped ahead, looking up and down the street before signaling her from her hiding place. She hurried over to him under the dirty windowpanes and attempted to peer inside.

Cullen wiped away his smile at her attempt to hop up enough to catch a glance. On her third try, he wrapped his hands about her waist and lifted her straight up.

"Oh!" She flailed, her hands grabbing wildly and smacking him in the nose, trailing down his jaw before landing atop his hands at her waist.

"Ouch."

"Sorry."

"Stop flailing." He kept his head away from her hands, uncertain if he could trust her not to grab his nose if she felt like she was falling. "I've got you. See if you can make out anything inside."

She leaned forward, and he heard the squeak of fabric against glass and grimaced at the obvious mark it would leave behind.

"I see canvases draped over piles that *have* to be the sugar.

There are loads more in here besides the wagonful tonight. Whoever is using your warehouse has been tapping off the company for some time."

Cullen lowered her feet to the cobblestones. "I think it's best we return home. Do you trust me to investigate this and discover who is using my warehouse without my knowledge?"

"Of course. And now that I know for certain about the stealing, I can hire a guard for the sugar shipments until we can find the thief." Her stomach rumbled, bringing a pretty hue to her pale cheeks. She pressed a hand to her petite waist. "This helps explain our slower year."

"I *did* promise you dinner. If we are finished sleuthing for the night, perhaps you'd like to join me?"

She gestured to her plain gown. "We can't go anywhere dressed like this."

He shoved his hands into his pockets, hunching his shoulders against the cold. "Maybe not anywhere that you would know, but back in my boxing days, I would frequent many places in this area. There's a respectable restaurant a couple of blocks away, if you are interested."

She looked around, tensing, as if suddenly aware of her surroundings. Cullen held out his hand to her. "No one will bother you when you are with me."

She wrapped her hands around his, a little firmer than usual, betraying her uneasiness. "I know."

He drew her away from the dark building and its ghosts, walking at a clipped pace until they reached a flickering streetlamp and slowed in its reassuring glow, his focus on the corner eatery and its guests whom he could hear from here. "Better?"

"Much. Thank you for today."

"I regret that we didn't work together, but I think we made up for it while waiting for the thief." He grinned. "Something I would very much like to repeat in the future."

She ducked her head sweetly but did not admonish his boldness, which led him to believe she wanted to kiss him as much as he did her. He held the door for her, the once-cheery red paint peeling from years of exposure to the elements, the sounds of merriment greeting them, the guests rowdy with the lateness of the hour. He found a table for them, not in the corner as he had hoped, but in the middle. Seating Willow, he waded through the group to fetch two coffees and place an order for Irish beef stew, keeping her in the corner of his eye at all times. Seeing a fellow approach her, Cullen tossed his coins to the man behind the bar and didn't wait for change but wove back through the guests to her side.

"I said I am with someone." She gave the fellow her regal scowl, drawing herself up as much as possible while seated.

The fellow chuckled, lifting a mud-encrusted boot onto the opposite seat, leaning on his knee toward her. "Then he shouldn't have left such a pretty girl alone."

"*He is right here,*" Cullen growled, squaring his shoulders and raising himself to his full height. "I suggest you listen to the lady and step away."

"As I live and breathe, it's the Irish Wild Man," someone nearby shouted, bringing the room into awed murmurs, every eye turning to him, which made the fellow at once dart back from Willow.

He lifted his hands, taking another pace backward and bumping into guests. "I don't want no trouble. Sorry, miss."

"You won't have it if you listen to the lady," Cullen shot back before taking his seat across from Willow and glaring at the man until he vanished into the crowd.

"Welcome back, Cullen. What's been keeping you away for so long from my fine establishment?" the round proprietor asked in a thick brogue, sliding a coffee to Cullen and setting one before Willow in clean albeit chipped mugs.

"This one has been keeping me on my feet." Cullen reached across the table, taking her hand and sliding into the familiar accent he had been trained to curb once his family had moved to Fifth Avenue.

"Glad to see you settling down." He looked to Willow, his toothless grin overtaking his features. "We knew it would take a special lassie to keep Wild Man out of the ring. Nice to see our hero smiling for the first time since I've known him."

She turned to the proprietor with a smile, bringing those delightful dimples to light at the corners of her bottom lip. "Was our hero always so focused?"

He nodded, his fuzzy gray brows rising. "Pity the man in the ring where those Irish eyes were fixed." He rubbed his hands down his filthy, mottled apron. "Well, let me know if you have need of anything else. It's on the house for the Wild Man."

Willow turned sparkling eyes to him. "They love you here. I take it that you frequented this establishment more than a handful of times."

He leaned forward on the scarred tabletop, gripping the mug in his hands. "After every fight. 'Tis an Irish restaurant if you haven't figured that part out yet."

"May I ask why your brogue isn't usually stronger? I catch whispers of it occasionally in your words, but never more than that." She gestured to the proprietor. "But when you were speaking with him, you sounded like another man."

"My mother and father drilled it out of me. When I am exhausted, or comfortable, I usually slip into the lilt." He shrugged. "It's not as if I am still *trying* to omit my brogue anymore, but it has been so long since I was allowed to speak so around my mother. When we moved to that mausoleum on Fifth when I was ten, I was told to leave behind the old ways."

"And yet, in the ring, you claimed your heritage." She tucked a curl behind her ear and reached for her cup. "How did you come about the name of Wild Man?"

He grinned. "Before every bout, my mentor told me to 'fight

like a wild man,' and well, the name stuck. I added the Irish part later."

"I am glad you did. It is important to remember where we come from and the people that made us who we are today."

A serving girl laid two beef stews on the table along with spoons, her hand grazing across Cullen's shoulder as she departed, earning a scowl from Willow.

"I was told that your set did not like to parade about such things as ignoble beginnings." He shoveled a boiled potato in his mouth, the delightful herbs bringing the simple vegetable to life.

"Ignoble? Is that what your mother and father taught you?" She set down her spoon. "Then allow me to set the record straight. I am the great-granddaughter of French *peasants*, hence Dupré."

"But you *are* descended from English lords, as well," he gently corrected. Try as she might to relate with him, she did not know what it was like.

"My mother is the granddaughter of a baron, and as one of the lower lords, there were no subsidiary titles to pass on to their children or grandchildren." She lifted her brows as if her point was made, but the complicated English aristocracy family tree had always eluded Cullen. "I could go on and tell you the origin of all the new money residents who have managed to secure a position in the New York Four Hundred, but I don't think it is necessary. Money does not make us noble. Character does."

Character. He shifted in his chair. He thought he had character once, but one poor decision made in fear had become a second and then a third, until he had become so ensnared in his lies that he hardly recognized himself. But since he had been with Willow, Cullen had remembered who he was and returned to the feet of Jesus.

"Cullen, I want you to feel relaxed around me. I want nothing but the real Cullen. And if it helps"—she looked up at him through her long lashes—"I find your brogue striking."

"Very well, *macushla*." *My darling*. He stroked her hand, never wanting this evening to end and wishing he could be the man she thought him to be.

Stews finished and second cups of coffee consumed, he glanced at his worn gold-plated pocket watch, the positions of the hands sending him to his feet. "We've let time get away from us. We best make our way home at once lest your father send the police looking for you." He flipped the watch face for her to see.

Her jovial expression disappeared. "They're going to be livid."

In moments, Willow was settled in a hired carriage beside Cullen, pulling over the Brooklyn Bridge that was quite eerie at the hour. Only a few pedestrians tottered past, swaying in the center lane, and they did not look like the sort of people he wanted near Willow. He decided, though, that with the trolley line separating their lane from the pedestrians, they were safe enough. Soon they were off the bridge, and the ensuing silence covered them like the fog hovering over the cobblestone streets.

"Thank you for trusting me and showing me part of your world." She took his hand in hers. "Thank you."

Cullen's confusion wedged in his throat. "Willow, I want to share everything with you, but there are things you would not—" The carriage halted in front of the mansion, and Cullen grimaced at the lights ablaze in the parlor. He had missed his feeble chance to confess. *Probably for the best, until Flannery gives me the signal*. He sighed, digging into his pockets for a few coins to hand the driver. *Lord, help me be patient.*

"Make haste. We cannot linger." She scooted across the cracked leather seat and hopped out of the carriage before he could help her and led him past Beckwith, her parents appearing in the hall at once.

Mr. Dupré glared at him. "You do realize you are making it quite difficult for me to keep my daughter's reputation pure when you are out, heaven knows where, until *eleven o'clock?*" He turned his frown to Willow. "Your mother was sick with worrying over you for the past hour. We sent a messenger to Flora's brownstone, only to find that you were *never* there. What do you have to say for yourself?"

Willow shed her shawl. "I know it was foolish, but—"

"And what are you wearing?" Mrs. Dupré clicked her tongue, grazing Willow's sleeve with her fingertips.

The twins poked their heads over the second-floor balcony, watching them, jaws dropped as if this were the most diverting novel they had ever read.

"I beg your pardon, sir. I lost track of time," Cullen admitted.

"Someone in Willow's position does not have the luxury to lose track of time," Mr. Dupré crossed his arms. "I expected more from you, Dempsey, and I fully expect an explanation in the morning."

The disappointment edging his voice was almost too great to bear. "I sincerely apologize for causing you all such worry, Mrs. and Mr. Dupré. I never would have—"

"Willow, do you know how difficult it is to entertain two gentlemen who are acutely aware that their sweetheart is off with another man *unchaperoned*?" Mrs. Dupré interjected, pinching the bridge of her nose and drawing in a deep breath. "Please at least tell me that you were in a public location for the late hour?"

"We were well-chaperoned in a restaurant. No one recognized me."

Mrs. Dupré released her breath. "Well, at least there is that. Now, get yourself to bed. You all have a fitting tomorrow morning for your costumes for Alva Vanderbilt's ball. The invitation arrived here while we were in Newport and no one thought to forward it, so we must make haste. We have less than three weeks to prepare for what is being touted as the grandest ball New York society has ever seen."

Willow gritted her teeth. "Did you say costume?"

"It's a costume ball, and as you *must* all wear a costume, I have taken the liberty of designing a piece for you and the gentlemen." She lifted her hands, shooing everyone to the stairs. "Now to bed. I expect *everyone* to be ready for their fittings first thing in the morning, when I also expect a *full* explanation for the pair of you being found wearing such drab clothes."

Twenty-One

In the weeks since Willow's adventure as a factory girl, Cullen assured her that he was on the cusp of having enough evidence to get a conviction for the man he suspected was behind the thefts. So, Willow entrusted him with a key to the back gate and a key to the servants' entrance to help him tend to the situation without much ado from the staff. With his promise to keep investigating and her hiring of a guard for the shipments, Willow rested in the fact that while they had yet to catch those responsible, they had at least stopped the thieving and so the numbers would be up in next month's report.

She then shifted her focus to her relationships with Teddy and Fritz, partly to make up for her insensitivity regarding her private dinner with Cullen. And it seemed her efforts were rewarded, as the hostility between Fritz and Teddy had ebbed a bit. She had even found them playing cards together. As for Teddy, she brought him to the office a half-dozen times, always followed by a private tea or meal, with Flora or the twins acting as chaperone. Yet the more time she spent with Fritz, the more she wavered in the choice that lay before her. Fritz was impossibly kind and thoughtful, but would those traits be enough for a marriage?

As the day of Alva Vanderbilt's costume ball neared, so did her final laurel ceremony. Another week and she would be engaged, but thankfully society was so distracted with preparing for the ball that parlors across New York were no longer filled with only the fantastical stories surrounding Willow but with hushed whispers of who was escorting whom. This was closely followed by hints of elaborate costume gowns being created by the city's best one hundred and forty seamstresses, who were busy working day and night to finish the orders in time. Willow had heard that twelve hundred invitations had been issued, and those who had not been invited were devastated, a fact her mother reminded her of in the days leading up to the ball during the countless fittings of her costume between outings with her gentlemen.

Now that the evening for the ball had finally arrived, Willow could see why her mother had been so determined that her gown be perfect. It was indeed a masterpiece, and for once she felt like the queen society had dubbed her. For this one evening, she would set aside her cares of repairing the damage of Archie's continuous scathing articles, of theft and of choosing a husband, and enjoy herself. Willow smiled at the three gentlemen seated in her closed carriage as they rolled up to the Vanderbilt mansion on Fifth Avenue and 52nd Street, five minutes to the eleventh hour, already in line behind several carriages.

Teddy leaned out the window and commented, "Seems to be quite the line. It's a good thing we arrived a little early or we would not have been able to get so close to the door." He settled back into the tufted leather seat, chuckling to himself. "You should see the costumes coming out of the carriages. I wouldn't be caught dead in some of those outfits."

"Speaking of costumes," Cullen said, turning to Willow, "you still haven't even hinted at what you are wearing."

She kept her full-length golden cloak with its pearl-lined

hem firmly fastened about her gown so as not to reveal her costume before she was inside. Clutching the heavy velvet bag her mother had thrust into her hands as they departed for the party, she replied, "And neither have you, given you were all wearing your outerwear before I had a chance to discover your costumes."

Fritz sighed. "I really don't like not knowing things, but I hope it will at least explain why your mother put us in such uncomfortable costumes."

Willow laughed as the carriage pulled up to the door and the men piled out first, Cullen and Teddy lifting their hands to escort her down from the carriage. The onlookers pressed in from all sides, blocked only by the presence of the police, who had formed a chain with their arms to keep the people at bay, their arms shaking with the effort as they dug their heels into the sidewalk, leaning back on the persistent, clamoring crowd. Cullen kept one arm around her, throwing out his other to block the flowers being showered upon them, while Teddy kept her arm tucked firmly in his as Fritz waved to the crowd, caught a rose and lifted it to her, making the crowd go mad with the romance of it all when Willow accepted it.

"I'll take your second choice, Miss Dupré!" a lady called out.

"I'd take any of her castoffs! I'm not picky," another called, sending the crowd into laughter.

Teddy sent the ladies a wave, and the trio strode through the dazzlingly white marble doorway into the stone hall with its oak-paneled ceilings lit by Japanese lanterns dangling from ribbons between the matching stone columns. Willow's eyes widened at the crowd within, which appeared to be pressing toward the French-styled drawing room.

"If you will take the stairs, there is a bedroom where the lady may refresh herself." A butler in blue livery and sporting a bored expression held out his hand to her, motioning toward the stairs.

"I have no need to refresh myself at the moment, but if you would help me with my cloak?" She pushed back her hood.

Cullen moved to take the golden cloak from her shoulders, but Fritz was already there.

"Willow . . ." Cullen's jaw dropped as she turned. "You are—"

"I am Queen Guinevere." She released her hold on her train and adjusted the long flaring sleeves of her emerald medieval gown, running her hands down the bodice with its hundreds of pearls and diamonds sewn into the centers of embroidered crimson roses, which cascaded down to her waist to a golden belt forged in the image of laurels that encircled her slim hips. The gown's emerald silk imitated a waterfall of embroidered vines and more roses with diamonds that shimmered and fell into the train behind her that swept the floor. She lifted her hand to ensure her golden crown of laurels was still firmly in place and pulled her long braid over her shoulder. "And now, sirs, prithee show yourselves."

The men shed their capes, and her heart clenched at the sight of them as they bowed to her dressed as knights in chain mail with her mother's family crest upon their chests. Teddy was King Arthur. Cullen, Sir Lancelot. Fritz . . . ? She tapped her chin. "And you are?"

Fritz moaned, shaking his head. "See? No one thinks of Sir Gawain."

"It is an honor to be escorted by you, sirs. Now for the finishing touch to our ensembles." Willow stepped aside as King Lear and his three daughters passed by, the girls all craning their necks to catch a glimpse of Willow's gentlemen. Pausing in the hall before a towering, cascading display of roses arranged for a waterfall effect, Willow opened the velvet bag her mother had handed her, instructing her to open it in the foyer in front of the crowds. Willow inhaled sharply and withdrew three crowns that matched her own. Mother had thought of everything. "I will now crown my King Arthur, and knights, Sir Lancelot and Sir Gawain."

She lifted the first crown and held it out to Teddy. He knelt, drawing cries from the crowd behind him at the bottom of the stairs outside, who could see all through the open door, causing the arriving couple to frown that Willow was stealing their spotlight. After placing the crown on his head, she moved to Cullen, repeating the action and earning even more wild applause when Cullen caught her hand and kissed it.

Fritz bowed to her, his hand resting over his heart as she set the final crown atop his fiery locks. "And just because I am a lesser-known knight in the story does not mean I shall not try to win the fair maiden's hand. I'm only grateful I managed to convince your mother out of the Merlin's beard and costume she had originally chosen for me."

"Thank goodness for that," she laughed, then motioned her knights to draw near. "Shall we pay homage to Mrs. Vanderbilt?" She took Fritz's and Cullen's arms, positioning herself safely between the two of them, with Teddy breaking their way through the crowd. She adored the way they looked, crowned in laurels and clad in chain mail that accentuated their broad shoulders. Willow could feel the stares of everyone as she nodded to ladies she had long since known but had never truly held a decent conversation with beyond the niceties, though she admired their choice in costumes. "Lovely Phoenix costume, Mrs. Lorillard." She curtsied. "Your red wig is splendid for your Queen Elizabeth costume, Mrs. Stevens." She passed a Miss Fish but did not recognize the royal costume with its pointed cap and gold gown. "Magnificent choice, Miss Fish."

When it was their turn to approach the settee, where Mrs. Vanderbilt and Lady Mandeville perched greeting the guests, Mrs. Vanderbilt motioned her forward, Willow openly admiring her impressive Venetian princess costume of white-and-yellow brocade. Willow curtsied as her men bowed.

"If it is not New York's fairest rose, Queen Guinevere." Mrs. Vanderbilt's gaze went at once to the gentlemen at Willow's side. "It is a pleasure to finally meet the remaining three suitors in your competition. How will you ever decide which one of these delightful knights to wed?"

"Mayhap she is simply being polite, for we all know the only choice is me." Teddy grinned, his comment earning retorts from Cullen and Fritz, which sent Mrs. Vanderbilt and Lady Mandeville into giggles behind their fans.

"Delightful. Now, Miss Dupré, I know your competition ends in a few days' time, with a wedding no less, so I hope the ball I have planned will illuminate which fellow you wish to marry. I feel compelled to warn you, however, that all the ladies will be after your beaus tonight. For with the press you have been receiving regarding your gentlemen, they have become the most eligible bachelors of society." Mrs. Vanderbilt winked at Willow and gestured for her to continue onward. "Enjoy the evening, my dears. You had best return to the grand staircase lest you miss the descent of the quadrilles."

"We don't want to miss that sight," Cullen whispered in Willow's ear as the next in line greeted Mrs. Vanderbilt and Lady Mandeville. "And once the quadrilles have been performed, I wish to escort you to the first dance."

Teddy tensed. "I should have thought of that. Why am I always a step behind?" he muttered under his breath.

"You shall have the first, King Arthur the second, and Sir Gawain the next. After that, there are no rules and you all must seek me out."

"Miss Dupré?" A cough sounded behind her.

Recognizing the nasal lilt at once, she turned to find the phrenologist. "Good evening, Harold."

"It is *Mr. Harolds* to those ladies I am not courting." He adjusted his tricornered hat and held a hand to his bullfighter's jacket, a perfect mirror of a matador. "Have you regretted your decisions thus far?"

Cullen tensed while Willow gently rested her hand on the gentleman's forearm and answered, "Mr. Harolds, I am confident I will find my husband among the remaining three men I have at my side tonight."

He pushed his spectacles back up his nose, studying the men. "I was wrong in my initial assessment of Fritz. With the crown upon his head, I can see by the bit of shape over his ear that he has the propensity toward destructiveness."

Cullen and Theodore laughed, but Fritz looked to be alarmed by the comment.

Willow frowned. "Maybe you should return to studying, Mr. Harolds, for I've never known a gentler soul than my Fritz."

Mr. Harolds adjusted his spectacles again. "Be that as it may—"

A trumpet sounded then, which thankfully gave Willow the excuse she needed to step away with her gentlemen and turn her attention to the quadrille groups descending the grand Caenstone staircase.

Cullen enjoyed watching the quadrilles perform to music from Gilmore's band. The hundred ladies and gentlemen performed admirably, setting his foot to tapping, and he wondered when the rest of the guests would be able to dance when the final quadrille was announced and the star quadrille, performed by ladies with a single star upon their foreheads, began. Willow, Queen Guinevere to his Lancelot, swayed with the music, her lips slightly parted with wonder at the perfect performance. Though he had initially thought it odd that Mrs. Dupré would choose such a scandalous tale for the costumes, he supposed it was a sort of parallel to the competition, a nod to the mystery of whom Willow would end up loving and choosing for a husband.

Someone knocked into his shoulder, and Cullen turned to find a guest dressed as a colonial highwayman in a mask, broad-brimmed hat, and a wooden model pistol in his belt. Cullen waited for the man to beg his pardon, but instead he simply stared at Cullen and tilted his head to the side door of the ballroom before weaving around courtiers, a swan, another Queen Elizabeth, and several pirates toward the exit. Seeing Theodore in his possessive stance beside Willow, Cullen slipped away unnoticed, keeping the highwayman in his view, who made his way up the grand staircase to the third floor where Cullen found himself in a makeshift forest of sorts, with palm trees, brilliant magenta flower-covered vines, and orchids filling every space.

Cullen's fists curled at his sides, his right bumping into the wooden sword at his belt. The build of this man was nothing like that of Agent Flannery, who never would have sought such a public place for a private audience. "Show yourself."

The highwayman appeared between potted palms on Cullen's left. "You betrayed me. And those who betray me will pay their forfeit."

Cullen's shoulders tensed. *Is he speaking of my trip to the warehouse with Willow? Or does he know about my involvement with the Pinkertons?* "Wellington. What do you want?"

"What I've always wanted—your loyalty." Wellington's eyes narrowed behind his mask, and Cullen could see the heat of his anger radiating through his grimace.

"I've given you what you've wanted."

He held up a gloved finger. "You gave me one pathetic hint of a factory and yet I still gave you the gift of time, and this is how you repay me?"

Still uncertain as to which betrayal Wellington was referring, Cullen laughed. "Are you going to expose my father's sins to the world and ruin my sister's chances because I failed in giving you more information?" He rolled his shoulders back. "Your threats are not good enough anymore. Willow taught me that there are more people like her than I was raised to believe, people who will look beyond the sins of my father and judge me and my family on our own merits."

"Like the merit you displayed by deceiving the city's darling?" He trilled his fingers against one another. "Society will not welcome you with open arms after a stunt like that."

Cullen frowned, not liking the man's pointed truth. He had acted like a cad in the beginning and now he must pay the price. Once more, Cullen prayed that Flannery would allow him to tell all to Willow before it all came out in the papers, and that his and Willow's relationship would make it through the storm ahead. "Whatever you throw at me for my punishment for not doing your bidding, I will take."

Wellington sneered and perched on the arm of an oversized velvet settee. "I went to warehouse seven. Where are my goods?"

Flannery moved them? His heart lifted. *If Flannery made such a telling move, then surely I can tell Willow any day now.* "I'm assuming you're speaking of the tons of *stolen* goods that you were keeping there to await relabeling."

"Who says they were stolen?" Wellington withdrew a cigar and held it to a nearby candelabra, lighting the end and drawing in quick consecutive puffs, bringing the cigar to life.

"Judging from the steady decline in profit of Dupré Sucré's sales, you've had this scheme in motion for quite some time."

He flicked his cigar, sending ashes fluttering atop Cullen's leather shoes. "Circumstantial."

Cullen locked eyes with the man. "Willow knows."

Wellington's cigar broke. He sputtered the wet pieces from his mouth. "What did you tell her?" He closed the distance between them before a slow smile pulled at his lips. "The public records will out you in a heartbeat. You just saved me the trouble of exposing your part in all of this, you love-sick fool."

"I told her the truth—that it was my warehouse, and that it was most likely *you* behind the theft. What I did not say is that

I know how to press men into confessing things . . . things that would leave you rotting in jail." At the flicker of fear behind the man's eyes, Cullen grinned. "And now I believe you see that I have the leverage I need to have you leave my family alone and allow me to gracefully bow out of your command. I will, of course, finish paying my debt to you, but I wish to have no further ties with you regarding the competition." Cullen turned on his heel to seek out Willow.

"You won't ever be done with me!" Wellington shouted after Cullen as he took the stairs two steps at a time. "Ever!"

Twenty-Two

Willow stifled a yawn, the clock on the Vanderbilts' mantel in the dining room chiming two o'clock in the morning. A footman removed her soup bowl, a note appearing on the golden charger that she had not noticed before. She looked over to see if Teddy had one, but as conversation was moving to the left, his head was not inclined toward her, and Cullen had mysteriously disappeared during the final quadrille. He had missed his dance with her and had not yet returned, though he had requested to be her partner for dinner. Fritz, seated across from her, sent her a questioning look over a floral arrangement before the lady beside him in a Joan of Arc costume of white china crepe that shimmered with fleurs-de-lis over solid-silver chain mail began speaking to him once more.

Willow slid her finger under the seal and unfolded the note.

> *Tonight you must select*
> *The suitor who is correct,*
> *Or the one to whom your heart belongs since first sight*
> *Will be destroyed the morning of your wedding at first*
>   *light.*

Willow jerked her head up to see if anyone had noticed her read it. *Is this a jest?* But all those about her were absorbed in their conversations. She read the note again, flipping it over. If it was a jest, it was in poor taste. She studied the fine penmanship, frowning. *Archie is no doubt overplaying his hand again.* Even still, her hand trembled as she moved to place it in her pocket before remembering that her costume did not have pockets like all her other dresses.

She crumpled the note in her fist and glanced around the table before dropping it under the tablecloth to the floor and ripping it to shreds with her silk slipper, wishing she could burn it. For a fleeting moment, she wondered if she shouldn't have left the note intact under the table in case one of the servants happened upon it and, seeing her place card directly above on the table, concluded that one of her beaus was in danger and then alerted the police. *Well, it would serve the writer of the message right if he were thrown in prison for such a cruel jest.*

"I am so sorry," Cullen said, returning to his seat. "I was pulled away during the quadrille by an old business acquaintance with a message for me, and when I returned, I found I had missed the opening dance and then was surrounded by a group of mothers and their daughters as dinner was being announced, and I barely escaped. What did I miss?" Looking at his empty charger, he gave a sigh. "Obviously the soup. I wait all night for a meal and then I miss it because I was trapped by husband hunters. Tell me, who serves a meal at two in the morning?"

Willow handed him an extra bread roll she had saved for him. "Hopefully this will stay your hunger pains until the next course."

"Was the soup delicious?" he asked after swallowing a mouthful of bread.

Willow patted her waist. "Oh yes. I overheard Mrs. Vanderbilt saying it was prepared by the chefs from Delmonico's. Did your friend keep you long?"

"Not really. But like I said, I kept getting stopped by mothers and their daughters." He frowned at his plate as he finished off the roll.

She ignored the thought of socialites throwing themselves in his path. "Was the message urgent?"

He waved a hand dismissively. "Not as important as missing our first dance of the evening and a meal from the best restaurant in New York beside my lady, I can tell you."

"Well, you really should not disappear without telling me where you are going and when you will be back." *Not when I am receiving notes like this.* She swallowed back her rising tone.

"Is the fair queen worried about her Lancelot?" He reached for her hand beneath the tablecloth.

"Well, Lancelot was the knight Guinevere favored most." She returned his jest with a weak smile, attempting to keep the note from ruining her mood. She had received threats before and had handled them, although this was the first one in regard to her beaus.

"I'll have to thank your mother with a gift for allowing me the honor of being the one the queen loved most. Dare I take that as a sign as to which knight she would choose for her daughter?" He gestured toward Fritz. "Poor fellow had to resort to being Sir Gawain. Most have no idea of his part in the Round Table."

Willow giggled and almost chided him that he should not take it as a hint, and yet her mother never did anything by chance. She glanced to Teddy, thoroughly engrossed in his conversation with Flora, who was dressed as a fairy queen in a filmy blush gown with gold embroidery. *She made Teddy the king . . . her preference is evident.* "I know she was deliberate in her choice."

"Then that makes this cumbersome chain mail and these itchy leggings quite worth it." He winked at her.

She lowered her voice, leaning toward him. "While I am

loath to change the subject, we have only six days left until the crowning."

He nodded, his expression somber. "I am well aware, which is another reason I am so sorry for keeping you waiting."

"I've been meaning to ask you . . . why *did* you agree to join in the competition?" Just then the next course arrived, a delicious-smelling chicken stuffed with butter and herbs that made her mouth water despite her serious question to Cullen.

Cullen nodded his thanks to the server but didn't bother lifting his fork and knife. "I'll admit that while my initial motives were not pure, the moment I met you, everything shifted in my heart. And all thoughts of saving my family and my business, though still important, were not as important as you."

Her heart thudded at his confession. "Why? What could I have possibly said or done to bring about such a drastic change?"

His hand once more found hers under the tablecloth. "It was your heart. I had heard of you, of course, before the competition. About how you were a calculating business-minded woman, and I am afraid that I assumed it must have been true if you were still single with such wealth tied to you."

That stung. She reached for her crystal glass to hide the pinch in her expression.

"Yet throughout that first night, I saw that you were kind to all, even those who were rather odd and ungentlemanly. And then, throughout this journey, I've seen the woman behind the rumors. You are gifted in business, but you have your faults."

She stiffened. This was not going as she had intended.

"The important thing, however, is that once you see that you are in the wrong, you own up to it." He ran his thumb over her hand. "You are lovely, inside and out. And fortune or no, any man would consider himself blessed to have you as his partner in life."

Willow lifted her lashes to meet his ardent gaze.

"Now, you must allow me to ask *you* something." He leaned toward her. "Why did you give me the first crown?"

She felt her cheeks flush and cleared her throat. "I say, the chicken will be too cold to eat if—"

"Please."

She exhaled and folded her hands, whispering so low that Cullen had to lean ever closer to hear her. "Because you intrigued me. A giant of a man who loves to dance. A man who is not from my usual circle but was invited to court me. A man who displayed confidence even when admitting to me that his business nearly failed, which means you had more experience than most men who simply inherited their fortunes or were given a successful business." She picked up her fork and knife, more to give her hands something to do than to eat. "And yes, I'll admit, I was taken by your looks. But there is a good heart in you, Cullen Dempsey, and I do not wish to see the last of you."

He grinned, but before he could respond, the conversation turned. Relieved to set aside the heaviness of the previous topic, the rest of the meal finished in a flurry of conversation with Teddy until soon Willow found herself being led by Cullen to the dance floor at long last.

"I have missed dancing with you." He turned her seamlessly in time to the Viennese waltz.

"As have I." She loved being this close to him as they glided silently around the ballroom floor with the crowd looking on. Cullen's question had awakened her to the fast-approaching deadline that had been lost in the blur of preparing for the ball. Following the ball, though, nothing would keep her from the glaring reality that was time.

If he would only confess his love for her, she knew she could end the competition at once. What was taking him so long? *Maybe he's not attracted to me?* He said she was "lovely," but that didn't mean he was attracted to her. She knew she wasn't a great beauty like Flora, but Willow had hoped Cullen would fall in love with her by now. But, remembering their kisses, she knew that lack of attraction couldn't be it.

If she had to choose today, she knew Cullen would be her instant choice, yet was passion enough for a marriage? Certainly they had enjoyed wonderful conversations together, and she greatly relished her time with him exploring the warehouse . . . and his kisses, but did she know him as well as she thought she did? Enough to gamble her business, her very life? And then there was Teddy, a man she knew from years before. And dear Fritz, who had taken her heart by complete surprise . . .

Lord, help me make the right choice come Saturday.

"You act as if you will never see her again." Theodore slapped Fritz on the shoulder, but the chain mail made the action sting his palm and did little to wake Fritz from the stupor he had been in since dinner.

"You are one to talk. You were seated beside her, with me across," he mumbled, leaning against the doorframe and watching Willow dance with Cullen *again.* "Joan of Arc never ceased her constant flow of questions even when the conversation turned, so I only caught parts of Willow's conversation." Fritz wiped at his brow with the back of his hand, wincing as the edge of the chain mail caught his forehead. "Joan was nice enough, but I am feeling the pressure of the final ceremony." He gestured toward Willow, laughing in Cullen's arms, whirling past them. "Don't you feel as though she is slipping away from you? And with her, your future happiness? Why aren't you in a panic like me?"

Because I know Willow shall pick me in the end. She may not be completely in love with me, but I know she does love me. He adjusted the sword on his belt that kept twisting to his backside. "She doesn't know Cullen well enough to pick him."

"She knows him as well as she does me, and *that* has me in

a frenzy." He pulled at the collar of his costume, revealing an angry red line at his neck. "And this chain mail is chafing me."

"Take a deep breath," Theodore said, glancing sideways at the Robin Hood character and his Maid Marian who were staring at them, whispering away to each other. "You are drawing undesirable notice."

Fritz scowled. "By all means, let us not show any undesirable traits when the woman I love is falling for someone else right before my eyes and kissing another behind my back."

"How romantic that this process is working." Flora approached in a cloud of soft pink, her golden and diamond-flecked wings sparkling in the candlelight.

Theodore bowed to her. "Care for a dance?" Without waiting for an answer, he swept her onto the dance floor, thankful to get his mind off Fritz's troubling observances.

"I hardly think dancing with another woman will help your case, Teddy," she teased. "You should know by now that your every action will be written about in tomorrow's papers."

"My apologies, but I had to escape from Fritz. I do believe he's cracking." He clicked his tongue and tapped the side of his head.

"The situation is enough to drive any young lover to madness." She shook her head, sending her curls to bobbing beneath her floral crown. "I don't know if I would have had the stomach to endure what she has put you all through."

"The thought of having her hand at the end of all this is the *only* thing that has kept me going."

She tensed under his hands. "You are confident then that she will choose you?"

"If I wasn't, I wouldn't be here."

At the end of the polka, Theodore did not tarry once he left Flora to distract Fritz. He wove through the guests to where Cullen had led her away from the suitors. "Will!" he called over the crowd for fear he would miss catching her. "Will!"

Nearby, ladies tittered behind their fans, but instead of parting for him, they drew closer, blinking their lashes at an astounding rate and arching their backs in such a way as to draw attention to their assets. He craned his neck to see over the ladies, calling desperately one last time for Willow when a hand grasped his shoulder.

"My king?" Willow grinned up at him, pulling him onto the dance floor for a slow waltz as the ladies groaned, murmuring how all the good men were taken by Willow's competition.

"Thank goodness you found me. The ladies here are relentless, and Fritz is positively overwhelmed with the timeline . . . even more so than me, which is hard to imagine."

"You are feeling overwhelmed, as well?"

"Of course. We only have until Saturday for you to make up your mind regarding whom you are going to marry on Sunday." Teddy inclined his head toward her, his expression subdued. "Can I ask you a question that has been burning inside me?"

"By all means, Teddy. You know you can ask me anything."

He guided her around a couple, who had fallen out of step with the rhythm. "If you don't know at this very moment who it is you are in love with and wish to marry, how on earth will you know by Saturday? And if you do not know yet and decide the morning of the final laurel ceremony, how is the man you choose going to know that you chose him because you *love* him and not because he is the one you fancied most that day?"

Willow bit her lip. "You were never one to sugarcoat your words and so neither will I. That very quandary has been plaguing me, as well. Regardless, I can tell you this, I've been taking careful accounts of our times together and will make an *informed* choice and not allow myself to be swept up in the emotion of the moment."

He sighed. "Will, I'm not talking about an informed business dealing. I'm talking about marriage. Two lives joining as one for *life*. Such a choice *does* affect the heart."

Willow shrugged, biting her lip again. "I don't know how to answer your question, but I know I will be ready when the time comes."

Teddy scowled, dissatisfied with her response. Still, glancing down at her furrowed brow, he nodded and gave her a smile. "Thank you for being honest. I know it must be difficult for you as well as for us. Now, let's talk about something more pleasant and, just for tonight, lose ourselves in the moment." Theodore twirled with her, pulling her closer. "For if losing ourselves means that I get to hold you in my arms until dawn, one night free from any thoughts of tomorrow cannot hurt."

The dancing lasted long into the night, and at dawn a Virginia reel was announced, which Alva Vanderbilt herself led. And when the final bar had been played, the party ended. Slowly the rooms began to empty of guests, all unwilling to return home after the social event of the century despite the hour.

Theodore sank down in a daze in the carriage seat beside Willow, the other two men sitting across from them. Willow stifled a yawn and waved to a friend as they rolled away from the mansion.

The streets had begun to come alive again, and a boy on the corner shouted, "Paper! Paper! Get your paper." He lifted high a newspaper, and Theodore could make out the large bold font crying *Vanderbilt* . . . and something else he couldn't quite read.

"At last, a story that doesn't revolve around me or my gentlemen." Willow closed her eyes with a contented sigh and rested her head on Theodore's shoulder.

Twenty-Three

I know you had a late night, but you have an announcement to make at the upcoming ball." Father lifted his cup to Beckwith at the family's afternoon tea in Mother's private salon, and the butler at once refilled it. "And with that in mind, we need to discuss the next item on our list this afternoon—Mr. Blythe."

Willow covered a yawn with her hand. It had been a chore to get out of bed at all after only falling asleep at six in the morning. But to summon enough energy to go on an outing? She set down her teacup. "It is not on the schedule."

Mother selected an iced cake from the tiered plates the butler was bringing round to each of them, the twins selecting more than they should and earning a disapproving shake of the head from Mother. Together they each returned a cookie to the tier.

"Willow, I am usually fine with your living by your appointment book, but this is not one of those times. Your father and I discussed it last night at great length, as we chose to stay home from the ball to put the finishing touches on your wedding on Sunday, and if I haven't stressed this enough, I will repeat it once more. Time is of the essence."

Time. The thought was enough to quash her appetite. She waved the tiered tray onward, choking down her tea. She had a choice to make and her own ball to attend in less than a week, followed by a wedding once the license was secured. *But Mother probably already has a special license secured.* She rubbed her hand over her mouth. *I haven't even thought of where we would live.* That did it. She was going to lose her tea. She half rose when Mother shoved an envelope into her hands.

"Here is your first clue."

"We helped!" Philomena announced proudly, Sybil nodding vigorously, pink icing ringing her mouth.

"Open it. Open it!" Sybil clapped her hands in her eagerness.

Clue? Willow's head ached as she stood, but with one glance at the beaming twins, she swallowed her protests and mustered a smile. Willow broke the seal and read the scrawling script, *Love Will Find a Way.* She flipped it over and . . . nothing. She waved the note in the air. "Girls, could you be a little more specific?"

The twins' infectious merriment earned a smile from all in the room, including her father who had been in a ubiquitously sullen state since the whole Osborne business had begun again.

"Very well. I will help you with the first step. You must go to Fritz. He has the next clue." Sybil pushed Willow toward the door.

Giving a theatrical sigh for the girls, she threw up her hands in surrender. "I'm going. I hope I don't regret this." Willow checked the conservatory, waved to Teddy and Cullen in the library, but did not see Fritz. So she took the stairs up to the third floor and paused at the landing. "Fritz?" she called through the sea of rooms.

At the end of the hall, Fritz popped out of a room, already dressed for the day, tucking his ever-present journal into his pocket as he met her at the forbidden landing. "Miss Dupré?"

"Do you know anything about this?" She extended the card to him.

He studied her, taking in her olive cotton-sateen gown sprinkled with clusters of pink roses. "Lovely. And yes, your mother gave me a note and told me in no uncertain terms that I was *not* to open it until you arrived." He withdrew an envelope from his pocket, slipped out a single sheet of paper, unfolded it and read aloud, "'Find your clue beneath the cherry tree.'" He paused and read it again silently, then looked at her. "Sounds as if we are being sent on a hunt of sorts. Shall we fetch your wrap?"

"Yes, thank you."

They went downstairs to find the twins holding Fritz's coat and Willow's straw bonnet with its brim of matching roses and plume, giggling away. Her bonnet fixed, snug in her sleeveless olive velvet wrap, Willow followed Fritz out the back door into the courtyard, where the only cherry tree on the property stood, her hand tucked in his arm. She lifted her face to the sky, loving the warmth of the sun on her skin despite the chill in the air.

"I'm guessing that's the one?" He pointed to the tree at the corner of the courtyard with a red ribbon around its trunk and a card attached, its branches gracefully dangling over the stone wall.

"Yes. Father and I planted the cherry tree years ago on my tenth birthday. And judging by the growth of the tree, I fear I have at last given away my age to you."

Fritz made a show of walking around the trunk, studying its bark. "This is but a sapling, my lady. Surely you cannot be much older than a debutante."

Willow laughed at his teasing and tugged at the bow, freeing the ribbon from the tree, and handed Fritz the card. "Would you like to do the honors?"

"I hope this gets more difficult, or else we'll be done within the hour and my time with you won't be near as long as I would wish." He cleared his throat and read, "'Where Willow goes to rest.'" He waggled his brows at her. "That's easy."

"Is it?" She scrunched her lips to one side, thinking of her bedroom and how surely her mother would not allow the twins to send them there alone.

"It's the pond where you ice-skate."

"I wouldn't have thought of that for at least another hour." She pushed open the side door that led to the sidewalk. "I've never been very good with these games, no matter how obvious the clue. As a child, my parents would hide my birthday present and have me search for it, thinking it would make it more amusing for me, but even with my father's clues, I was hopeless. At the end of the day, he would take pity on me and show me where he had hidden it."

He took her hand in his, staying her. "Then it's a good thing you're with me. But before we go, allow me to give you your blossom of the day." He removed a bouquet hidden behind the bench.

"You knew the first clue?" Her laughter bubbled in her chest. "If so, you had an unfair advantage."

"Unfair advantage?" He rolled his eyes. "Will, the note said *exactly* where to find the clue. But no, I did not know. I told the twins to hide this wherever the clue led us." He handed the bouquet of crimson tulips to her, their meaning clear.

An avowal of love. She accepted them and buried her nose into the blossoms. "Thank you. As always, you are too kind."

He gave her a sad smile. "It's not kindness that prompts such a flower, but love," he corrected. "Now, I know you do not wish to carry flowers with you all day, therefore . . ." He plucked a single blossom, set the bouquet on the bench, and tucked the flower into the band of her chapeau. "There. The twins said they would see to the flowers being set in a vase. Shall we?"

Her hand secured in the crook of his elbow, Willow allowed him to guide her through the courtyard's arched doorway toward the park, yet her thoughts would not stay with Fritz. She kept thinking of her conversations with Cullen last night, and the one weeks ago when he intimated that it was difficult *not* to love her. If he would only declare his love like the others had, her choice would be much clearer. But how could she choose him if she wasn't certain Cullen would propose? Even so, with Fritz's and Teddy's obvious devotion, she knew it would be difficult to say good-bye to either of them if the time came with Cullen declaring himself. Nevertheless, she needed a husband in the end, not a broken heart . . . and Kit had already taken a piece of it. *Kit*. He was likely back in Charleston by now. What would it be like to meet him in Newport during the summer with a husband at her side? *Husband*. A beautiful and nerve-wracking thought.

"No doubt the end of the competition is on your mind," Fritz said, breaking the silence, rubbing his finger over his bottom lip. "And I was wondering . . . are you any closer to making a decision?" He held her hand as they crossed a muddy patch on the path.

She looked sideways at him, knowing he would not like hearing that if this were a race, he would have ranked in the final position. But she would never be so blunt, not with him. "I've narrowed it to the top three."

He wiped a hand over his brow. "Whew. I was afraid you had left a few of the men in the attic and had not told me."

"Just Archie, for who else could be trusted to get my private conversations with my beaus correct?" She paused at the bench she always used while skating and looked out at the pond, ducks already swimming about.

Fritz squatted down, peering at the underside of the bench. "Found it." He handed an envelope to Willow and bowed with a flourish of his hand. "Hopefully, the twins selected something more challenging for our next clue."

Willow broke the seal to find an old-fashioned key and read aloud, "'Take the carriage to the Blythes' country estate and search for your namesake beyond the gate for your next clue.'"

"Not exactly difficult to interpret, but a drive to the country sounds lovely." Fritz grinned, rubbing his hands together.

Willow studied the typed note. *Seems a bit improper to venture so far into the country without a chaperone, but Mother did say I should be more spontaneous.* She glanced at her watch pin under her wrap, weighing how long it would take to travel there and back. It was almost four o'clock now, and by the time they returned, it would be dark. *I wonder if Father knows . . .* After her disagreement with Mother this afternoon, she needed to prove to Mother that she *could* leave behind her diary and have unscheduled amusement. Willow nodded. "Then we best summon a carriage."

"Already taken care of by your mother, it seems." Fritz pointed to the other side of the pond, where a small buggy with a pair of fine, dappled gray horses stood waiting with a groom Willow did not recognize holding the reins.

Swept up in the mystery of her family's making, Willow allowed herself to forget her worries and her conflict over choosing a husband and instead immerse herself in this adventure with her suitor. Fritz helped her into the buggy, then hopped in himself, spreading a soft plaid over them both. Extending his thanks to the groom, he snapped the reins and the geldings took off at a trot, the wind whistling through Willow's wrap. She tucked the plaid closer about her legs, but even then it was not warm enough, so she slid a bit closer to Fritz, who straightened his shoulders as he guided the horses in the direction of his country estate.

Willow relished seeing this new level of confidence arise in Fritz. Around the others, he tended to be more reserved. She ran her finger over the flower in her bonnet. She would miss his sweet attentions. She paused at the realization. It was as if her heart had at last let her mind in on the secret she had been harboring for so long. Fritz loved her, of that she was certain, but she wasn't in love with him. She bit her lip and stared at his strong profile that hinted at his sweet nature with his softer jawline. Now that she knew she could not love Fritz, suddenly the joy and ease of the day lost its luster. And she did not wish to cause him any more pain than necessary by drawing out their outing when she knew the truth at last. "Fritz?"

He turned to her, and the moment their eyes met, his mirth faded and she could see he understood what she was going to say.

"Don't." He turned and stared at the road ahead, the muscles in his neck cording.

"Like you said, there are three of you left and days until the end of the competition." She paused at the crack in her voice. "How can I say good-bye to you, dearest Fritz?"

"Please—"

"Fritz, it is my prayer that when we part, you will start your journey to finding the love of your life."

"It is a journey that began and ended with you." He blinked madly away, shaking his head against her words. "Let's not speak of it. Not yet. Just give me today, Will. One last glorious day with you."

She dipped her head, unable to deny him. "Very well."

Leaving the city behind, Fritz sent the horses into a gallop. Willow gripped the side of the buggy and the back of the leather seat. Knowing the twins, they had likely planned an entire afternoon and evening of amusement for her and Fritz, although she was still surprised Mother had approved of her taking this trip without a chaperone, especially after the incident with her and Cullen on an outing by themselves until eleven in the evening.

Fritz slowed the pace of the horses to a trot, then leaned back in the seat, his foot propped up on the front of the buggy. "Tell me something about yourself, Will. What is it you enjoy that you've never told anyone else about?"

"If you check under my mattress, you will find a dime novel. I pretend to read only Mother's collection, but the truth is that

I have my maid pick up a new book for me every week, and she disposes of the previous week's shameful read." Her cheeks reddened at the mention of her bed.

Fritz threw his head back and hooted. "I never would have guessed that the businesswoman has a thirst for romance."

"Let's keep that between us, shall we? I would hate for any-one to know that behind my business façade, there beats the heart of a woman." She clenched her hands on her lap, the air turning cooler in the shade of the passing trees.

"You don't have to be so guarded, you know." He flicked the reins, that scowl returning.

"Do you know something about the board that I do not?" She laughed, attempting to break the growing tension between them.

"I know that the heart of a romantic can live inside a man, as well." He turned to her. "Every one of your board members is married, and that means at one time they each had to woo a woman. Don't be fooled by their haughty attitude."

They rounded a corner to find a wagon with a broken wheel and two men examining it blocking the main road. Fritz pulled back on the reins, the horses tossing their heads at the abrupt change. "Can I help you, sirs?" Fritz called to the strangers.

The men sauntered around the wagon, but instead of an-swering, the men seized their reins, making the horses jerk back their heads and whinny while the shorter of the two men charged the buggy, brandishing a knife. Willow recoiled in fear and let out a cry.

Fritz threw his arm out in front of Willow. "Would you threaten a lady? What do you want?"

"Your pretty buggy and horses . . . and perhaps a turn with the lady." He sneered, his blade grazing the hem of her skirt.

Willow curled her legs back, away from the man's knife. "Fritz!"

Fritz launched himself over Willow, diving atop the man.

They rolled in the dirt, making the horses prance nervously to the side. The thug drew back his blade and drove it down toward Fritz's collarbone. Willow screamed, and Fritz blocked the knife's trajectory with his forearm against the man's wrist before kicking him between the legs, crippling him. The other man dropped the reins and charged at Fritz, aiming a punch at him. He was unable to duck in time and the blow caught Fritz on the jaw, sending him reeling backward into the path of the horses' hooves.

"Fritz!" Willow leapt from the carriage, but the rocking of the buggy disquieted the horses and threw off her footing. Willow rammed into the hard-packed dirt, knocking the wind from her lungs. Gasping, she crawled to her knees, then scrambled up and grabbed the horses' bridles to guide them away from Fritz, who had now grabbed the knife and rolled himself to standing. He held out the blade before the thugs. "Run, Willow!" he shouted. "I'll hold them off."

Drawing a full breath at last, she heard Fritz cry out from behind the buggy. "Fritz!" she screamed into the wind, praying he was unharmed, praying that this was somehow part of the plan. She searched frantically for something to use as a weapon. She couldn't leave him behind.

Fritz appeared around the buggy, gasping and clutching his side as he hoisted her back into the buggy and climbed in after her, the reins in his fist. She wrapped her arms about his neck, but he shook her off and snapped the reins, guiding the horses around the wagon. "We have to move. I tied them up, but we need to get you away from here. Somewhere that is safe."

"Are you hurt?"

He slapped the reins again, and the horses sprang into a gallop. "Nothing that time cannot heal." Breathing heavily, Fritz gave an inane laugh. "That was close."

"Close? Fritz, you were almost killed." She wrapped her hands around his arm, thinking how she could have very easily lost him forever, and the thought terrified her. "Why were they after us?"

He did not look at her as he pressed the horses onward. "They wanted you for ransom."

"What? But how could they have known I'd be here?"

He scowled. "They were hired, Will."

Her hands trembled, and she tucked them under her arms for warmth. "How do you know that?"

"I am not proud of it, but when I turned the knife on them . . . I drew blood at one of their throats." He groaned.

"One cannot judge you for that. Who hired them? Wellington?"

"That's the unfathomable part." He frowned. "They said they were hired by Cullen Dempsey to see to it that I was eliminated from the competition."

Her breath caught. *No. It can't be.* She pressed her gloved hand to her mouth. *But why would Fritz lie to me, and why would the thugs lie about such a thing?* She slid off the seat onto the floor of the buggy, gripping her knees to her chest. "Cullen. No. No." Her heart could not make sense of it all, but what she did know was pain unlike anything she had ever endured.

Fritz grasped her shoulder. "It's difficult for even me to accept. Yet why would the thieves lie about who hired them?"

Willow dropped her head to her knees, withdrawing from her feelings. This was why she did not wish to fall in love. There was too much pain in it. Had she come so far, opened herself after years of building up walls around her heart, only to have her heart crushed and her greatest fears come to fruition?

"Will, we need to get you warm. I fear you may become hysterical." Fritz drew the buggy slowly around a bend and up a drive where he hopped down to open the iron gate before grabbing the horses' bridles and guiding the buggy inside. He secured the horses to a post and scooped her into his arms, carrying her up a brick walkway. Willow couldn't think clearly enough to release her hold about his neck but allowed him to carry her up the steps. A dog barked, and at the sound she lifted her head to see they were at a white mansion with wood shakes for siding and a turret at the front. She pressed her hands to his chest, and he set her down as he unlocked the front door, using the key from the envelope.

"Fritz, where are you taking me?"

"Inside my country estate. Like your mother said to in the clue."

"Now is not the time for a silly game. We need to summon the authorities." She shook her head, almost annoyed by his persistence to continue their outing . . . though she at once felt guilty. After all, hadn't he just saved her life?

But instead of agreeing with her, Fritz swung open the door. "We need to get you inside where no one else can harm you. Then, once your mother arrives with the dinner, we will send one of her footmen for help."

Twenty-Four

Cullen gripped his hat and scanned the gentlemen's social club, searching for Wellington. Laughter sounded to the left, and there Wellington sat on a velvet settee in the corner of the smoky gilded room, along with three others. "Wellington."

Wellington looked up, slowly bringing his cigar to his fat lips and drawing a long draft before exhaling in a huff, creating a ring of smoke. He waved Cullen over with the two fingers around the cigar, flicking ash onto the wood floor in doing so. Cullen strode forward, his gaze darting to the men in Wellington's company.

"Cullen, my dear boy. Come to tell me more delicious secrets about your dear Miss Dupré?"

Cullen stiffened at the man's comment, his temper rising. "Sir, you're smashed. You best heed your tongue."

"I have never been more lucid in my life. Loosen your corset, Cullen, and join us. We are celebrating." He spread his arms to the group of men, who raised their glasses and cheered.

"I don't feel like celebrating," Cullen growled. He ran his hands over the brim of his hat. "Why did you send for me? I told you, I have no further business with you. But if you wish to speak with me, do so alone or not at all."

Wellington snorted around his cigar. "Anything I have to say to you can be said in front of my comrades."

Cullen leaned against a carved wood column. "Have it your way. Let me be or I will go to the police, *tonight*."

Wellington sat up straighter, and his friends leaned forward. "Perhaps we should speak in private, after all. Gentlemen, please excuse us." He waved away the portly fellows and motioned for Cullen to assume a vacated seat.

"I came as a one-time courtesy for our relationship of old. Do not summon me again, Wellington."

The man's grin spread in a way that sent a chill down Cullen's spine. "You didn't ask me what I was celebrating."

"That's not important," Cullen snapped.

"I beg to differ. Go on. Ask me, my dear boy."

Cullen's fists curled. "You know what happens when I get angry. Do not tempt me, Wellington."

"Very well." He released a sigh. "Such a spoilsport. I was celebrating a breakthrough in a rather spontaneous courtship. Your sister, this very afternoon, has agreed to marry me."

"Liar!" Cullen's fist connected with the man's nose.

Wellington held his hand to his gushing nose as gentlemen gathered round to see. He waved them away, rage turning his skin crimson. "You broke my nose! I'll have you sued for this."

"How dare you? What did you say to my sister? Did you threaten her?" Cullen grabbed the man by the collar and lifted him from his chair, shaking him, his feet dangling in the air. "*What* did you say to my sister, sir?"

"The *truth*." Wellington grinned, his teeth bloodstained. "That by doing so, she would ensure her mother's standing in society, and that her brother's debt would be wiped clean and his secret kept, allowing him to marry the love of his life. It was a simple enough transaction. For sixteen, she is quite astute."

He shook Wellington again, snapping his neck back and

forth, the man's grin still in place. "She is a child. And she would have told me . . . unless you *threatened* her."

"She is a romantic. I have been paying court to her since I first had the idea of wedding her. I told her to keep our meetings a secret, just like all the other secrets of yours she's kept."

Cullen dropped him onto the chair and raised his fist again.

Wellington thrust his arm out before him. "Keep your hands to yourself, boy, or I swear, at the next blow, I'll forget the years we have spent together and see you rot in prison."

Cullen wiped his hands on his jacket, disgusted at his powerlessness, hating that despite his urge to strike the man, he could not do it again. "You break it off with Eva Marie, and don't you dare print anything in the papers about it or I will finish you. I am *done* with you, Wellington. You hear me? Done."

Wellington leaned forward. "Cullen, my boy, you do not get to be as wealthy as I without having multiple plans in place when the first two will inevitably go awry."

"What do you mean?"

He gave a maniacal laugh. "There is *always* a security in place to catch my plan should all fall apart."

Cullen's blood turned cold. "What other security could be worse than your pressing my sister into an engagement?"

Wellington withdrew a second cigar from the box atop a side table and lifted it to the tabletop lighter. Pulling its pearl handle to release the flame, he drew the cigar to life before exhaling. "You have crossed me for the last time. It's time you drop this Miss Dupré and return to my side as my partner like we always planned. Once you do, I'll release Eva Marie from our engagement without suing for breach of promise." He flicked the end of the cigar, watching the ash drift into the tray. "And since I foresaw you ignoring my magnanimous warning at the ball, I had my third plan set into motion. Archibald Lovett owes me a debt, one that he will gladly fulfill. For what man wouldn't wish to erase his debt through such delightful means? And I told him that tonight was the night."

Cullen's blood turned cold. Willow was alone with Fritz this afternoon, most likely still on an outing, and therefore unprotected and vulnerable. "Where is she?" He reached for the man, seizing the lapels of his jacket. "Tell me where, or so help me, I will kill you."

Willow eyed the dark hallway, the hair at the nape of her neck rising on end. "Fritz, if Mother approved this next clue, shouldn't there be a dinner awaiting us?" *Or a dozen servants to chaperone with the house full of light?* Mother wanted her to be adventurous, but she was not foolhardy. "Perhaps we should return."

Fritz pointed to a chair with a box atop it, its satin ribbon shimmering in the moonlight. "Ah, never fear. Seems your mother's plan has not led us astray. Shall we see what's inside?"

Willow pulled the ribbon and lifted the box top, pushing aside the tissue to find a snowy gown trimmed with the finest lace. A typed card lay on top, which read, *Please don before dinner arrives.* Willow's hands shook as she lifted out a wedding gown. "Mother has to be jesting."

He ran his hands through his hair. "No harm in playing along. You can use the powder room."

"I couldn't manage the buttons alone. We should wait on the veranda until they arrive. If they don't appear in the next ten minutes, we should be on our way. It isn't proper to be alone, much less here at your family's estate." She returned the gown to the box.

Fritz closed the front door, locking it. "I think we should stay."

Willow moved away from him and bumped into a round foyer table that was covered with a white cloth. "You're frightening me."

Fritz struck a match. "Forgive me. I didn't mean to alarm you, but what I meant was that the thugs are still out there." He held the match to the wick of a hurricane lamp, then replaced the rose-painted glass dome and turned the wick up until it brightened the foyer. He reached for her hand and drew her closer, despite her leaning back to show him that she did not wish it. "You know, I sensed that today was the day you were going to release me. I did so wish not to have a broken heart."

She exhaled, relieved that he was only speaking of their parting. "And I am sorry for it. Perhaps I should have spared you and sent you away with Kit, but there was hardly time for me to discover my feelings before the next ceremony was upon us."

He stroked a curl behind her ear. "I read the papers. I knew long ago that I was not your preference."

"Oh? How could you know that from Archie's articles when I did not know myself?"

He gave a mirthless laugh. "Because of the way you follow Cullen with your eyes as he walks about the room. The way you smile when he comes near and how you lean ever so slightly toward him whenever he is at your side. You are in love with him."

Her heart stumbled. "How can you be certain?"

"Because you care for Theodore like a dear friend, someone you find handsome and yet you do not intend to marry him." He dropped his hand. "I only wish I could have made you see how much I loved you. Every day I tried to let you know. Every day I gave you flowers." He withdrew his journal and placed it in her hands. "Every day I worked diligently on finishing my own dictionary of the secret language of flowers, all for you."

"For me?" She flipped it open and read the dedication. *To Willow, whose name will mean "forever love."* She lifted her gaze to him. "You gave my name a new secret meaning?"

He nodded, tucked another wild curl behind her ear. "It is the author's privilege to invent a meaning should he desire it.

And I *do* desire it. I'm going to have this published and make my own fortune to prove to you that I am worth something on my own."

His declaration took her aback. "You *are* worth far more than a fortune, Fritz Blythe." She shook her head, clearing it of the romantic gesture. "Perhaps if we had more time, or if we had courted before . . . But there is no sense in our speaking of what might have been when we know for certain what *is*."

"You never even allowed me to kiss you." He looked to her lips, and not wanting to give him the chance, she ducked away through the open door of an eerie-looking parlor. The room's curtains were bagged and the shades drawn, the furniture covered with white cloths. Even the mirror above the fireplace was covered over.

"We should leave before—"

"Willow, you know that once word hits the papers that we were seen leaving this mansion alone, you will have to marry me."

"My mother would never allow me to be unsupervised. She will appear at any moment. I am certain she meant to arrive before us, but as I said, it is probably for the best that we await her on the front porch, even with the thugs we left behind still at large."

He ran his hand over the back of a chair, smoothing its dust cover. "Did you really think she would have sent you unchaperoned to my country estate?"

"W-what do you mean? Why wouldn't she when she helped the girls plan it?" Willow took a step back, bumping into the furniture in the overcrowded sitting room.

"I mean that I looked at the clue the twins left with me this morning, which gave me plenty of time to go along the route and change the clues to suit me."

She clasped her hands to keep them from shaking. Fritz was

a good man. He would not harm her. After all, he had saved her from the highwaymen. Why would he hurt her now?

"I knew I was last in line for your heart, so I thought I would remove any impediments."

"By sullying my reputation?" She darted to the French doors that led to the veranda, pulling on the handles, frantic for an escape. *Lord! Help me.*

"Please. Don't be afraid. I would *never* take advantage of you. I love you too much. I know trapping you into a marriage is underhanded, but after the reporters arrive, there will be little else for you to do but marry me. So, if you are agreeable, we can send for the minister. If you wish to wait, we can simply announce our engagement in the papers tomorrow."

Willow's blood pulsed. He had forced her into a corner. *He's right. The only way out of this is a wedding . . . if I am caught.* "Fritz. Is this really how you wish to have my hand? By ruining my good name by insinuation?"

"At this point, I know it is the only way. I know you're fond of me. And you keep saying that if we had time, things could be different. Well, I'm giving you that time. A lifetime." He ran the back of his fingers down her arm, grasping her hand. "I am only sorry that you are not as in love with me as I am with you."

The man is mad. Shaking, she lowered her shoulders in an attempt to appear resolute. "I see no way out of this with my reputation intact. But I need to use the powder room. It was a long journey, and well . . ." She dropped her gaze, hoping he would catch her meaning.

"Certainly. Still, to secure your *staying* in the building, I would have you visit the second-floor powder room." He gathered the box and the lamp and escorted her up the stairs to the second-floor landing. On either side of the landing was a small chamber, one for the ladies and one for the gentlemen. "I'll wait for you here." He placed the box in her hands along with the light. "Change for me? It would be better for the reporters to think we are having a wedding. Perhaps it can salvage just enough of your reputation to delay until the real wedding. I'll secure any buttons you cannot reach."

Stiffly, Willow slipped into the smaller, second room in the chamber that served as the necessary and closed the door behind her. She spied a window set high above the toilet. Dropping the box and setting the lamp atop the vanity, along with her wrap and hat, she climbed atop the closed cane back lid of the toilet, then reached up to slide open the window, which gave an obnoxious creak. Grimacing, she paused to make sure that Fritz had not heard and then breathed a silent prayer of thanks.

As Willow hoisted herself through the small opening feet first, her bustle became wedged between the window and frame. She pulled, twisted, and jerked until her skirts ripped free, then had to catch herself against the window frame to keep from pitching backward and falling. Tapping her feet, she found a narrow ledge and slowly eased herself out, creeping to a position above a bed of rather soft-looking bushes. Panting, she lowered herself further, sliding along the wall until she was able to grasp the ledge. She then slid her legs past the ledge and dangled for a few seconds by her fingertips before releasing her grip and dropping.

Twenty-Five

Cullen sat low in the saddle, urging his mount to remain at a full gallop. Lather spotted the horse's neck as it strained with the effort to keep its frantic pace in their rushing toward the country estate.

At last, he reined the horse into the drive, its hooves scattering pebbles as they slowed in their approach to the mansion. Outside, a buggy and a carriage were parked near the front entrance. The only places where he could see any light was in a room off the second floor, and a flicker in one of the downstairs rooms where he saw four male figures through a paned window. Cullen tied the reins to a low-lying branch and darted up to the window, crouching low and listening.

"I don't see why you are all bent out of shape, Archie. All of New York will know of the scandal by morning, so get off my back. This is my wedding, after all. Why would it matter if I wed her tonight versus the original date set for the competition?"

Wedding? He stiffened. *Lord, please watch out for my girl. Protect her.*

"This is about more than a blasted girl," Archie snapped.

"Shut it. You had best remember that I *love* Miss Dupré, and while you are under my roof, you would do well not to speak of her in such a callous manner," Fritz fired back.

Where are you, Will? He crawled away from the window and peered up at the second story to see a dainty foot poke out of the window. He sucked in through his teeth and stood beneath the window as petticoats followed the well-turned ankles and stockinged calves and out scooted Willow, her legs dangling about as her toes searched for a hold. He didn't dare speak for fear the men would hear him and come running, so he slipped behind some bushes as close to the house as he could manage and outstretched his arms, praying he wouldn't miss. *Can she not see me in the dark?*

Willow eased out farther, then slowly lowered herself until she was hanging by her fingertips, still a good ten feet from the ground. Whimpering, she released her hold and plummeted to the earth. Cullen dove for her, barely catching her in his arms. But the odd angle and her weight knocked the wind from him as they fell backward into the bushes, whose branches dug into his jacket and very narrowly missed gouging out his eye.

Willow gasped, twisting around to see who had caught her. "Cullen." She wrapped her arms about his neck, her voice cracking. "Thank the Lord. Cullen!"

Still unable to draw a breath, Cullen lifted a finger to his lips, rolling over and gasping for air. "We need to get you away from here. Fritz might never intentionally harm you, but when someone acts so irrationally as to trap someone in a marriage—"

"I couldn't agree more." She took his hand and pulled, helping him to his feet.

"Where do you think you two are going?" Archie sketched away on his pad, no doubt a rough draft of his depiction of finding them entangled in the bushes. "This will do quite nicely for the headline tomorrow."

"Archie." Willow's voice turned fierce.

Cullen tucked her behind him. "You destroy that picture and kill the story or you will live to regret it."

Archie licked the stub of his pencil and continued scribbling away while the other two men moseyed in front of him, eliciting a gasp from Willow.

"You're the thugs who attacked us on the road. Archie, it was *you* who had us attacked? And for what? A story?"

Cullen had little time to react to that bit of news as Archie laughed, tucking the pencil behind his ear and shoving his notepad in his pocket.

"If I had wanted them to truly hurt you, do you think Fritz Blythe could have managed to get away from two trained boxers? It was part of Blythe's plan to be the hero and hopefully become your choice, Willow, but I suppose once he realized this morning that you were going to cut him today, he panicked and contacted me and added that ridiculous part with the wedding gown and having me report it, forcing you into an engagement. But what Fritz doesn't know is that the thugs he hired are *my* men. You see, I knew who I was dealing with. Any reporter worth his salt always does a background check on those in his story. I thought maybe that you would have recognized these two fellows from your last year in the ring, Wild Man."

"I know who they are." Cullen cracked his neck and lifted his fists, shifting himself into his familiar fighting stance. "If you had done your research, Archie, you would've known that I knocked both Tanner and Cliff out with one blow."

Archie grabbed for his pencil. "Yes, but *not* at the same time with a woman to defend."

Willow raised her own fists. "I am no defenseless woman."

Archie chuckled. "Says the woman who has never sparred a day in her life."

Cullen looked to her, pride filling his chest at her willingness to join him in a fight. "I can take them."

She dropped her fists, a flicker of relief in her expression. "I have no doubt."

The men charged him, and Cullen dodged, jabbing left and right, ducking and whirling. Tanner tripped over a tree root, and seeing his back exposed, Cullen reared his arm back and, with the full force of his body, slammed his fist into the man's kidney, sending him crumpling to the ground just as the second came at him. Cliff punched Cullen in the gut. Cullen, having taken many a blow before, tightened his muscles before the impact, lessening the force of the strike.

"Cullen!" Willow screamed.

He jerked around in time to see the fallen giant had risen and had slipped on a set of cast-iron knuckles. Cullen set about dodging the brute's fists. If Tanner caught him on the jaw . . . Cullen might not wake again.

With a yell, Willow leapt on the man's broad back, wrapping her thin arms around his throat in a manner that seemed to block the assailant's ability to draw a full breath. He grabbed for her arms. *If he manages to catch hold of her, he could very easily break her wrists.* Desperate, Cullen threw a powerful punch that crumpled Tanner to his knees, Willow falling atop him, her arms pinned beneath his body. Hearing Cliff's boots on the gravel behind him, Cullen whipped his arm around and backhanded Cliff with such force that it sent the assailant to his knees. Followed by a second blow, Cliff fell face-first, unmoving.

Cullen's chest was heaving as he rushed to help Willow when a board struck him on the back of his head. Spots formed in his vision. He staggered forward, falling beside Willow, who shrieked and tugged herself free in one motion, only to throw herself onto Cullen's back.

"Archie! No!"

"It will be in defense of your honor, or so the papers will say." Archie's cackling laughter rallied Cullen. "This will be the story that will redeem my reputation after your father had me fired from my position."

With a groan, Cullen shoved Willow behind him as he lifted his forearm to block the second blow, shattering the board against his tensed arm. He rose, rolling his shoulders back. "You *dare* threaten her?" He threw his fist into the reporter's face, enjoying the crush of bone beneath his knuckles, felling Archie backward, his nose gushing and his front tooth dangling from a thread of gum.

"I'll have you imprisoned for this!" Archie screamed, spitting blood with each word.

"Then we shall be cellmates." He drew his arm back again, but Willow wrapped her hands around his bicep.

"Don't, Cullen. He is incapacitated. Can't we tie them up? You don't need to sink to his level."

Cullen looked back to the house before tugging off his neck-cloth and fastening it around Archie's hands, who continued to spew threats. "We aren't out of danger yet. Fritz is still about."

Willow's eyes widened. "He wouldn't have done this to us. They must have betrayed him, as well." She pulled on his arm. "Please, he may be hurt. No matter what Fritz has done, he was only motivated out of a misplaced love for me and would never have allowed any harm to come to anyone."

"Only your reputation." He tilted his neck, cracking it again, and straightened his shoulders. His knuckles were raw without his gauze strips and gloves to protect his hands.

"Like I said, he is misguided but not dangerous."

Cullen nodded, silently agreeing with her. The flower-loving fellow was not the violent type. Nonetheless, he stepped into the house first, keeping an arm in front of Willow. "Blythe? Are you injured?"

A muffled cry came from a nearby room, and Cullen slipped inside the dimly lit parlor to find the man tied to a chair. He stopped thrashing at the sight of Willow behind him. She removed the gag so tenderly that it made Cullen uncomfortable.

"Willow, I'm so sorry. I never meant for any of this to happen. Forgive me. Forgive me," he cried over and over again as Cullen worked on freeing the lout's hands from the arms of the chair. His hands free, he leapt to his feet and cupped Willow's face in his hands. "I love you. I have the moment I saw you on the ice, and I always will."

"I know, Fritz. I know." She placed her hand on his chest, a gesture that had Cullen's skin crawling. "But you have to understand that I cannot marry you. Don't you?"

He dipped his head, his tears falling unabashedly. "Yes. I'm a fool for ruining my chance with you, a blasted fool who will be ostracized for his actions done in blindness."

She drew in a shaky breath. "It would not be wise for me to withhold this from the police, but if you can promise to stay away from me and my family, I will keep silent on this score. However, if you come near me or my family again—even once—I will be forced to report you."

At Fritz's stiff nod, Willow turned to Cullen. "Can you not mention his part in this night?"

Cullen gritted his teeth, hating that she was protecting a man who very nearly ruined her reputation for life. If she could so easily forgive Fritz for his misdeeds, would she be able to forgive Cullen for his deceit? "I'll not mention it." *Even though he is fit for the asylum after this scheme.*

Fritz reached for her hand. "I treasure your heart more than all the flowers in the world."

Her lips began to tremble, and Cullen fought the urge to turn around to give them privacy, though not from consideration but rather the discomfiture of the situation. Fritz's eyes filled as he shifted away from her, their fingertips separating. He swiped at his eyes with the back of his cuff. "Cullen, you see to it that you take care of her now. Cherish her as a husband should."

"What makes you so certain it's me she wishes to wed?"

"It is in her eyes and in the words she does not say." He caught Willow's hand once more and pressed a kiss to her palm. "Farewell, my queen. I'll be sending the police to collect the men." With those words, he bowed to her and stepped into the buggy, snapping the reins and leaving Willow to Cullen's care.

Cullen lifted her chin. "Is it true? Am I the one you desire?"

"What say you?" she whispered.

I say that I've loved you since the moment you taught me how to toboggan and cared for my injuries as if there were no one else's name on your heart but mine. And I will go on loving you for the rest of your days if you will allow me, macushla. "I say that we need to get you as far away from Archie as possible and make certain he does not print his sordid version of what happened in any of the papers. No telling what that slimy reporter has up his sleeve."

Willow sighed. "Very well."

Cullen wrapped his arm about her waist and led Willow to his horse. She glanced up the drive to see Fritz turning his buggy onto the road, her heart breaking at the sight. He was gone forever. Because *she* had sent him away. *Stop this. The man fairly kidnapped you and here you are defending him.* She needed to be rational. That had never been a problem before. She was Willow Dupré. She could not allow herself to be caught up in the shock of the evening or his heartbreaking declaration or their past. Whatever it was, her heart was sore from losing him, for he had never behaved so before tonight and she truly believed desperation had driven him to such lengths. No matter his decision this night, he loved her.

Cullen lifted her onto the front of the saddle before climbing on behind her. She rested her head against his chest, enjoying the nearness of him for a few moments longer, tears streaking down her cheeks at the hurt she had inflicted on such a pure heart. Was she so wrong for keeping Fritz when deep in her heart she knew it wouldn't work? Not when Cullen was courting her? And dear Teddy . . . how could she bid him farewell before she knew of Cullen's intentions? She could not bear to break a second heart, not if she could help it.

The ride home was quick and thankfully uneventful due to the cloak of darkness drawn about them. As they reached a more populated street, Cullen turned his horse onto Sixth Avenue, then directed his mount into the wooded area of the park and down the path that would lead them to the Inventor's Gate.

"I figured that no one would be in the park at such an hour. At least no one you would know." He coughed and shifted away from her. "May I ask why was it so difficult for you to release Fritz tonight? I would think after—"

She drew back, not expecting him to question her. "Because he loved me."

"And you love him?" he returned, his tone sharp.

"In a way, but not the kind of love one needs for a marriage." She had to get off the topic for fear her emotions—which she had no control over these days—reared their red-nosed, puffy-eyed head. "So, did you find out who was using your warehouse and gain enough evidence to arrest him?"

The change in his posture was immediate. His shoulders tensed, he sat straighter, and his arms tightened as well as his voice. "I did, but I'm still waiting on the results of the money trail from a friend."

"Who is it?" She turned to watch his face in the moonlight, swaying with the horse's steady rhythm.

Cullen tilted his neck from side to side, cracking it in that practiced manner she noticed he used before fighting. "Will, you are not going to like it."

"Wellington. He needs to be thrown in jail for what he's done to my family." She balled her fists, but he placed a steadying hand over them.

"Yes. But I'll tell you right now that the man will not be caught unless my friend finds the money in one of Wellington's accounts. While you can arrest the men he hired, I guarantee you that it will be nearly impossible to bring him to justice with all the protections he will have set into place. The men you would imprison are merely among his hundreds of pawns."

She grunted. She needed to work off her anger before she did something rash, like stop by the police office before they had sufficient evidence to arrest Wellington. "Can we walk? We are nearing the concert ground, which, as you know, is one of the more populated paths, and a lady holding on to a gentleman on a single horse will send the gossips to banging on my door."

"Of course." Cullen reined in his mount and slid off before turning to help her.

Willow did not linger in his arms but moved a few paces away to gather her tumultuous thoughts, for now there were only two potential grooms standing, and the only one she wanted had not yet proposed.

At the steady clip of a horse approaching, Cullen gripped her elbow and motioned for her to hide behind the trees lining the path. "The dark should hide you, and your reputation will be safeguarded."

She stepped behind a cherry tree and exhaled. *You are safe. Cullen is here. No one will take you again.* And with that overwhelming fear, any pity she had for Fritz suddenly dissolved. *He* had done this to her. She willed herself to cease shaking and focused on Cullen's broad back as he bent to examine his horse's hoof.

"So, you thought you could double-cross me?" called a gruff voice.

She leaned around the tree and nearly gasped at the man sitting on a snowy gelding before Cullen. She had only met him once and that meeting had been short and offensive.

Cullen's back stiffened as he rose to his full height. "What are you talking about, Wellington?"

How does he know Cullen? Did their paths cross while he was investigating Wellington?

"I *made* you, boy. You should know by now that I would've had you followed after you attempted to break your promise to me."

Cullen's mentor is Wellington? Willow pressed her hand to her mouth. She silently slid down the rough bark of the tree to the withered grass, drawing her knees to her chest, focusing on exhaling and inhaling to keep from exposing her hiding place.

Wellington gave a short, mirthless laugh. "Your love for Miss Dupré betrayed not only me but yourself . . . and Agent Flannery. Did you really think I'd allow you to turn me over to the Pinkertons so easily? I have not garnered my wealth so quickly without being astute." Wellington's booming voice was impossible to ignore.

Agent Flannery . . . She closed her eyes as if that would keep the awful thought at bay. If Cullen was working for the Pinkertons, then he *wasn't* in the competition for her and never had been. He was in it to bring down Heathcliff Wellington. She brought her hand to her mouth again, suppressing her cry. She had been a fool. *This is what happens when you open your heart, Willow. You become weak, and in that weakness you will be destroyed.* She swiped her tattered olive sleeve over her eyes and forced herself to peer around the cherry tree, her fingernails digging into its thick bark.

"Agent Flannery, you say?" Cullen patted his horse's neck. "I am not familiar—"

Wellington leaned forward in the saddle, crossing his wrists over his thigh. "Do not treat me like a fool, Cullen. I summoned you to the club tonight to give you one last chance before I acted and you failed me. And yes, I *knew* of him. I arranged a little accident for him in the East River. Tonight, Hell Gate claimed yet another victim in its shipwreck-filled waters." He ran a hand down his crop, making his mount dance to the side. "Poor fellow should not have gone fishing in such terrible currents. Smashed into the rocks so many times, it will be difficult for the authorities to identify him."

Willow swallowed a sob as Cullen bowed his head, and she wondered if he and the agent had been friends. "Why are you telling me this?"

"Because if I had an agent killed, what do you think I would do to my fiancée, dear Eva Marie, if you step out of line again?"

Cullen lunged at him, but Wellington pulled his horse out of reach, lifting his riding crop.

Willow gasped. So this was the sort of man Cullen had for a mentor. She shook her head, which swirled with questions. *Was the mentorship a lie, too?*

"I'd stop before you hurt your sister. Now, if you'll excuse me, I want to be home in time to read the *New York Times* and *The World*." He gave a laugh, kicking his mount. "I hear there is going to be quite the exposé in both about one of Miss Dupré's beloved suitors. I will not insult your intelligence by telling you who."

With shaking limbs, she pushed herself to standing, running into the darkness, away from them. Tripping over a tree root, she fell and sprawled in a patch of mud. With a groan, she flicked it from her hands, and when she attempted to stand, she found her ankle was unable to bear her weight.

The pounding of hooves sent her scrambling into the shadows, where she spied the rider. Cullen dropped from the saddle and ran to her. She wanted to scream at him not to touch her, but instead she allowed him to help her out of the mud. "Why, Cullen?"

He sank down beside her, mindless of the mud, their backs

to a tree in a secluded bend of the park. "Deceiving you broke me, Willow. It brought me to my knees and back to the feet of Jesus, a place I never should have left. Instead of giving Him my burdens and fears of providing for my family, I allowed those fears to control me and make me into a man I am not proud of, nor someone I wish to be any longer."

"Was any of our time together real," Willow whispered, "or were you always working with the Pinkertons? Laughing at the plain heiress who couldn't help but fall in love with the dashing, mysterious Irish Wild Man?"

Cullen caught her hands, covering them with his own. "You need to understand how deep I was in with Wellington. You heard him and the threats he made against me and my family. You heard with your own ears his confession to murder."

She pulled free from him and dropped her head in her hands, thinking of their moments together . . . all tainted with lies. "It was *all* a farce, Cullen."

"*No*. It wasn't. I am merely telling you this for you to understand how my love for you was enough to wake me, to drive me to become the man you thought me. Wellington wanted me to spy on you, to gain your trust in order to ruin you. But—"

"You have been using me. This entire time." She could not think as the searing pain returned, blinding her to his explanation. She forced herself to look at him, to read it in his face for herself. "Tell me you did not give Wellington my Paris factory."

"I did not wish to." Cullen's grief-stricken face blurred again. "But by that time, I was working with Agent Flannery, and he insisted for the good of the case that I needed to satiate Wellington somehow to keep him from revealing—"

Lord, no. Please, no. Willow pressed her hands over her mouth to keep from crying out. Her dream had been destroyed by the man she loved. *Willingly* destroyed. She sat forward, the meager contents of her stomach reaching her throat. She leaned to the side and retched, Cullen holding her shoulders.

She shook him off. *No. No!* She stared at his contrite expression, his beautiful, brilliant emerald eyes filled with concern, remorse, and longing. "Who are you?"

He flinched, but before he could answer, Willow heard Theodore's shout. She scrambled to her good foot, holding on to the tree for support.

He caught her elbow, steadying her. "Please, Willow, give me a chance to explain everything. You don't know—"

Once more, she ripped herself free from him. "Do not follow me, Cullen Dempsey. It will not end well for you if you do."

Twenty-Six

Theodore searched the park near where Mrs. Dupré said she had left the first clue, praying he would find some sort of answer as to where Fritz had taken her. He was about to leave when he spotted a crumpled piece of paper at the foot of a tree near Willow's park bench. He bent and painstakingly smoothed the paper enough to make out Mrs. Dupré's fine penmanship. *To the book shop you will go, where you will find your next clue in a book by Victor Hugo.* Willow would not have discarded the clue. She would have held on to it, re-reading it every few minutes to ensure that she had not mis-interpreted it.

That flower fanatic changed the clues. He shoved the note into his pocket, wracking his brain trying to think where Fritz would bring her, when he heard voices coming from around the bend. It sounded like Willow, crying . . . unless he was imagining things in his anxiety. He trotted down the path to find Willow limping out of the tree line toward him in a torn, disheveled gown. "Will!" He bolted for her, leaping over patches of mud. "Will." He enveloped her in his arms. "What happened? Are you well?"

Willow drew back, a weary smile lighting her face. "It's a

long story, which I shall divulge to you and my parents once home. But I'm well enough after being kidnapped."

"Kidnapped? How did you escape?" Theodore asked, unwilling to allow her to leave his side after the haggard evening of waiting and wondering where she had been taken when she had not returned home after the final clue, which was apparently supposed to lead her to a romantic dinner in the library. While her parents merely laughed, saying that their daughter was terrible at scavenger hunts, Teddy did not agree and at last, slipped away to go looking on his own without the Duprés' knowledge.

Willow turned her face into his chest and sobbed. He paused. Willow never cried and never this hard. *Dear Lord, what happened to her?* "Did Fritz . . . ?" He swallowed against the foul question. "Did he hurt you?"

She gave a slight shake of her head. "No. Please, just take me home. I want to go home."

Theodore tugged her closer and, feeling her shiver, noticed that one of her mutton sleeves had been torn. "I've got you, Willow. Lean on me. I'll see you home."

"Thank you, Teddy."

He ached to ask her what had happened, yet it was clear that she was in no state to explain. And even though Fritz had not harmed her, something terrible must have happened to have her in such a state. The questions swirling in his heart were almost too much to bear, but with one look at her tear-stained, mud-encrusted cheeks, he swallowed every last question. He would support Willow in whatever way she needed, and right now she needed him to keep her safe and see her home in silence.

Within a quarter of an hour, the pair reached the Duprés' mansion and as society members would likely be returning from dinners or leaving parties, there was a greater chance of their being spotted at the main entrance, so they slipped in through the servants' entrance to keep observers to a minimum.

"Mr. Beckwith?" Theodore called. The butler huffed into the

dim hallway, his wiry brows lifting almost as high as his hairline at the sight of Willow and her suitor in the servants' hall. Beckwith reached out a hand for her, but Theodore shook his head. "Please send a tray for Miss Dupré to wherever the family is waiting."

"The parlor, sir."

"Thank you." Theodore kept his grip on Willow and took the stairs to the main floor and directly to the parlor.

She put a hand to his chest, staying him outside the parlor door. "I better walk in unaided lest they think the worst."

"I think they already will once they see the state of your gown," Theodore replied.

She reached up and brushed back his hair. "I always could count on you, dear Teddy, to save me. Thank you."

"Always," he whispered, threading her hand around his arm, offering her support and all his love with the touch.

"Thank goodness, you are safe. The doctor said your ankle should be just fine with a day or two of rest." Mother fussed over Willow's comforter, tucking it about her daughter's feet once the stories had been told, everyone fed, and the twins and Teddy sent to bed. "I never would have guessed Fritz would take such measures to secure your hand . . . nor Cullen."

Willow closed her eyes against his name.

Father kept a firm hold on Willow's fingers from his seat beside her bed. "While there is nothing we can do regarding Cullen's deceit, as he *was* working for the law, the police have secured Archibald Lovett and his two hired thugs. The question remains, what do you want us to do about Friedrich Blythe? Are you still certain you do not wish to press charges? I wish you would let me."

"Please, protect Fritz from the papers. He was only acting out of misguided love for me, and as long as he stays away from us, I wish for him to be free from charges."

Father cleared his throat. "I hate to be callous and bring this up, but as you only have one suitor left . . ." He let the question hang in the air.

"Teddy does not know about Cullen yet. I need more time to come to terms with Cullen before I can make my choice."

"So long as you have an announcement March thirty-first as to whom you are going to wed, you may keep it a secret from all, Willow." Mother dabbed at her eyes with a handkerchief. "And I could not have selected a better gentleman for you than Teddy Day." Mother wrapped her arms about Willow. "I'm afraid it is bedtime, my darling. Try to rest if you can."

Bidding all good-night, Willow blew out her hurricane vase lamp, and though her body was exhausted from the trials of the day, her mind raced. After a half hour of tossing and turning, she slipped from her bed and knelt beside her nightstand, then removed the card from the drawer where she had copied her verse, although she did not have to read the script to recall it. She pressed it to her heart and lifted her chin, closing her eyes.

"Lord, you have taken me from near despair at the thought of a loveless marriage and have given me a new dream, a song for an even better future than that of the one I imagined all these years. And now. Now I'm so confused. Please guide me . . ." She swallowed as Cullen's face appeared in her thoughts, closely followed by Theodore's. "Let me not be blinded by what I want. Let me choose correctly."

Twenty-Seven

After following Willow as far as when she reunited with Teddy, Cullen had taken to walking the streets. He had felt an undeniable pull toward his old neighborhood, and having nothing but time, he gave in to the urge, soon leaving behind the fine mansions and reaching the row upon row of now-dilapidated brownstones without a single Knickerbocker in residence.

He paused in front of his old brownstone home that held the only fond childhood memories he had left—when they were happy . . . when his father loved him. Ripped from his childhood home after his father had made his fleeting fortune, Cullen was made to leave behind their Irish traditions, his brogue, and his friends—clinging only to what was acceptable by the society his mother so desperately wished to return to, which left precious little of anything familiar. The only time he had not been lonely was when he had taken up boxing and had made friends in the ring. His mother did not know it wasn't a gentlemen's boxing club, and he never felt the need to tell her. There, he could just be Cullen.

The gaslights flickered dimly above, still not having been replaced with the bright electric lights the upper class took for granted on their pristine avenues. Mother would have hated living here even more now. He sighed and kept walking, his feet taking him to the only church in which he had ever felt at ease. The exterior, though showing signs of age, looked well kept. He pushed open the small iron gate, which released a long, scraping rasp. *I wonder . . .* He tried the front door and it swung open, silent and well oiled. He swiped off his hat and stepped into the sacred house, his boots clicking on the stone floor as he made his way down the aisle to the simple cross hanging on the back wall. He slid into the third pew on the right. The familiar smooth wood of his family's pew brought him back to his boyhood. They had occupied this place with pride. Until, of course, it was no longer fashionable. He propped his forearms on the pew before him, bowing his head with the weight of his transgressions. *Lord, how am I supposed to let her go? I thought I was obeying you, listening to you when I met with the Pinkertons. Was it only me again? Trying to force my will?* At the silence, he rose and stuffed his hands into his pockets and moved through a side door to the back room behind the ancient massive organ, where the children met for Sunday school.

A bucket of coal that Cullen remembered filling sat at the ready beside the Franklin stove in the back corner. Along the wall stood a blackboard with what he assumed was the week's Scripture written across it—the book of Psalms, fortieth chapter.

He crossed his arms in the cold stone room and read, *"I waited patiently for the* LORD; *and he inclined unto me, and heard my cry."* Cullen shifted, his heart piqued. *"He brought me up also out of an horrible pit, out of the miry clay . . ."* He sank onto the bench. *". . . and set my feet upon a rock, and established my goings. And he hath put a new song in my mouth, even praise unto our God: many shall see it, and fear, and shall trust in the* LORD. *Blessed is that man that maketh the* LORD *his trust, and respecteth not the proud, nor such as turn aside to lies."*

He bowed his head, tears tracing down his cheeks. If only he could be rescued from the filthy mire of his choices. Again. "Lord, hear my cry. Get me out of this mess I have created by relying on my own stupid strength. It has failed me again and again and yet I continue to rely on these . . ." He opened his hands, palms up. "These hands that have destroyed lives in and out of the ring." He sank to his knees. "God, I beg you to pull me out of this pit, set me on ground that will not give way. Place a new song in my heart and . . ." Dare he pray it? "And in Willow's. Anything I say only makes it worse. I know I do not deserve it, but let her trust me. Please, Lord. Show me what to do or *not* to do." He lifted his eyes and read, *"Withhold not thou thy tender mercies from me, O LORD: let thy lovingkindness and thy truth continually preserve me. For innumerable evils have compassed me about: mine iniquities have taken hold upon me, so that I am not able to look up; they are more than the hairs of mine head: therefore my heart faileth me. Be pleased, O LORD, to deliver me: O LORD, make haste to help me."*

And with that prayer on his lips, the burden of not telling Willow that had been strangling him fell from his shoulders. He still had Eva Marie to protect. And with God's help, he would see her out of that engagement. His thoughts whirling, Cullen rose to return home. Breaking into a jog, he wove about street vendors, not caring what anyone thought of him, for wasn't that what had gotten him into this mess? His incessant need to feel valued? His father never valued him—not after his sister was born. But if he had only stopped to speak with God instead of running and leaning on his own strength . . . none of this would have happened. It would not happen again.

Cullen unlocked his front door and slipped inside, calling out, "Eva Marie? Mother?" He set to lighting a candle on the foyer table.

"Darling?" Mother appeared at the top of the stairs in her

dressing gown, followed by Eva Marie. Seeing Cullen, the two hurried down to greet him.

Eva Marie trailed her fingers over a bruise on his cheek. "What's happened?"

"You haven't started up boxing again, have you?" Mother pressed her lips into a thin disapproving line.

"No. It was in defense of Willow against Wellington's thugs."

"Heathcliff promised me he would not hurt you. He promised," Eva Marie whimpered.

At the sound of Wellington's given name upon his little sister's lips, he opened his arms to her and rested his chin upon her hair, his anger at Wellington and his grief over losing Willow threatening to overtake him. "Why did you do it, Eva? Why didn't you come to us before promising yourself to a man thrice your age?"

"He told me that in doing so I would be saving you from disgrace and setting Mother's standing in society forever." She wiped her wrist under her nose. "He didn't seem like a cruel man."

Cullen groaned. He had fallen for the same façade as Eva in his youth, thinking Wellington his savior. A crown that belonged to no one but the Lord.

Mother looked away from the pair of them, twisting her hands. "I begged him to leave her alone. I begged."

"You've spoken to him? I didn't know you were on speaking terms." He spoke at last, his voice hoarse from suppressed tears for his sister's willingness to sacrifice herself.

Mother stroked his hair behind his ear. "I knew Heathcliff Wellington long before your father. He was not always cruel and never to me. Before I met your father, Heathcliff and I courted without my father's knowledge and consent. And I loved Heathcliff . . . which led to a complication."

Eva Marie stiffened while Cullen jerked backward, rubbing his hand over his mouth, unable to speak with the truth he already knew in his gut. *Complication . . . me?*

She twisted the simple gold ring about her finger that she had yet to set aside. "I was madly in love with Heathcliff. We were to run away and marry. It was only one moment of recklessness the month prior to our planned elopement, but you see, he only had one business trip to complete before we could wed and, well, I gave in to him." At Eva Marie's gasp, Mother looked down to her folded hands, knuckles white against the green silk dressing gown. "Father found me leaving Heathcliff's brownstone, and seeing the state of my hair, he knew. And before I could even tell Heathcliff what was happening, I was locked in my rooms and soon found myself wed to your father, Donavan Dempsey. He had little money to recommend him to society, but he had a modest factory and I needed a husband who wasn't abroad."

Cullen ran his hands through his hair as he sank onto the bottom stair. "I cannot believe what I am hearing. I am Wellington's son?"

"No. You are Donavan Dempsey's, of that I am certain. Donavan was elated with my dowry and more so to have a son so soon, but when Eva Marie was born soon after moving into this house, and he saw that you two looked nothing alike"—she reached out and stroked Eva's long braid—"with Eva Marie's auburn hair, porcelain skin and freckles, while your hair was darker and your complexion free of freckles, he began to ask me about Wellington. And when he learned of my indiscretion, he could not see reason that you were, beyond a doubt, his own, which led to the gambling away of my inheritance, other women, and debts." She lifted her hands. "All I can say is that the lost love, or perceived lost love, of *the* woman can drive a man to madness."

"So that's why you tried to keep us apart," Eva Marie whispered, her freckles stark on her pale cheeks as she pressed a hand to her throat.

"We will break the engagement, Eva Marie. Even if we have to leave New York for good." Mother's voice quavered.

"I doubt it will come to that. I've spoken to the police, and they will be collecting Wellington shortly . . . after I speak with Willow and have her agree to testify."

"Then you must go to Miss Dupré at once." Mother wrapped her arms around her daughter. "We cannot risk being tied to that fiend one moment longer."

He nodded. Pressing a kiss to his mother's cheek, he stepped out into the fog. With a renewed spirit of purpose and hope, Cullen rushed back to the mansion to attempt to make things right with Willow as dawn's light peeked through the buildings.

"Paper! Paper! Get your paper!"

Cullen blanched at the headline the boy was waving over his head. *Dempsey Spies for Sugar Competitor*. Cullen ran up to the paper boy and purchased the lot, praying that Willow would not happen upon the article before he had a chance to explain, to confess his underhanded part in the competition.

"You are the fellow on the front—"

Cullen lifted a finger to his lips and handed the boy a half dollar.

The lad grinned and pocketed it, nodding to him. "Thank you, sir. Good luck with Miss Dupré. You are going to need it."

Tucking the papers under his arm, he returned to the mansion through the back gate, his hands shaking as he fit his key into the lock of the servants' entrance. The family was still safe in bed after the long night, so Cullen darted into the servants' hall, then paused to hear if anyone was about. All was quiet. Quickly, he gathered the morning papers before the footman had a chance to iron them, stuffed them into his greatcoat pockets, and climbed the stairs to the second floor. The family would most likely be abed until noon after the long ordeal, but he could not risk her hearing the truth from anyone but him. Taking a chair from the second-floor study where the fire was already lit, he tossed the stack of papers onto the flames, save one, and positioned himself outside her door. If she opened it, she would stumble upon him. With gritted teeth, he opened the single newspaper and began to read.

"*Source says that he managed to secure Cullen Dempsey an invitation to the Dupré competition. In exchange, Dempsey would gather invaluable information on the business and send to competitor. The motivation for this was so Dempsey could keep his family from the scandal of impending bankruptcy.*"

Cullen paused and read that last part again. *Wellington is at least protecting his new fiancée.* If Wellington betrayed Father's reprehensible behavior, both in business dealings and private, and true cause of death, then Eva Marie would suffer. He lifted his gaze to the ceiling. *Thank you, Lord, that he spared her from my foolhardiness in trusting the wrong man of desperation. Please show me a way of rescuing my sister from this marriage. I cannot do this alone.* Reluctantly he returned his focus to the paper and read on about his traitorous actions, knowing that Willow would be cut even more deeply with all of New York abuzz with his betrayal.

A stirring in Willow's room caught his attention. Cullen rose and ran his fingers through his hair and lightly tapped on the door in the trill that he had seen the sisters do before entering each other's apartments. He took a step back, waiting and praying that it was not too late.

Willow poked her head through the doorway, her smile faltering. "Cullen? What are you doing here?"

He leaned forward, whispering, "I apologize, but I must speak to you before another moment passes."

"I'm not dressed to receive you." She clutched the top of her robe, pulling it closed at her neck, resting her weight on one foot. "And if I were, I wouldn't let you in. What if one of the servants sees you here this early? Go away before you do even more damage."

"Join me in your study then?"

She pulled at the collar of the blush silk dressing gown hugging her petite figure.

Cullen averted his eyes. "There is much more I need to tell you."

Sighing, she whispered, "Very well. I'll join you there. Go quickly now before anyone sees you."

Cullen hoisted up the chair and strode into the warm study, the stiff paper in his jacket pocket chafing against his chest, unnecessarily reminding him of his choices, of all he was about to disclose to Willow. He stared at a picture of her and her family on the desk, a casual portrait taken during their last summer in Newport. His fingers traced the sweet smile of Willow. Such a lovely creature, within and without.

The door creaked behind him, and there stood Willow in a billowing blouse and simple navy skirt, curls haphazardly braided over one shoulder and tied in a crimson ribbon, making her look far younger than she was.

"Cullen." Leaning heavily on a cane, she stood on the other side of the room, chin jutted forward. "What on earth do you think you can say that will keep me from throwing you out now?"

Cullen crossed the room toward her, then stopped short, his hands outstretched as if wishing to gather her into his arms. He let them fall to his sides. "I promise you, I gave Wellington only what I had to in order to keep him from discovering the case against him, from stealing my family's business, telling the family's secrets and destroying any chance of happiness for my dear sister."

"What secrets could Wellington possibly hold over you that would do all of that?" Cullen looked away, but she lifted his chin with two fingers, forcing him to face her for his betrayal.

As much as this conversation pained her, she needed to know. "I'm giving you a chance to speak. Tell me your side."

"Wellington knows the innermost secrets of my family. Of my father's murder to pay for his gambling debts, of the parade of women he kept company with, of the fellow Irishmen he paid pennies to for a full day's work, and—"

"And what?" Her voice rose with her indignation. "None of that is enough for you to commit such treason against me."

"I believe he used his past with my mother and my debts to threaten my sister into securing her hand at the tender age of sixteen."

Her mouth went dry. If someone threatened to take away Philomena's or Sybil's future because of a sin *she* had committed, wouldn't she have moved heaven and earth to spare them? "What past?"

He lowered his gaze. "He was the reason why my mother wed Donavan Dempsey. He, uh—"

Willow pressed her hand to her mouth at the connection, of the girl's choosing to sacrifice herself to Wellington to save her brother. *She must love him dearly.* She shook away that thought and focused on the most pressing question. "And the competition. Was any of it real?"

He slowly reached for her, cupping her face between both of his rough hands. She hated herself for leaning into his palm.

"You have to know before another moment passes that I never thought it possible to feel this way. I love you, Willow. I have from the moment I hit that tree in Central Park and you so painstakingly saw to my wounds with a tenderness that wove through my scars into my long-since shattered heart." He laid her hand on his chest and knelt. "You've taught me that love *is* possible for even one so wretched as me. And it's my greatest desire to marry you."

Willow's breath caught at his declaration, her body responding before her words. *Cullen loves me. He loves me.* She released her cane and wrapped her hands about his neck. *Stop. Stop!* She tucked a lock of hair behind his ear, and he made a move to shake his hair to free it, reminding her that he did not like to show his ears to anyone, but then halted, allowing her to see him. Her fingers shook as she stroked his hair, the news of his association with Wellington flaming to life. She pulled away, her ankle throbbing and her heart flinching with his fallen expression. "It's too late for us, Cullen. Too much has happened."

"Willow, I am begging you. Please, give me another chance. If I had not been so bound to the man in loans, I never would have started this. But don't you see that with this discovery tonight, and your acting as witness, Wellington's attempt to rule is over? Forever. You are free—"

"You never would have been given an invitation in the first place without his help. Your very presence here is tainted." Her voice cracked. With one look at the handsome fellow kneeling before her, she knew the choice she *wished* she could make, but knew the choice she would make.

"I promise you that I was going to tell you before the final ceremony and before everything was out and all was printed," Cullen whispered.

"How can I be certain your repentance is from the heart and not because you were going to be caught in your lies in front of all of New York today? You have broken my heart." Her arms hung limply at her sides.

He rose and gathered her to himself, his chest swelling. "Please believe me. What they print today may not tell all. I *am* working with the Pinkertons. I can prove it. And though my start was not honorable, everything else was. I love you, Willow. God help me, I love you so, *a stór mo chroí*. My darling treasure of my heart."

Willow, numb, extricated herself from the man she loved above all others, tears racing down her cheeks. Cullen attempted to take her hand, but she folded her hands over her heart, shying away. "Good-bye, Cullen. I hope you find a bit of happiness one day . . . though it will not be with me."

"What are you saying?" His chest was caving in. He couldn't draw a full breath.

"I'm going to marry Teddy."

He flinched, his heart raw. "You can't. Not when you love me."

"I never said I did."

"You never said you didn't." He grasped her hands, but she shook him off as if he were something foul she did not want soiling her.

"Leave your keys."

"Willow, please." He felt as if he were being wrenched in two.

"Leave them."

Slowly, he reached into his pocket and laid the two keys on a side table, feeling as if the action was severing something between them, a sweet secret that had turned. "Just promise me you will think long and hard before marrying a man you do not love."

"I respect Teddy, which is more than I can say about you." She nodded again to the door.

He gathered his greatcoat from the chair where he had abandoned it and moved in a daze down the hall to the servants' stairs, leaving his things behind in his room so as to avoid facing the others. He could not bear to think of the hurt on Sybil's and Philomena's faces when they learned of his deception. He thought of Mr. Dupré and the anger he would rightly feel, and of Mrs. Dupré, a dear thoughtful lady, hurt by his choices. All the people wounded in his wake because of his weakness in not standing up to Wellington, for valuing society's appraisal of him over his true character. The hope he had in his position with the Pinkerton Agency for redeeming his character in the family's eyes, which had shone so brightly before tonight, was nothing more than a dim flicker now.

Slipping on his coat, he took to the servants' hall and exited by way of the kitchen, even as the staff looked at him questioningly as he left through the back door. Unwilling to wait for the back gate to be unlocked, Cullen jogged for the wall and grabbed the thick vines growing along its stones, then pulled himself up and over the ten-foot wall and dropped to his feet on the other side, ignoring the gaping mouths of the few people passing by.

He tugged his coat straight and made his way to the Pinkerton Agency's office on foot, needing the exercise. *Lord, I know you forgave me, but help me endure the consequences of my actions. Help me make right the injustices I have committed against Willow. Not in my power but yours, Lord, help me mend my wrongdoings to the Dupré family.* He bowed his head against the wind. *And, Lord, help Agent Flannery's family bear the news they are about to receive.*

Twenty-Eight

Theodore greeted the woman behind the counter and placed his order for half a dozen French pastries and a cup of strong coffee, handing her a bill. "Please keep the change."

"Thank you, Mr. Day." The woman nodded, her cheeks turning pink. "I recognized you straightaway from your pictures in the papers and magazines."

He dipped his head, used to others' odd fascination with the competition by now. "It's a pleasure to meet you, miss." He pointed to the table by the window. "I'll be over there, soaking up the morning sun, if you wouldn't mind bringing me my coffee. And would you please box up the pastries? I want to bring some back to Miss Dupré."

The baker fanned herself with her plump pink hand and sent him a smile. "Anything for my favorite contender for Miss Dupré's heart."

With a tip of his hat, Theodore sat at the front table, pleasantly surprised to find a newspaper on the seat, left by a previous patron no doubt, folded open to more news on the Vanderbilt ball. As a rule, he did not usually read anything printed concerning society's happenings, but today he decided to peruse the article for a few minutes before turning his attention to the front page.

Beaming, the baker brought the coffee and box of pastries to him. "I added an extra éclair for you, sir, since I know you are fond of chocolate. And mine are the best in the city."

"Why, thank you. I shall be telling my friends of your lovely establishment." He popped open the box, his mouth watering at the perfectly oblong, chocolate-covered pastry.

This brought a flush to the matron's already-ruddy complexion. "You're too kind, but that's why you're my favorite. That other one is too mysterious for my liking."

"Another good reason for her to choose me over that *other one*. I'll have to tell Miss Dupré of your vote." Theodore winked at her and took a bite of his pastry as the lady slipped behind the counter to see to her queue of customers. He snapped the paper open to the front page, his jaw dropping at the headline. *Cullen . . . is an interloper?* He scanned the article, his shock at Cullen's deceit mounting with each word he read. He stood so quickly, he bumped the table, his coffee sloshing onto the saucer, but he had only one thought. *Willow.*

He raced down the street, weaving around pedestrians and dashing across, nearly getting trampled by a milk wagon. As much as his thoughts focused on comforting Willow and beating that boxer senseless, there was a small voice in the recesses of his heart that whispered *he* was the last gentleman standing. Willow's final choice. *But will she truly be choosing me? Does she actually wish to marry me, or am I the consolation prize?* Regardless, he knew without question that he would choose her, no matter if her heart held only friendship for him. Darting into the mansion, he ignored the butler's protests. "Where's Miss Dupré?" Theodore panted.

"I-in the conservatory. But, sir, I must say one should *wait* to be allowed inside—"

He trotted into the conservatory to find Willow in a heap on the marble floor, her arms draped atop the stone bench, her shoulders heaving in silent sobs. Theodore knelt beside her and gathered her into his arms. "Will, I was out getting pastries for you when I read the news. I'm so sorry."

She lifted her tear-stained face to him, her nose red and eyes swollen. "It wasn't a shock to see the article, but it still hurts." She rubbed her fist over her heart, drawing a ragged breath. "How could he, Teddy? How could a man willingly do this to a woman he professed to love?"

Theodore fought against the choice words he wished to call the cad, his anger burning in his chest. "The man is a dog. He doesn't deserve to walk the same earth as you. Is he still here?"

"No. I sent him away, of course, and he left at once." She shifted away from him and raised her hands to her face, using the back of her cuff to dab at her nose. "Do you have a handkerchief? A dripping nose is not seemly to behold."

He removed a plain cotton handkerchief from his pocket and softly dabbed beneath her lashes. She grasped it, turned from him, and blew her nose.

She gave him a wobbly smile. "I think I shall have to get this laundered before I return it."

He stroked a lock of hair behind her ear, unable to jest with her for once. "Do you want to go for a walk? Perhaps get some air?"

"I'm afraid someone in the park will recognize me and I shall have to endure their pity. I cannot endure any more pain today lest I break, and I cannot break in front of the public." She sniffed, twisting the damp handkerchief in her hands. "Teddy, I didn't want it to end this way."

"End?" He stiffened. "You cannot mean to send me away? Not when I am in love with you? And then there is the business to consider . . ." He sounded desperate even to his own ears.

"Yes. The business." Her tone was hollow.

He took her hand in his, rubbing his thumbs over her icy palms. "I suppose the question is . . . do you still want to save the business at the expense of marriage?"

"Absolutely," she whispered, her eyes filling with fresh tears. "I am tired and *lonely*. I want to marry because I desperately need a friend, someone I can trust and be comfortable with at the end of the day. But you need to know where my heart lies now." She swallowed. "I don't wish to have feelings for Cullen. I truly don't, but—"

Theodore lifted a finger to her lips. "Say no more. Miss Dupré, I have loved you for longer than either of us knew. Will you marry me?"

She gave a little cry and pulled him into a fierce embrace. "You're the dearest friend anyone could ask for, and I know that in time our friendship will blossom into something beautiful."

He grinned, not caring that it was only friendship that she felt for him at this point. "Is that a yes?"

"If you will have me as I am, brokenhearted, I would be honored to have you for my king." She pulled his hands to her lips and kissed them.

"Always." He swept her into his arms and twirled her about the flowers until she laughed.

"You will wed Theodore, then?" Mother asked, embroidering a pillow beside Sybil as the girls played chess in the parlor, with Father harrumphing over the newspaper every few minutes.

"But we thought you loved Cullen," Philomena said, capturing one of Sybil's pawns, her round eyes full of hurt, though Willow could tell she was attempting to act like an adult by keeping her tears in check and focusing on the game.

Willow rose and paced the room with her cane. For despite the pain, she could not sit still. And she could not endure being around her family any longer, not with the piteous looks they were sending her way, nor the anger electrifying the air of the chamber, nor the constant flow of questions. She wished she could escape from it all, but she still had to speak with Teddy whenever he returned from his afternoon ride about their plans for the future. Hopefully he would have a peaceful ride, although she was certain the city was already buzzing with the scandal, which was why she had not sought the comfort of a ride in the park along with him.

"Yes. I will not be humiliated by having no one at the end of the competition." Facing the window with her back to them, Willow discreetly wiped at her cheeks with the back of her hand. She loved Cullen, but she had never uttered those words to anyone, not even Cullen. For that, she was thankful—that she had not given up that sacred moment to a man unworthy of her devotion. "Besides, Teddy loves me. And I have always loved him as a friend."

"Well, that is a promising start, my dear. Many do not begin with even so much as friendship." At Mother's grunt, Willow turned to find Mother had stabbed her needle through the pillowcase too far, pricking her finger, betraying her nerves. Mother never made a mistake. She set her work aside and wrapped her finger in a handkerchief before looking up at her daughter. "I want you to know that your father and I are thrilled to have him as a son. Thank you for your willingness to save the family's legacy."

Willow straightened her shoulders, heartened. It felt good to remember *why* she had agreed to the competition. Her family. "I know our relationship can grow. With such love from him, how can it not blossom into more?" Feeling the knot swell in her throat, she had to escape before it was too late and she cried in front of her little sisters. She turned on her heel. "I need to be with the maids when they pack Cullen's things, to see what else he has been hiding from me." She crossed the room and slowly, painstakingly took the staircase to the third floor and made her way to the room where Cullen had been staying. She strode inside just as the footman was placing into a trunk

Cullen's two other suits, the ruined one on top. She grazed her
fingers down the sleeve of his favorite blue shirt. The scent
of sandalwood lingered on the fabric. "Have you found any
papers of his here?"

A maid stripped off the comforter from the mattress and
checked underneath for anything hidden. "Atop the desk, miss.
I found them rolled and stuffed inside the toes of his shoes,
and I figured I would ask before I packed them in his trunk."

"Thank you." She picked up the top letter and opened it to
find a short note from Eva Marie.

> *Brother, judging from your previous letter, I would risk
> saying that you are completely in love with your Miss
> Dupré. Do not ruin this.*
>
> *E. M. D.*

Willow suppressed a laugh that at once turned bitter as she
caught sight of the date marked on the note, which was about
the time of her Parisian factory loss. Cullen's betrayal bit her
again. She filtered through the stack of letters, fully intending
on reading them again later before burning or forwarding them.
At the bottom, inside an envelope with Eva Marie's handwrit-
ing on it, she found a telegram that had been carefully folded
and tucked inside.

> *After your little outburst saying that you will not work
> for me anymore, I think a forfeit is due. Send me notice of
> something that will hurt the Dupré business or I will call
> in your loan and ruin your mother's chances of a future
> by releasing your stories to the press. As for Eva Marie, I
> have something special planned.*
>
> *H. W.*

Willow shook her head against the despicable man's threats. *Why did he keep this one letter from Wellington when there are no others?* She pocketed it along with the rest and poked her head into the closet, spying something hanging over the edge of the topmost shelf. Using her cane, she attempted to push it from its perch. It fell, and the brush of something brittle greeted her fingers as she caught it. *He dried a laurel crown? Perhaps I did mean something to him if he kept one.*

She held the dried laurels to her heart, remembering the ceremony when she had given him the first crown. *Lord, why does this hurt so?* She set the faded green crown in his trunk. Perhaps he would see it and feel remorse for the pain he made her endure. It was time to let him go and embrace her future. "Nancy, please have Cullen's things sent to his home. But if his trunks happen to get dropped by accident in the Hudson River along the way, I would not be opposed."

The maid looked up as if waiting for her to say she was only jesting. Instead, Willow turned on her heel and headed for the conservatory for a bit of nature to cool her thoughts, her cane thumping against the marble floor as she walked among the potted orchids that spilled splashes of brilliant color along the cold marble columns. *Lord, I trusted you to give me a new song. Is this it? A ballad of a broken heart?*

Twenty-Nine

Willow and Teddy decided that it was best to keep the original wedding date on Sunday, as her mother had already booked Delmonico's to cater the event and issued the invitations. It had been a peculiar way to send invitations when no one knew who the groom would be, but Willow did not wish to endure any more of society's piteous, curious stares than she had already. Her parents, of course, were ecstatic that she was marrying Teddy, despite the circumstances, though no one was allowed to breathe a word on the identity of her groom. Even the dark ending of the competition dimmed some for Willow and the twins in the flurry of dress fittings for a new trousseau and a wedding gown.

Keeping busy was key to not dwelling on her pain, so Willow insisted upon returning to the office with her father and Teddy at her side to protect her from the cruel judgments of the occasional comment. Her fiancé was not only helpful as a supporter, but she discovered that he was also a shrewd businessman. Teddy threw himself into the pile of work at her desk and labored relentlessly to lessen her load.

After a long morning of work on Friday, Willow received a note requesting an appointment to speak with an inspector at her home that evening, which negated her entire plan of keeping busy so as not to think about Cullen. And, seeing her distracted state, Teddy finally convinced her that she needed to take the afternoon to herself to help clear her thoughts before the crowning ceremony tomorrow and the wedding the following day. Despite her need to keep busy, her head ached from the suppression of nagging thoughts, so she reluctantly agreed, giving him a peck on the cheek in thanks.

Taking up her horse's reins, she gave him a swift kick and sent him trotting toward the Brooklyn Bridge. She had only ever traveled this way escorted or in a closed carriage, so it made her slightly anxious to take it by herself. Still, she knew Teddy would never send her somewhere dangerous, and besides, it was silly to shy away from something as simple as riding unescorted across the bridge back home, even if she wasn't as accomplished in riding as her twin sisters.

Perched on her sidesaddle, she rode at a trot across the bridge, keeping her attention from the men driving wagons, riding in carriages, and pulling horse carts surrounding her. She swallowed hard as she felt their stares on her straight back, regretting her decision more than once. She was counting the seconds until she reached the other side of the bridge when a man's lewd remark made her start and she dropped her whip in the line of sight of her mount. The horse pranced fearfully to the side and into the man leading his cart, knocking him to the ground before his mules.

"If you can't control your horse, you best keep to a carriage, woman." He glared at her and swiped his hat off the ground, grunting. "Look at that. You have gone and spoiled it."

"Then you shouldn't have spoken to me so rudely." She moved to turn her mount, but the man gripped her horse's reins.

"Then *you* shouldn't be out unattended."

"Release me at once!" She narrowed her eyes at him from behind her riding hat's netting.

"You aren't going anywhere until you pay for my hat," he snarled.

Hoofbeats thundered behind her, and she hated her traitorous heart for leaping at the sight of the handsome fellow. Had it really been only three days since her conversation with Cullen?

"Release her or pay the consequences." Cullen Dempsey's powerful voice cracked the air.

The man must have recognized the fury in the former boxer's expression, for he released her at once and pulled his mules into the line of moving wagons.

Cullen reached out for her reins and urged the horse alongside his, calming her mount with the presence of his own horse. "Whoa there. Whoa, fellow."

She drew a deep breath and met Cullen's bewitching green eyes. He was even better-looking than she remembered.

"Willow, are you well?"

"It is *Miss Dupró* now, Mr Dempsey," she replied curtly, lifting her chin. "And I was controlling my mount just fine without your assistance."

"While I may not be in your competition any longer, I vividly recall your distaste for riding sidesaddle, especially alone. And where is your knight in shining armor?"

"You mean my *King* Arthur," she corrected, her teasing him coming back like an old habit. She smoothed her face once more. Cullen was no longer her concern, and she would not give him the satisfaction of knowing that he plagued her every breath with *what if*s and that the very sight of him was enough to wrench her heart in two. Hiding behind a false show of strength, perfected from her years spent in front of a hostile board of men, was the only way for her to remain composed. She shifted atop her mount. "If you'll excuse me, sir, I must be on my way." She directed her horse forward, but Cullen did not leave her side. "I cannot afford to be seen with you, especially not in so public a place as the Brooklyn Bridge, which as you can see, we have reached the end."

Cullen nodded. "I happen to be traveling in the same direction."

She would have urged her mount into a gallop, yet she didn't think she could stay in the saddle for anything more than a trot. It would take a half hour to reach home, and she could not endure a moment more with him at her side without giving in to the tears clogging her throat. She kept her focus straight ahead. "While I thank you for your assistance with that brute, I cannot have you beside me. It's . . . it's too much."

"Because you still love me despite all that I have done?" Cullen's bold words drew her gaze to his, and she found her pain mirrored there.

"I never said that I loved you."

"You didn't have to, *macushla*."

"Do not call me that when it is not true," she whispered.

He drew his horse closer to hers. "I'm living in agony, Willow. To know that I lost you because of my foolhardy beginning."

"Something that I must live with, as well. Your choices have hurt more than just you. But that is all behind me now. I've made my choice. The announcement party is still on schedule, along with the wedding."

Cullen pulled his horse in front of hers, his free hand propped on his thigh, the intensity in his expression undeniable. "You're making a mistake, Willow. You know how good we are together, and we could be wonderful partners in business too, if you would forgive me."

"Forgive? It's not only my forgiveness you need. You have also hurt my parents and my sisters. The girls wept when they heard of your betrayal."

He ducked his head.

"But I dried their tears when I told them I would marry Teddy. He will be a wonderful husband, a catch in his own right as well as from an old family, not to mention he adores me and would *never* act as you have. *He* is willing to give up his place in his family's riverboat business in New Orleans to be by my side, aiding me in *my* dream." She shook her head. "I do not deserve a man such as he to love me."

Cullen pressed his lips into a firm line. "You do. How could you say otherwise?"

She gave him a knowing look. *If you could know how much I love you, then you would understand how cruel it is for me to marry someone who loves me but whom I do not love back.* She directed her horse down the avenue and decided to end the ride by stopping at Flora's brownstone residence. "This is where we will part. I do not expect to see you again before I am wed."

He dismounted and reached up for her. His hands wrapped about her petite waist, and she loathed herself for the tears threatening her stoic façade. Her hands lingered on his arms for half a second before she stumbled back over her long, crimson riding skirt. "Cullen, please." Her voice trembled. "Leave me be. When I am married, I do not wish to see you again, *ever*."

"I can't, Willow. Until the vows are spoken, I cannot give up on us . . . even if you have. I will love you until my dying breath, *a stór mo chroí*."

His words echoed with every step she took to the front door. She lifted the knocker and tapped in rapid succession, her focus forward, knowing that Cullen was still below. The door opened, and Willow darted inside, breathing a sigh of relief that she had not looked back. Such an act would have required a confession to Teddy and she would not betray his trust, not when she knew what the act felt like on the receiving end.

"Miss Flora is in the parlor, Miss Dupré. I'll have another cup sent with her afternoon tea cart." The butler bowed to her.

Willow retreated into the cozy room, which enveloped her in its warmth.

"Will." Flora held her hands out to her friend, squeezing

them as she drew Willow over to a chair. "You have come at a perfect time. My sisters and parents are out, and I have tea and chocolates coming, which I will happily share, for I believe you need them more than I after your week. I could hardly believe the papers." She shifted her attention to the fireplace, lowering her voice. "I, uh, tried to come to you earlier, but every time I called, your mother said you were out or too busy."

"I know. I'm sorry I haven't called back sooner. I have found that idle hands are not my strong suit when I have too much on my mind." Willow pulled off her black riding gloves before lifting the netting of her riding hat and removing the pin securing it in place. She chucked the gloves into the hat and set it on a side table so as not to soil Flora's fine carpet. "It has not been formally announced yet, as Mother is having a ball for the final ceremony tomorrow as you know, but I will be wedding *Teddy* on Sunday."

Flora blinked, her lips parting. "What? So soon? I was not quite prepared for that after all that has happened," she said, her voice shaking slightly.

"Whyever not? He was among the top two contenders and is the only one left who has not lied to me." Willow dabbed at her neck with her handkerchief. The cozy room was turning into an inferno in her high-collared gown.

"Because I thought you loved Cullen." Flora rose, pulling the cord once more, muttering, "Where is that tea?"

Willow leaned back in the stiff Louis XIV chair, hurt by her friend's callous response. "Aren't you going to issue me congratulations?"

A blush reached Flora's cheeks. "Forgive me. I was merely taken aback. If you are happy, then I am happy. Congratulations, my dear friend."

Willow did not quite care for this answer, no matter her friend's kind tone. "Why wouldn't I be happy?"

Flora twisted her lips. "I wish you would stop pressing me to speak."

Willow snorted. "Flora, you were never one to need pressuring to speak your mind. Do so now or I will think what you are withholding from me is quite awful."

"It is."

Willow sat up. "Now you *must* tell me."

"If you insist." Flora cleared her throat. "I saw you at the ball. Any fool could tell which of the gentlemen you preferred even if you could not."

"That's utter nonsense." Willow stood and turned toward the fire, kicking her skirts behind her. "Why do you even care?"

"If you are marrying Teddy for the wrong reasons, I care a great deal." Flora planted her hands on her hips as if Willow's retort had made Flora's point for her. "Do you have any misgivings as to your motives?"

Willow stretched her hands to the heat to give herself the excuse not to look at her friend. "Of course I do. While I am marrying Teddy, I can't help but worry at his attentiveness with the business these past three days. I know he must only be trying to help me with this cloud of doubt hovering over me, but what if his focus on the business is the true reason for his interest?"

Flora gasped, pulling Willow's shoulder to face her. "Bite your tongue, Willow Dupré. I was referring to the state of *your* heart, not his. If you are looking for a reason to dismiss yourself from this marriage to such a good man, then by all means cut him loose, move on with your life, and let Teddy have a chance at true happiness."

Willow straightened, surprised by her friend's passion. Flora had always been rather sensitive whenever Teddy came into the conversation, but was there a reason beyond what Willow could see at the surface? "Flora, why are you so piqued?"

"Because I'm tired of hearing you make up all manner of feeble excuses in your attempts of escaping matrimony with Teddy." Flora crossed her arms and lifted her chin. "There are *plenty* of females who would jump at a chance to have Teddy's affections."

"Including yourself?" Willow's voice rose.

Flora pursed her lips. "Even if I had feelings for him, would you think me capable of such treason? I am your *best* friend. And no matter the gentleman you wed, I will support you and your marriage to ensure that it is a success. I would *never* jeopardize it no matter how I felt."

Willow enveloped Flora in her arms. "It seems I am continually surrounded by those who are too good for me. I do not deserve you, Flora Wingfield." At the chime of the mantel clock, Willow pulled away. "I'm afraid I do not have time for tea, after all. I have an inspector to meet before dinner."

"And that's all I have for you, Agent Nolan." Willow folded her hands around her teacup in her father's study. "Do you have any more questions?"

Agent Nolan set down his pencil inside his black book and closed it, the pencil keeping it propped open a bit as he leaned toward her in the wing-back chair. "May I speak plainly to you, Miss Dupré?"

"Of course." *Weren't we doing so before?* She could hardly imagine speaking more plainly to a man she had just met, whose line of questions left her blushing one moment and pale the next.

"Cullen Dempsey, in his seeking out the Pinkerton Agency, was *choosing* the difficult path. It would've been far simpler to keep this information to himself, woo you and marry you without your having any knowledge of subterfuge. But Dempsey is an honorable gentleman, as a lesser man would not have sacrificed all." The agent cleared his throat and lowered his gaze. "And I think it is important for you to know that Dempsey's supervisor, Agent Flannery, gave his life seeking justice for his sister, who died as Wellington's factory worker and tenant at the tender age of five and twenty."

Willow pressed a hand to her chest. "I did not know."

"That's what makes Dempsey's and your sacrifice so important. We may never know everything that Wellington held over the immigrants who work for him, living in his ghastly apartments, but most likely his workers earned mere pennies in his factory, and while Wellington initially extended grace to them in their rent, he gradually increased it until it was too much for them to handle. And being the charlatan he is, he acted as if the debt meant little to him. Before long, though, they were so indebted to Wellington, he decided to call in their debts, essentially having free labor and sending his profit margins soaring."

Willow's fists curled on her lap. "Despicable man."

"Yes, but it wasn't illegal." The agent shook his head. "Because of Agent Flannery working with Dempsey, paired with your witnessing Wellington's confession, these people will have a fighting chance in America. Like Dempsey, they trusted the wrong man, and like Dempsey, they are now free because of the two of you."

Her heart thumped. Had she been too harsh with Cullen? She had listened to his story, but until today, had not *heard* it. Now, despite her bruised pride, she could see the difference Cullen had made, not just for his immediate family but also in the lives of hundreds of Irish workers.

Agent Nolan removed a second, worn leather book from his jacket pocket. "Agent Flannery kept careful accounts of all his meetings with Dempsey and reported to me at the end of each week." He flipped the book open. "Allow me to read you the entries—well, part of the ones I think you would find interesting. '*Seventh of January*, Dempsey offers aid and asks when he can tell Miss Dupré. *Twentieth of January*, Dempsey again asks when he can share with Miss Dupré. *Seventh of February*, Dempsey sends telegram asking if he can inform Miss Dupré of the plan.'" He looked up at her. "I could go on and name the dozen times your gentleman requested to tell you. And each time he asked, Flannery states in his notes that it was apparent Dempsey was falling more and more in love with you." He handed her the book, allowing her to see the entries for herself. "This is not normally in my line of business, but I would hate to see a man like Dempsey be punished for choosing the right path. For being so close to Wellington, it is a miracle he did not turn out to be a criminal. Instead, he was instrumental in taking down Wellington." He coughed, distilling the rising tension in the room, his neck crimson as he pushed himself up from the chair.

Willow rose with him. "Thank you for your honesty."

"Honesty is my job. Thank you for your time, Miss Dupré." He extended his hand to her, and she shook it. "We will be in touch about the court date."

Teddy paced in the foyer, pausing when he heard the thump of boots on the stairs. The agent nodded to him as he showed himself to the door, and once the door closed behind the agent, Teddy took the steps three at a time to the second-floor study. He drew in a breath to steady his pounding heart and gave a light knock on the half-open door, spying Willow beside the fireplace, head buried in her hands. "Will?"

The moment she lifted her tear-stained face, his gut twisted . . . and in that moment he felt as if he were losing her. He knelt beside her, his hand at her shoulder, patting. "What happened?"

She swallowed. "Wellington will no longer be a problem."

"Well, that is no reason to be crying now, is it?" He tried to infuse his comment with lightheartedness.

She straightened her shoulders and presented him a weak smile, a pathetic attempt to appear fine. Yet he took his cue from her and extended his hands, helping her to standing.

"You know what I think? You need some amusement. You have been shut away in your rooms and office for far too long."

"It's only until the ball when we announce our engagement." She shrugged. "It is not too great a burden to bear."

He shook his head, not giving in so easily. "It isn't healthy to be so sedentary. What shall it be, my lady? Boating in the park? Horseback riding? Lawn tennis? Badminton in the drawing room?"

She slipped her hand into his and leaned her head on his shoulder, sighing. "You know that I am always up for breaking an expensive vase whilst playing badminton in the drawing room."

The woman in the shadows kept pace with him, so that after a couple of blocks, Cullen ducked into the alley between buildings and waited for the apparition. She passed his hiding place, whipping about looking for him. He was surprised she could see two feet in front of her, what with the widow's weeds she was wearing. He grasped her arm, eliciting a shriek from behind the widow's veil. "You should not be following a man in this part of town."

The woman swatted his hand away with surprising force. "She does if she wants to relay a message."

The familiar voice made him drop his hold on her at once. "Flora?"

"Shh!" She waved her hands at him, tugging him farther into the alley, sending a few tin cans and crumpled newspapers scattering in their wake. "Do you want to alert the entire block of my presence? I only just managed to evade the press outside my door. And then there are the gamblers to account for with their bloodthirsty need to know which gentleman Willow is choosing. Apparently, there are quite a few large bets being placed throughout the city on the outcome."

"I'm guessing the correct answer is no, I don't want to alert them? So, why are you here?" he asked, keeping his voice low.

She crossed her arms. "Because Willow is miserable, and I want to know if you are worth my fighting for."

"Pardon?"

She gave an exasperated sigh and lifted her veil over her ebony bonnet to reveal reddened cheeks and matted, golden curls. She narrowed her stark blue eyes. "Willow listens to me. And as her dearest friend in the world, I want her to be happy, and therefore she will forgive me for the transgression of over-stepping my bounds by finding you and asking . . . why should I help you redeem yourself in Willow's eyes?"

"Miss Flora, if you would speak kindly of me, it would mean the world. And to show you that I am a changed man . . ." Cullen reached into his pocket and withdrew the package he had just secured, tugged out the documents within, and placed them in her hands.

Flora flipped through them, her face brightening under a sheen of sweat. "Now *this* is something I can use. Tell me, what are your feelings on breaking and entering?"

Thirty

Willow greeted her guests, all of whom expressed their excitement over the upcoming announcement at the end of the ball. For although the papers had spread the news of Cullen's betrayal, her ride with Cullen had been spotted by several society matrons, which had sent the speculations into a frenzy of not knowing upon whom Willow would bestow the final laurel crown. And the fact that the final ceremony would be carried out at the party made the invitations as coveted as the invitations to Alva Vanderbilt's costume ball had been.

Standing in the receiving line just beyond the foyer, in a gown of cream silk with puffed sleeves and an elegant lace pattern that traveled from her collar to her waist, her hair perfectly coiled with a tiara fashioned of golden laurels atop, she caught a glimpse of someone who looked exactly like Cullen in the waiting crowd outside that had spilled onto the sidewalk. *No, he wouldn't dare show his face here, not when my parents would throw him out for all to see.* She blinked and the striking figure in the crowd had vanished.

Flora clasped Willow's hand. "You are exquisite in that ensemble. One could almost say you have a bridal glow about you." She leaned closer to Willow and lowered her voice. "When is the announcement? I promise to look surprised along with everyone else."

"As soon as I greet the guests, I shall return to my chambers for a few moments, allowing time for everyone to get settled, and then I will make my grand entrance and announce it for all to hear, after which I will open the dancing."

"Did you have a chance to read that note I sent round?"

"Yes, Flora." Willow sighed, shaking her head over the long letter proclaiming why she should give Cullen a chance to speak his mind once more. "It's too late. I've already accepted Teddy."

"Very well. I need to be on my way then." Flora patted her on the arm and added, "So you can greet your other guests, of course."

Willow felt as if lost in a fog, greeting guests and smiling, yet she wasn't certain how she was going to make it through the guest line without bursting into tears. She had not realized the extreme lengths her heart had been given to Cullen. She had thought she had protected herself. If it had only been her dream that he had dashed, she could have forgiven him for sneaking into the competition solely to spy on her, because that was *before* he knew her. Before they fell in love . . . But every time thoughts of his betrayal threatened to consume her, Inspector Nolan's conversation blazed to the forefront of her heart, and the black-and-white hurt of before blurred into a jumbled mess. Teddy was right—the heart was not like a business transaction.

The four-hundredth guest greeted, Willow ducked behind the footman in his crimson livery, followed him to the parlor and slipped past the door behind the screen that the servants used, and took the staircase up to her room. Her cream skirts trailing behind on the marble steps as she leaned heavily on the wooden railing.

"Begging your pardon, Miss Dupré, but do you need assistance? You look pale."

She waved the footman off. "Thank you, Marvin, but I will be fine. It's just these steps that have me moving slower than usual." *Along with my broken heart.* She padded down the hall with its thick carpet to her now-dark room. The maids must have forgotten she would be returning and turned down the gas. She closed the door behind her and moaned. *Lord, help me through this. My head knows what it must do, but my heart does not wish to follow.* She went to her bed and knelt there, praying for direction, for strength to do the right thing no matter how difficult.

"Come on." Flora waved Cullen in through the side gate, despite the footman's glare.

"This is highly irregular, Miss Wingfield. I'm supposed to guard this door and not let anyone pass "

Flora lifted a single brow to him. "I know, but since I am Willow's dearest friend in the world, you know that she would not mind *my* taking a liberty here or there."

"Then why not take him in through the front door like the rest of the guests?" He narrowed his gaze at Cullen. "This staff is extremely loyal to the family, and while we would never speak of their affairs outside the house, you should know we are all aware of your past sins, sir."

"I am aware." Cullen tugged at his dinner jacket's silk lapel with one hand and held on to the gift for Willow in the other.

"You do realize that tonight is when she will announce her fiancé." Flora crossed her arms at the dedicated footman. "And I am certain that the staff do not know whom she will choose, as even the lady herself does not know who shall have her hand."

Cullen's heart leapt at this news, and he lifted his face to the heavens. *Thank you, Lord.*

Flora elbowed him in the ribs, making him wince. "Isn't that right, Mr. Dempsey?"

"One can only hope," he replied and rubbed at the sore spot. Flora was surprisingly strong for such a lithe woman.

With an exaggerated lift of his chin, the footman waved them forward. "Very well. But I will not take the blame for this one, Miss Wingfield."

"I know I have put you through a lot in the years you have worked here, James, but you will not be blamed." Flora patted his arm in passing and grabbed Cullen's hand, tugging him toward the servants' staircase.

Cullen stared at the narrow stairs that snaked along the passage up and up to reach the attic where the servants slept.

"She will be announcing her engagement any minute! Go. Go!" Flora gave him a little shove, and he did not need a second prompting. He took the stairs two at a time, leaving Flora at the bottom. Opening the door at the second-floor landing, Cullen slipped into the hall and counted the doors to Willow's chamber. Drawing a deep breath, he let himself inside. "Willow?" he called into the near darkness, a small fire casting the only light in the room.

At the sound of his voice, she gasped and straightened in her wing-back chair beside the fireplace. "Cullen?" She leapt to her feet. "You cannot be in here! Do you seek to ruin me completely?"

Cullen crossed the Persian rug and joined her side. "I've come to give you something." He lifted a rectangular box with a satin ribbon securing it. "Please, open it."

She looked up at him, the firelight flickering across her features, where he saw a mixture of curiousness, confusion, and anger in her expression. She was right to be angry with him, but he prayed that these documents would at the very least serve as a balm to her wound.

Willow pulled the ribbon and lifted the lid, holding the top document up to the light. She inhaled sharply. "How did you—?" She whirled and locked eyes with him. "These are the last shares. My cousin would never have parted with these unless you gave him something he could not refuse."

"The price does not matter. What matters is that I repair some of the damage I caused to the purest heart I have ever met." He reached out to caress her face, then stopped, uncertain if the action would be welcome. He dropped his hand. He did not deserve to touch her. "Please, look at the second set of documents."

"There is more?" She pulled an envelope from the bottom of the box and broke its seal. "This is a deed."

"For the Parisian factory. I know how much that dream meant to you and to your family."

"Oh, Cullen." She pressed her hand to her mouth. "What did it cost you to purchase this from Wellington? And how on earth did you persuade my cousin?"

"My mother visited Wellington in prison, and in the course of their conversation, she discovered he had something on Osborne. At her request, Wellington released my sister and sent a note to Osborne, promising to no longer blackmail him if he sold the shares to me for a fair price . . . which was the entirety of my remaining shares in the shipping company." He shook his head. "I do not know how Mother moved him to such an action, but I did not stop to question his motives until I had the shares in my possession."

"You sold your business . . . for me?" As she reached out for the settee to steady herself, he grasped her hand in his, supporting her. "And the deed to the refinery, what did that cost you?" Willow whispered.

"With my family's blessing, I signed over my mansion to Wellington's second-in-command, who apparently had no interest in the property, preferring a Fifth Avenue address more." He shrugged. "A small price to pay if it meant returning your dream to you."

"You would surrender everything for me without even a promise from me? How will you live?" Willow's lovely eyes sparkled behind a sheen of tears.

"By God's grace. He gave me a talent that I can use again if He is willing and provide for my family that way. I would gladly give up all and more if that is what it takes for you to see that I am a changed man because of *you*. My love for you brought me to my knees before God. I have been relying on my own strength, but seeing you embrace this new life, despite your best-laid plans . . ." He pressed her hand to his chest. "It awoke a passion in me that I had allowed life to squelch. With this gift, I want you to know that I believe in *you*, Will. You have one of the sharpest minds in the business world, and I know that if given the chance, you will change the industry in ways that the businessmen cannot even fathom. I know this does not excuse my deceiving you, but I pray you'll forgive me in time."

"I already have." She held the documents to her chest. "Inspector Nolan told me everything. I now know why you did what you thought necessary."

"Will, I love you. I am finished with all the subterfuge, and I stand before you, a man with nothing to offer you but his love and support." Cullen tucked a lock of her chestnut hair behind her ear. "Please, tell me I am not too late, *macushla*." *My darling.* He drew her into his arms, loving the nearness of her.

A soft knock sounded at the door, and Willow leapt away from him. "You must hide at once! I cannot have anyone find you in here with me, especially not alone."

"Promise me you will at least think on what I have said before it's too late."

She hesitated for only an instant before answering, "I promise. Once I leave my room, wait a moment and then take the servants' stairs down to the party. The guests expect to see you before I appear again. Theodore should already be mingling with them."

"Until the vows are spoken, I will wait for you." He repeated his promise as Willow slipped out the door, giving him a furtive glance over her shoulder. And his heart soared at the soft smile gracing her lips.

Thirty-One

"Nicolette." Willow closed her bedroom door, still clutching the documents to her chest, relieved to know her heart at last. "Have you seen Teddy . . . I mean, Mr. Day in the ballroom?"

Her brow furrowed at Willow's blocking the door. "No, miss. I only came to see if you were ready for the announcement as per your mother's orders."

"Not yet. I need you to find Mr. Day and bring him to me at once in my study. It's imperative."

"Yes, miss. I'll return directly." She bobbed into a curtsy and hurried away.

Willow slipped into the study, surprised to see the hurricane vase glowing brightly atop the desk she shared with her father. "Father? Are you hiding away from the party, as well?"

Father motioned her forward, and she perched herself on the corner of the desk. He cupped her face in his hands. "Despite tradition, not once have I ever thought that you needed a man to help you run the company." He swallowed hard. "And even though you are not in love with him yet, Theodore will make a good husband."

Willow straightened her shoulders. "I agree, but not for me."

346

His jaw dropped. "So, you have decided at last then? You will surrender the company to Osborne? But you were so determined this morning . . ."

"Things have changed since we last spoke." Willow showed him the documents and explained what Cullen had done for her.

Her father rubbed a hand over his mouth, aghast. "And at such a cost to himself. You and I both know your cousin wouldn't have taken less than a fortune for his shares. Because he knew what he was giving up."

She nodded, unable to control the happiness bubbling inside her. "But don't you see? This changes everything. Cullen has changed. When he first arrived, all he cared about was protecting his family and keeping up appearances, and he allowed those fears to dictate his future. Without any assurances from me, he has given all away, his legacy, his home . . . and his place in society for the sake of my happiness."

Father scratched his chin and laughed softly. "Well, the man is not the cad I thought him to be. He must truly love you to sacrifice so much. And you love Cullen?" He cupped her chin in his hand once more. "Because your unhappiness in marriage is something I could not bear. My dear, clever daughter."

"I love him and would be well loved in return, Father. But are you certain you can get over his past connection with Wellington?"

"If you can be happy with Cullen, so can I."

Theodore appeared at the door, his face pallid. "Happy with Cullen? Willow, what are you two discussing?"

Mr. Dupré shut the door as he left the room, giving them a moment of privacy. Willow reached out her hands for Theodore and guided him to the fireplace as her body trembled uncontrollably. Theodore wordlessly pulled her into his arms and rested his chin atop her hair, her crown stabbing his throat, but he did not care. "What's happened to cause you such distress on an evening that should be the happiest of our lives?"

"Teddy . . ." Her voice cracked into a sob. "My heart feels like it's breaking anew."

He closed his eyes against the words, tears pricking at his lashes. *No, Lord, no*, he prayed. Yet he had known since the inspector's visit that something had shifted in her, and in his heart he knew that she was not his. "Please think about it, Will. Please do not do this. Do not give in to the moment. Are you willing to throw away a future together for someone who betrayed you? Can you truly cast me and my heart aside so easily?"

With a little cry, she reached up and grasped his face between her petite hands, pulling him down to her. She pressed a kiss to one cheek and then the other, her tears trailing down her chin. "Forgive me, my dearest Teddy. Forgive me." She bowed her head to his chest and dissolved into tears. "I never wanted to hurt you. Never, my dear Teddy."

The words bent his knees, sending him to the carpet, kneeling before her with her hands in his. He bent his head to her hands, his shoulders shaking from suppressing his breaking heart.

She knelt at once and wrapped her arms about him. "Please don't cry. I cannot bear it if you are broken, too."

He drew a steadying breath. "But if you feel such pain for me, how can you be certain you're doing the right thing in releasing me?"

She rested her forehead to his, her voice cracking again. "Because *I love him*, Teddy."

"And you do not love me?"

"Not in the way I should for a marriage." She rubbed her thumbs under his eyes, drying his tears. "Please, say something."

His gut twisted within him. "And what do you expect me to say? That I'm happy for you?" He pulled himself to his feet.

"Because I am not. I think you are making the biggest mistake of your life."

"I really do believe that your true love is out there waiting for you," Willow returned, gathering her skirts and standing.

He faced the window. "Well, that makes me feel loads better." He shook his head, thinking of his family downstairs, of the lifetime he had imagined with Willow as his bride and the mother of his children, all of it dashed now. He rolled back his shoulders and braved a smile for her sake. For no matter how she felt about him, he loved her and could not bear willingly hurting her. He caught both her hands and kissed her palms. "God help me. It will take a lifetime for me to see you without feeling pain." He held her hand to his cheek, memorizing the feel of it against his skin and aching at the thought that this would be the last time he would ever hold her. "I cannot watch you promise yourself to another."

She pressed her forehead to his. "I understand. Thank you, Teddy. For everything."

Thank you? The words cut him. "If I had known that the last time I kissed you would be the last time, I would not have ended things with a kiss to the cheek." He pulled away from her and ran from the house and did not stop running until long after the sounds of merriment faded into the night.

Willow waited for the dip of the violins, followed by a trumpet blast, before descending the grand staircase, her skirts trailing behind her in a cream cloud. The crowd hushed, all staring at her as she glided toward the throne her parents had once more affixed to the middle wall, where two columns stood on either side of the platform bearing massive vases filled with roses. Silently she walked over to the table that bore a single crown of gold laurels and lifted it. She drew a deep breath and turned to face the crowd at last, all eyes transfixed on her.

"Ladies and gentlemen, I want to thank you for your overwhelming support in my finding my husband and the ruler of my family's sugar empire. At the beginning of this competition, I could not imagine I would actually find love, but I am thrilled to say that I have found the truest and purest love for a gentleman."

The crowd gasped, some of the women rapidly fanning themselves at her words, young women fairly giggling in delight. In the crowd, she caught sight of a few of the contenders from the very beginning. She waved to Chandler Starling, who pointed to the girl beside him, sending her a wink. Sebastian Jones with his plate of cheese. And Lord Peregrine with not one but two ladies on his arms. "I also want to thank those gentlemen who paid me the highest honor of considering me for their bride. I do not take that lightly and will remember their kindness for years to come." She turned to her parents and sisters. "Thank you for pushing me to do something I was uneasy about. Because of your love, I have found my future husband. That is, if he will have me."

She looked about the guests, seeking him. Her heart pounded. *Surely he did not leave?*

He stepped from the shadows, his eyes hungrily answering her. She smiled at him, the crowd murmuring and gasping as they parted for Cullen. The hundreds watching them faded away in his presence. She remembered the first time she had given Cullen a crown, thought of that day he ran into the tree, their many conversations, their time undercover, his saving her on the bridge, and his constant, ever-present love and how he had sacrificed his entire fortune for her dreams. Despite his beginning, he was the man she thought him to be. He was true. He was good. And she knew that with him at her side, nothing else would matter.

He climbed the steps and knelt before her. "Because of you, I have discovered a love that is deeper than anything I have ever experienced. Because of your kindness and pure heart, you have awakened me to a beautiful thing. You are my guardian angel, my queen. Willow Dupré, will you do me the honor of becoming my bride?"

For her answer, she threw her arms about his neck, nearly knocking him to the ground. "Yes, my darling. Yes."

"Yes?"

"Yes!" She laughed as he lifted her in his arms and twirled her in the air, pausing only to kiss her again and again. He set her down to the cheers of the guests, and she lifted the crown. "Now, I have a question for you, Mr. Dempsey. Will you accept my final laurel crown?"

"With all my heart, *macushla*." And with those words, he kissed her until the applause melted away and a new song filled their hearts, a song of promise and love.

Epilogue

VENICE, ITALY
APRIL 15, 1883

Willow drank in the stars beside her husband at the out door table of a little café in Piazza San Marco, finishing off their cups of melted chocolate.

"It's wonderful that the board agreed to an eight-week wedding holiday." Cullen's hand found hers, as well as his gaze. "I wish this time with you could last forever."

"Well, now that we control the company *without* the threat of losing the majority share to my wayward cousin or Wellington . . ." She waggled her brows.

"You can be a tyrant? And do whatever you wish?" Cullen guessed with a laugh, taking another bite of his *baci de dama* cookie and offering her the last of the chocolate-filled hazelnut cookies.

"Exactly." She winked at her dashing husband. While their meeting had been unconventional and tumultuous at times, Willow knew she had made the right choice in listening to her heart. Their whirlwind wedding had been splendid and filled with well wishes, but these sweet moments alone with Cullen were all that she desired.

Finishing the sweet, she tossed a few coins atop the table and seized his hand and pulled him to his feet. Together they ran through the piazza, devoid of tourists save for a few lovers strolling in the blessedly cool evening, only stopping when they reached a bobbing gondola. "Do you know why I wanted us to travel to Venice for our wedding trip?"

He grinned, helping her into the gondola, his hand steady as the vessel swayed with her stepping inside. "Take us to your favorite destination," he called to the gondolier.

At the Italian fellow's quizzical look, Willow stumbled through her translation and settled on the seat at the front of the gondola atop the crimson cushions with Cullen at her side.

"Tell me why, *macushla*," he whispered into her ear, the name sending chills up her arm as it always did.

"I toured here when I was seventeen and fell in love with the romance of the city and promised myself that one day, I would bring my husband back here and take a ride in a gondola with him."

"How romantic of you." He smiled, tucking an escaped lock behind her ear.

"And kiss him senseless in a gondola," Willow finished, biting her lip at the ridiculous admission.

"How positively scandalous, Mrs. Dempsey." Cullen leaned toward her, pausing a breath away.

"Truly." Her eyes settled on his lips.

And with the moonlight enveloping them, Cullen swept her into a kiss that left stars in her eyes and her sighing for more.

AUTHOR'S NOTE

I don't think I've ever had so much fun writing a book as this one. I hope you enjoyed my Gilded Age romance! I wanted to address a couple of things that may have caught your eye in the reading of *My Dear Miss Dupré*.

Though the term *bachelorette* did not become vogue until the early 1900s, as our heroine is a trendsetter, I let her set the trend.

In the story, I mention quite a few blooms that aren't in season, so I researched the use of forced blooming, which to my surprise has been in practice far longer than I thought and worked perfectly for my budding botanist, Fritz Blythe, and allowed me the freedom of using the various blooms mentioned in my Victorian dictionaries of the secret language of flowers, a fascinating practice where couples or friends could pass along hidden messages in the bloom itself. After two months of meeting and dating, my husband-to-be presented me with crimson tulips on my birthday. *An avowal of love.* He didn't know what they meant at the time, but a Victorian lady would have swooned. After we were married, I told him what the flowers really meant.

Stay tuned for Book Two in the AMERICAN ROYALTY series to read more about some of your favorite characters from *My Dear Miss Dupré*. Happy reading!

ACKNOWLEDGMENTS

To my husband and best friend, Dakota. You are a dream of a man and the inspiration for all my heroes. I love you forever.

To my darling little boy and baby girl. I love being your mama.

To my family, Dad, Mama, Charlie, Molly, Sam, Natalie, and Eli, thank you for your tireless enthusiasm for my writing dream.

To my betas extraordinaire, Theresa, McKenna, and Bonnie, thank you for your encouragement and help in working through those messy first drafts. Your critiques have saved me from falling into many a plot hole!

To my agent, Tamela Hancock Murray, thank you for your years of encouragement and for helping me live my writing dream. You are wonderful and I am blessed to have you on my team!

To my ACFW writing friends, Crystal Caudill, Deanna Fugett, Tisha Martin, Sarah Sundin, Jen Turano, and many more, thank you for your overwhelming support and encouragement over the years!

To the team at Bethany House Publishers, Dave Long and Luke Hinrichs, thank you for believing in this story!

When I was a young girl of twelve, I would go to the library and scan the spines of books in the fiction section, selecting books solely because of the Bethany House logo, for I knew any book by that house would be a clean, romantic read, until I had read every historical fiction work by BHP I could find in that library. Today, you hold in your hands a dream of a young girl that was sparked in a library. A special thank you to the St. Tammany Parish Library, Douglas County Library, and Ascension Parish Library!

To the reader, thank you for taking the time to get to know Willow Dupré and her many suitors. I hope you had as much fun reading this story as I did writing it!

And to the Lord who has given me a new song in my mouth, *You* are why I write.

Grace Hitchcock is the author of *The White City* and *The Gray Chamber* in the True Colors series, as well as a number of novella collections. Grace is a member of ACFW and holds a master's degree in creative writing and a BA in English with a minor in history. She lives in southern Louisiana with her husband, Dakota, and their son and daughter. To learn more, visit her at www.gracehitchcock.com.

Sign Up for Grace's Newsletter!

Keep up to date with Grace's news on book releases and events by signing up for her email list at gracehitchcockbooks.com.

You May Also Like . . .

When his reputation is threatened, Aaron Whitworth makes the desperate decision to hire a circus horse trainer as a jockey for his racehorses. Most men don't take Sophia Fitzroy seriously because she's a woman, but as she fights for the right to do the work she was hired for, she finds the fight for Aaron's guarded heart might be a more worthwhile challenge.

Winning the Gentleman by Kristi Ann Hunter
HEARTS ON THE HEATH, kristiannhunter.com

More from Bethany House

After his father's death, Kevin Hunt inherits a ranch in Wyoming—the only catch is it also belongs to a half brother he never knew existed. But danger follows Kevin, and he suspects his half brother is behind it. The only one willing to stand between them is Winona Martin—putting her in the cross hairs of a perilous plot and a risk at love.

Braced for Love by Mary Connealy
BROTHERS IN ARMS #1
maryconnealy.com

Luke Delacroix's hidden past as a spy has him carrying out an ambitious agenda—thwarting the reelection of his only real enemy. But trouble begins when he falls for Marianne Magruder, the congressman's daughter. Can their newfound love survive a political firestorm, or will three generations of family rivalry drive them apart forever?

Prince of Spies by Elizabeth Camden
HOPE AND GLORY #3
elizabethcamden.com

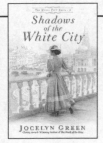

When Sylvie Townsend's Polish ward, Rose, goes missing at the World's Fair, her life unravels. Brushed off by the authorities, Sylvie turns to her boarder and Rose's violin instructor, Kristof Bartok, for help searching the immigrant communities. When the unexpected happens, will Sylvie be able to accept the change that comes her way?

Shadows of the White City by Jocelyn Green
THE WINDY CITY SAGA #2
jocelyngreen.com

⬥BETHANYHOUSE

More Historical Fiction

When a stranger appears in India with news that Ottilie Russell's brother must travel to England to take his place as a nobleman, she is shattered by the secrets that come to light. But betrayal and loss lurk in England too, and soon Ottilie must fight to ensure her brother doesn't forget who he is, as well as stitch a place for herself in this foreign land.

A Tapestry of Light by Kimberly Duffy
kimberlyduffy.com

After receiving word that her sweetheart has been lost during a raid on a Yankee vessel, Cordelia Owens clings to hope. But Phineas Dunn finds nothing redemptive in the horrors of war, and when he returns, he's sure that he's not the hero Cordelia sees. The two of them must decide where the dreams of a new America will take them, and if they will go there together.

Dreams of Savannah by Roseanna M. White
roseannamwhite.com

In 1946, Millie Middleton left home to keep her heritage hidden, carrying the dream of owning a dress store. Decades later, when Harper Dupree's future in fashion falls apart, she visits her mentor Millie. As the revelation of a family secret leads them to Charleston and a rare opportunity, can they overcome doubts and failures for a chance at their dreams?

The Dress Shop on King Street by Ashley Clark
HEIRLOOM SECRETS
ashleyclarkbooks.com

BETHANYHOUSE